Ghost of a Chance

Kim Beall

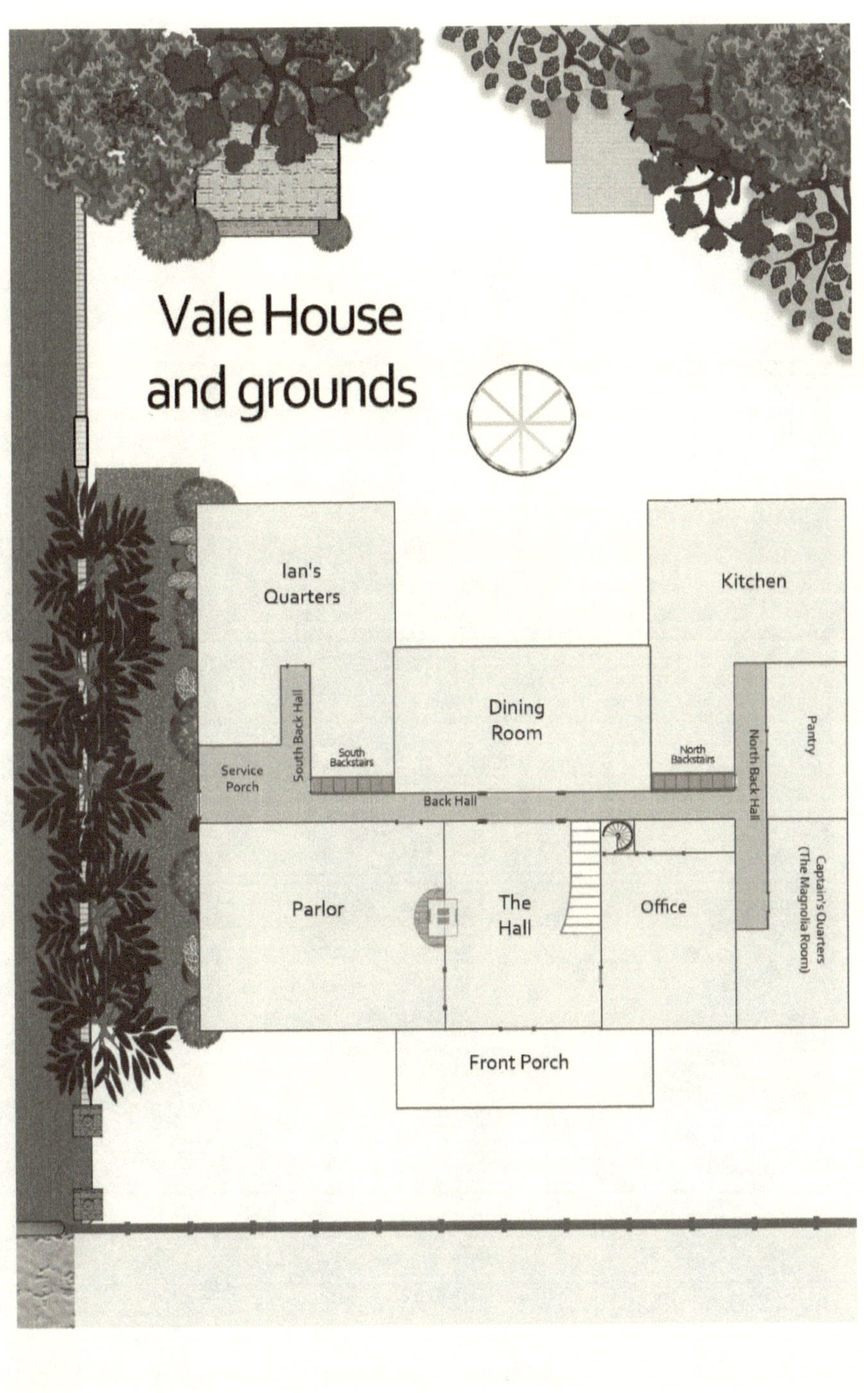

Vale House and grounds
Ian's Quarters
Kitchen
Dining Room
South Back Hall
South Backstairs
Service Porch
North Backstairs
North Back Hall
Pantry
Back Hall
Parlor
The Hall
Office
Captain's Quarters (The Magnolia Room)
Front Porch

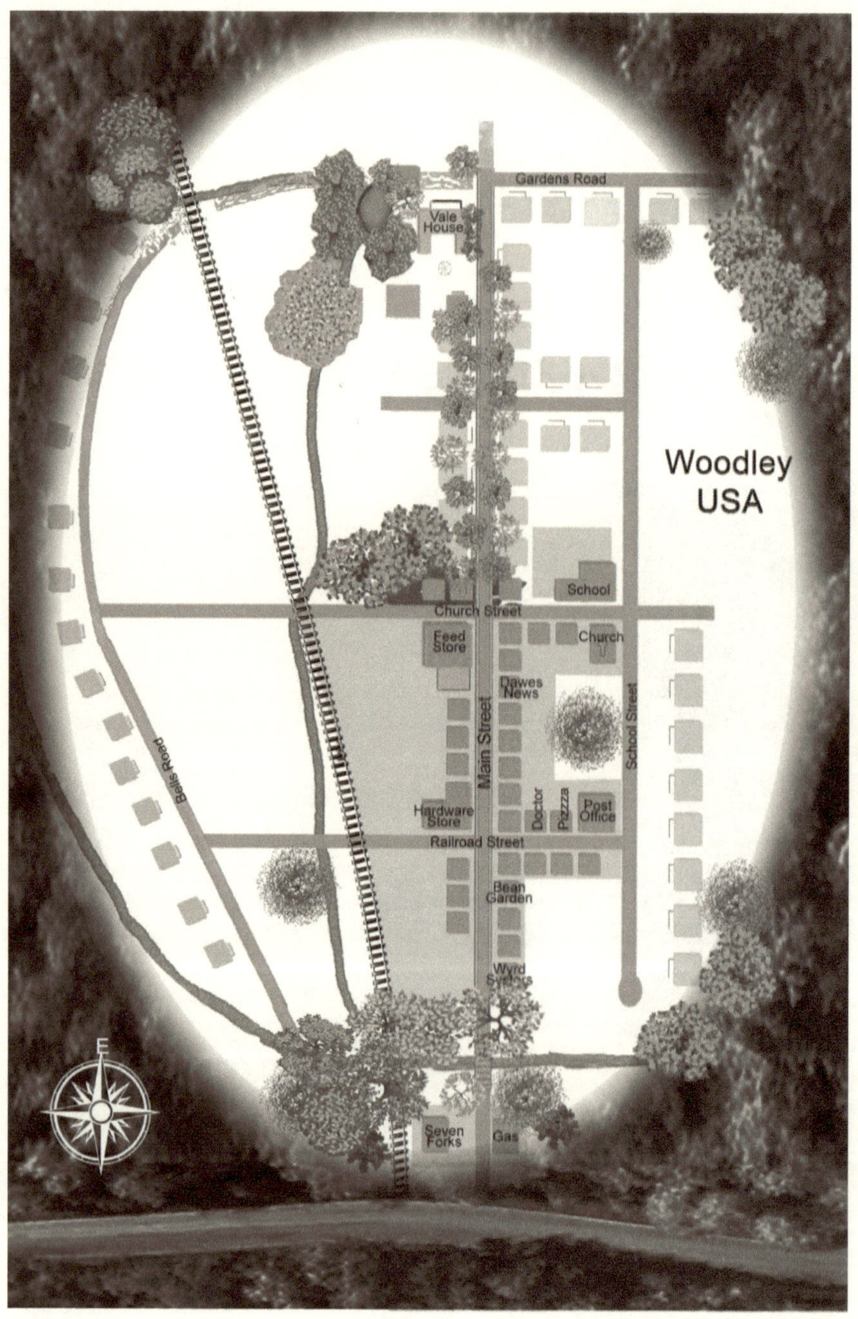

Woodley
USA
Gardens Road
Vale House
School
Church Street
Feed Store
Church
Dawes News
School Street
Main Street
Bells Road
Hardware Store
Doctor
Pizza
Post Office
Railroad Street
Bean Garden
Wyrd Systems
Seven Forks
Gas
E

To my daughter,
who is so beautiful in All The Ways

Acknowledgements

I am grateful to the Franklin County Arts Council for their support of local creators, and particularly for their Writers Guild. Such an amazing resource to have discovered in a rural county. Whod've thunk it?

Thank you, Johnny Sinatra, for permission to use a snippet of your amazing lyrics in this book. I wish I could have included them all, but then I would have had to change my genre to "Best Rock Lyrics of All Time" or something like that.

Thank you Charles de Lint for the encouragement you've offered over the years, including a good, swift kick in the butt when I needed one. Thank you especially for encouraging me to try Vellum. On all counts: you were right!

Special thanks to my copy editor Donna Campbell Smith. Thank you for your sharp eye, and for taking me on, on such short notice. I can't believe I missed all those little things. (Um, well, yes I can!)

I also wish to acknowledge the contributions of my Beloved Beta Readers. You are too numerous to list here, but your input – every single one of you – has been tremendously valuable. This book would completely different without your insights. I truly appreciate you!

Thank you to Suzanne Lucey at Page 158 Books in Wake Forest, NC. Right from the beginning, your support and encouragement have meant the world to me (and, I'm sure, to many other local authors as well.)

Last, but absolutely not least, I loudly proclaim Wake Forest Coffee Company to be the finest coffee shop in all of time and space. I am infinitely grateful for your wonderful staff and your cozy table in the back where I can sit and write for hours on end because 1) you let me and 2) your excellent lattes both soothe and fuel my brain.

CONTENTS

CONTENTS

A Text Chat Between Old Friends Who've Never Met

Emerald<< So how's your novel coming along?

Cally>> Em, I know you only ask me that to pick on me.

Cally>> I'm behind schedule with it, of course.

Emerald<< You always are - - but it seems to work for you!

Emerald<< People like your stories - - even though you end up finishing them in a frantic rush before deadline

Cally>> I guess. Speaking of finishing. That's something I've been wanting to talk with you about.

Cally>> What do you suppose happens to the characters in a book if the author never finishes writing it?

Emerald<< Interesting question - - I can't imagine

Emerald<< LOL, why? Do you feel guilty about making your characters wait so long to find out how their story ends?

Cally>> Hah! No, I was thinking more along the lines of that story you sent me.

Cally>> The one that seems to be your unfinished autobiography.

Emerald<< Oh! Well, I'm not sure I'm to blame for that - - I'm not even sure it was me who wrote it

Emerald<< I mean - - it's almost certainly about me

Emerald<< Even though I only remember some of it ever happening to me

Emerald<< Other parts seem like pure fiction - - and there are huge gaps in the narrative

Emerald<< But then - - there are huge gaps in my memory

Emerald<< It's all pretty sketchy

Cally>> Yes. It is. It's rather like an unfinished first draft.

Cally>> But don't worry, I wasn't blaming you.

Cally>> In fact, I think I'm pretty sure, now, you didn't write it at all.

Emerald<< I concur - - at least, that would certainly explain why I can't remember writing it

Cally>> So here's the thing.

Cally>> The main reason I don't think you wrote it is because I came across another copy of the story. On an old-fashioned floppy disk.

Cally>> This was a few months ago, and I apologize for having put off telling you for so long, but I had a hard time finding a way to access the data.

Emerald<< A floppy!

Emerald<< Wow - - it must have been written by someone much older than us

Emerald<< Do you have any idea who it was?

Cally>> Careful, Em. I'm old enough to remember people using floppy disks.

Emerald<< LOL Sorry 🙂

Cally>> You are so not sorry.

Emerald<< OK now - - basically you're telling me I'm just a character in an old story someone never finished writing?

Cally>> No! Well, not as such. I'm just speculating about how these things might work.

Cally>> I'm still investigating. I'm sorry if I upset you.

Emerald<< You haven't upset me - - I asked you to help

me figure out who I am, after all

Emerald<< I don't want you to be afraid to tell me whatever you figure out

Emerald<< No sense shooting the messenger!

Cally>> I still haven't quite figured it out. And I do apologize for that.

Emerald<< I'm just trying to decide whether it's better or worse than being a ghost in a machine - - like Melissa in the old television set

Emerald<< I was hoping I was some kind of feral Artificial Intelligence or something like that

Emerald<< Turns out I'm just an abandoned fictional character

Cally>> Em, you are not "just" anything. You are a person! Just like Melissa and George.

Emerald<< At least they were alive once!

Emerald<< Sure - - they died

Emerald<< But you have to be born and be a real person - - to have had a life - - in order to die.

Cally>> I can tell you're a real person, Emerald, because I can feel how upset you are.

Cally>> Whatever you are, you're my friend, and I love you.

Emerald<< Whatever I am - - or am not

Cally>> There is no "am not" about you.

Emerald<< Whatever - - Do you have any idea who wrote the story?

Emerald<< Where did you find this floppy disk you're talking about?

Emerald<< Was it there at Vale House?

Cally>> *I'm not really sure who wrote it but...*

Cally started to type what she had planned to say, even before she'd sat down to start this conversation, this text chat with the friend she'd met online so many years ago but had still never met in person.

But, as she watched the cursor winking at the end of the line, a stab of guilt pierced her. It wasn't technically a lie, saying she wasn't sure who had written Emerald's story. But it wasn't the whole truth, either. She was, at the very least, almost sure now. She backspaced a few characters.

Cally>> I'm not really sure, but I have a few more questions.

Cally>> I need to talk to some people. It's an ongoing investigation.

Emerald<< Just like in one of your stories

Cally>> Kind of like that.

1 – Ordinary World

Blackthorn looked so different in the daylight, Cally suspected she might have found her way into the wrong town. The last time she'd been here had been at night. The sidewalks had been full of people, with cars parked in every spot along both sides of the street. The lamplit night had been filled with the sound of music flowing from the open door of The Fountain.

Now the little town was bright with warm, spring sunshine, but it was devoid of any automobile or foot traffic, and silent except for the calls of sparrows and blackbirds flying between the rooftops of the brick storefronts.

The Fountain stood where it should be, though, halfway along the north side of the street, its door open to the sidewalk. Cally braked gently and let out a breath of relief to realize she had finally found this enigmatic place on her own, with no assistance from anyone.

Even better: she had no trouble finding a parking spot directly in front of the little neighborhood bar. She got out and reached back inside to retrieve her purse and the silver flask lying on the passenger seat.

The inside of The Fountain was silent and dim, lit only by the sunlight slanting through the front windows. She could smell food cooking – probably one of the place's signature burgers – somewhere inside. Only one other person was there, sitting at one of the wooden tables just inside the door. Cally waved and nodded as she passed him on her way to the bar at the back. The roundly-built, gray-bearded man acknowledged her greeting vaguely. He seemed to be staring at the open door as if he were expecting to see someone else come through it any minute.

The man behind the bar, however, greeted her warmly. "Good morning, My Lady," he said, wiping the bar in front of him and setting out a glass of water for her. He was a short, slim man, and he had a gray beard, as well, but his was neatly trimmed. He wore a gray woolen cap with a peaked brim. Cally had seen him before – he always made her wonder if the beatnik style of the 1950s was coming back.

"It is a good morning," she replied, sliding onto a wooden stool and accepting the glass of water. He continued wiping down the bar while Cally looked around, breathing in the atmosphere of the room. Somehow, the dust motes drifting lazily through the blue and magenta lights above the empty stage only made the place seem more magical than it did at night. She noticed the old man at the table was tapping his foot and bobbing his head as if there were an invisible band playing on the stage. She thought he looked a lot like Jerry Garcia.

Looking past him, across the room to the row of wooden settles against the far wall, she saw the booth where she and Ben had once shared burgers and beer, and the memory brought a smile to her face. It seemed so very long ago, though it had really only been just over a year. One of these nights, she promised herself, she was going to bring him back here.

"Any news about your new grandson?" The bartender's voice interrupted her reverie.

Cally jumped and turned back to face him. She didn't even bother to ask how he knew about her soon-to-be-born grandson. She had learned well, by now, that everyone knew everything about everyone in these small, Southern towns. Especially in *these* small, Southern towns.

"He could arrive any day, now," she said. "All of us are very excited about it."

"Yes," said the man, gazing away for a moment through the open door, just like the other patron in the place. "We are." Then he shook himself a little and looked back to Cally. Draping the towel over his forearm he asked, "What can I get for you?"

She put the silver flask on the bar. "I need a suggestion," she said, "about what to put in this. A very dear friend is coming home today, and I'd like to share a special toast with him."

Picking up the flask as if it were made of delicate glass, he held it up to the light. The stage lights reflected off it to throw glittering red and purple rainbows around the room. (Even these did not seem to draw the attention of the old man at the table.) The bartender ran his thumb lightly over the etching of a dancing stag on the curved front of the flask.

"Well," he said. "Well now, there's a thing I haven't seen in quite some time."

"You recognize it?"

"I could tell some stories." He grinned and set the flask back down on the bar. "But if I did, nobody would tell me any of their stories ever again."

She laughed, understanding.

He said he knew just the thing, and excused himself to disappear through the low, arched door behind the bar. Cally sipped her water while she waited, watching the old man headbanging to unheard music at the table near the door. The glass at his elbow was still full of pale, yellow beer that looked to be completely flat, now, and Cally wondered how long he'd been sitting there.

When the bartender came back, a green bottle tucked in the crook of his elbow, Cally leaned across the bar and whispered to him, "Is that really Jerry Garcia?"

He grinned. "Why, My Lady," he said, barely above a whisper, himself. "I would think you'd know: Jerry Garcia passed away years ago."

"Yes." Cally grinned back. "I know. But...is that him?"

Instead of replying, he set the green bottle upright on the bar and wiped so much dust off it he had to exchange the smudged towel for a fresh one. "This should be just the thing for the upcoming festivities," he said, turning it to face her. Instead of a label, a dull metal medallion, hammered in the shape of a sun with many rays, was set right into the glass.

"What is it?" Cally asked. A waxed cork sealed the bottle, but the light over the back-bar shone through the liquid inside, revealing it to be only about three quarters full.

"It's triple-distilled," said the bartender. "Which technically makes it an Irish whiskey. But it's not from Ireland. It's... locally made."

"I understand." She did understand.

"Don't worry, it's very smooth."

"You've sampled it," Cally observed. This in itself didn't worry her, but she glanced through the door to her car parked at the curb. She was thinking she didn't want to have to drive home with an open container of alcohol in her car. Then she remembered that sort of thing probably didn't matter around here, even if any form of law enforcement could ever find this place.

"There have been only a few occasions worthy of toasting with this spirit," the bartender was saying. "Please, if you don't mind, I pray you have a drink in my name, as well, when you toast Ian May's health tonight."

Cally nodded her promise to him and didn't bother to ask how he knew who the drink would be for. She slipped off the stool and stood up. Collecting the silver flask, she tucked it into her purse and fished out her wallet.

"What do I owe you?"

"Never!" The bartender drew the green bottle back and held it with both hands, looking levelly at her. "Never, My Lady. It is we who owe you. Never forget that." He continued looking at her, unmoving, until she nodded, and only then did he settle the bottle gently into her hands.

She couldn't help trying, one last time, to get the old man to speak to her as she walked to the door. "It's been a long, strange trip," she suggested conversationally, pausing beside his table. He nodded as if he agreed – or maybe it was just that the tempo of the music in his head had changed at that moment. She waved to him anyway and stepped back out onto the sidewalk.

The weather was growing much warmer, bordering on hot, as the sun crossed the horizon above the buildings on the other side of the street. Cally took off her sweater and, still cognizant of the laws of the ordinary world, wrapped the bottle in it and tucked it securely between the spare tire and a cardboard box full of books by Callaghan McCarthy in the trunk of her car.

Then she paused a moment beside the driver's side door, looking up and down the quiet street. The stillness of the town seemed almost preternatural, as if everyone who lived there was suspended in some enchanted sleep. Perhaps, Cally thought, remembering how lively the place had always been at night, they really were all indoors sleeping it off, preparing for another night when the town would come alive again.

She put a hand up to her throat, hesitated a moment, and then ran her finger under the fine chain around her neck to draw out the pendant attached to it. The crescent-shaped silver amulet, about the size of a half-dollar coin, reminded her of a day-old moon, with a flat crystal suspended between its two points. She held the crescent up at eye level so she could look at the buildings through the crystal.

She saw exactly what she expected to see. She saw nothing, except, as she slowly turned, two lanes of black asphalt stretching east to west. Empty fields rose and fell in all directions, covered with scrubby weeds and even scrubbier clumps of thin trees, sweetgum and slash pine, the types of trees that always grew back first over a retired hayfield. There were no buildings, no sidewalks. Even the birds that had been chattering on the rooftops could no longer be heard – only the soft hiss of the breeze through the brush.

Though she had been expecting this, Cally still had to put her hand on the doorpost of her car to steady herself. She dropped the pendant back inside her blouse, and the town of Old Blackthorn was there again, all around her, just as real and solid as the hills and scrubby trees she could no longer see.

And she knew: it really was there, just where it should be. Just as the field and trees were, just as she and her red Corolla were. Only, they were not all in the same place. Not really. She sensed that, back inside the Fountain, the bartender was smiling through the open door at her with quiet amusement. After all, she was the one out of place and time, here. Maybe. Probably. She threw her purse into the passenger seat and got behind the wheel of the car, reminding herself to be proud that she had managed to find this place at all on her own.

Now, she thought as she turned her car around in the empty street, all she had to do was find her way home again.

2 - Honey I'm Home

The road dipped down a gentle hill, crossed a stream, and when it rose again on the other side, she could no longer see Blackthorn in her rearview mirror. She drove now through fields dotted with clumps of scrubby trees. The pavement swung gently in a wide, sweeping curve to the left, then turned left again until it headed more-or-less north. The sun had crossed overhead into the west so that, when the road began to parallel a wooden fence on her right, Cally could see the shadow of her car running along it. Ahead, nestled in a line of oaks and willows, the town of Woodley, USA rose and slowly spread across the horizon.

Three horses stood on the other side of the fence, black, white, and chestnut, their heads stretched out and ears pricked forward as if watching for her. When she passed, they all broke into a run just fast enough to keep pace. The white mare kicked up her heels, and the chestnut shook her head up and down, challenging the red car to a race. Cally ignored her and slowed down as she neared the Woodley town limits.

Here the road became a residential street, with a green sign reading "Gardens Road" marking the place where the sidewalk began. Shady oaks and stately older homes ranged along the left side, all facing across the pavement into the meadow. Passing a gable-fronted yellow house, Cally saw her son, Brandon, sitting cross-legged in the lawn tinkering with an ancient lawnmower. His girlfriend Rosheen was tending the neat flower border next to the house, the very picture of grace despite – or perhaps because of – her advanced state of pregnancy. Cally didn't stop, only slowing down enough to wave at them. She knew she would be seeing them again in just a few hours.

She finally braked to a crawl in advance of the intersection with Main Street. To the right of this intersection, Main Street ended at a sagging metal gate to become a pair of dirt ruts winding away into the meadow. The horses stopped chasing her, here, putting their heads down to graze, paying her no further mind.

Directly across Main Street, Gardens Road ended, also, at two widely spaced masonry gateposts topped with pineapple-shaped finial lanterns. Cally drove carefully between these onto the grounds of the Vale House Bed and Breakfast.

Ignacio, the caretaker, was mowing the grassy parking area between the fence and the white-sided antebellum mansion which, like the houses on Gardens Road, also faced directly into the meadow. Cally parked in a spot he had already finished mowing, beside the old pickup truck under the oak tree next to the barn. As she got out of the car and retrieved her sweater, along with the bottle wrapped in it, she glanced down the slope beyond the barn. The farm pond at the bottom of the hill glittered in the afternoon sun. Cally noted with concern (or sorrow – she could never tell which) the absence of the derelict fishing boat that had once sagged against the pond's near bank.

"He won't get here until dinnertime." Two women were sitting on the wooden porch steps, snapping green beans into a colander between them; it was the older of the two who had spoken. Bethany was the receptionist at Vale House. As Cally reached the flagstone walk leading up to the porch, she saw Bethany had brought a telephone handset outside with her.

"But our Nellie is here!" said the younger, rounder, and shorter of the two women. Katarina was wearing a brightly flowered and heavily floured apron. She tilted her head toward the screen door behind her. "She's in your office, trying to get that stupid old TV to work!"

"Oh, that's wonderful!" Cally meant it. "About Nell, I mean, not about the old TV." She stepped around the women and hurried up the steps. Ignacio had swept the porch well and had even, apparently, scrubbed the white wicker chairs until they gleamed in preparation for Ian's homecoming. Nell's little calico cat, Cyndi Lauper, sat curled in one of the chairs with what looked like a contented smile on her tiny face. The other Vale House cat, Doctor Boojums, hovered like a gray Foo-Dog between Cally and the door. Cally stopped with one hand on the handle, wondering if she should ask him to move, or just walk through him.

"Oh, Cally." Bethany paused her bean-snapping to turn around. "I nearly forgot to mention. The Iversons have arrived early! When I told them on the phone that Ian would be back in town this weekend, they moved their vacation up a week so they could be here to welcome him. They're taking their usual tour of the old railroad museum right now, but they promised to be back before dinner. Ian is going to be so tickled!" She smiled and wrapped her arms around herself with delight. "They're not just customers, anymore, you know. They've become like family. I've invited them to stay for dinner. I hope that's alright with you?"

Cally still felt awkward whenever Bethany and Katarina treated her like she was their boss. At most, she was just the Vale House office manager. "It's Kat you should be asking," she pointed out. "She's the one who'll have to do the extra cooking."

"Oh, I don't mind!" Katarina, still snapping beans, nodded across the lawn to where Ignacio was putting the mower away in the barn. "Anyway, Ignacio will be happy to help! There's nothing my husband can't do, you know!"

Cally had often thought if she were to cast Katarina in a novel, she would have to use a lot of exclamation points. "You're right, Kat." She looked down and noticed Doctor Boojums had disappeared. "And it will be nice to see the Iversons." She opened the door and went in.

Inside the Reception Hall, a slender young man with brown skin was sitting in the chair behind the desk. He looked like he was trying to get the chair to spin around. He was not succeeding, but he was smiling anyway. "Hey, Cally!" he said. "Nellie is home!"

"So Bethany told me." She paused in front of a carved, oaken door near the foot of the grand staircase. "She's in there trying to talk to Melissa. You should join us, Georgie."

George's hair was done, today, in dozens of braids with blue beads at the ends which swayed and rattled when he shook his head. "I don't like that room." He frowned at the door to Cally's office.

"But you used to enjoy talking with Melissa. Come on."

"Maybe some other time." He vanished. Cally shook her own head, sighed, and opened the door.

Ian May's daughter, a young woman in her mid-thirties with

a head of uncontrollable auburn curls, was sitting on the office sofa staring into the cracked screen of an old console television set. She looked up, brushing hair out of her face, when Cally entered.

"Helen May," said Cally. "It's so good to see you! Welcome home."

"It's good to see you, too!" Nell stood, holding a clunky old remote control in one hand. "I'm so happy to see Georgie, and Melissa, and everyone again!" She turned, waving the remote at the television screen. "I have to go, Melissa. Talk to you later!" As gray static faded from the screen, Nell crossed the room and took Cally by the elbow. "Come on. Let's go find a funnel."

"A what?" Cally often had trouble following Nell's train of thought, but she went with her anyway back out into the Hall.

"To transfer the whiskey into the flask. You don't want to spill a drop of it!"

Now Cally struggled to keep her mouth shut. As far as she knew, Nell was a perfectly normal human being. Well, normal with neurological challenges, but still, one hundred percent human, anyway. There was no way she could have known what was wrapped inside the sweater in the crook of Cally's elbow. But Nell often seemed to know what people were thinking, and often knew other things there didn't seem to be any way for her to know.

Nell laughed as she walked past the reception desk and through the wide doorway into the dining room. "Don't worry, Cally. I didn't read your mind. George told me about it. He's been following you around all morning."

"Nice of him to let me know." While Nell opened the top sideboard drawer to search for a funnel, Cally glanced up to the gallery above the dining room. George was looking over the railing from the upstairs hallway, and he bowed cheekily at her scowl.

"I'll talk to *you* later!" she called up to him before he vanished again.

Nell, who was one of the few people Cally didn't have to be careful not to talk to ghosts in front of, shut the considerably disarranged drawer and opened another.

"How are you enjoying school, Helen?" Cally knew Nell liked to be addressed by her formal name, though most people preferred to refer to her by its affectionate diminutive.

Nell looked up from a drawer full of napkin rings and bottle openers. "I'm learning so much," she said, brushing curls back from her face. "More than I ever dreamed of. But it really is exhausting. You should follow me on Instapics – you'd know all this already!"

Cally frowned. "I don't know. I'm too old for that kind of stuff."

"There are those who would say I'm too old to start medical school," Nell reminded, trying another drawer. "And too sick. But I don't let that stop me, do I?" Nell resumed her search as Cally gave her a sheepish grin. "Besides, you're a famous author. Authors need to do all that social media stuff!"

"I'm not famous."

Nell let out a little yelp of delight, then straightened and turned to hold a small, plastic funnel out toward Cally. "Ta-daaaaa!" she declared.

The funnel, held upright between Nell's fingertips, flew sideways as if it had been slapped out of her hand. Both women turned to stare as the funnel bounced with a hollow *tonk!* off the front of the open drawer, then fell and rolled across the hardwood floor. Before Cally and Nell could turn back to look, open-mouthed, at one another, the drawer slammed shut so hard the crystal goblets on top of the sideboard rattled against one another.

"George!" was Cally's first thought, and she spun around to scowl up at the gallery. Nobody was there.

"Don't be silly." Nell tucked her hair behind her ears and stooped to retrieve the funnel from where it was still rolling along the baseboard. "Georgie can't touch things. And even if he could, he would never do a thing like that."

Nell was, Cally knew, right on both counts. Still, she looked carefully at the younger woman as she straightened with the funnel once more in her hand. Nell sat calmly down on the opposite side of the dining table, patting the tablecloth between them. "Come on, Cally. Bring the bottle."

"That didn't bother you at all!" It was more a question than a statement.

"Well." Nell grinned from behind the curtain of hair which had once again fallen across most of her face. "I did grow up in a haunted house, after all."

"Yes, but..." Cally sat down and withdrew the whiskey bottle from its sweater wrappings. "None of our ghosts has ever done anything like that!" She was slightly appalled to hear herself referring to them as "our ghosts." Still, it was true: even the melancholy Preacher's ghost had never done anything more violent than annoy her with its silent, brooding presence.

"I'm sure it's fine." Nell reached out a hand and Cally put the bottle into it. While Nell regarded the medallion on the front with a gentle smile, it occurred to Cally that this was just the way Nell had acted in the presence of her controlling former husband, carefully ignoring and explaining away the monster he really was. Then she checked herself. They had all been guilty of conveniently failing to see the kind of person Foster had truly been.

But Foster was gone, now, she reminded herself. She took the silver flask out of her purse and set it upright beside the bottle. She held it steady while Nell inserted the funnel into it, and her expression softened. The flask had been a gift to her from one of Vale House's most beloved former residents. Cally could almost feel him sitting there in his favorite chair at the end of the table, nearest the sideboard and its brandy decanters. Even so, she knew, the Captain was no longer one of the ghosts hanging around the Vale. She had personally watched him cross over to green grass and high tides. Even now, in spite of her smile, her eyes misted over at the memory as she took back the bottle and began to fill the flask.

"Careful!" Nell laughed at her. She had nearly missed the funnel as she poured. "Callaghan McCarthy, don't make me cut you off before you've even had any!"

Cally laughed, too, but she noted Nell was gripping both the flask and the funnel far more tightly than necessary as her large, brown eyes flitted about the room.

The liquid trickled like a stream of diamonds from the bottle into the flask, flashing tiny rainbows in the sunlight slanting through the tall windows. There were no further mysterious mishaps, and Nell set the funnel to one side and screwed the cap back on the flask. Cally replaced the cork in the bottle, which was still more than half full. She had meant to place it on the sideboard, to display it among the crystal goblets and decanters, but now she wasn't sure it would be safe there.

"I'll just take this to the kitchen," Nell offered, snatching at the funnel as it rolled – probably perfectly naturally, Cally told herself, not believing it for a second – across the tablecloth.

"And I'll put the whiskey away in my office." Cally watched Nell walking away down the narrow back hall. She seemed to stumble as she reached the turn toward the kitchen, or had she been pushed? Cally shook her head – she had been spooked, so her mind was starting to interpret everything as a supernatural event. She stood, collected the bottle and the flask, and went back through the wide doorway.

As she crossed the Hall on her way to her office, a red light on the telephone console began to blink, the phone to ring. Cally leaned across the desk to answer it, but before the second ring she heard Bethany's voice, out on the porch, saying "Vale House Bed and Breakfast how may I help you?" all in one breath.

By the time Cally had stashed the bottle and flask safely in her desk and returned back through the oaken door, Bethany was standing in the Hall beside the desk, putting the finishing touches on a new entry in the guest ledger.

"We have more guests coming this evening!" the older woman announced as Cally closed the office door behind her. "An old friend of yours!" She winked.

"Oh. No." Cally felt her shoulders tighten. "He is *not* my friend!"

Bethany's puzzled look quickly gave way to understanding. "No, no!" she laughed. "I don't mean Mr. Teine. There will never be any vacancies here for *him*. Never again! I'm referring to that young Miss Danya Barry."

"Ah." Cally was only marginally less dismayed by this clarification.

"Now." Bethany *tsked* at her. "None of what happened last time was Ms. Barry's fault."

"Oh, I know that," Cally admitted. "Just...I don't know. Just bad associations with not-so-pleasant memories, I guess."

"And besides, she's bringing two more paying guests with her. A charming couple – you'll have heard of them. They're famous TV ghost hunters!"

Cally said "Terrific" in the most enthusiastic tone she could muster, which was not very enthusiastic at all. Then, seeing Nell returning through the dining room doorway, wearing her usual shy, quiet smile, she thought maybe a visit from some "famous ghost hunters" might not be such a bad turn of events after all.

3 - The Sailor Ashore

"Ahoy, there!"

Cally heard Ignacio calling from the porch, and that could only mean Ian and Sofie had arrived home. She pushed open the screen door in time to see the white-haired old couple walking up the sloping lawn to the flagstone pathway. Cally knew if she should crane her head out the door far enough to look down the hill, she would see the derelict old boat back in its usual place, half grounded on the bank of the pond.

Ian supported Sofie by the elbow but the old woman, dressed in a navy sailor-style dress, seemed to float up the stairs as if she were weightless. Ian himself had to grip the railing and pull himself up each step, and it was all Cally could do to stop herself running down to assist him as he waved away everyone's help with his free hand.

"It's fine," he insisted. "I just haven't got my land-legs back yet!" His gentle laugh was interrupted by a grunt as he ascended the top step and put an arm around the porch column to steady himself.

"He's much heavier, here," Sofie said by way of explanation, smiling sweetly but not meeting anyone's gaze.

"Mama, you look so tan!" Nell ran to hug her mother; Sofie accepted the embrace with a nervous smile.

"You both do!" Cally agreed. "It looks good on you." She had almost said, "It makes you look so healthy," but thought in time to avoid that topic.

Everyone on the porch surrounded the couple, waiting in turn to hug Ian, and then standing back thoughtfully to let Sofie decide whether or not she felt open to being hugged. The old woman opened her arms to Bethany and Katarina, but then she drew back, clinging to Ian's arm. The un-hugged remainder of the welcoming committee graciously respected her space.

While Katarina ran inside to fetch refreshments, Ian helped Sofie into one of the wicker chairs. Bethany informed Ian, who settled with a soft groan into his own favorite chair just beside the door, that William and Celeste Iverson had rearranged their vacation plans this year in order to be at Vale House when he arrived home, and that they would soon be returning from their visit to Coppersmith.

"We must be sure to invite them to dinner!" Ian declared as he reached to accept a glass of iced tea from Katarina. "They're like family, now." Bethany assured him the invitation had already been issued and accepted, and Cally was grateful Joan Cromwell, the former B&B office manager, was no longer around to remind them all that "This is a Bed and Breakfast, not a Bed and Three Meals a Day!"

"It might be a bit awkward, though," Bethany pointed out. "Three more guests are also arriving this evening. If they turn up before dinner, it will seem snooty not to include them as well." Everyone's eyes turned to Sofie as Bethany said this. Sofie tended to be anxious around large crowds.

She waved a hand airily in their general direction. "We must have a big do tonight. With Doc and the boys, too. A nice, big party."

"Um..." A look of panic flitted across Katarina's face. Cally knew she must be wondering how, even with Ignacio's help, she could stretch the meal at the last minute to accommodate not just three, but eight additional people.

"After all," Sofie concluded, "Johnny and I will be leaving tomorrow!" She smiled and nodded with apparent pleasure at this announcement.

Now several other mouths also opened, but everyone managed to hold their tongues. Sofie's mental condition, similar to Nell's, often made it difficult to know what, if anything, she was really talking about and their incomprehension could, in turn, upset her. They all looked to Ian, instead, to explain what Sofie might have meant.

The old gentleman smiled and patted his wife's hand. "That's a wonderful idea, sweetheart." His blue eyes twinkled as he turned his smile to everyone else. "Ms. McCarthy, please telephone Doc for me. Ask him to get the word out to the rest of the boys. Ask if they would all do us the honor of joining us on the porch for drinks tonight, after dinner. Maybe they'll all bring their instruments.

Wouldn't that be nice?"

Katarina let out a sigh of relief.

Cally wanted to ask Ian to also clarify what Sofie had said about the couple leaving tomorrow. They had only just arrived home, and everyone had understood they were finished with their sailing adventures and would be settling back into Vale House, now.

It was Ian's expression that reassured her. He looked comfortable in his wicker chair, gazing fondly across the lawn to the barn and beyond it into the meadow. He didn't look like a man who had any intention of sailing off again any time soon.

4 - The Seating Chart

"We don't have enough men." Bethany stood beside the dining table, cradling a stack of white china plates in her arms and shaking her head.

"What kind of thing is that to say?" Cally looked up from the freshly laundered dinner napkins she was folding. "Bethany, I thought you were a strong, independent woman!"

"No, no – look!" Bethany referred to a sheet of paper in her hand as she walked around the table, setting one plate at a time on the linen tablecloth. "Ian, of course, goes at the head of the table. And it will be so nice to see him there again!" She paused and smiled fondly at the empty chair while Cally smoothed a napkin beside the plate and placed silverware on top of it. "Sofie on the distaff, at his left hand, of course, and you at his right...

"Don't argue!" She waved a plate at Cally before she could protest. "You *are* his right-hand man, now. You've handled the running of this B&B while he's been gone, and that is where you should sit, now. Unless the president of the United States or someone like that shows up." Her expression showed she would be annoyed, but not surprised, if this should happen. "Now, normally we would have placed Foster here, at Sofie's left, then Nell, and so on, boy-girl, boy-girl, all the way around, but of course Foster is out of the picture now." She did not say what she thought of this, but her satisfied nod spoke volumes. "I guess I'll just seat Nell next to her mother. She helps calm her, anyway..."

"How selfish of Foster to mess up the seating protocols by getting himself killed," Cally said, and laughed quickly lest Bethany sail a plate at her. "Anyway, I think Nell is perfectly content without a male person sitting beside her."

"She's better at taking care of herself than that man ever was at caring for her!" Bethany tapped the tablecloth with the edge of a plate. "OK I'll put Ignacio and Katarina at Nell's left. They pretty much raised her anyway.

"Now, Cally, are you sure your young man won't be joining us tonight? You know what? I'm going to set a place for him anyway, just in case you can talk him into it. That way we'll still have boy, girl, boy, girl even if Mr. Dawes is only there in theory. If Danya Barry and the Tollers do turn up in time, we'll just have to put Danya beside me. And, please, do try to encourage young Ben to attend! I start to wonder, sometimes, I really do!"

Cally put up a hand in protest as Bethany set a phantom place to the right of her seat, but she knew it was pointless to argue. She had tried, many times, to remind Bethany that her not-so-young man could not attend evening meals, not ever, but Bethany had never accepted this. It might have been, Cally understood, because she had never explained just *why* Ben had very little say over how he spent his time in Woodley. She knew she really should explain, and promised herself she would do so at her earliest opportunity. Maybe.

That discussion would have to wait, however, because the sound of car doors slamming let them know the dinner guests were beginning to arrive. Cally ran into the Hall where she could see, through the screen door, an elderly couple getting out of a silver sedan. Ian had stood up from his wicker chair to make his way to the porch steps, while Ignacio ran past him, down into the yard to gather the shopping bags the Iversons had acquired during their day's outing.

William and Celeste Iverson were just a few years younger than Ian and Sofie May, and Cally could tell, as she watched them slowly cross the lawn, that their traveling days might be nearing their end as well. While Ignacio politely refused the tip William tried to offer him, Celeste, her coiffed hair tinted a soft sunset shade, waved with delight up to Ian on the porch.

"We're so glad to see you home!" she called, preceding the men up the steps. When she reached the top, Ian bowed and took her hand, kissing the back of it. Ian and William exchanged a hand clasp while Celeste continued to enthuse, "Vale House just wouldn't be the same without you here!"

"Sofie and I are glad, as well, that you could be here tonight." Ian waved the couple toward the screen door as Cally opened it. "We insist you join us for a nice, little family dinner."

"We couldn't impose." William tried, perfunctorily, to

decline the invitation, but rich aromas of roast chicken and freshly baked bread filled the Hall, and the couple's objections were easily overcome.

Katarina excused herself, dashing off to see to last-minute preparations. Ignacio followed her, while everyone else moved through the doorway at the left side of the Hall, gathering in the parlor for a pre-dinner aperitif. Ian, in the Captain's absence, started to serve small cordial glasses of brandy, but he tired quickly. As he sank into one of the wing chairs beside the fireplace, Cally took over for him. Sofie sat in the chair opposite Ian, nodding happily but not answering Celeste's polite inquiries about the identities of all the people depicted in the framed photos on the mantelpiece.

"And have you encountered any ghosts yet during your visit?" Ian asked the Iversons, ever the perfect Haunted Bed and Breakfast host.

With a little gasp, Celeste turned around and set her cordial glass on the mantelpiece. "I still haven't met any of Vale House's ghosts, not personally, but..." She began digging in her purse. "Look!" She withdrew her phone and fiddled with it until she found what she was looking for. "Look!" she exclaimed again, turning the screen toward everyone in the room. Mr. Iverson took the phone from her and handed it to Ian.

"Well, now. Isn't that something?" Ian smiled at the screen, though it wasn't clear he could see what Celeste was talking about.

Celeste nodded, nearly bouncing on her toes like a little girl. Ian handed the phone to Nell, who gave Celeste a wide smile as she passed the device on to Cally.

Cally squinted at the screen. The photo appeared to be of Vale House's photogenic grand staircase, with its hand-carved white railing curving smoothly up from the Hall to the upstairs gallery. A shadow seemed to obscure the steps halfway up, though, and if she looked closely Cally could make out the figure of a slender, dark-skinned man dressed in gray trousers and a white shirt. His wide grin was his clearest feature; the specter looked very pleased with himself.

"That's amazing, Celeste. It does look like you've caught something there." She passed the phone to Bethany.

"I do believe I have!" Celeste gazed delightedly at the photo as Bethany handed the phone back to her. "The figure wasn't there when we checked in. That's when I took the photo of the stairs. And I didn't see anything unusual when I went through my photos on our way to Coppersmith, either. But when I looked again on our way back this afternoon, there it was!"

"Well." Mr. Iverson smiled indulgently at his wife, "No self-respecting antebellum home should be without at least one ghost running up and down the stairs!"

While Celeste put the phone back in her purse, Cally glanced toward the parlor doorway. She didn't see George there, but just in case he was listening, she whispered "That was really nice of you."

She declined to serve herself a cordial, meaning to remain alert at least until after the rest of the evening's guests had checked in. In fact, it was not long before they all heard more car doors opening and closing. One, two, three... and, as a small grin widened across Cally's face, a fourth door slamming. She did not bother to explain her delight to Bethany as she insisted "No, don't worry, I'll check them in!"

She dashed into the Hall to see an elderly gentleman with dark silver hair, smoothly combed back, holding the screen door open for two women and a man. She also saw a dark-suited man standing just to one side of the desk, staring at the portraits on the wall behind it. She had learned a long time ago to ignore this ghost, who never did anything but stand there and look morose.

"Good evening, Doc!" She addressed the man who was holding the door as she dashed behind the reception desk to retrieve the register.

"I'll just go and say hello to Ian," he answered, nodding to Cally as the other three entered. Softly closing the door behind the others, he bowed and saw himself into the parlor.

The new arrivals made their way to the desk. "So nice to see you again, Ms. McCarthy," said the wide-eyed, dark-haired younger of the two women. She held her hand out, but not quite all the way, as if she feared Cally might stab it with the desk pen.

Cally paused, pen in hand, listening. Her small grin expanded into a smile edging on laughter when she heard Bethany's voice, from the other room, exclaim, "Doc! Oh! I wasn't expecting..."

The smile remained on Cally's face as she reached across the desk to clasp Danya's hand. Though she failed to quite express pleasure at seeing the other woman again, she did manage a polite "I trust you had a pleasant trip, Ms. Barry?"

Danya let out a sigh, visibly relieved. "Yes. Thank you. Um, please allow me to introduce Anderson and Geraldine Toller." She stood aside to let the couple accompanying her approach the desk.

Cally's hand was still out, and Mr. Toller, a broad-shouldered, middle-aged man in a beige suit, grabbed it firmly. "Our trip was fine," he said, squeezing hard. "But this town is damned difficult to find! We would still be out there wandering up and down the interstate if Ms. Barry hadn't stopped at the exit to flag us down!"

Cally nodded and rubbed her bruised knuckles. "Many people would agree with you," she said. "I had trouble finding Woodley, myself, the first time." And the second, and the third, she thought but did not say. "Still, people do seem to manage to find us somehow!" She turned to offer her hand to the small, bird-like woman standing beside him.

Geraldine Toller did not reach back, and in fact she did not look up to meet Cally's eyes. Her mouth formed a straight, serious line.

"This place is full of spirits!" she declared.

This was something people claiming to be mediums often said upon entering Vale House, whether they could actually "sense" anything or not.

"Yes." She had a feeling Mrs. Toller was not pretending, even though she was gazing up the stairs and not at the Preacher's ghost standing right beside her. Cally began to give Geraldine the standard Vale House reply. "Many do say they experience..."

The woman interrupted with a "*pfft!*" and a wave of one thin hand as she turned her eyes from the stairs to Cally. "You couldn't swing a dead cat around here without hitting at least six entities!"

Cally snapped her mouth shut. It was all she could do to stop herself turning and looking up the stairs to see if George was standing there. It wasn't just the woman's words that took her aback – it was that she had first heard almost exactly this same expression from George himself.

The sound of laughter from the parlor helped her regain her composure. She looked away from the woman and addressed Mr. Toller instead. "I understand you'll be staying one night, the same as Ms. Barry?"

"Please forgive my wife," he said. "She's highly sensitive to these things."

"I understand," said Cally. "We get many mediums and spiritualists at our establishment. None quite so famous as you, of course," she felt compelled to assure Geraldine Toller, though she also felt inclined to replace the word "famous" with something else. "Ignacio will be along in a moment to take your luggage to your room for you. If you'll just sign here..." She laid the plumed guest pen in the crease of the register just as Bethany appeared in the parlor doorway.

"Cally, may I speak to you, please?" Bethany flashed a brief, professional smile to the Tollers, and then returned her glare to Cally. "In private."

Cally struggled to stifle her laughter as Bethany strode briskly to the rear of the Hall, reaching out, as she passed the desk, to seize Cally's elbow. She let Bethany draw her through the dining room doorway until they stopped at last beside the table. Here Bethany turned to face her, hands on hips. "Doc wasn't supposed to be here for dinner!"

"Oh, Bethany, I'm so sorry." Cally watched a flush of red creeping up from the older woman's neckline. "I completely forgot to mention! When I called Doc, earlier, to tell him to gather the guys for music on the porch tonight, I took the liberty of asking if he would be so kind as to join us for dinner as well. He is Ian's oldest and dearest friend, after all. Don't worry, there are still two seats left at the table. Three, if you count Ben's. We can just move Danya down one, and seat Doc between you and Celeste. You know, boy, girl, boy, girl – just the way it should be!"

The redness had crept up to Bethany's cheeks. "If this is supposed to be your revenge for me advising you to get more serious about Ben Dawes, it won't work. Doctor Tanahey is a good man," she conceded, nodding toward the parlor. "But he and I are just friends. I do not think he belongs at my right hand like some kind of dinner date!"

Cally was already in hot water, so she went ahead and pressed her luck. "You should wear that ring he gave you for Christmas."

"It's not that kind of ring!"

"No, no, of course not. That's why it would be perfectly alright for you to wear it. It would match your dress nicely."

Bethany let out a snort. "I'll go and get another plate." She headed down the back hall toward the kitchen, then turned back. "And I expect to hear the real dirt about your Mr. Dawes and you, very soon!"

Cally chuckled under her breath at Bethany's retreating back. Behind her, she could hear Celeste Iverson entering the Hall from the parlor, gushing her delight at meeting the Tollers as Ian shepherded all of his guests toward the dining room. Bethany returned with the final plate, but she stopped just short of setting it down on the table.

"You know..." she murmured. Cally saw her eyeing the empty place that had been set for Ben. "I think maybe we could seat..."

"Oh! You're absolutely right!" Cally interrupted just a little too loudly. "Danya should sit there!" She turned to address the dinner guests pausing in the dining room doorway. "Ms. Barry, will you be so kind as to take the place beside mine? We have so much to catch up on."

Danya nodded, though her expression was somewhat perplexed, and moved toward the seat at which Cally was pointing. This left only one open place setting, the one at Bethany's right, for Doc. Bethany gave Cally a look that would have curdled fresh milk. Still, as Bethany turned away and directed everyone else to their places according to what was left of her mutilated seating chart, Cally noticed the opal ring Doc had given her had somehow appeared on her hand.

"Thirteen..." Ian had pulled out Sofie's chair for her, but Sofie remained standing, looking around the table, her eyes quickly flitting over and over the place settings. "Thirteen." Her voice was soft, but her hands had begun to tremble.

Bethany hurried to the end of the table and put down the fourteenth plate.

5 - Dinner Party Crashers

Due to the dearth of male dinner guests, Doc intuited it was his job to assist both Cally and Danya with their chairs, and this earned him a smile of approval from Bethany. Danya stopped just short of sitting down, however. Her wide eyes grew even wider when she saw Ignacio and Katarina, who had donned crisp, white aprons over fresh dinner outfits, coming from the back hall with serving dishes in their arms.

"Oh, my god! Mr. Munoz!" Danya ran around the end of the table, reaching out with both hands toward Ignacio. "I am so sorry! I swear, I didn't mean to... I would never..." She stammered and looked back to Cally, clearly uncertain of what she was so sorry about. "I mean, what I put you through, last time I was here. I... anyway, please, forgive me!"

Ignacio put down the crystal salad bowl he was carrying, turning back to take both of Danya's hands between his. "It's alright," he said. "It was an honest mistake. There is nothing to forgive."

"What are you two talking about?" Katarina cast a meaningful look at the young woman's hands in her husband's. Danya pulled away and stood back awkwardly. "I...I'm not sure," she confessed. "I remember, I seem to remember, I said or did something to hurt him, last time. To hurt both of you. But I..."

"It was just a case of mistaken identity," Ignacio assured her, looking past her to Cally.

Cally nodded. "Danya may have unintentionally said something, last fall, which cast Ignacio in a bad light." As far as Cally knew, only she and Ignacio had any memory of that particular timeline, but apparently Danya also retained some of what had happened. Seeing how sorry Danya felt, now, over someone she barely even knew, made Cally reconsider her haughty judgement of the young woman. "It's all in the past, now," she assured everyone.

Ignacio gave her a private little smile, as if she had made a joke that only he and she would get.

Bethany was gesturing impatiently toward the two places she had set at Nell's left. "Mr. and Mrs. Munoz, will you do us the honor of joining us for dinner?" It wasn't really meant to be a question. Ignacio and Katarina took off their aprons and sat down.

Danya shook her head, as if to clear it, and returned to the chair Doc was still holding for her. Once she had settled herself, he turned again to draw out Bethany's chair. Then he raised what was left in his cordial glass and addressed the table, just as the Captain had used to do.

"To your health, all of you!"

"*Mae govannen!*" Nell agreed, raising her glass in turn, and Ian began to cut up the roast chicken set before him. Cally's heart filled near to bursting at the sight of the master of Vale House sitting once again in his proper seat at the head of the dining table.

Celeste Iverson had been engaged in intense conversation with Geraldine Toller, showing her the photo of the alleged ghost on her phone and telling her all about her own lifelong interest in ghosts and spirits. Geraldine smiled and nodded politely at Celeste's photo, but didn't seem to find it remarkable. Instead she turned and nodded sharply at Nell.

"You are recently widowed," she observed.

This was not news to anyone present, but it was an uncomfortable topic for a near stranger to bring up so abruptly. Nell only smiled sweetly at Geraldine. "I am."

"You don't seem to be upset about it."

"I try to remember to always see the good in life." Nell took a roll from the basket in front of her and passed the basket to her right.

Celeste Iverson put her phone away and cleared her throat. "I would love to hear Ian tell us about his trip at sea!" she suggested by way of a change of subject.

"Yes!" Anderson Toller nodded his agreement as he cut all the meat, vegetables, and potatoes on his plate into tiny pieces. He looked up only long enough to waggle his fork at Ian. "I heard there were some pretty fierce storms this past winter. I hope you steered clear of those."

"There was a dangerous storm, right here, just a week ago,"

Geraldine put in, gazing vacantly at the light fixture above the table. Cally wondered how someone who was visiting from hundreds of miles away even knew about that, since summer storms around Vale House tended to be extraordinarily – some would even say supernaturally – localized.

Ian winked at Cally as he buttered his roll. "I am confident Ms. McCarthy handled it masterfully."

"She did!" Bethany asserted. "Just as well as you ever did, Ian. But we missed you, all the same."

Cally had to agree with that.

Ian nodded. "Well, Mr. Toller, my little boat is no longer in any condition for open water excursions. We stayed well within sight of land, for the most part. Though we did make it all the way down to the Port of Tirrane and enjoyed a leisurely cruise through the straits of Repenglow before rounding the point at Kingsfall to begin our return journey. The weather was very fine where we sailed, for the most part, though sometimes a bit foggy."

Cally had never heard of any of these places, but Anderson Toller answered as if he knew all about them. "Apparently you stayed inside the intercoastal waterway. Good idea." He was stirring everything on his plate together into a homogenous mound. This he tucked into with gusto, while his wife served herself a small spoonful of green beans.

"Oh, you've seen such exotic places!" Celeste Iverson enthused. "They almost sound like lands you'd only see in fairy tales. William, we really must take a cruise ourselves, sometime."

Mr. Iverson nodded indulgently. "Preferably on a haunted pirate ship like Ian's, I assume?"

"Ian, is it true your pirate ship is haunted?" Celeste asked hopefully.

Ian skirted the question by explaining that his boat was not a pirate ship, but an old fishing trawler that had once belonged to his uncle. He then launched into a little treatise on types of boats. Most of the people at the table had heard this at least once before, so they took the opportunity to eat in silence as Ian carefully explained the differences between trawlers, schooners, and sloops, including the number of masts and the types of keels each possessed. Geraldine Toller ate green beans, one at a time from end to end, and watched him from the side of her eye. Ian concluded as usual with his favorite Sailing Fun Fact: "The most popular type of ship for pirates was actually the sloop!" Sofie applauded as if it were the first time she'd ever heard this.

Anderson Toller began to fill his plate again. "I admire you, sir. I can't even imagine spending the winter in a little boat like that. Not at my age, let alone at yours!"

"Oh, no, we were fine!" Sofie piped up. "When winter came, we put in and stayed with the fairy queen as her guests of honor. She is such a gracious hostess. She made us very comfortable."

They all heard a sharp rap as Geraldine Toller put down her fork down and stared at Sofie. Cally wished she were sitting on the other side of the table so she could explain quietly about Sofie's condition into Geraldine's ear, but Katarina had it covered.

"It's alright." Katarina reached around Anderson Toller's plate (avoiding the stream of gravy he was pouring over the top of his well-mixed meal) and put a hand on Geraldine's forearm. "Sofie May is, well, she has a unique talent for being able to see things most of us can't." She winked carefully at Geraldine, and Celeste smiled reassurance across the table for good measure.

"I understand," said Geraldine, but she was still looking at Sofie. "You are touched by the hand of God."

"That's how some put it..." Cally began, but she could see by Sofie's wide smile that she had taken this as a compliment.

"We all love Sofie," Bethany stated firmly. "She's a ray of sunshine to the entire household."

All this should have been enough to make the newcomers understand that though Sofie was neurologically atypical, she was respected, but Geraldine Toller had apparently not taken the hint.

"You shouldn't dabble so carelessly in matters you don't understand," she advised the old woman in an ominous voice. She didn't seem to notice that now at least five pairs of eyes around the table were fixed firmly on her.

Cally felt Ian's hand on hers before she realized she had started to rise from her seat. As always, Ian exuded gentlemanly demeanor.

"My apologies, Mrs. Toller," he said. "I'm afraid I have neglected to include you in the conversation. I'm sure we would all be fascinated to hear more about your experience in these matters. I hope you understand you may speak freely, here. In this household, all voices are heard and respected."

It still wasn't clear to Cally that Geraldine had taken the point, but the woman did at least look away from Sofie as she began speaking again, in her singsong voice, apparently to the empty air about three feet above the table.

"There are many mysteries in this world," she began, "of which the average person is unaware. I have spent my entire lifetime studying these mysteries, pursuing them into dark corners, delving into the shadows, and laying them to rest. It is no task for the inexperienced! And I tell you again: This house is full of unexplained spiritual manifestations. The forces of evil are nothing to trifle with!"

Cally slipped her hand out from under Ian's and gave him a smile to assure him she was not going to lose her cool. She took a careful breath and said, "Mrs. Toller, with all due respect, I hardly think any of what you call 'manifestations' in this house are evil. Some may be a little eccentric, but..."

Geraldine turned from gazing at the air and focused on Cally. "And what would you know about it?"

Before she could stop herself, Cally glanced up at the gallery railing above the dining room. She saw George, there, looking down at her from the railing, but he was not grinning this time.

Without following her gaze, Geraldine said, "I see. So, you are well aware of the demonic forces surrounding you."

That did it. Cally stood, balling up her napkin in her fists. "Demonic?" She threw the napkin onto her plate. "Now wait just a minute! Why must all you 'ghost hunters' and your TV producers insist on conflating ghosts with demons? Ghosts are people, too! Well, they were, and anyway I don't see why they should be any more inclined to evil and mayhem than the rest of us! Which I have to admit, right now, I..."

"Ms. McCarthy." Cally felt Danya's hand tugging at her elbow. "It's alright. The Tollers don't think all ghosts are demons." As Cally slowly sat back down, Danya launched into a description of a TV episode in which Geraldine and Anderson Toller had recovered the lost spirit of an innocent little girl and helped lay it to rest.

Before Cally could decide whether she wanted to apologize or not, Geraldine resumed speaking, but in a much less grating tone. "I will be happy to do the same for any of the lost spirits here at Vale House. I can sense that many here are ready to cross into the light, where all are welcome."

"We do not charge for this service," Mr. Toller added. "All we ask is that..."

Before he could finish, the empty plate at the end of the table sailed past his face. It flew almost the length of the table before swerving to pass between Nell and Sofie's heads, where it finally shattered against the wall behind them.

Celeste Iverson screamed and covered her face, then continued to scream softly between her fingers. She didn't seem as thrilled as she'd always told everyone she would be, should she ever see real evidence of a supernatural manifestation.

Geraldine Toller only directed a curt nod at Cally. "I rest my case," she said.

6 - A Talk with George

Bethany had turned off most of the lights in the dining room and parlor, until the downstairs was illuminated only by the light over the dining room sideboard and the green shaded lamp on the reception desk. A blue light on the telephone console winked softly to assure Cally, as she passed through the Hall toward the grand staircase, that the phones had been forward to voicemail for the night. Through the screen door, she could see evening creeping into the sky above the meadow. The sound of voices and laughter outside grew more raucous as an increasing number of visitors arrived on the porch.

As she started up the stairs, Cally saw Doc coming from the dining room into the Hall. He was holding several stemmed glasses from the sideboard in one hand, and a crystal decanter in the other.

"Doc, let Kat get you a tray for those!" Cally shook her head at him. "No, on second thought, ask Bethany." She winked.

Doc paused, grinning. "I tried using a tray. That's why Kat had to go fetch a broom. It seems the dishware around here has a mind of its own, lately! I thought it might be safer to just keep my hands on the glasses that survived." He started for the door again and then turned back. "By the way, Ms. McCarthy, don't think I don't notice, or appreciate, your matchmaking efforts. Just between you and me, I think it's starting to work."

"I hope so." Cally glanced around to make sure Bethany was not in earshot. "You and Bethany would make a cute couple."

"Well, we'd make half of one!" He laughed as he backed against the door, pushing it open with an elbow. Bethany appeared on the other side and said, "Oh, Doc! Here, let me help you with those!" Cally continued up the stairs.

At the top of the stairs, she looked in both directions along the hallway between the rows of closed, white doors. Each door, where most lodgings would normally display numbers, was identified by a botanical flower print in an oval frame. Cally could hear the Tollers talking in animated tones behind the door of the Hydrangea Room. She didn't try to make out what they were saying.

"George, are you here?" She kept her voice low. If he was there, he would hear her even if she whispered. She didn't see the ghost at the gallery railing, though, or near either of the butler's desks at the ends of the hallway. He was seldom there anymore, since his haunting range had become so much wider than it had once been. Sighing, she crossed the hallway to stand outside the door of the Rose Room. This was where she had used to see the ghost most often. In fact, it was where she had first met him. Tonight, the Rose Room was occupied by Danya Barry.

The door of the Wisteria Room opened, interrupting her reverie. Mr. and Mrs. Iverson stepped out, each carrying sweaters draped over their forearms.

"It looks like you've decided to join us on the porch after all!" Cally said, genuinely pleased.

"Well." Celeste grasped Cally's elbow and gave it a firm squeeze, as if she were trying to steady herself. "I admit I'm still a little rattled. But, you know, mostly I'm embarrassed that I turned out not to be as brave about...you know...as I used to think I was!"

Cally gave the woman's hand a reassuring squeeze in return. "I can't say I blame you at all, Mrs. Iverson. That was a little more startling than what we normally get around here."

"Please call me Celeste," she insisted. "Maybe all I need is a sip of that brandy!"

Mr. Iverson chuckled. "I think we all do. May we walk you down to the porch, Ms. McCarthy?" He offered her his free arm.

"Please call me Cally. Thank you, sir, but I'll be down in a little while. I have a couple small errands to take care of first."

It was not until the Iversons had begun to descend the stairs that Cally finally spotted George. He was facing the door of the Hydrangea Room, standing quite still with his hands on his hips.

"It's not nice to eavesdrop," she told him.

He didn't turn to look at her. "I don't like those Tollers!" he declared.

Cally smiled. "I don't disagree with you," she admitted. "But they're only staying one night."

When George turned to face her, his usual innocent smile

had returned. "She can see me, you know. But not the same way you do."

Not for the first time, Cally wished she could hug him. He was wearing a Psychostick t-shirt with the sleeves cut off, ragged jeans, and no shoes. His hair was done in a sort of fro-hawk that stuck up like spikes.

"Speaking of seeing, George, do you know who threw that plate this evening?"

His expression grew serious. "It wasn't me!"

"Oh, don't worry. I know that. You can't touch things anyway."

Even though this fact exonerated him, he seemed to resent it. "I'm practicing," he insisted. "I'm getting better at touching things!" He looked around for something upon which he might demonstrate and spotted the paper *"Do Not Disturb"* tag hanging from the doorknob of the Tollers' room. He flicked at it with his fingers, but they passed right through. The tag didn't sway even slightly.

"It's okay, Georgie," Cally reassured him. "I know you can learn anything you set your mind to, given enough time. And apparently, someone has! Who do you think it was? Do we have a new ghost around here, all of a sudden?"

Even as she said this, she and George locked gazes, and both bit back things they didn't want to say.

"Well," he said at length, drawing his words out in a most careful execution of his quasi-Jamaican accent. "It's not really so sudden, is it?"

Together, they turned and looked over the gallery railing to the dining room below. There they saw Nell coming out of the back hall, passing the sideboard on her way through to the Reception Hall. No crystal or silver, at the moment, lifted itself to fly at her.

"I mean," George continued, "he has had to practice, too, to learn just like anyone would have to after they are discorporated. It's just a matter of what his priorities were. Are. He's getting better at it."

"Apparently he..." Cally still couldn't bring herself to use the name she was almost certain this new spirit had probably once borne. "Well, whoever it is, it seems they are most interested in moving things around. George, maybe we really should avail ourselves of the Tollers' services."

"I don't..."

They both jumped as they heard a shout behind them, but it was only Bethany calling up the stairs. "Hey, Cally, the sun is setting! We're all waiting for you, and your Mr. Dawes will be arriving any minute!"

While Cally called back her promise that she'd be right down, George resumed trying to move the tag hanging on the guest room door. Cally turned away to the door of the Dogwood Room. This was her own room, and it was connected by a narrow stair to her office below. She meant to stop there and retrieve the Captain's silver flask from her desk drawer.

Before she managed to get her key into the lock, however, Geraldine Toller burst out of the Hydrangea Room. She fixed the doorknob tag with a murderous glare, which she then turned on Cally. "Who is there?" George had vanished, but the tag was swinging wildly. "Who was that?" Geraldine demanded.

"I don't see anyone," was Cally's honest answer. "Will you be joining us on the porch?"

The woman refused to be distracted. "Was it that evil man?"

"Now, Mrs. Toller." Cally took a deep breath to keep her temper under control. "As I mentioned before, I hardly think he's evil."

Geraldine stepped to one side of the doorway to make room for her husband behind her. While Anderson acknowledged Cally with a polite nod, Geraldine gestured with one hand and a scowl toward the stairwell. "He has a very dark aura," she intoned in her airy, quavering voice. "He's a tall man, in a dark suit. But that's not the only dark thing about him. He has a long, pale face and he is highly disturbed about something. Something unrighteous, unwholesome... He was there at the reception desk when you checked us in."

"Oh!" Cally nearly laughed out loud with relief. "You must mean the Preacher!" Geraldine returned her attention to Cally as she told the couple about the spirit she had dubbed "the Preacher" due to his serious demeanor. She told them many guests had sensed this brooding presence in front of the desk, but that few had seen him visually. "He's completely harmless," she assured them. She did not tell them the rest of what she had only recently learned: that this preacher had, in his lifetime, caused great harm indeed, and now existed in a limbo of regret.

"Well, he's not here now," Geraldine admitted, looking up and down along the hallway.

"No, he's not. He only shows up now and again."

"We would be happy to cleanse this place of his presence and help him cross over," Anderson Toller reminded. He reached into his shirt pocket to retrieve a business card. "I mean, my wife would." He smiled and took Cally's hand, pressing the card into her palm. "I am merely her assistant."

Cally thought she wouldn't mind being rid of the Preacher's gloomy presence in the Hall, as it could really get on her nerves sometimes. But she knew this spirit and George had a history, and she wouldn't want to do anything without consulting him first, so she changed the subject.

"It sounds like the rest of the band has arrived." She gestured toward the stairs, where they could hear strains of guitar music drifting up from the porch. "You're welcome to join us if you like. They tend to play a lot of Eagles songs."

Though she walked briskly to the top of the stairs, Geraldine did not seem to be interested in Eagles music. She pointed a long, red-nailed finger down the stairs at the space in front of the desk where the Preacher often stood. "I wasn't talking about him. The spirit I am talking about wore glasses, in life." She turned and looked back at Cally, pantomiming a gesture that almost caused Cally's stomach to flip over. "They keep slipping down. He keeps pushing them up. You're lucky. He can barely see a thing."

7 - One of These Nights

Cally escaped at last into the Dogwood Room. What she really wanted to do, just then, was throw herself onto her bed and pull the pillows over her head, but she could see through the casement windows that the sky outside was darkening to silver. That meant Ben would soon have to leave for the night, and opportunities to see him were precious and not to be squandered. She opened her closet door, quickly exchanging her jeans for a flowered skirt with huge pockets, then continued on to the back of the closet, where another small door opened onto spiral stairs leading down to her office.

She ran across the room to her desk and removed the silver flask from the drawer. As she turned to leave, she heard a soft chime from the laptop computer on the desk. Her beloved long-distance friend Emerald was the only person who ever contacted her through the laptop's ancient (as technology went) text chat program, but Cally didn't have time to respond. She slipped the flask into one of the deep skirt pockets and hurried outside to join the festivities already in progress.

Apparently, every business in town had closed early this evening, as their proprietors were all sitting or standing on the Vale House front porch. Cally was greeted, as she shut the screen door behind her, by Merv Arkwright from the feedstore, Andi Kilmarten from the coffee shop, and Jud Thornton from the hardware store. Jacob Lucas, who everyone called Luke, had brought a stack of boxed pizzas from his gourmet-pizza and computer-repair emporium. Merv stood up from his seat and offered it to Cally. She waved a "no, thanks" to him and crossed to the porch steps instead.

Even the news store seemed to have closed early. It's proprietor, Ben's sister Bree, was just then preceding her brother through the gateway. Bree Dawes caught Cally's eye and scowled. Ben himself, when he looked up and spotted Cally, smiled his usual mellow smile, and that helped her ignore Bree. He patiently matched Bree's hobbling pace as they approached the porch, and Cally didn't mind that he didn't hurry. She liked watching him walk toward her. She liked everything he did.

When the pair reached the porch, Ben helped his sister to a chair. He paused to shake Ian's hand and welcome him home, then he returned to stand at Cally's side at the top of the steps. Slipping an arm around her, he drew her close to his side and, even though it was a warm evening, she basked in his nearness. They turned together to watch the band warming up.

The town elders, Ian's lifelong friends (all save the Captain, who had passed away the previous summer) had brought their customary instruments. Merv had brought his guitar and Doc his mandolin, while Jud produced a harmonica from his pocket. The sheriff, Dunn Mahon, some decades their junior, was fairly new to their little group. He had brought a ukulele and was trying to figure out how to fit its sound in with the other instruments.

Sofie sat next to Ian with a crocheted throw from the sofa around her shoulders. "Johnny, you should get out your drums!" she said.

"Oh, I'm too old for that, now," Ian held up his knobby, arthritic hands as evidence, but he smiled happily all the same. Cally still couldn't manage to picture Ian, even as a young man, playing drums in the rock band he and his friends had formed in their youth. She did note, though, that he still drummed on the arms of his chair as Merv and Doc began to cover an old Allman Brothers tune. When Ian joined in singing harmony, she was astounded at how rich and full his voice still was.

When they finished the song, Ian lifted the full brandy glass Katarina had stood waiting to hand him and proposed the first toast of the evening.

"I drink to your health when I'm with you," he said to his cronies. "I drink to your health when I'm alone. I drink to your health so often, I sometimes worry about my own!"

Laughter rang out across the lawn and into the darkening hills beyond the meadow fence. The sun had finished setting on the other side of Vale House, so that the last silver glow above the meadow had taken on a tarnished look. A waxing half-moon hovered above the farthest dark hill.

Doc had lifted his glass, prepared to quip a traditional toast of his own, but he fell silent as Cally stepped away from Ben and took the flask from her pocket.

"We don't need any glasses for this," she said, handing it to him.

Laughter turned to gasps as everyone recognized the flask. Doc accepted it from Cally with a trembling hand.

"Well, now," said Ian. "Isn't that something?"

Sofie applauded.

"I think maybe Mervyn should start," Doc suggested. He held the flask out from himself as if it were likely to bite him.

Merv set his guitar aside and stood, taking the flask gently between thumb and forefinger as if it were a bubble of blown glass. "Well, I had a silly old toast prepared, but..." He shook his head as he discarded his original plan and, clearing his throat, twisted off the silver cap.

"Here's to friendships." His voice quavered as he spoke. "Old ones and new ones. And to every love and every heartache we'll ever share, and every breeze around us, and every star that shines above us."

While everyone on the porch applauded this, he took the first sip straight from the flask and began to pass it around. Nobody corrected Sofie when she remarked how thoughtful it was of the Captain to share his whiskey with them.

When the flask had passed through Ben's hands and back to Cally's, she handed it to Doc to start it around again. By this time, Doc had loosened up and was able to recite a humorous toast about oak trees and old age.

"Oh, I have one!" Sofie piped up. "I have one!" She took the flask from Doc and held it up between herself and Ian, beaming at him over the top of it as she spoke.

> "Wine comes in at the mouth
> And love comes in at the eye;
> That's all we shall know for truth
> Before we grow old and die.
> I lift the glass to my mouth,
> I look at you, and I sigh."

Cally noticed she wasn't the only person on the porch trying not to sniffle out loud as Sofie nodded solemnly and informed them all: "That's by William Butler Yeats." She took a ladylike sip and handed the flask back to Doc.

"And on that note." Cally felt Ben's breath on her cheek when he spoke into her ear. She looked across the lawn to the now black sky above the eastern horizon and nodded to let him know she understood it was past time.

They walked down the steps and out of reach of the porch light, passing arm-in-arm across the lawn. As they neared the fence, their arms wrapped more tightly around one another until, by the time they reached it, they had turned face to face in a close embrace.

Cally always had to struggle to stop herself saying, "I wish you could stay, just for one night." Sometimes the words did slip out, and when they did, she knew they hurt him as much as they hurt her. This time, she succeeded in silencing herself by pressing her lips hard against his while the first stars winked into life above them.

When at last they stood back to regard one another he said, "That was a nice touch, using the Captain's flask. And you got the whiskey from the Fountain in Blackthorn, am I right?"

"It was good," she said, nodding. "Much lighter and smoother than what the Captain used to keep in it." Ben fixed her with a smile and waited for an answer to his question. Even in the dim moonlight, his eyes shone a deep china blue, crinkled at the corners and patient. She laughed and looked down. "Yes, I found the way there by myself, finally," she confessed.

He was silent a moment longer, brushing stray wisps of hair back from her face. "I try hard not to worry," he said at last. "About you doing this sort of stuff on your own. You know that, don't you? I know you're strong and capable. I know you've got this. I hope you don't hate that I do worry, sometimes."

She reached up to trace the streaks of silver in his beard. "Maybe we just both wish you could be with me, when I go there. I really would like to go back to the Fountain with you again, one of these nights. It was fun, that time. Or maybe, during some full moon, we can go to Seen's Mill."

Behind her, she heard more guests arriving to the party. In particular she heard the high giggle of Errin, one of the local teenagers, and that meant her friends Mima and Zenbe would be right behind her. The banter and laughter on the porch shifted again to music, an Eagles song, this time: "One of These Nights."

Cally sighed at how appropriate the title was to their situation, but she told Ben, "When I was a kid, I used to think they were saying 'One of these knights.' You know, like, knights in shining armor."

"I'm sorry you've had to settle for a knight in rusted, dented armor instead." His grin deepened the crinkles around his eyes, and she couldn't help putting up a hand to touch them.

Barred owls in the oak trees along Main Street responded to the music on the porch with a few experimental whoops of their own. From their midst, Cally heard a man's voice and a woman's call: "Hi, Mom!" "Hello, Dad!"

She turned to see her son Brandon, chivalrously supporting Ben's daughter Rosheen by the elbow as they entered the grounds and crossed the lawn, even though Rosheen didn't seem to need any support. She walked so lightly she might as well have floated up the porch steps. Ben waved and gazed after the couple wistfully until they disappeared into the crowd. Then he looked back across the meadow to the dark horizon.

"I guess you have to get going." Cally willed her hands to release him, but he pulled her against his chest and kissed her softly.

He took a deep breath when he finally let go. "I'll see you in the morning," he promised, just as he promised every night. Grasping the top rail of the fence, he vaulted over it to land in the tall grass on the other side.

She watched him walking in brisk strides, not looking back, east and a little south, until she could no longer hear his footsteps through the grass or discern his from among the rest of the shadows over the hills.

8 - Front Porch Music

The drinking and toasting went on far into the night. Cally did her best to sing harmony to some of the old Southern Rock songs the men covered. Brandon had brought a small, square drum he called a cajón, which he offered to Ian to play. George put in an appearance, as well, and did his best to participate, though only Cally and Rosheen (and possibly Luke) could hear the notes he played on his invisible electric bass.

They played more Eagles classics, they played "One Chain," they played "Green Grass and High Tides" with much shorter guitar solos. When they played "Seven Turns," it was Ian who covered Gregg Allman's hauntingly beautiful descant at the end.

The two young women who owned the Wyrd Systers Gifts and Books store had, apparently, kept their shop open until its normal closing time, because they arrived late in the evening. Cally greeted them vaguely, careful not to attempt calling them by their names. She knew they called themselves "Raven" and "Willow," but she could never be sure which was which. After complimenting Cally on her skirt (which she had bought in their shop) they offered free tarot readings to whoever might be interested. Then, undismayed by the lack of any response, they turned to join the other young guests who had gathered, away from the old men and their instruments, at the quieter north end of the porch.

Danya Barry came out of the house shortly after this, looking around bemusedly, and Cally apologized to her for the noise. "We should have given you a room facing the back of the house, where it would be quieter."

Danya smiled and shook her head. "It's fine," she said. "In my profession, I seldom get to sleep before four in the morning."

Luke spotted Danya and invited her over to join the other young people. "I knew you'd be here," he told her. "So, I made sure to bring a one hundred percent kosher pizza." He removed the last square box from his pizza warmer and held it out to her. "I keep my cheese in a separate refrigerator and everything!"

"Oh." She gave him an awkward smile. "That's sweet of you, but you didn't have to do that. Anyway, I just had a big dinner."

Luke looked disappointed, but Rosheen grabbed the pizza box eagerly from his hands. "Not a problem!" she said. "I have to eat for two, after all!" She put an arm around Danya to let her know she was welcome in any case to join them.

"You sure there's only one baby in there?" someone called from the crowd around Ian's end of the porch, and Rosheen smiled patiently. Luke appeared to cheer up considerably when Danya leaned against the railing beside him.

Cally turned to see how other incipient romances were coming along on the porch that evening. Bethany was sitting in the wicker chair next to Doc's. She had made no attempt to sing along with the music, but she had been watching his hands on the strings of his mandolin.

"Hey, Luke!" Merv set his guitar down and called out toward the crowd of young people. "How do you fix a broken pizza?"

Luke gave him a hard stare. "With tomato paste, ha ha."

Cally was inclined to agree with Luke about how funny that joke was not. "That was really cheesy, Doc," she said, getting more of a laugh than he had.

Danya had a better one. "I knew a hipster once who badly burned his mouth eating pizza." She waited until everyone was looking at her, then explained. "He ate it 'way before it was cool."

Cally had suspected Luke was crushing on Danya, but now he couldn't seem to take his eyes off her. The young people continued to crack jokes until someone warned Rosheen that if she laughed any harder, the baby might come sooner than expected.

"Oh, no," she assured them all. "Adam will arrive on Midsummer's Day. He's told me so in no uncertain terms."

The Iversons were the first to give up and go inside. "We have a long drive ahead of us in the morning," Celeste explained. Ian thanked them warmly for their patronage and friendship.

The sheriff, also, excused himself. "It may come as a surprise to you all," he said, "but there are other towns in this county I need to make my rounds of." He reached a hand to Bree and offered her a ride home in his patrol car. She stood stiffly, but instead of casting her usual scowl at Cally in departure, she turned around and, standing in front of Ian and Sofie, gave them what Cally could almost have sworn was a curtsy.

"Thank you for always making me feel welcome here," she said, in an uncharacteristically kindly tone. "I will see you both again, someday." Then, accepting the sheriff's arm, she stumped off down the porch steps.

Ian's jokes and toasts were beginning to sound decidedly muzzy, and Bethany's head slumped occasionally onto Doc's shoulder as she dozed off, but it was Sofie who decided to officially declare it a night. "We have a long trip ahead of us in the morning!" she said, cheerily echoing what the Iversons had said, and everyone agreed not to disagree with her as they all rose to begin saying their long-winded Southern goodnights.

As he finally stood, himself, and turned toward the door, Ian thanked Cally for all she had done for him, for Vale House, and for Woodley. "I am profoundly grateful you were sent to us," he said, taking one of her hands in both of his and patting it gently. "And, Ms. McCarthy, I'm so glad I finally got to hear you sing."

"I'm glad I got to hear you sing, too, Ian." She reached out to steady him as he stumbled. "You really should get to bed, though! I'll see you in the morning."

He peered at her as if he wondered what she meant by this, until Nell came and took him by the arm. He reached out to collect Sofie with his other arm while Cally held the door open for all three of them. She watched their retreating backs through the screen, until they had gone out of sight around the bend into the back hall, and then she turned to help Luke break down the empty pizza boxes. Katarina and Ignacio began picking up glasses and, Cally couldn't help but notice, piling them into a basket rather than collecting them on a tray.

Jud offered Doc and Merv a ride home, but Merv explained that he had walked, and would like to walk back. Donning his battered old baseball cap, he asked Cally if she would do him the kindness of walking him home. "I want to show you a shortcut," he explained.

9 - The Shortcut

Cally had hoped to check her computer, maybe read the message she'd received from Emerald before falling into bed at last, but she couldn't refuse the old gentleman's request. This was not just because it would have been rude for a young (or, at least, younger) person to refuse such a request from an older person, but also because any time Merv offered to show her a secret about Woodley, it held the potential of being anything but mundane. And she had so many questions...

Merv offered his arm and led the way down the porch steps. Here he turned, to her surprise, not toward the street but in the opposite direction, crossing the lawn to where it sloped down to the pond. He skirted around the pond on its western side while they both gazed, without speaking, at Ian's old boat listing there, more than half grounded on the bank.

He stopped at last next to the short, white fence surrounding the May family cemetery.

"You know where that nice little flask came from, don't you?" He placed his free hand over Cally's before she could withdraw it from his arm.

She didn't see the point in lying. "The Captain gave it to me. This past autumn, just after the closing on the Yellow House. He wanted to thank me for taking care of his old family home." She didn't need to remind Merv that the Captain had already been dead and buried for several months prior to this.

Merv nodded and released her hand, turning to look into the cemetery. The moon had begun to slide down the western sky, and only a few stray streaks of its light managed to pass through the oaks on the other side of the little patch of hallowed ground. One of them illuminated a headstone they both knew had no body beneath it; it's inscription, in the daylight, displayed the name "Sofia Arkwright May." The Captain's grave lay a few feet beyond this, in soft shadow.

"The last time I saw that flask," Merv said, more to himself than to Cally, "Doc and Ian and I were tucking it into the Captain's jacket pocket, just before we closed his casket."

Cally was not surprised when a shiver ran through her. What did surprise her was that it was a warm shiver, not a cold chill. She couldn't help herself; she reached over and wrapped an arm around Merv's shoulders.

"He's gone now," she reassured him. "Really gone, I mean. He's at peace now – he's done everything he meant to do."

He returned her embrace and said, "Thank you." Then he turned away from the cemetery, leading the way once again, past the pond to where the ground rose gently toward the railroad track embankment. Beyond the tracks, a row of lights twinkled welcomingly from the front windows of all the cottages along Bells Road.

"I am honored to know you, Callaghan McCarthy," Merv said as they walked. "I'm not completely sure how you found us, but I'm glad you came to live in Woodley. May I ask, how is your new book coming along?"

"Please, Mr. Arkwright, call me Cally." She was sure he never would, so she answered his question. "My new novel is selling well. I guess I had more fans left from my first one than I expected. I'm just glad they're willing to forgive me for having taken so long to write another book."

"You're not working on a new one now?"

She groaned softly in the back of her throat. "I'm kind of behind schedule."

"You always say that," he said with a little chuckle. "Yet you always pull something out of your hat at the last minute."

"I guess I do," she admitted. She didn't bother to give him any excuses about being too busy running Vale House. She knew she had plenty of time to write. "It's just that I'm kind of taking a departure from what I've written before."

"All life is a departure from what has been before."

"That's..." She tried to decide whether she wanted to say "wise" or "philosophical" or "deep." She ended up saying, "True."

Pausing beside the railroad tracks dividing the field in half, Merv broached a different topic. "Jud is very pleased about the new business taking root in town, lately. And it is not lost on him you've had something to do with that. He thinks you're the bee's knees, now. Your friend Danya Barry is also helping to put Woodley back on the map."

"Danya's not exactly my friend." Cally gave a little snort. "And I hope she's not going around telling the whole world to feel free to come and trample all over an Authentic Haunted Town, despite what Jud may want."

"No, nothing like that," Merv said. "Ms. McCarthy, you know this town is hard to find."

Cally did know that. Woodley did not appear on any maps, and showed up most unreliably in GPS databases. "But people still manage to find it," she said, and waited for Merv to explain why. She knew he and the other town elders not only knew why but had something to do with making it so. She had been waiting over a year now for them to let her in on this secret, and she hoped Merv was about to do just that. "I have a responsibility, now," she pointed out.

"And life is short."

He looked eastward along the tracks. The gravel of the berm was choked with weeds, and dog fennel grew between the ties. This had never been allowed to happen before, when the tracks had been in use. No trains had come along them for many months, now, ever since an incident had damaged the trestle over the culvert by which the tracks crossed the creek. The official explanation had been "frost heave," something that almost never happened this far south.

"Opinion is divided as to whether the trains should go through or not," Merv said.

"Well, they certainly shouldn't until the trestle is repaired!"

"There are those who say," he went on, "that the tracks should never have been built in the first place. Jud, of course, strongly disagrees with this train of thought." He laughed a little at his own joke. "The Thornton family, back in the day, was one of the early proponents of a freight stop in Woodley. But others warned that the rails, the iron rails, would hold down energy that needs to flow into the world."

Cally nodded her understanding. She had seen this energy herself. "But what is it, exactly? Is it good or is it bad?"

"Good and bad aren't useful concepts, here. Maybe all we

can really say is that our interference has caused problems. It's always a judgement call. We make decisions the best we can, but none of them are without drawbacks as well as benefits. And we're all getting older. We need to pass these kinds of decisions on to you younger people. Someone needs to man the switch, I guess you could say. Ms. McCarthy, we all admire your capacity for discretion. That's quite rare in a youngster such as yourself."

Cally laughed, a little too loudly, causing a dog in one of the cottages to bark. "Youngster!" she said. "Mr. Arkwright, if you're trying to flatter me, it isn't going to work. "

Merv laughed, also, but more softly. "Only because you've already fallen for someone else." He turned and winked at her. "You do realize Young Bennet is actually much older than I am, don't you?"

"So he tells me," Cally said. "Mr. Arkwright, was there something else you wanted to tell me? Maybe you want to show me where I might find this...switch?"

He stepped over the tracks and headed toward the unmarked stretch of blacktop that was Bells Road. Cally followed as he began to tell her a story instead.

"When we were all kids – Doug and Ian, Jud and I – I guess we knew something was going on around here. I mean, we didn't realize it was any different from how things were in the rest of the world. We'd never been outside Woodley, except once in a while if we went with our parents to the big grocery store in Blackthorn. Ha, we thought that was The Big City!" He laughed as they stepped onto Bells Road and turned left. "It wasn't until we started high school. We had to go to Blackthorn for school, then, because the school here only goes through middle school. New Blackthorn, I mean, not the old version of the town. I think you know what I mean. Anyway, we noticed people always looked at us funny. At first, we figured it was because Woodley is so small and backward, but other kids would say things like 'Your town doesn't even exist!' They would tease us and accuse us of being ghosts or something. We had to get into some trouble to prove we weren't!" He laughed. "A girl I took a fancy to in my senior year asked me quite seriously why Woodley doesn't show up on maps, but, that's a whole different story..."

Here he paused next to a white picket fence surrounding one

of the cottages. Though it was late, small lights shone from the front windows of almost every cottage. Merv's cottage, set well back from the road, was no exception. Cally wondered why Merv, such a decent and kind man by all accounts, and a respected member of one of the great, old, land-holding families of Woodley, lived all alone here. That was just one of dozens of questions she would have liked to ask him.

Merv turned to face her, resting one hand on his front gate but not opening it. "I guess that was when I learned to be so evasive with my answers to direct questions. Which proved to be a useful skill, later on, so let me apologize, Ms. McCarthy, for my lack of skill now in giving you straight answers."

He turned and looked back the way they had come, across the field and the pond and up again to the dim, distant Vale House porch light. "In those days, it was James May – Ian's dad – who was the Armadeur of Vale House. We didn't know anything about that, of course, back then. Even Ian didn't know. All we knew for sure was the fishing was pretty good down at the Mays' pond, but if you followed the creek through the culvert, under the tracks..." He gestured toward the dark culvert, and then beyond it toward the bulk of the woods surrounding the meadow, curving like a soft, green arm behind all the cottages. "You could follow the stream on into the meadow. At some point, it would flow into the woods, with a deer trail – we assumed it was a deer trail – running alongside. One day we followed it for hours, just to see where it went. We thought we were heading straight north." He turned where he stood, describing their journey with a waving hand. "But when we came out of the woods at the other end, wouldn't you know it, we were standing right here. These cottages had not been built yet, in those days. We were facing down this slope, toward the pond there, and looking across at Vale House."

Cally found herself shuddering, following his gesture to Vale House's porch light. "We were a little freaked out, but we figured we'd just got ourselves turned around. Except... there were no railroad tracks.

"Well, we were boys, so there was nothing for it but to go and investigate. A weird blue light seemed to be coming from the windows of Ian's house, so we decided to go and check that out first, though I have to admit, it did freak us out a little and we proceeded carefully. We snuck through the trees around the pond, and when we came around to where Ian's boat is now, we saw a little old man in greasy overalls sitting on the bank fishing."

"Rum!" said Cally. Merv turned to her with a puzzled frown. "No, that was his name," she explained. "Is his name. Rum – I've met him, too." She tilted her head toward the fence, which was where she usually saw the Vale's local land-wight.

Merv smiled and nodded. "He didn't tell us his name, but I guess we didn't ask. You don't normally see strangers in Woodley – we thought he must be some kind of itinerant hobo or something. We didn't run away, though. He was pulling fish after fish out of the pond. Amazing fish! I've never seen any like them, before or since. We got so distracted by that, we ended up sitting down to fish with him. Caught a bunch, too, though none as big as the ones he was catching. It was getting on toward evening by the time we remembered about our plan to investigate the house. We gave the old man all our fish and started on up the hill toward the house. But Michael Dawes came around the corner from the back garden, just then, and he stopped us.

"Mr. Dawes, he was your Ben's father. He disappeared a long time ago, but he was already in the habit of disappearing by then anyway. I have a feeling you may have heard Ben's side of that story! Anyway, he came around the corner and he spoke to us very sternly. 'You boys better be getting on home now!' He pointed back the way we had come, toward the woods at the north end of the field.

"We told him that was exactly what we were trying to do. After all, Vale House was Ian's home! But Dawes pointed back toward the woods and said, 'No, you need to go back the way you came. Follow the exact path you took to get here and do it before the sun goes down.' He was kind of scaring us anyway, after the things we'd heard about him, the way his wife had disappeared and he, himself, would disappear into the meadow for weeks at a time, so we just did what he said. We ran back to the woods and back along the trail beside the stream until we came to the meadow again, and then to the culvert. Ran under the railroad trestle and back to the pond. There was no more blue light coming out of Vale House, no more Mr. Dawes and no more old man fishing – Rum, you say his name was?

"Well, the years went by. Old man Dawes finally disappeared for good. We boys formed our band and started to travel outside of town for gigs. That's when we really began to put together how different this place is. Eventually, we all met our sweethearts and tried to settle down. Ian married Sofie. A few years later, Ian's dad passed on, leaving the house to him. I guess we all figured it out little by little. A little bit at a time, we all shouldered our share of the mantle that had formerly been borne by Michael Dawes and James May and a few others. Became the caretakers of this odd little town. This gateway between two worlds. One of many gateways, I'm fairly certain, and I hope so, because we've never been quite sure we're doing it right. I don't know if our fathers were ever sure, either. We do the best we can."

He took Cally's hands and held them gently in both of his. "Dear Cally," he said. It was the first time he had ever called her anything but "Ms. McCarthy." He peered earnestly, as best he could in the dim moonlight, into her eyes. "We are not hiding anything from you. Not anymore. Only..." He looked past her shoulder, down Bells Road to where it seemed to end at the meadow fence, where the houses stopped and the fence crossed the horizon, dividing Woodley from the meadow beyond. "Well, you'll see. No, I mean that quite literally. We would answer all your questions straight out, but the truth is, you won't understand most of it until you see it for yourself. You are seeing more and more, these days. I think you're going to be alright." He released her hands and opened his gate.

Cally wanted to say, "Thanks, Mr. Arkwright, for once again telling me nothing." Instead, as he stepped onto his walkway and shut the gate, she asked, "Merv, when you put that flask in the Captain's pocket, what was in it?"

"Well..." He paused, his hands resting on the top of the gate. "Of course, we filled it full of his favorite rotgut whiskey. Why?"

Cally laughed. "I thought so. Then you should be pleased to know, when he gave it to me, it was empty."

10 - Green Grass and High Tides

The best, and the worst, thing about the fast-approaching summer season was the fact that the sun came up earlier every day. Cally was not ready to wake when it rose, but she slipped out of bed eagerly anyway, because sunrise also meant Ben was returning.

She stepped through the open casement window onto the belvedere above the front porch. This afforded her an unobstructed view of the meadow, where the silver light even now shifted gradually to gold above the furthest hill on the horizon. A small, dark spot of movement appeared at the edge of this light. As the sky above grew bluer, the shape drew nearer until she could make out the figure of a man walking, in well-practiced, ground-devouring strides, toward Vale House.

Knowing he was watching her, too, Cally slipped her nightgown down over her shoulders, stepped out of it, and hung it on the edge of the window frame. By the time she had gone back through the window, crossed the room and unlocked the door to the spiral stair, she could hear his footsteps on the porch. She smiled and slipped back under the covers.

When she woke again, much later in the morning, she edged gently away from him so as not to wake him. He looked utterly peaceful in his sleep, and she knew sleep was something he seldom had a chance to do.

The smell of coffee drifted into the room, and the muffled sound of doors opening and shutting in the hallway outside her own door. Breakfast was being served. Bethany and Katarina understood why Cally tended not to come downstairs until later in the morning, these days, and in fact her new morning schedule had been devised with their emphatic encouragement. She still couldn't help feeling a little guilty about leaving them with the earliest morning duties, even though her own work in the office was not as urgent.

She let Ben sleep while she went into the Dogwood Room's tiny en suite bathroom to wash up. He would not have to leave to help Bree in the family store until noon, and Katarina would make sure she got breakfast into him before then. Breakfast at Vale House was the only opportunity Ben ever had to enjoy a real, home-cooked meal. Their life, Cally admitted, was not by any means a perfect happily-ever-after, but it was perfect enough for her. It was absolutely much better than she had ever hoped, at one time, it could be. Her heart, as she brushed her teeth, was full of gratitude.

Wrapping a fluffy Vale House bathrobe around herself, she returned to the vanity in the bedroom. Ben was snoring softly, which made her smile all the more while she combed out her wet hair. When she set the comb down, her eye fell on a little fired-clay box, a gift from Nell, next to one of many piles of notebooks and pens. With one eye still on Ben, she lifted the cover of the box. The inside provided only enough room for the silver moon necklace, the glamour-piercing talisman. Her hand hovered over it, considering whether or not she would have any reason, today, to wear it under her clothes.

She felt a little guilty, glancing from the box to Ben, as she had still never told him about having this object in her possession. She'd been procrastinating about it ever since Christmas, because she knew he was not on good terms with the man who had given it to her: his father, Michael Dawes. Now she looked from Ben to the silver talisman in its box, and back again.

Ben had always insisted he was human. Even though his mother was the queen of the local Daoine Sidhe court, he disavowed his faerie side and preferred to embrace his humanity. Still, ever since she had been gifted the talisman, Cally had wondered. If she could see through any faerie glamour that might encompass Ben, would he look different? She knew he was much older than he appeared to be. Did he only maintain his mellow, middle-aged appearance by using faerie glamour, and did he appear, in reality, to be the nonagenarian he actually was? It was even possible, she realized, his faerie side might manifest by way of some feature such as stag's antlers, or reptilian skin, as some of his faerie kin possessed. Maybe even both. She had no doubt at all that she would love him regardless of his true appearance, but it was hard to not want to really know...

She let the lid of the little box fall shut. No, if he wanted her to know what he looked like, he would already have shown her. Anyway, it didn't matter.

She turned and opened the closet door, reaching inside for a clean blouse. Then she shut it quietly and went back to the vanity. Before she could stop herself again, she had raised the silver semi-circle to her eye.

She steeled herself to remain calm no matter what she saw, but the sigh of relief she let out when she looked at Ben was so loud, she feared it might wake him. He only stirred a little, however, and then fell back to softly snoring. Cally calmed her breath, gazing through the crystal in the center of the pendant. Lying on the pillow next to hers she saw only a man. Just a human man, as he had always insisted he was. A wave of guilt as profound as her relief washed over her, and she began to lower the pendant from her eye. That was when she noticed it.

In the sunlight slanting across the pillow, she noticed that the gray streaks through his hair and beard – which she had always loved, likening them to rays of sunlight – were not there. Neither were the crinkles around his eyes which always deepened when he smiled. His hair on the pillow was as brown as rich earth, as thick and full and free of silver as that of any twenty-year-old.

He turned onto his back, and Cally's heart rose into her throat, but he settled back to sleep. The sheet had slipped off him and there, in the middle of her bed, lay the taut, firm body of a young man, with no trace of the paunch all young humans dreaded eventually developing.

The talisman fell from her hand to the carpet. That, of all the things she had imagined she might see, had been the last thing she would have expected. She choked on her own breath as she stooped to pick up the pendant, and when she turned to put it back into its box, she found herself facing her reflection in the vanity mirror.

A middle-aged woman was looking back at her. A woman whose appearance, until that moment, she had felt to be quite within the limits of acceptability, especially for someone who was about to become a grandmother any day now. Now all she could see was the spiderwebbing of silver throughout her once golden hair. Yesterday she had rather liked this, as well as the fine smile-lines around her mouth. Now, as she leaned closer to the mirror, she raised a trembling finger to the little, white hair on her lip she had been meaning to pluck for the past two days. She nearly jumped into her own reflection when a knock came at the door.

She jammed the talisman back into the box and shut it so hard she feared she might have chipped it. Ben was sitting up, looking at the door with the sheet tangled around his body once more. He appeared again as he normally did, but now Cally could not un-see what she had seen.

The knock came again. It was an odd knock – more like a hollow boom happening just outside the door. Cally let out her breath. That was George's knock. He had never mastered the art of making his aethereal knuckles interact with the door, but he could project sound from his imagination to those who were able to hear ghosts. Cally sighed and wrapped her robe tighter around herself, giving Ben a "just go back to sleep; I'll handle this" look while she opened the door a few inches.

"What is it, George? I'm kind of..."

"I didn't mean to disturb you, Cally. I'm so sorry." He truly did look sorry – his large, brown eyes glittered with unshed tears. "But Miss Sofie wants to say goodbye to you, and she promised not to go into anyone's room anymore without permission..."

"What? Goodbye?" Cally opened the door the rest of the way and stepped out. Sofie stood near the butler's desk at the north end of the hallway, wearing the flower-sprinkled nightgown she'd always worn back when everyone had thought she was a ghost. "But you've only just arrived!"

She suspected Sofie was having another one of her spells, and composed herself to be as reassuring and gentle as possible, inching closer to the old woman. "We're all so glad you and Ian are home, Sofie. We were hoping you'd stay at Vale House for a good, long while, now." She reached out gently. "Why don't you let me help you get dressed, and then we can all have a nice breakfast together..."

She stopped just short of touching Sofie's arm because, she noticed, she could see the lamp shining through her.

"No, no, it's alright," Sofie was saying. "Johnny has already gone on ahead of me. I really should follow quickly, or he'll feel awful about leaving me behind." Cally had never heard her speak so lucidly, had never seen her look at anyone with such a direct, unabashed gaze. "You see," she went on, nodding, "that was always his greatest fear. For me to wake and find him gone. He would have gone a long time ago, but he was waiting for me. Everything he ever did was for me..."

She looked away through the walls toward what Cally knew was the east, where the sun was now hanging over the meadow. "He gave up so much, in life, for me," Sofie continued, then looked back at Cally. "That was why I made my wish, to the Fairy Queen, for him to be able to go sailing at last, like he always wanted to do, but never could because of me." She nodded solemnly. "He would have died this past winter if we'd stayed here, but in Faerie the cancer couldn't touch him. It was the queen's gift to him, you see. In return for all he's done for this Vale. Don't you forget..." she added, glancing behind Cally to where Ben now came out of the bedroom door. "She'll owe you just such a gift, one day, too. Don't be too proud to ask for it."

And with that, Sofia Arkwright May smiled, and nodded, and vanished.

At her side, Cally heard George intoning something in a language she didn't understand – some kind of prayer or benediction. She turned around to look, open-mouthed but unable to speak, at Ben standing in the doorway wrapped in the bedsheet. The tears standing in his eyes showed he had at least heard the conversation, and Cally was grateful not to have to explain it to him. She ran back to huddle in his arms until they both heard footsteps running downstairs, and Katarina crying in the dining room.

11 - Never Die Young

Katarina had found them.

It had been Ian's habit, for all the years he'd been master of Vale House, to appear at the breakfast table at 8:30 a.m. sharp. When he and Sofie hadn't appeared as expected, Bethany had suggested Katarina might bring them a tray of tea and pastries. "I'm sure they're exhausted from last night."

The tray, tea, and pastries sat forgotten now atop the spare quilt at the foot of the bed. The Vale House staff: Katarina and Ignacio, Bethany, and Cally, stood beside the bed with their arms around one another while Ben, having dressed hastily, stood shifting awkwardly from foot to foot in the doorway between the bedroom and the study. Nell's little calico cat lay curled asleep beside Sofie's knee while Nell herself sat silently, one hand on her mother's cooling shoulder, in the bedside chair.

Doc put his stethoscope back in his bag. "I'm going to call it about five o'clock this morning," he said. Bethany's choked sob covered the sound of his.

Katarina had stopped crying out loud, but tears still ran freely down her cheeks and dropped off her chin. "How sweet that they went together like that," she said. "It's just what Ian would have wanted." She sniffed hard and picked up the tea tray.

"They were circles around the sun." Nell looked up at them all with a reassuring smile. She was the only person in the room whose eyes were dry, and this made Cally concerned for her.

Cally shifted her gaze to Doc and saw that he was also looking at Nell with the same concern in his eyes. "I'll contact the county coroner," he said in a voice that would have sounded more authoritative if it hadn't been pinched with emotion. "I understand Ian left instructions with you, Ms. McCarthy."

Cally looked past Ben's shoulder to the antique desk in the study. "Yes. A copy of his will is locked in the desk, and I have the key in my purse." She already knew what was in the handwritten letter accompanying the will, the main thing being his wish that Cally should take care of everything. Assuming responsibility for Vale House had seemed easy enough, before, with Ian only gone on holiday, but now that he truly was not ever coming back, she already felt the weight of it crushing her.

As if reading her thoughts, Nell said, "You always tell everyone I'm stronger than I seem. You need to let me help you."

Cally didn't have the strength to argue. She only wondered aloud, "What should we tell the guests?"

They all exited the suite together. Cally paused, as they passed through the study, beside Ian's desk. The old ghost-cat Doctor Boojums lay purring in the middle of the desktop, apparently snoozing, amongst sea charts, sticky notes, and a copy of "The Return of the King" with a bookmark halfway through.

"I guess he really was trying to tell me something," Cally said to no one in particular. "Last fall, when he gave me the key to this desk. I didn't want to hear it, then. I still don't."

Doctor Boojums opened one eye to look at her, then slowly closed it again. Cally followed everyone out the door at the opposite end of the room.

The Iversons had abandoned their breakfast and were hovering near the end of the back hallway, just inside the dining room. Celeste looked like she had already been crying, and when she saw their faces, she gripped her husband's arm and said, "Oh, I knew something must be wrong!"

Doc (*"God bless him,"* Cally thought) shouldered the burden of informing them of what they already seemed to know, and Celeste burst into fresh tears. Cally led the couple back to the table, where she appropriated the napkins from under a few place settings and piled them in front of Celeste.

"You are absolutely welcome to stay a few more days," she told the couple. "At no charge, of course. So you can be here for the..." She swallowed with the effort of saying it. "For the funeral."

Celeste seemed to be considering this, but William quietly reminded her that they had promised to be home in time for a granddaughter's birthday. Celeste blew her nose and nodded reluctantly. "Anyway, you're going to need all the rooms," she said. "Family will be coming from out of town to pay their respects."

Cally had to admit she was right, and cast a sympathetic eye to Bethany who, as the oldest family friend, would end up being the one to shoulder most of the responsibility for calling all of said relatives. Ignacio went upstairs to collect the couple's luggage. With many a tearful hug goodbye, William and Celeste Iverson departed the house just as Anderson and Geraldine Toller came down the stairs.

"Death has recently visited this home," Geraldine proclaimed when she reached the bottom step.

"Don't," Cally thought with all her might at the woman. *"Just don't."*

"There's fresh coffee on the sideboard," Bethany informed in a flat, robotic voice as the couple walked into the dining room. Katarina ran to the kitchen to fetch that morning's hot entrée, as well as napkins to replace the ones Celeste had used. Bethany stepped into the Hall and took a sheet of paper from beside the phone. This she placed, along with a pen, on the tablecloth next to where the Tollers had seated themselves. "If you'll just sign here, you'll be all checked out, and then you can take your time finishing your breakfast. Ignacio will fetch your luggage and put it into your car."

"That won't be necessary," said Anderson Toller. "We've decided to stay another night."

"But..." Bethany looked to Cally for support.

"I'm afraid that won't be possible." Cally began to explain, as levelly as possible, the reason why they were about to need all of the guest rooms.

"Nonsense," Geraldine interrupted. "I just heard, over the railing upstairs, that other couple declining your invitation to stay longer. We can avail ourselves of their vacancy."

"Anyway..." Anderson plucked a cinnamon bun from the platter in the middle of the table. "With the shade of death hanging so closely over this house today, you'll need us here more than ever."

Cally closed her eyes and tried to think of what Ian, ever polite and diplomatic, would have done. It still took every ounce of self-control she possessed to reply calmly, "That remark, Mr. Toller, was in very poor taste."

It was probably not what Ian would have said.

"It's alright." Nell had been standing, completely silent, in the back hall just outside the room. Now she came closer and put a comforting hand on the back of Cally's shoulder. "Mama and Daddy are at peace. You know this. Mama spoke to you. They won't be hanging around the house, because they know they've left it in capable hands." Cally turned and saw that Nell was not looking at her, but at the Tollers. To her astonishment, Geraldine Toller was unable to meet Nell's eye.

Nell's hand on Cally's shoulder made the weight on them feel so much lighter, and she suddenly felt ashamed of being so touchy. It should have been she who was comforting Nell, not the other way around.

"We will check out tomorrow morning," Anderson Toller assured them all. "This should be no problem for you, as our room will be vacated in plenty of time to freshen it for visitors arriving from farthest away."

With a dazed look in her eye, Bethany picked up the paper and went back into the Hall to annotate the guest registry.

"In the meantime," said Geraldine, "we need to do some shopping." She took a napkin from the stack Katarina had brought and wrapped two cinnamon buns in it. "Is there an antique shop in this town? I need to buy at least six objects."

Cally blinked to clear her head. "What sort of objects?"

"They should be easily held in the hand." Geraldine held up the bundle of pastries to demonstrate. "Attractive, but not too reflective, and ideally they should be previously owned. Stoneware or glass is best, but wood or metal will do."

Cally's mind was not at all on the topic at hand, but her mouth formed an answer regardless. "A woman recently opened a new shop on Main Street. Not antiques, per se, but a little boutique of knickknacks and things from estate sales."

Katarina elaborated. "It doesn't have a sign in the window, yet, but it's right next to Dawe's News."

Geraldine nodded and tucked the buns into her purse. "That will do nicely." With a wave, she turned and walked into the Hall, Anderson following closely. He paused, when the couple reached the door, and turned around.

"I'm sorry for your loss," he said as he and his wife let the screen door bang shut behind them.

12 - Dumbo's Feathers

Ian May had been respected by many, and most of the out-of-town friends and relatives Bethany telephoned with the sad news informed her they would be leaving for Woodley immediately. Even counting on the Tollers vacating the Hydrangea Room, Bethany had to warn them Vale House would be quite crowded, and that some of them might have to double up.

Danya Barry came downstairs too late in the morning for breakfast. She seemed sincerely sorry to hear of Ian and Sofie's passing and promised to vacate her room as quickly as possible. Bethany assured her there was no need to hurry, as mourners would be not arriving until late afternoon at earliest. Katarina offered to reheat some sausage for her, and to make a fresh pot of coffee.

"It's alright," Danya assured them. "It's almost lunchtime anyway. I'll just stop at the pizza shop on my way out of town. I want to talk with Luke, anyway."

The Tollers returned, carrying shopping bags, late in the afternoon. Cally, who was relieving Bethany at the reception desk at the time, did not bother to call Ignacio to help them take their purchases to their room, but that didn't seem to be their plan anyway. Geraldine stopped in the Hall and began unpacking the bags, setting tissue-wrapped bundles on the desk.

From a lavender gift bag, emblazoned with the words "Wyrd Systers" in a curly font, she drew a round lump of gray rock about the size of a lemon. This she held up to show Cally how it split into two halves to reveal white and purple crystals lining its hollow interior. "These have already been cleared!" she announced with apparent delight. "Those two girls who run the place, Raven and Willow, they certainly know what they're doing!"

Cally had a different opinion about that, but she kept it to herself as the woman continued to unwrap her purchases on the desktop. "The old dame who runs the news store, though, she's a real piece of work."

"She certainly is." That was one thing with which Cally could agree.

"I had to ask her son where to find more objects," Geraldine went on.

"He's not her son. He's..."

"Had to go across to the hardware store to find this," Geraldine interrupted, unwrapping a ball of newspaper from around a highly detailed wooden train engine. "It's new, but it will do quite nicely."

"Do nicely for what?" Cally didn't actually want to know, but she couldn't look away from the odd assortment of MacGuffins ranged across the desk blotter. In addition to the geodes and toy train, Geraldine had lined up a starfish-shaped candy dish, a brass candlestick, and a small red vase Cally thought looked vaguely familiar. Instead of packing her purchases back up, then, Geraldine wadded all the tissue paper into one of the bags and stuffed this into her purse.

"Do you mind if we set up in the next room?" Without waiting for Cally's answer, Anderson Toller gathered up the objects and turned to carry them into the parlor.

"Set up what? Mr. and Mrs. Toller, we are getting ready for a..." Cally still choked whenever she had to say the word. "For a funeral. We don't have time to host a ghost hunt or a séance or whatever you're planning."

"Do not worry." Geraldine reached across the desk and patted Cally's arm with a bony hand. "We will set out the objects in unobtrusive places. That works best. And then we will retire to our room. I will call to the spirits from there, completely out of your way. Each spirit will find its object by morning, and when we check out tomorrow, we will simply take them away with us. You won't be inconvenienced in any way."

While Cally was still trying to parse all this, Geraldine followed her husband into the parlor. Cally considered following as well, but the phone rang, and she answered to find herself talking to a woman who introduced herself as Merv Arkwright's daughter. "I'm so sorry," she said. "Ian was always so nice to me when I was a kid, and Nellie and I..."

Cally was barely listening. Instead, she followed the sound

of Geraldine's and Anderson's voices around the parlor. Geraldine was intoning something in a singsong voice.

"Don't go to any trouble," Merv's daughter, whose name Cally hadn't even caught, was saying. "I won't need a room at Vale House. I'll just crash on Dad's couch. See you tomorrow."

Bethany came from the dining room into the Hall as Cally hung up the phone. "I feel so useless," she said. "Kat and Ignacio have got all the food planned, and even rented extra chairs. I don't know what else I can help with, and I have to do something or I'll just start crying again."

Cally looked at her notepad full of things she still needed to take care of. "Well, I've already contacted the funeral parlor in Blackthorn to order the caskets. Do you think you could call around and find out where we might buy a nice guestbook? It'll help us remember, later, who we need to send thank-you notes to. I'll call about the headstone, and..."

Bethany snatched the entire list from Cally's hand. "Got it!" she said with obvious relief, taking over the desk chair as Cally rose and followed the sound of the Tollers' voices into the parlor.

"You will be safely cared for," Geraldine was saying. She turned in the middle of the room, nodding toward each of the objects her husband had nestled amongst the already considerable quantity of knickknacks displayed throughout the room. "No, not there," she added, returning her focus to her husband as he set the red vase on an end table. "Put it next to his widow." She pointed at a small, silver-framed photo of Nell on the mantel, then resumed her exhortations. "You will be safe while we transport you to your new home, and..."

"Wait a minute!" Cally gazed at the toy train on the bookcase. "Are you intending to...trap? The spirits in these objects?" She had suddenly thought of George and his *zemi*, the little wooden carving to which he had until only recently been bound, and from which he was so happy to have been freed at last.

"Trap?" Anderson Toller's expression was one of mildly offended patience. "Oh, no, my dear. I wouldn't call it that at all. We merely transport them to our workshop, where we then release them safely to the other side without harm to anyone."

Cally couldn't imagine what to say to this. *"Very well, then, proceed,"* was right out, but she had to admit it would be refreshing to be rid of the Preacher's annoying presence, not to mention the new and violent spirit that was probably Foster.

"But I... Well, I just don't feel right about this." She started to say she would have to ask her boss about it. This was an excuse she had found handy in the past, whenever she needed to say no to something without upsetting a guest. But that just reminded her she didn't have a boss anymore, and fresh tears of grief sprang into her eyes.

"I understand." Anderson laid a hand on Cally's shoulder. She knew he probably meant for it to be comforting, but she found it heavy and irritating. "This sort of thing would be unusual to you at the best of times, and you have a lot going on right now. Let my wife handle this for you. Being rid of the negative influences in this house will only make your life a bit easier, especially over the next several days..."

She turned and ran from the room. Bethany only glanced up at her as she crossed the Hall. "No, don't be silly!" she was saying to someone on the phone. "We would never charge you! You're part of the family, and anyway..."

Cally took the stairs two at a time and was out of breath by the time she reached the top. Pausing to wipe tears from the corners of her eyes, she called "George!" She didn't bother keeping her voice down. "Georgie! Are you here? Where are you?"

When he didn't appear, she ran to the desk at the north end of the hallway and yanked open one of the little doors in its front. Digging through a mess of brittle rubber bands and yellowed envelopes, her fingers finally seized upon a triangular lump of wood, carved with deep lines and not a few cracks and canine chew-marks. This she snatched up and held to her breast. "Oh, George, I know you're not bound to this thing anymore but, right now, I wish you were." Her thumbs ran over and over the carvings in the ancient wood, and she found comfort in this, just as she imagined George must have in life. She put back the envelopes she had scattered and shut the little door. "I'll just take your *zemi* with me into my room," she said, in case he was listening. "To keep you...to keep it safe. And yes, you can consider that an invitation."

George did not appear until well after midnight. "It's so quiet, tonight," he observed. Cally, sitting up in bed, looked up from her laptop to see him standing beside the vanity.

"Oh, my god, Georgie!" Relief ran like water down out of her clenched shoulders. "I'm so glad to see you! That Toller woman..."

"Are you talking to Emerald?" He nodded at the laptop. "Tell her I said hi!"

Cally looked at the screen as if she had forgotten what it was. "Oh. Oh, yes." She typed George's greeting to Emerald, then looked back up at him. "Georgie be careful. That woman...I'm not sure I approve of what she's doing. Even if she is doing it to you-know-who. I should have put my foot down and told them to leave this morning!"

George's smile was gentle and not at all concerned. "It's alright. It's like Emerald said. You're new at this Being In Charge thing, but you have all of us to help you. Under the circumstances, it's amazing you're thinking at all, never mind thinking straight."

Cally sighed into the light emanating from the laptop screen. That was what Emerald had just said. In fact, it was exactly what she had said, word for word...

"George, you were eavesdropping, weren't you?" She shook her head, but she couldn't be angry with him. "I'm so relieved to see you. Please, just stay away from the parlor. Be careful!"

He laughed his musical laugh and shook his head. "Don't worry. Remember, I know, now. That being bound to an object stuff was all in my head. She can't fool me now. Honestly, I doubt she can fool any of us, except maybe Foster, and...sorry, I meant, 'he who must not be named'!"

Cally felt a passing pang of guilt for hoping he was exactly right, and then, quite suddenly, she realized how tired she was.

"I think I can get some sleep now," she said. "Now that I know you're alright." She said this aloud to George and then typed it into the chat for Emerald's benefit. "George, feel free to stay here in my room tonight. Your *zemi* is in my dresser, and ..."

She managed to power the laptop down and close it before

she drifted off to sleep, but she did not get as far as removing it from her lap to the nightstand. She dreamed all night that it was a weight like a coffin, pinning her down as she lay half buried in a cave.

13 - Kings and Queens Bow

"And thank you so much for your hospitality." Anderson Toller signed his bill and handed it, along with the key to the Hydrangea Room, to Bethany. Cally stood in the parlor doorway watching Geraldine Toller circling the room. The old woman was chanting something to herself as she tucked her assortment of random objects into a padded satchel. When she finished with the red vase from the mantel, she looked up at Cally and smiled.

"You will find the atmosphere in this house to be much lighter, now," she announced. "This house is clear!"

It didn't feel any different to Cally. She turned and glanced up to where she had last seen George at the top of the stairs. He was still there, and he winked when he saw her looking at him.

He disappeared just as Ignacio, coming down the stairs, was about to walk through him. Carrying the Tollers' bags, Ignacio preceded the couple out to their car. Anderson paused in the doorway to reach for Cally's hand. Instead of shaking it, however, he patted it as if it were a dog. "I assure you they will be safe with us. And may I just say again how sorry we are for your loss." He took the satchel from his wife and hoisted it onto his shoulder. The screen door would have banged shut behind the couple, except for the fact that even as they left, the entire town of Woodley began to arrive.

Ian's own family had not been especially large, but he had been well loved by many members of the community, and they did have large and far-flung families. Cally had offered, at breakfast, to move into her office temporarily so the Dogwood Room would be available for guests, but Bethany had refused to hear it. "You will not believe how tired you're going to be by tonight," she'd said with the authority of experience. "Latecomers can get rooms at the Motel Nine in Blackthorn. You will sleep in a real bed tonight, not on the sofa in your office!"

Ian had left instructions for a small, simple service to be

conducted in the Vale House parlor as soon as possible after his passing. As it turned out, the service could not have been considered small by any stretch of the imagination. It was simple, however, and intimate with everyone crowded into the room along with two caskets in front of the hearth and a head-high spray of white lilies that had been sent by William and Celeste Iverson.

Afterward, all of Ian's old friends, as well as Ben (who had been released from his daytime duties since Bree had closed the store for the day) and Luke and Brandon carried the caskets down the hill to the May family cemetery. Sofie's empty grave had been re-opened and, this time, she was actually interred within it, next to the new grave that had been dug for Ian. Rosheen had crafted a cross from beech branches and Nell had draped it with summer flowers. This was set up as a placeholder for the shiny new headstone that would soon be placed next to Sofie's well-weathered one.

Evening fell, warm and clear. Cally said goodbye to Ben at the fence as usual, then returned to the house. In true Scots-Irish fashion, after the funeral proper, all of the out-of-town guests, friends and neighbors had reconvened in the parlor. She brought out the green whiskey bottle from the Fountain once again, but this time it seemed more appropriate that everyone use glasses. She noted with some relief that no mysterious forces manifested to throw any of the glassware around.

Bethany had been right: she was already exhausted, and the gathering was only just getting underway. She stepped out to the Hall on the pretense of checking to make sure the telephones had been forwarded to voicemail for the night. They had been, but she sat down in the desk chair anyway to take a break from the crowd and noise. She was a little disappointed, then, to feel the familiar sense of someone watching her from the front of the desk. When she scowled and looked up, though, she did not see the Preacher's ghost.

She still felt she was being watched, however. Rising, she walked toward the front of the Hall and realized the feeling was coming from outside. She stepped out onto the porch and peered across the tops of all the cars parked in the front lawn. She expected to see Rum there, but a much taller dark figure stood, instead, on the other side of the fence. It resembled Ben, but Cally knew it was not him.

"Michael," she said, weaving her way between the cars toward him. "It's good of you to come. I wish I could invite you inside."

Ben's father bowed to her as she drew near. "I'm sorry for your loss."

Cally always wanted to put her arms around him, any time she saw him, but the best she could do at the moment was reach across the fence and lay a hand along the side of his face. His eyes were just as remarkably blue as Ben's, but they were filled with an infinite sadness, and his shoulders stooped as if under a burden.

"I've been sent to ask a favor of you," he said gently. "Could you please, just for this night, open the gate? There are some on this side of the fence who would like to pay their respects."

"Well, yes, of course. I could open the gate, but I don't understand. Why do you need me to open it?"

"It's made of iron." Michael gave her a puzzled frown, as if he expected her to already understand this. "I mean, *I* could open it. But it's not my place to do so. Not anymore."

She put her hands on the top rail of the fence. "But the fence itself is only made of wood. Why can't they just hop over it, like Ben always does? For that matter, I suspect most of them could walk right through it." She looked away past his left shoulder and could almost see (though she did not look closely) ranks of tall, fey figures spread out behind him, waiting silently among the dark hills.

Michael smiled and shook his head. "It's the principle of the thing," he explained. "Faeries are a very rules-bound people. The gate is just a symbol, but symbols are absolutely real to them. They cannot cross it without permission. *Your* permission, to be precise."

Cally shook her head but did not argue. She walked southward along the fence and passed between the pineapple-topped masonry pillars into the crossroads. Here she unhooked the loop of chain that held the iron gate shut across the end of Main Street. Michael helped her drag it across the ground until it stood wide.

Suddenly, a host of beautiful and terrible folk appeared all around her. Ben's mother, Rianwynn, queen of the Sidhe, was among them. She did not pause to speak to Cally (possibly because Michael still stood next to her) but held her head high as she quickly skirted the cars in the parking lot to the Vale House porch steps. The silent Sidhe began to follow like a broad stream of fluttering gold and silver leaves, giving the cars a wide berth.

As Michael retreated back toward the meadow, one particularly beautiful Sidhe woman, tall and pale with ruby hair flying around her shoulders like a cloak, paused to speak to Cally. The rest of the host parted to go around them.

"Sorry for your loss," the woman said, extending a long, white hand. Cally recognized Aileen, Ben's ex and the mother of his eldest daughter Ana. "Isn't that how you people say it? I'm afraid I don't understand much about this whole mortality thing."

It took a bit of self-control for Cally to be able to reach back and accept the woman's cool handclasp, but she was sincere when she answered, "Yes, that's correct, and thank you for saying it. It means a lot that you would come." She turned, looking through the crowd of Sidhe for Ana, but was not surprised to see she was not in attendance. Ben's eldest had never been sentimental about family matters.

"We are duty and honor bound," Aileen was saying. She enclosed Main Street and Vale House in a gesture with her pale arms. "Ian May was a big deal around here. Now, you are a big deal around here, Callaghan McCarthy! By the way, we brought Ben with us." She tilted her head toward where Ben had stopped in the darkness just beyond the gate.

He was looking along the fence to where Michael was standing, and he was not smiling. Cally looked in time to see Michael hold his son's gaze for a moment before bowing and drawing back into the shadows among the hills.

"The queen has given special dispensation," Aileen continued as Ben walked forward to join them. "He may stay here tonight and help keep the vigil. Have fun!" She waved and followed the others into the house.

"Um, not exactly fun..." Cally muttered at the faerie woman's retreating back, then shook her head, turning to Ben as he stopped behind her. "She can be so inappropriate," Cally told him. "But I can't help liking her."

Ben chuckled in a low tone, his breath warm on her cheek. "How are you holding up?"

Holding up was almost literally what she was tempted to ask

him to do for her as they walked back to the house. All the seats in the parlor were occupied, so they stood in the wide doorway between the Hall and the parlor, listening to the toasts and the stories Merv and Doc were telling about Ian's youth. The room seemed impossibly crowded, with the Sidhe jammed shoulder-to-shoulder with all the humans in the room, but only Cally and Ben, and a few others such as Nell and Rosheen and Luke, could see this. The Sidhe had brought silver flagons of some sort of cordial of their own, and they sipped from these each time one of the mortals in the room proposed another toast. Nell sat silently in her mother's old overstuffed chair next to the hearth, a gentle smile on her lips as she listened to the stories. Cally couldn't help smiling, too. She knew Ian would have approved of the increasingly raucous wake following the solemnity of the funeral.

After many, many more toasts, though, all Cally wanted to do was sleep. She could see Bethany and Katarina were also emotionally and physically exhausted. At some point, Ignacio came into the room bearing a fresh tray of hors d'oeuvres and bent to speak quietly into Katarina's ear. She nodded and stumbled wearily down the back hall, and that left only Bethany standing at the rear of the parlor, watching owlishly with an empty cocktail tray in her hands, waiting to see if the company needed anything.

Ben kissed Cally on the cheek and excused himself to cross the room, where he gently took the tray from Bethany's hands. Doc nodded to him, producing car keys from his pocket, and offered Bethany a ride home. She was too tired to decline.

While Cally smiled at Ben's thoughtfulness, Aileen appeared at her shoulder. "You two really need to start planning your wedding," she said.

"We don't talk about weddings at funerals!"

Several people nearby turned to see what Cally was grumbling about. She muttered "Excuse me," and left the room in Bethany's and Doc's wake.

Nobody else was on the porch, as the taillights of Doc's car left the grounds, and all the wicker chairs were empty. Cally sank gratefully into one of them, then pulled another around in front of her to put up her aching feet. She could still hear the susurrus of voices through the parlor window behind her, but she tried to focus on listening instead to the crickets in the meadow and to the sound of her own breathing.

"But you really should."

Aileen had followed her. The faerie woman stood under the porch light, moths flying around her head like little fey devotees. "Now that you're both the incipient queen of the local court and the Armadeur of this house, you and Ben should be wed."

"Aileen, don't even say that out loud!" Cally put her feet down and looked nervously out across the dark meadow. "Don't you remember all the trouble the general of the Fomorians caused over the mere possibility of my ever becoming both those things? He literally started a war!"

Aileen laughed and waved a dismissive hand toward the night over the hills. "Don't worry about Eladha! We've got him under control. He's bound to the Nocksgall with a chain made of crow whiskers and unicorn tears..." When Cally frowned, trying to imagine this, the faerie woman said, "Never mind. Anyway, he can't get loose again."

Cally was not as confident about that as Aileen seemed to be. "I may be the proprietor of Vale House now," she allowed, "but please. I'm not the queen of anything, and I'm not ever going to be. Adam will be your king, when he arrives."

"You just keep telling yourself that!" Aileen crossed the porch and turned around, leaning her curvaceous hips against the railing and looking back through the window into the parlor. She pointed to where Ben stood, drink in hand, deep in conversation with Merv. "Anyway, I'd think you'd at least want to marry him for romantic purposes. Isn't that what you humans do? Fall in love and marry the people you love. Isn't that what you want?"

Cally twisted in her seat to follow Aileen's gaze. "What I want is irrelevant," she muttered.

"Oh! Oh, now, do I sense trouble in paradise? A human-style lovers' spat, perhaps?"

"What? No!" She looked back to the flawlessly beautiful creature who had been Ben's first lover, in his youth. The youth he, apparently, still retained, whereas Cally, while she did not consider herself chopped liver by any means, had never been half as stunning as Aileen, not even in her twenties. Why was she even talking to this woman about the man she loved? And yet, if circumstances had been different, she knew she would very much have enjoyed Aileen's friendship.

"It's just..." she began. "Well, where would we even live?"

Aileen apparently had an opinion about this, but as she opened her mouth to give it, Cally spoke again. "And then, there's this!"

She slipped the crescent moon pendant out from under her blouse and held it up for Aileen to see.

"Oh!" A smile spread so wide across Aileen's face, Cally thought her head might split at the ears. "Oh, ho! Where did you get *that*?"

"Ben's father gave it to me. This past Christmas."

Aileen giggled like a little girl. "So that's who stole it!" She looked through the window into the parlor again, nodding. "You should have seen the fit Rianwynn had when she realized it had gone missing."

"I'll give it back to her, then." Cally started to rise from her chair. "I don't want..."

"I wouldn't, if I were you." Aileen stepped between Cally and the door. "Don't even let her find out you've been in contact with Michael Dawes. Seriously."

Cally realized Aileen was probably right. She nodded and found herself wondering if she really should consider this faerie woman a friend.

Aileen cocked her head. "So, you've looked at Ben through that thing. Right? That's what's bothering you."

Cally had to nod. "I guess. And now I'm not sure what I should do. Even less sure, that is. Knowing he had to leave for good someday, after Bree dies, I was coping with that. And even though he was only aging at half the normal rate – or so I thought – because of having to spend half his time in Faerie, I didn't think I'd be too old for him by then, myself. In my mind, when I imagined that big, dramatic, final parting scene, I pictured two people who at least looked to be roughly the same age. But now that I know he's never aged a day since..."

"No, he certainly hasn't." Aileen cast an appreciative leer through the window. "He still looks as fine as he did when I last bedded him!" She grinned at Cally as if they were sharing some delicious secret, completely oblivious of how awkward it made Cally feel.

Cally paused to give Aileen a chance to say what a human woman might say: supportive, well-intended platitudes about beauty being on the inside and age not mattering, etcetera. Aileen merely nodded as if she understood perfectly why Cally should be feeling so inadequate, and waited for her to go on.

Cally swallowed and went on.

"The thing about it that bothers me most, though. Well. It feels like he's deceived me. I allowed myself to trust him, even though I had once sworn I'd never trust any man ever again, and it turns out he's been pretending all along to be someone he's not."

Aileen continued waiting, as if she didn't see what was wrong with someone deceiving a lover. When Cally did not elaborate, Aileen looked at the pendant from the side of one eye. "You seem, I mean, I'm guessing, here, but you seem to be under the impression that glamour is something we do intentionally."

Cally shrugged, shaking her head. "I guess. I don't understand much about glamour at all."

Aileen nodded. "Well, it's like chameleons. You know about them, right? It's a survival instinct, not something we do consciously. Not most of us, anyway. Rianwynn and her ladies can deliberately weave glamour, and beautifully, too. But for the most part, when something mortal sees us, such as cats or genetically quirky humans, the glamour simply responds with whatever semblance is safest for both of us. I don't know, I think cats might actually just see us as we are. They're kind of weird. Anyway, then there's our dear Ben. He's half mortal, himself, so he's easily fooled by glamour. Even his own!" She laughed.

"You mean." Cally didn't laugh. "He doesn't know what his glamour looks like? What he looks like to me?" She turned and looked at Ben again. He was laughing at something Luke had said, nearly spilling his drink.

"What I mean," said Aileen, "is that when you look at him, you're not seeing what he wants you to see. You're seeing how he feels about himself. He honestly believes he looks like that."

Cally drew in a long breath and let it out in an even longer sigh. Yes, of course. Ben had always insisted he was fully human. It was what he truly wished to be: an ordinary man.

"Do you want to look at me through that thing?" Aileen offered.

"What? Oh, no, Aileen, that's alright. I think I'm done with invading people's privacy." She released the pendant and let it fall back inside her blouse.

"No, seriously!" The fairy woman leaned down to slip a cool finger under Cally's collar and raised the talisman again so that it hung between them. "I'm curious, now. Tell me what you think!"

Cally had only to move her head a little to the right and she would be able to see Aileen through the crystal. She wasn't sure why she hesitated. Of course, Ben's former lover was only as beautiful, to human eyes, as her glamour, and Ben, of all people, knew that. It was ridiculous for Cally to have ever entertained any insecurity about the matter.

"Alright," she said. "I have to admit, I'm curious now, too." She took the semi-circle of silver from Aileen's hand. The faerie woman smiled and struck a pose against the porch column.

Through the frame of encircling silver, the tall, voluptuous woman with waves of ruby hair took on a completely alien appearance. Her limbs, much longer in proportion to her body than a human's should be, seemed almost insect-like but were shapely nonetheless, made of something resembling pure, solidified moonlight. Her hair was a magenta aura which surrounded her entirely, and her eyes were vast pools of night. Cally felt both intimidated and reassured at the same time.

"You are astonishingly beautiful," she breathed, and she meant it.

Aileen nodded in agreement.

Cally slipped the chain over her head and held the pendant out in her palm. "You should keep this," she said.

Aileen crossed both hands in front of her. "Oh, no, no! I wouldn't want Rianwynn to catch me with that thing. If you want to be rid of it, you'll have to find some other sucker!"

Well able to relate to the fear of Rianwynn's wrath, Cally wrapped the fine silver chain around the pendant and tucked it into her pocket. She resolved to return it to her room as soon as possible, never to keep it on her person again.

"You and Ben are still going to have to figure out what you're going to do, though," Aileen persisted. "Bree hasn't got that much time left, after all."

When the wake broke up at last, Cally helped Ignacio collect empty glasses in the parlor. Ben drove his sister home in the Dawes family vintage Daimler, and then returned to Vale House for the night as the queen had promised he would be allowed to do, though it was nearly morning, anyway. When Cally dragged her weary body into bed at last, she was too tired to worry about the apparent age of the comforting arms that surrounded her. It was not "one of these nights" as she had always imagined, but she was thankful for the deep and dreamless sleep his presence brought her.

14 - Close the Gate

The scent of coffee woke her, or maybe it was the sound of birdsong through the open window. Cally lay awhile with eyes closed, relishing both, as well as the warmth of Ben's sleeping body beside her. Then she shouted an unladylike word and leapt out of the bed.

"What?" Ben sat up and seemed, in the gray light, to be reaching to his side for a weapon that was not visible to Cally's eyes.

She pushed open the window and stared down at the trampled front lawn. "I forgot to shut the gate!" She flung off her nightgown and grabbed her skirt from the back of the chair where she'd draped it the night before.

"I'm sure it's alright." Ben rose and stood behind her, laying hands on her shoulders. He tried in vain to get her to turn around and look at him. "Cally, what are you so worried about?"

She didn't know what she feared might happen with all of Faerie still free to wander at will through Woodley, but she shoved her way past him to the dresser and snatched a t-shirt out of the drawer.

He hurried to dress, as well, in the clothes he'd been wearing the night before, but all the while he repeated his assurance that everything was alright. Cally opened the door and ran out into the hallway. Looking down over the gallery railing, she saw the dining room teeming with people, all dressed for travel and quaffing coffee, most of them politely declining Katarina's offer of breakfast.

In the minute she spent combing the crowd with her eyes, looking for anyone who did not appear to be, strictly speaking, human, Cally heard at least three people say, "Oh, we really must get together again soon. And this time let's not wait for someone else to die!"

"Well, that's a thoroughly human thing to say, anyway." Cally was only marginally reassured. She cast a quick look at Ben behind her, then hurried down the stairs. She wished, for once, he would not follow. She badly wanted to break last night's promise to herself and get the moon pendant out of her pocket, just this one last time.

Nell stood beside the front door, giving and receiving hugs as groups of people filed out, each expressing their sympathies once again before departing. Bethany waved at them from behind the telephone console, wishing them safe journeys.

"Well," Bethany said as Cally and Ben drew abreast of the desk. "As soon as everyone's gone, I'm going to sleep for a week. But at least, for once, I haven't felt that dark presence in this Hall this morning." She tilted her head toward the perfectly empty space in front of her. "And our dish-throwing poltergeist appears to have gone away, too. Maybe that ghost-hunter woman really did the trick!" Her jovial mood seemed forced, as did the smile she plastered across her face as she jabbed at the phone console to take the line off voicemail. "I wonder if the interwebs will still list us as a haunted B&B, now?" Before she could finish fake-laughing at her own joke, another knot of guests came into the Hall from the dining room.

Cally headed for the door ahead of them, pausing only long enough to tell Nell she'd be right back. Still closely followed by Ben, she ran down the porch steps and dodged a couple of departing cars to run across the lawn and out into the crossroads at the end of Main Street.

Ben had apparently been right; she'd been worrying needlessly. The Sidhe delegation stood ranked like banks of morning mist just outside the open gate, with the exception of a few individuals standing on the sidewalk at the corner of Gardens and Main, waiting for an opportunity to cross without danger of coming into contact with a car.

Ben's mother, her hair shining like molten silver in the growing sunlight, stepped away from the group and came to stand in the gateway before Cally. "All are present and accounted for," she said, and Cally knew she could take Rianwynn at her word.

Then, to her astonishment, the queen of the Sidhe bowed to her.

Cally managed to keep her wits about her enough to realize the most diplomatic thing to do would be to bow back, and she bowed more deeply.

From somewhere out in the meadow, Aileen's voice called,

"Don't forget what I told you!"

The Sidhe, now gathered into one group beyond the gate, turned away as if in a military drill. They walked silently toward the eastern horizon, fading from visibility into the fog that was probably not really fog curling over the hills. Cally looked over her shoulder at Ben as he, too, watched them depart, and wondered if what his blue eyes were seeing was the same as what she saw, or if it was completely different.

When he saw her looking at him, he smiled and bent to grasp the middle rail of the gate. Together, they drew it shut and Cally replaced the loop of the chain that held it tight against the gatepost. Nell appeared, then, walking across the mostly empty parking lot to stand between the masonry pillars, waving at the now empty horizon.

While Cally considered how to ask – and get a straight answer – about how Nell was feeling, the younger woman came closer and regarded her with an impish smile.

"Callaghan McCarthy, you are standing at a crossroads!"

Cally laughed. She was, in fact, standing where Main Street crossed Gardens Road to pass, mostly invisibly, into the meadow. Here, also, Gardens Road crossed Main Street and continued on to the crumbled and forgotten stretch of Bells Road running beneath the Vale House lawn. But Cally knew Nell meant this in a much more lyrical way.

"You're right," she agreed. Turning her back to the gate, she held out her right hand and gestured toward Vale House. "On one side of me, my mentor lies resting in his new grave, while on the other..." She gestured with her left hand toward the Yellow House a little way along Gardens Road. "...my first grandchild is about to be born."

Nell grinned and nodded her approval of Cally's apprehension of the situation.

Cally continued. "Behind me lie vast unknown – well, mostly unknown – realms of faerie mystery." Finally, she nodded her head to indicate the shady sidewalk, stretching away before her until the overhanging oak trees gave way to sunny downtown Woodley, USA. "And before me lies a perfectly mortal little human town, though I have to say, it's not that much less mysterious."

Nell applauded softly, adding, "And we are standing here with you."

"Yes." Cally reached out to hug her. "Yes, you are." She put out an arm to include Ben in the hug. "And how are you feeling, yourself, Helen?"

Nell's small smile fell at last. "I'm feeling worried," she said.

"Worried?" That was one emotion Cally would not have expected Nell to be struggling with today. "What are you worried about?"

"I haven't seen Georgie," she said. "I can't find him anywhere."

15 - Bethany's Confession

"I'm sure he's okay," Cally told Nell. Or was she telling herself this? "I saw him just yesterday morning. He goes off by himself a lot, lately. Remember the time he got lost in the modem?"

"He was only gone a few hours, then."

"It's alright. I'm sure it's alright. Let's try not to worry." Cally put an arm around Nell and started heading back toward the house. "We've got the reading of the will tomorrow. He'll probably show up to make a few remarks only you and I will hear, and we'll have to struggle to stop ourselves laughing at an inappropriate moment."

It was still early. Ben didn't have to be at the news store until noon, but Cally discovered she had mixed feelings about him following her back to Vale House, now. Normally, he and she would have enjoyed a leisurely late breakfast until it was time for him to go, but so many things hadn't been normal, these past couple of days.

Nell stopped short of the porch steps. "I don't want to go back inside." She gazed past the house, through the side garden toward town. "I was in the middle of a painting. I need to get back to my apartment to finish it."

Cally looked carefully at the side of Nell's face. The younger woman's expression was calm, if a little sad. "Are you sure you're going to be okay? Come to the kitchen and have some coffee with Kat and Ben and me. Maybe Bethany will join us. We could all use a good talk."

"No, I'm alright." Nell pulled away and took a few steps toward the crossroads, before looking back with a wry grin. "And yes, don't worry. I already took my medication."

Cally knew Nell's landlady, who was also the proprietor of the coffee shop, knew how to make sure Nell was okay. But with all the out-of-towners passing through Woodley this morning, she knew Andi would be having a particularly busy morning. She turned to Ben as Nell walked away. "Would you go with her? I'll follow in a little while, I promise."

He ran a gentle hand over her hair and pressed his forehead against hers. "I can take a hint," he said. "You need some time alone. I understand."

"No, it's not that. I just..."

He drew her close and held her for a moment. Cally caught herself recoiling so that her considerably-not-flat-anymore belly wouldn't protrude against his actually flat one. If he noticed this, he had other explanations for it. Kissing her swiftly, he said "I'll see you this evening."

"Really, I'll be along in just a couple hours," she insisted. She didn't look back to see if he acknowledged this or not. Instead, she hurried up the porch steps, muttering "Everything is alright." This time, she knew it was herself she was trying to reassure.

She entered the now quiet Hall to find Bethany bent over the guest book, sniffling softly and dabbing at her eyes with a tissue as she filled out small thank-you notecards for everyone who had attended the funeral.

Cally went around the desk and lay a hand on Bethany's shoulder. "Just bring those to me when you're done. I'll address them and take them to the post office."

She forced herself to maintain a normal pace as she turned and went up the stairs, whispering, once again, "I'm sure everything is alright." She realized she was echoing Ben's words from just a short while ago, when she had awakened so abruptly. He had been right, then. She told herself she was just, understandably, in a state of heightened emotion today.

Even though George was not in the upstairs hallway. Of course he wasn't. He wasn't bound to the butler's desk anymore. She walked to the south end of the hallway and opened a narrow door across from the Calla Lily Room. In this little electrical closet, Ignacio maintained the Vale House modem and router and other wi-fi equipment. Green and amber lights were winking merrily, and all appeared, to her untrained eye, to be perfectly normal. She didn't think George was likely to have gone modem-surfing again, anyway, after his first and last experience, which had turned out to be much less fun than he had anticipated. She mentally shook herself by the shoulders, ordering herself not to spend the entire day concocting worst-case scenarios.

Shutting the door, she walked slowly toward the other end of the hallway, calling George's name softly until she came to the Wisteria room. Through the open door she saw Katarina inside, stripping the sheets from the bed and piling them in a basket. She borrowed Katarina's ring of flower-coded keys and went back along the east side of the hall, gathering more used bedding from the vacated guest rooms. Ending with her own room, she left the sheets piled outside the door and went down to her office via the spiral stair in the closet.

Bethany had already left a small stack of cards beside her laptop. Cally pushed them to one side and, nudging the computer mouse to clear the screensaver, saw the chat icon illuminated with a number in the corner, indicating Emerald had left seven messages since yesterday. She sighed; a chat with a thoughtful and supportive friend was just what she needed to settle her nerves.

The messages were not ones of sympathy or support, though, and definitely did not settle her nerves.

Emerald<< George said to tell you he went willingly

Emerald<< Went where? What do you suppose he could

have meant by that?

Emerald<< Have you spoken with him recently?

Emerald<< Cally? Are you there?

Emerald<< I'm sorry - - you must be so busy with the

funeral and everything - - please get back to me when

you can

Emerald<< Good morning, Cally - - have you seen George?

Emerald<< Cally please answer - - I'm worried!

She sat down quickly and clacked away at the keys, fighting to keep down the sick feeling rising in the pit of her stomach.

Cally>> Went where? Sorry, I know you don't know either.

Cally>> Did that ghost-hunter woman get him?

Cally>> Dammit I told him to stay away from the parlor!

Cally>> No, wait, you said he went willingly. Are you sure

he didn't mention

She jumped as the office door opened. Bethany entered, carrying another stack of cards. "Oh, I'm sorry!" she said. "I didn't know you were in here. I should have knocked." She added the cards to the top of the existing pile.

"It's okay, Bethany, I was just..." She nodded toward her hands, still hovering over the keyboard.

But Bethany, instead of retreating to the door, drew one of the side-chairs to the front of the desk and sat down. "I need to tell you something." She sat straight up in the chair, hands folded on her knees, looking across the desk at Cally with red-rimmed eyes.

Cally glanced at her computer, then back at Bethany, then tapped "enter" to send her unfinished message. Compelling herself to keep her eyes off the screen, she nodded to the older woman.

"Of course, Bethany. Anything you have to say is safe with me."

"Good." Fresh tears sprang into Bethany's eyes. "Because I loved Ian May."

"Oh, Bethany." Cally pushed a box of tissues closer to her. "I know you did. We all loved him."

"No, I mean. You know. I was in love with him."

Cally did, in fact, know this. Most members of the household had understood that Bethany's regard for Ian had not been strictly platonic. She didn't think it would be kind to say so, though. Instead, she said "It must have been so difficult for you."

"It was." Bethany sniffed and wiped the corners of her eyes, glancing back through the open doorway to make sure nobody was standing in the Hall. "Well, yes and no. The whole time Sofie was gone, when we all thought Ian was a widower, well at first, I was just being supportive of an old friend. I honestly was. After all, I was a widow myself. I knew – I thought I knew – what he was going through.

"But eventually it became more. For me. Never for him, of course. I thought he was just unable to move on, and I could sympathize with that. Some people even encouraged my pursuit of him. They thought it would help him.

"I never realized: I never even had a chance at all! It was a shock to all of us when we discovered he was actually just being faithful to a wife who was still very much alive. And I was happy for him when we found out. I really was!"

Cally started to stand up so she could go around the desk and put her arms around Bethany, but Bethany put up a hand, gesturing for her to sit back down.

"So, the thing, now," she continued, "is, well, now I feel like I've been widowed all over again. I feel like I should be wearing black, but it's not my place to do so. The love of my life has passed away, but I can't talk to anyone about it."

Cally had to pull a tissue from the box herself, then.

"You can talk to me about it," she said. "And I'm sure you can talk to Kat, and even Ignacio. I know they'll understand." *They already do,* she did not add.

Bethany sat back and, to Cally's relief, let out a little laugh. "Well, now I also think I understand what I've been putting Daniel through. I've been completely unavailable to him, despite how sweet he's been to me, because my heart was given elsewhere. Even with all of you pushing me and him together. Don't think I didn't notice! I mean, Doc is a good man, but..."

Cally smiled and nodded. "But Ian May is a tough act to follow."

"I knew you'd understand." Bethany blew her nose.

From the corner of her eye, Cally saw a blink on the computer screen. Emerald had sent a reply to her message, but Bethany showed no sign of getting up or concluding the conversation.

"Well, now that I've poured out my heart to you," Bethany went on, dropping the tissue into the trash and taking a fresh one, "I wonder if you could tell me something. I mean, if I asked you something, would you answer me honestly?"

Cally hedged. "I can only promise to do my best. I guess it depends on what you want to ask me. And that's an honest answer!"

It lightened Cally's heart to see Bethany grin at that. "Okay, well. It's this. We joke around, here, about the ghosts supposedly haunting this house." She waved a hand around the room in general. "I mean, we don't deny they exist, because frankly the rumors are good for business. But we don't actually claim they're real, either. Even with that weird, dark presence I sometimes sense in the Hall, well, I don't really believe. I've always been sure there's a logical explanation for it. An allergy to mildew or something. Though..." She looked thoughtfully through the doorway into the Hall. "I do have to say, I haven't felt it lately. And that's great, because I don't think I could deal with it today. It's probably just something that Toller woman put into my head, bless her heart, but it's working. And Foster's ghost isn't going around breaking things today, either..."

"You knew it was Foster? I mean...I wondered, too."

"Well, it wouldn't have been the first time he's caused havoc from beyond the grave," she snorted. "A few broken dishes are nothing compared to flushing all Ian's money down a black hole."

"All that has been resolved," Cally assured her. "But I know what you mean." She knew, in fact, a lot more about the matter than Bethany would ever know, and she was glad to keep it that way.

"Well, what I wanted to know. What I wanted to ask you is: Who is George?"

As Cally sat with her mouth open, trying to think of how to answer, her eyes flinched to the computer. Emerald's brief reply hung in the middle of the screen.

Emerald<< When was the last time you saw him?

Bethany was continuing. "Don't think I don't hear you talking to this George all the time. I mean, I don't eavesdrop intentionally. But it always catches my attention, because I remember Nell had an imaginary friend when she was little, and she called him Georgie."

"He wasn't imaginary." The words were out of her mouth

before she had turned to look back at Bethany. When she did, though, she saw Bethany let out her breath and relaxed back in the chair, as if she was glad to hear the truth at last. "He was real," Cally continued, then quickly amended this. "George is real." She hoped he still was.

"Well, it's just that Nellie saw a lot of things when she was younger, before they found the right medicine for her."

"Yes. I mean, yes, she does also have schizophrenia. The medication helps her separate her symptoms from reality. As a result, she's also able to figure out what is actually real. George is real. I can see him, too."

"Why can't I see him?"

Cally shrugged and told her what George had once told her. "Some people can, and some people can't. Just like how some people can play music by ear or do math in their heads. Everyone's different."

"Tell me about him."

Cally should have felt relief at the freedom to talk openly about the ghosts surrounding her, but other concerns distracted her at the moment. She told Bethany, as concisely as she could, about the young Taino pirate and how he'd eventually found his way, as a spirit, to Vale House. She ended the story with a short summary of the day she'd met him, unwilling to proceed to where she now feared the tale might now be heading.

Bethany nodded, her expression noncommittal. "Well. It'll take me a while to digest all this, but I can't say I'm terribly surprised, after all." She stood and patted both sides of the stack of notecards to trim up their edges. "I hope I get a chance to meet him someday."

"I hope you do, too," Cally said.

She hoped it with all her heart.

Bethany replaced the chair and headed back toward the Hall, but she paused in the doorway, turning back to say, "Thank you for pushing me toward Doc. Life is short. I'm going to try, I'm really going to try, to give him the chance I never had."

16 - A Chat with Emerald

Emerald<< All he said was to give you that message - - that
he went willingly

Emerald<< It was about 7:AM yesterday

Emerald<< I knew you were busy with the funeral but I was
hoping you'd seen him since then

Cally>> I saw him in the morning before the funeral, while
the Tollers were checking out.

Cally>> That would have been about an hour after you
heard from him.

Emerald<< And since?

Cally>> I don't remember. Damn it. No. I haven't seen him
since then.

Emerald<< We mustn't panic - - he's a very old spirit and
anyway it's not the first time he's gone off on his own

Cally>> Last time he nearly got himself...whatever passes
for "killed," for ghosts. He got lost in the internet.

Cally>> Is that how he messaged you? Can't you search for
him from where you are?

Emerald<< No - - I don't see him in the wires - - he doesn't
use the modem to talk to me

Emerald<< I just hear his voice - - here where I am

Emerald<< Wherever that is

Emerald<< What do I know about where I am - - or who

any of you are - - or if I'm even real at all?

Cally>> I hear your frustration, Em. And I'm sorry about

putting that issue on the back burner so much lately.

Cally>> But I think we might find answers to both questions

if you can remember anything about when you first

met him.

Cally>> Where were you? What did he look like to you?

Emerald<< It was right there in your office

Emerald<< Actually I'm not sure I've ever seen any other

part of Vale House besides your office

Emerald<< It was a parlor then - - they called it "the small

parlor"

Emerald<< I remember - - George was hovering over

someone - - looking very concerned

Emerald<< I don't think it was me he was looking at though

- - I wasn't even born yet - - I mean

Emerald<< Shit I don't know what I mean

Cally>> It's OK. It makes perfect sense.

Cally>> It's because you were never born...

Cally looked at the last line she'd typed and managed to stop herself before she hit "enter." She did feel like she was zeroing in on the nature of Emerald's existence and, once she was sure, there would have to be a long, serious discussion about it. But that conversation would have to wait for a time when she would be able to give it her undivided attention. She backspaced over her words and sent a different message:

Cally>> I'm going to try talking to Bree Dawes. I think she

can help, if I can just figure out how to get her to give

me a straight answer.

Cally>> In the meantime, do you think you can contact

Melissa about George?

Emerald<< I tried - - Melissa is not responding to me

Cally>> Damn.

Cally>> OK, well, as you probably expected, that tidbit of

information means I'm going to have to go...

Emerald<< Understood - - please keep me posted

Cally closed the chat window but left the program itself running in the background. She shoved her office chair back and stood up, staring across the room at the obsolete console television set. The remote was still lying on the sofa where Nell had left it. Nell had spoken to Melissa just a few days ago, but Cally couldn't say she'd ever succeeded in doing so, herself. Now her legs trembled as she forced herself to cross the room and power on the old device. It hadn't occurred to her until now to be concerned for Melissa, and she felt a little ashamed of that.

It was probably, she reasoned, because she had never really got to know Melissa. She had never succeeded in seeing and hearing what Nell could so easily discern among the static and white noise. Anyway, Cally reasoned as she waited for the old screen to warm up, Melissa would probably have been safe from the Tollers' ghost-trapping scheme, since she was already bound to a physical object of her own.

"Melissa, are you there?" Cally said into the bulging, cracked glass. "Please don't be coy. Please be there, this time."

The screen filled slowly with snowy static, and the speakers hissed softly. Sighing, Cally sat down on the edge of the sofa and picked up the chunky remote. She pushed buttons, switching channels over and over with a growing resignation. The static on the screen changed shade or brightness, from channel to channel. The hissing sound changed timbre sometimes, but the only thing that coalesced on the screen was a brightness where the static tended to gather more densely around the crack across the middle. No matter how hard she squinted or, alternatively, tried to unfocus her eyes, Cally couldn't even trick her mind into seeing the pareidolia-triggered illusion of a human face. Her ears failed to ascribe any allusions to a human voice in the staticky hissing.

Twice before, she had heard – or thought she'd heard – Melissa's voice just as she was leaving the room, so she tried that, too. She turned and opened the door to the Hall, but she still didn't hear anything, except Bethany's voice as she looked up from the guest register and said, "Heading down to the store to see Ben, now?"

"Um..." Cally listened closely for the sound of any passing remark behind her, but there was nothing. "Um, yes, in a minute. Have you seen...?"

"Cally? Have I seen what?"

She shut the office door behind her. "Never mind, I'll go and look, myself."

"It's turning out to be a hot day," Bethany remarked as Cally crossed the hall to the front door. "Ignacio warned me it would be, when he saw the fog this morning."

Stepping out onto the porch, Cally observed absently that Bethany was right about the weather, but her attention was focused mostly on the porch railing. Little Cyndi Lauper sat drowsing in the sunlight on the railing next to the steps, her tail curled around her feet, but Doctor Boojums was nowhere to be seen. That wasn't so unusual, even for a living cat, she knew. Still, she found herself at the bottom of the steps, peering into the shadows under the shrubbery, whispering, "Boo? Boo!"

"Did you lose something?" Bethany was standing at the screen door, watching her. Even though she had just had a frank conversation with her about ghosts, Cally didn't really want to tell Bethany what she was looking for, at the moment. Doctor Boojums had been Bethany's cat, in life, and the woman still loved to launch into long reminiscences about him whenever the opportunity arose.

Cally didn't feel up to it, at the moment.

"I'm not sure," she replied honestly. "I think I'll head into town, now. If my agent calls, please tell her ... I don't know. Just tell her something. I'm sure she'll understand..."

17 - En Plein Air

Instead of leaving the yard through the front gate, she turned the corner of the house and ducked into the shade garden along its south side. Following the mulched path between the hostas and crape myrtles there, she called, "Doctor Boojums, here, Kitty!" into the shadows around the side porch. She was not surprised not to see him – he had never haunted that part of the grounds, and anyway he probably hated to be referred to as a "kitty."

Letting herself out through the little wooden gate at the back of the property, she turned right, onto the sidewalk under the oaks of Woodley's residential district. Here, the shady end of Main Street ran past stately, older homes set well back from the sidewalk. Almost all of them had cats sitting on their porches, but none of these were a fat, fuzzy gray ghost. Cally had always felt she was being watched from within these houses, any time she walked into town, but she'd never felt menaced by this. She'd become accustomed to it over the past year, and today the familiar constancy of it almost made her feel safe and protected.

Where the oaks ended, so did the houses, and the sidewalk ran on under bright sun through what passed as Woodley's downtown. The feedstore was the first establishment on the right and, as always, Merv Arkwright was sitting in a lawn chair on its loading dock. As always, he raised his baseball cap when he saw Cally approaching and said, "Good morning, Ms. McCarthy."

"Good afternoon, Mr. Arkwright," she replied. "It's well past noon, you know!"

"So sorry." He chuckled. "It's been a hell of a past couple days. I got up late this morning, and I'm behind on everything. How are you feeling this...afternoon?"

She almost answered "Worried," just as Nell had done earlier. She stopped herself and said instead, "I'm on my way to check on our Nell." Waving, she waited for a single car to pass down Main Street, then stepped off the curb.

Dawes News lay diagonally across the street from Merv's feedstore, and this was usually her destination whenever she walked into town. Today, however, she walked past the store with a wave through the window. She would stop in to see Ben, as she'd promised, once she'd spoken to Nell.

Andi's Bean Garden was about a block further on, two doors past Railroad Street. Cally could already smell, through the shop's open door, the aroma of the good coffee beans Andi always used. It was above this shop that Nell had rented a small artist's studio to assert her independence or, Cally suspected, to distance herself from Vale House and the unpleasant memories of her disastrous marriage to Foster Brentwood.

Nell had apparently decided to paint *en plein air* today. Cally could see her sitting on a wooden stool just outside the Bean Garden door. Nell and her easel faced the far end of Main Street, where it disappeared into the trees forming Woodley's western border.

The picture Nell was painting, however, did not at all resemble the view. Cally saw, as she stepped behind Nell's shoulder, the image of a waterfall taking shape on the canvas. Falling from a great height in a forest, past a cave mouth and into a pool at the bottom, the water looked so real Cally felt she could put her hand right through it into the cave behind.

"That's lovely, Helen," she said truthfully.

"Oh." Nell was dabbing at a patch of purple flowers near the edge of the pool. "Thanks. Honestly, I'm not happy with it, myself. There's something missing." She sighed.

Cally thought maybe Nell might eventually add some of the fanciful creatures, peeking out of the foliage, which almost always populated her paintings. "It'll come to you," she said.

Nell dropped her brush into the jar of paint thinner attached to the shelf under the canvas. Standing up, she came right to the point. "Have you seen George yet?"

There was no point in sugar-coating it. "I'm afraid not," Cally said, and then went ahead and got the rest of it out of the way, too. "Doctor Boojums and Melissa seem to have gone missing, as well. Oh, and the Preacher. And Foster." She watched Nell's face closely to see how this news affected her, but it was never easy to tell what Nell was thinking.

Nell merely nodded. Her face was a complete blank as she turned back to her easel. "I'd better get this stuff out of everyone's way." She began to fold the easel which absolutely no one was trying to walk around.

Andi Kilmarten appeared in the doorway of her shop, then, drying a white coffee mug with a bar towel. "Come on in," she told Cally. "I'll pour your favorite: a nice coffee-flavored coffee. On the house, today."

Cally held Nell's unfinished painting while Nell gathered the rest of her painting paraphernalia into a plastic box. Entering the shop ahead of her, Nell took the canvas and carried it through to the narrow stair at the back.

"Come join us for a coffee when you're done," Andi called after her. When they heard the door to Nell's apartment shut, Andi turned to Cally and sighed. "I'm worried about her."

The inside of the shop, warmly lit by the sunshine streaming through the wide front window, was quiet and mostly empty. Only the town's three feral teenagers, Errin, Mima and Zenbe, sat around a table near the back, with neon-colored drinks in front of them. Zenbe had a guitar across his lap, but Cally couldn't really hear the chords he was fiddling with because the guitar was electric and there was no amplifier. Mima and Errin were trying to get his attention with jokes, and laughing at him when he ignored them.

Cally listened to Nell's footsteps above as she followed Andi to the counter. "I'm worried about her, too." She was worried about George, as well, but she didn't add that part.

Andi twisted a few knobs on one of the incomprehensible, gleaming coffee machines Cally could have sworn she'd seen in a science fiction movie somewhere. "She hasn't said a single word," Andi told Cally over the hissing of steam, "about losing both her parents in one day. She just keeps talking about the ghosts at Vale House as if they're real people, and she's upset because she thinks they're in some kind of danger. I'm afraid all the stress is causing her to have a relapse. Should we call Doc?"

"I don't think so...at least, not yet." Cally accepted the mug of rich, black coffee Andi handed to her. Andi, like Cally, was a relative newcomer to Woodley. The two women had bonded over this, and over long discussions about their grown children and learning how to become Self Actualized Women of a Certain Age. Andi had once told Cally a story about a ghost she'd thought she'd sensed in this very shop, but Cally wasn't sure Andi was what one would call a "true believer," and she didn't know whether or not it was a good idea to speak openly about what was really bothering Nell.

While Andi prepared her own coffee and one for Nell (a concoction which seemed to consist of a small amount of coffee and a large amount of something that smelled like coconut) Cally perused the art on the shop's walls. Some of the artwork displayed there was Nell's. Cally particularly noticed her style on an extra-large bright yellow t-shirt tacked to the wall with a price tag taped next to it. It depicted a colorful unicorn dancing belly-deep in multicolored flowers. Cally leaned closer to look for the lettering. There was always a catchy saying somewhere on Nell's hand-painted t-shirts. She found it, flowing and twisting through the unicorn's mane, but she had to tilt her head in several directions to read it all. She thought she could make out the words "Sleeping Naked is for People Who Can't Handle Unicorn Pajamas."

The puzzled expression was still on her face when Nell came down the stairs, returned Errin's and Mima's waves, and accepted the mug Andi handed to her. The three women sat down at the table next to the front window.

"It's just that Melissa and George were my friends," Nell began as soon as they were all seated. "I probably wouldn't have survived my teenage years if not for them."

Andi gave Cally a "See what I mean?" look.

Cally reached over and took Nell's hand. "They are still your friends!" she said, despite Andi's presence. "Wherever they are, they will always be your friends. And they're probably ok." She wasn't sure whether it was herself or Nell she was trying to reassure. Either way, it didn't work.

The teens at the back of the shop got up and started toward the door. While Zenbe detoured toward the counter to drop some bills into the tip jar, Errin paused behind Cally's chair. "You should go talk to the Wyrd Systers about it," Errin advised with the authority of a teenager who knows everything. "Get one of those free readings they're always trying to give you."

"Errin!" Cally turned around sharply. "It's rude to eavesdrop!"

Errin made no attempt to excuse herself. "This is important," she said. "You need professional help."

"Professional help with our ghosts is what probably caused this mess to begin with," Cally said. "If I thought for one second those Systers could actually help, I'd be in their shop right now." She glanced out the window toward the end of town. The Wyrd Systers Books and Gifts Shoppe was the last storefront on this side of the street, just before the street ran into the trees. "I like Raven and Willow, but they're..." She scoured her mind for a kinder word than "airheads" or "dingbats." She finally settled on "young and inexperienced."

"Well, the thing is..." Andi had been looking, eyes wide, from Cally to Nell to Errin, and now she leaned across the table, her voice low and conspiratorial. "I'm relatively new around here, but I'm starting to figure a few things out about this town. I think some things, like Raven and Willow's mumbo-jumbo, and all the urban legends about ghosts in Woodley, well, maybe they aren't just urban legends. Maybe they're real. I've been dating Merv Arkwright, and he says..."

"You what?" Cally hadn't realized the tension in her shoulders had been suffocating her until she drew her first real breath in many hours. "Oh, that's wonderful! Why didn't you tell me?"

"Well...we weren't quite sure it was dating, per se, until recently. Then what with Ian's passing and all..."

Cally stood so she could go around the table to hug Andi. "It's just refreshing to see someone in this town managing to fly under the gossip radar, that's all!" She caught herself laughing perhaps a little too loudly.

Zenbe and Mima collected Errin and herded her to the door. As he followed the girls out, Zenbe bowed to Andi. "Thank you, Ms. Kilmarten," he said and then, bowing to Cally and Nell in turn, he added, "If I can help, count on me."

18 - Sunset at the Crossroads

Cally relented and walked with Nell to the Wyrd Systers Books and Gifts Shoppe, mainly to placate Nell, who seemed to be certain they could help. The two proprietors, Raven and Willow, were delighted when Cally finally accepted their standing offer of a free reading. For this, they used a deck they explained was not a traditional tarot deck but instead used "goddess magic" which was supposedly much better, for women, anyway. The taller and thinner of the two women laid cards out across the sales counter while the shorter and rounder of the two interpreted the spread. It was all about choosing a path but had nothing to say about what path to choose. It did not mention anything at all about ghosts, missing or otherwise. The whole experience left Cally feeling flat and no more inspired about what she should, or even wanted to, do next.

In the end, she let Raven and Willow sell her two more colorful long skirts with deep pockets, and then walked back to the coffee shop with Nell. She tried to convince Nell to come back to Vale House for the rest of her visit home, but Nell said she had to get back to her painting. Cally didn't try to persuade her that there was more than plenty of room to paint at Vale House. She suspected the ghost living in the coffee shop, as it had not been captured by the Tollers, might be a comfort to Nell. Slinging her Wyrd Systers shopping bag over her arm, she proceeded at last to the news store as afternoon stretched on toward evening.

The door stuck, as always. She tugged at it futilely a couple of times until Ben appeared on the inside and kicked it open for her.

"How is our Nell?" he asked. The inside of the shop smelled like a combination of dust, licorice, and coffee that had sat on the warmer far too long.

She wasn't sure how to answer that. She could only shrug and shake her head as Ben shut the door behind her. He drew her into an embrace that might have been more comforting if Bree hadn't been standing behind the counter, scowling at them over the top of a newspaper.

"You find out anything more about that little task you promised to take care of for me?" the old woman barked.

"I'm sorry, Bree. I'm still working on it." Cally knew she had given Bree this excuse far too many times already. It was the truth, but an excessively stretched version of it. She was frankly afraid of revealing her current theory about the old floppy disk Bree had given her, several months ago now. She would do it soon, she promised herself, but right now she just wanted to see the back of this long, horrible day so she could hide under her covers and cry.

Ben seemed to understand how she was feeling. Leaving her standing by the door, he approached the counter and stood in front of Bree. "Sister," he said, "I wonder if I could have your permission to clock out a little early today?" He smiled charmingly at the old woman. "I'll come in early tomorrow to make up for it."

The only times Cally had ever seen Bree's expression soften had been when she was looking at her brother. Ben seldom asked anything of his sister, and when he did Bree didn't seem to be able to say no to him. She couldn't say it this time, either. "Fine." She looked back down at her newspaper. "I'll cover for you this time. Just don't expect me to lie for you if the queen's toadies come around here asking questions!"

Ben walked with Cally, back through the residential district, to the metal gate closed across the entrance to the meadow. They leaned together on the top rail, watching the clouds around the shoulders of the farthest hills change slowly to saffron and crimson. It reminded Cally of the jewel city Shannish which sometimes appeared there, on clear evenings, when she stood at the gate waiting for Ben.

Now he was standing here with her, having stolen time from his contract with Faerie to be a comfort to her, and all she could think of to say was, "Ignacio would say those clouds are probably precursors more of drizzle than of a storm."

Ben chuckled softly and put an arm around her. "You're becoming as good at predicting the weather as Ignacio is," he said.

"Nobody is as good at anything as Ignacio is," she said. Then she glanced sideways at Ben. Well, she thought, maybe some people were better at some things than Ignacio, but she had no intention of testing this.

They stood a while in silence, watching the sky above the meadow fade from blue to gray as the sun sank behind them. Cally deeply appreciated Ben's presence and his concern for her. She knew she ought to say something, not about the weather, but she had no idea what else to say that wouldn't sound whiny and hopeless.

"Listen." Ben finally broke the silence himself. "I know you're not on the best terms with my mother but hear me out. Tonight, when I return to her court, I would like your permission to ask Rianwynn's advice about our ghosts. She is morally constrained to listen to me. Well, as far as faerie morals are concerned, anyway. And she's powerful in ways few will ever understand."

Cally sighed and looked up. The main thing she'd heard – what she had appreciated most, out of all he'd just said – was the way he'd referred to "our ghosts" as if this wasn't her problem alone. She wondered if she would ever be able to get used to not having to do everything by herself.

"I love that you would offer to run interference with Rianwynn for me," she said. "But I don't see what she could do about this. I mean, I know she's powerful. But she doesn't have jurisdiction over the dead...does she?"

She could tell by the way he closed his eyes and lowered his head that he knew the answer to this. "She does not," he admitted. "Not of the mortal dead. No more than she has over the mortal living." He sighed and returned his gaze to clouds on the horizon, colorless now under the darkening sky.

"Well," said Cally, "I don't suppose it can hurt to ask her advice, anyway."

She wasn't really sure it couldn't hurt, but she was moved by his wish to do something helpful. She thanked him with a swift kiss. He turned her to face him and, cupping her face in both hands, looked levelly into her eyes. "In the meantime, don't do anything crazy. I'll see you in the morning."

She watched him go, as she always did, until his shadow blended into the shadows of the distant hills, then turned her back to the gate to watch the porch lights coming on all along Main Street. The cooling breeze at her back, the rainy scent rising in the air, brought to her mind Woodley's famous "Crossroads Ghost" which often appeared here, exactly where she was standing, during thunderstorms. She had developed a precarious relationship with it over the past year, and now she wondered if the Tollers had got this one, too, since it was so closely attached to Vale House.

She didn't think so. Though urban legend referred to the cloaked and hooded figure as a ghost or a banshee, Cally suspected it was actually something else altogether. The dark, hooded figure had been, if indirectly, helpful on more than one occasion in mitigating threats to Vale House. She believed it was some kind of land spirit or earth goddess, more akin to Rum, the local land-wight who dwelt (most of the time) down by the Vale House pond.

She toyed with the idea of going back to the store and finally having that conversation she kept putting off having with Bree. Or maybe she could just go to Luke's pizza parlor and have a spinach focaccia. All she knew for sure was that she did not want to go back inside Vale House.

From where she stood, she could see Bethany had turned on the porch light. This meant Bethany would already have collected her purse and keys, ready to head home for the evening. Or maybe out to dinner with Doc, who knew? She sighed and went back to the house. Bethany was waiting on the porch. She hugged Cally, thanked her for being such a good listener, said her goodnights, and left.

Cally had never felt at all uneasy, before, about being alone in a huge house full of ghosts. Now she stood in the empty hall, turning round and round, not seeing George sitting in the office chair or standing at the top of the stairs, not even seeing the Preacher's annoying presence moping in front of the desk, and she didn't understand why the room didn't ring with echoes and cold wind. She didn't understand why the walls themselves weren't wet with tears, convulsing with sobs.

She locked the front door and switched off the porch light. As she passed through her office on her way to the spiral stair, she checked her computer to see if Emerald had left any messages. She had not.

Cally resisted the temptation to take the laptop up to bed with her. She was determined to get a good night's sleep, for once, so she could think more clearly in the morning and maybe even find a solution.

19 - Trouble in Paradise

Voices whispered in the dark. Rising, Cally shivered, her nightgown little protection against the cold, and made her way across the room until she could grope along the wall. Feeling for the doorframe, she tried to make out what the voices on the other side were saying. She couldn't discern any individual words – only a deep susurrus which slowly grew louder and more urgent. Turning her head to look over her shoulder, she wondered why she couldn't see the moon shining in through the window. She couldn't see anything – the darkness was complete, and the room around her was cold as the grave.

Finally her fingers fumbled across the light switch beside the door but, when she flipped it up, the light did not come on. She toggled it up and down a few more times in frustration, though she knew nothing would happen.

As the voices outside grew more strident, she made up her mind to open the door anyway. She felt her way down the frame until her hand encountered the knob. It was icy cold. She twisted the lock button in the middle and opened the door a crack.

As soon as she did, something pushed the door back into her face, opening it the rest of the way. A cold blast of air came from the hallway. Bright light flooded the room, almost blinding her. The voices rose to a roar, now, and most of them seemed to be weeping or lamenting. She put her hands up to her eyes and squinted between her fingers.

The hallway was full of people, all milling about, each trying to be heard above the others. But when she tried to step forward to see what was going on, she encountered a barrier, invisible but cold and hard like bars of iron. One face in the crowd turned toward her. It was George and, at first, she was relieved to see him. She called to him and waved, but he didn't seem to see or hear her. She tried to shout above the crowd, but she couldn't hear her own voice.

"Cally!" he was calling. "Cally!" He put a hand up to the invisible bars, but couldn't reach through them, any more than she could reach back. He called her name over and over as if he didn't see her standing right there in front of him.

"Cally!"

She sat up and nearly collided with Ben, who was leaning over her. Sunlight filled the Dogwood room behind him. "Cally, it's okay." He took her hands between his. "You were dreaming."

"Was I?" She pulled her hands away and wrapped her arms around herself. "It felt like... It was cold."

He made shushing noises and sat down on the bed to hold her until she stopped shivering, until she looked around the room long enough to feel grounded again in reality. It took a couple of minutes for the echoes of the voices to stop ringing in her ears.

"I was dreaming about George," she said at last. "It felt so real." She finally put her arms around Ben. "I think he might be in real trouble."

"We can hope it was only a dream."

Cally was thankful he did not go so far as to insist it could not possibly have been anything but a dream. He, of all people, knew better than to say anything like that.

"What time is it?" she asked.

"Late. I've been here for a couple of hours, but you were sleeping so deeply, I hated to disturb you. Don't worry, Kat fixed me a sausage biscuit!" He laughed. "But I have to say, I did miss seeing your nightie hanging on the window frame this morning." He grinned mischievously.

"Oh, I'm so sorry. Maybe we can make up for lost time?" She kissed him, but it was only half-hearted.

He held her by her arms, pressing her back gently, and said, "It's alright. You've been going through a lot, lately." He brushed her hair back from her face and kissed her eyelids each in turn. "I hope you know that's not the only thing I'm here for." He slid under the covers fully clothed and wrapped his arms around her, pressing his warmth all along the length of her.

She was grateful for the comfort of his embrace, so much so that she made an effort to return it more enthusiastically than she had over the past couple of days. She wondered, if she kept her eyes closed, if she might be able to forget she was a ruined older woman trying to make love to a beautiful young immortal. Then she realized, what she actually wished was that he would be the one to keep his eyes closed.

"It's just..." He sat up and propped a pillow against the headboard. His eyes were open, Cally noted ruefully. She pulled the sheet up to her shoulders. He waited until she was looking back at him before he continued. "Are we okay?" he asked. "I mean, I do understand you're going through a lot, but there seems to be something else. You seem, not distant. Not that. It feels like you're pushing me away, keeping me from being near enough to comfort you, to be any help to you at all. I keep getting this feeling I've done something wrong, maybe said something to upset or hurt you, and I don't know what it was. I want to make it right. Call me dense, but I need you to tell me what I did wrong."

She sat up then, as well, heedless of the sheet slipping from her. "Oh! No, it's not that! It's not..."

She bit her lip. She had almost literally uttered the words "It's not you, it's me."

"Oh, god," she said instead. "I never meant to do this to you."

She saw him close his eyes and hold his breath, fists clutching at nothing, preparing himself for her next words.

He thinks I'm about to break up with him, she realized, and again she said, "No!" She jumped out of the bed, bringing an anguished look in his face. Hurrying to the vanity, she opened the little trinket box. "It's just...this!" She turned around to hold the moon-shaped pendant up between them.

He opened his eyes to see what she was talking about, and she watched recognition slowly creep into his expression. He got out of the bed and came to stand before her, looking at the talisman, but he made no move to touch it.

"Where did you get that?"

She saw the pendant swinging back and forth, and realized it was because her hand was trembling. She forced herself to answer.

"Your father gave it to me."

She was not surprised, then, when he turned away. He turned his face to the window, his eyes shut tight. His jaw twitched as he set his mouth in a hard line, and his shoulders set, too, the muscles bunched in such tight balls she knew, without looking, that his fists must be clenched at his sides.

He wasn't looking at her, she realized, because he didn't want her to see the anger in his eyes. She couldn't think of anything more intelligent to say than "I'm sorry," but it was all she was feeling anyway. She was so very sorry and she wished with all her heart she could turn back time and un-make the stupid decisions which had led to this moment.

He opened his eyes and turned to her, but he still wasn't looking at her. His gaze was fixed somewhere far past her. "Why would he give you such a dangerous thing?"

She nearly wept with relief when she understood his anger was not directed at her at all, but at Michael Dawes.

"It's not dangerous," she began, and then, when his eyes did focus on her at last, she knew she was wrong. It *was* dangerous. It had already brought possibly irreparable harm to their relationship.

Ben's rigid posture collapsed so suddenly, then, he had to step back and sit down on the edge of the bed. "You've looked at me through it." It wasn't a question.

She had lied to him by keeping the truth from him. She swore to herself she would never do it again. "Yes." She sat down beside him, but she didn't feel she had the right to touch him. "I have. I shouldn't have, but I couldn't stop myself."

And then, to her utter surprise, he laughed, so heartily he had to put his hands on the mattress behind him to keep from falling over. "No, of course you couldn't," he said finally. "I knew from the outset I had fallen in love with a woman who can't stop herself from doing crazy things." He looked back at her at last and he looked like he, too, wanted to reach out but was afraid to.

"What did I look like?" he asked. "I suppose I am actually withered and white-haired and rheumy-eyed."

She had just promised herself she would never deceive him again, but it took all the strength she possessed to answer truthfully. "No," she said. "Not at all! You're beautiful. I mean, not beautiful like a well-aged oak tree. I mean, seriously, I would love you even if you were. Even if you were, I don't know, a dragon or something. But the truth is..." She was determined to tell him what the truth was, even if she had to force it past her teeth. "You're beautiful like a young sapling. Like the dawn of a summer's day."

As understanding filled his eyes, he slowly stood up. Now he did reach out, pulling her to her feet. She let the pendant fall to the floor, returning his embrace so fiercely she thought she might break him in her arms.

"I think I understand, now," he said into her hair. "Look." He pushed her back a little way so she could. "You don't need to put yourself through this, on top of everything else. Didn't you just hear yourself? You said you'd love me regardless of what I looked like. Don't you think I can love the same way?"

She laughed, then. He was right and, even though this transcendent sort of love didn't solve all the problems around his dual citizenship and the fact that she was mortal and he was not, it addressed what had been eating away at her and, thus, at them. Even more, he still loved her even though he knew she had deceived him. As long as they had that to start with, she thought, surely they could somehow figure out the rest.

He reached down to pick up the amulet, and held it spinning on the end of its chain between them. Cally thought about how close it had come to actually coming between them and, as if reading her thoughts, he said, "We need to get rid of this."

She reached out and closed her hand around it. "I think I know just what to do with it." She had a couple of ideas, actually. There were several hours left before the reading of the will. She went to the closet to get out another one of her skirts with deep pockets.

20 - These Dreams

Cally walked with Ben to the news store for the start of his mortal-world work day. As they passed the opening doors and emerging porch-cats of the residential district, he told her in low tones how his talk with Rianwynn had gone.

"She says she will only talk to you in person," he reported. "About the 'plight of these ghosts,' she called it. But I kind of got the impression she really wants to talk to you about something else entirely. Probably Adam, I would guess."

Cally sighed. Ever since Rosheen and Brandon had announced their pregnancy, she had come to understand why so many old faerie tales featured one good grandmother and another who was a complete vexation. "People who complain about their mothers-in-law have no idea," she said, and then bit her tongue. She should probably not, she knew, speak of Rianwynn as her mother-in-law, since she and Ben had never even discussed the topic of marriage. There would be no point in it – it could never be, whether either of them wanted it or not.

Ben said nothing about her *faux pas*. When they reached the end of the shady oaks, Cally mentally prepared herself for the impending battle of words with his sister, instead. Bree had a thousand and one passive- (and not-so-passive) aggressive ways of reminding her about her unfinished investigation. Sorting through her usual array of excuses, Cally hoped to get past this part of the conversation as quickly as possible so she could proceed to her real reason for visiting the store today: to offer Bree the amulet.

They waved to Merv when they passed the feedstore loading dock. Brandon was just leaving his morning shift at Dawes News. "I finally fixed that blasted door," he told them with a satisfied smile, pushing the infamous door shut behind him. "For good and real, this time!"

Cally and Ben asked him rhetorically if the baby had shown any signs of arriving yet. Brandon laughed good-naturedly, shaking his head as he walked away toward Gardens Road. Ben reached to grasp the door handle. He tugged at it, tugged again, and then pulled it open with a final determined yank.

Bree stood scowling into her newspaper as usual behind the sales counter. Ben nodded to her, then kissed Cally's cheek and said "Good luck" into her ear. Brandon hadn't left much unshelved stock, so Ben headed to the back of the store and picked up the feather duster. He had never interfered in any of Cally's conversations – or confrontations – with Bree, and she was grateful he was out of earshot by the time she approached the counter.

"Coffee?" Bree snapped, putting down her paper.

"Thanks." It was one of the nicer things Bree ever said to her, so Cally took a white foam cup from the stack beside the register. She poured some of the tarry liquid into the cup, took a sip, and did her best to control her grimace. "Bree, I..."

Bree interrupted, which Cally had expected, but this time she didn't harangue Cally about her unfinished task. Something else was on Bree's mind, today.

"Did you have a dream this morning?"

Cally choked and spit the coffee back into the cup, and not just because it was so vile.

"I can see you have," said Bree. "No, I wasn't reading your mind. I had the same dream."

Carefully, Cally put the cup down. "Tell me about your dream." Her voice came out in a croak that sounded more like it should have come from Bree's throat.

Bree didn't bother to share any details about her own dream but got straight to the point. "A friend of ours is in trouble. Don't look so surprised. He has other friends besides you."

"Georgie the friendly ghost." Cally didn't realize she had said it out loud until she saw an unexpected smile spread across Bree's face.

When Bree saw Cally had noticed this, her scowl quickly returned. "So," she said, "What are you going to do about it?"

"I don't know. What are you going to do about it?" Cally wanted to say, but had the good sense to stop herself in time. "I honestly don't know," she replied instead. "I was going to go down to the coffee shop and talk to Nell, after this. She's his friend, too,

and..."

Bree nodded. "That's a good start."

Cally felt a little irritated at herself for feeling all warm inside at having been given what almost amounted to a compliment from Bree.

"But," Bree went on, "I think you ought to consult Raven and Willow, too."

Now Cally wanted to ask the old woman who she was, and what she had done with the real Brigid Dawes. "I thought you held those two in high disregard?" It was one of the few things she and Bree had ever agreed on.

"There's a time and a place for everything," Bree said. "Especially in a time and a place where places and times are so..." She stopped with her mouth open for several seconds, apparently searching for the right word. "Tangled," she finally said, nodding.

She fixed Cally with her gaze again. Cally felt as if she were falling into the old woman's eyes, thinking about how they were so exactly the same color as Ben's yet so exactly unlike them. She struggled to remember what she had come here for. A favor. She had meant to give Bree something, to pass a burden on to her, but she couldn't remember what it was. Something about Nell. Yes, that was it. She needed to go and see Nell.

"I guess I'd better get going," was all she could say.

"Yes, you'd better."

But before Cally could reach the door, Nell came rushing in through it. Cally didn't have time to wonder why Nell had no trouble getting the door open, because Nell ran straight to her and seized her by both arms.

"Come on. We have to get going."

She turned back to the door, still gripping one of Cally's arms, but it was the urgency in Nell's voice that made Cally follow. They were already outside on the sidewalk before Cally could ask "Going where?"

"I had a dream about Georgie this morning. We need to talk to Raven and Willow."

She elaborated as they walked briskly along the sidewalk and crossed Railroad Street, heading toward the Bean Garden. In Nell's version of the dream, George had been standing on the other side of the railroad tracks, his back to the Bells Road cottages. He had been trying to reach across the tracks to Nell, and Nell had been trying to reach back.

"We need to figure out how to get to where he is. He is definitely not on the Other Side," she concluded. "We're going to try a different deck of cards this time!"

She led Cally past the coffee shop and on toward Raven and Willow's storefront. Through the store's plate-glass display window, Cally could see the taller of the two young women (Cally guessed she was Willow) standing on a ladder, hanging crystal-bedecked dreamcatchers. The shorter of the two (probably Raven) was waving to them from near the cash register. She had already spread a colorful deck of cards on the counter.

"Nell, wait. This wasn't very helpful yesterday. I don't see how trying it with a different tarot deck is going to make any difference. Those two don't know anything about ghosts." Cally didn't think they actually knew anything about anything.

Nell nodded as if she understood and let go of Cally's arm. She turned away from the storefront, then, but she didn't head back to the coffee shop. She walked right past the Wyrd Systers' store, toward where the sidewalk ended and Main Street became a two-lane blacktop road running slightly downhill through a tunnel of overhanging oaks.

"It's true they didn't know anything, at one time," Nell was saying as she gestured for Cally to keep up. "But they took a, sort of, crash course, you might call it. You actually had quite a lot to do with that, you know."

"I? How?" She followed Nell into the sun-dappled shade along the shoulder of the road, wondering if she should be worried. Little of what Nell was doing and saying was making any sense. She patted her purse to make sure her cell phone was in it. If Nell's behavior got any weirder, she was going to call Doc.

Nell kept walking. "Just talk to them. You'll see."

"But we just walked right past..."

"At the diner. We'll talk to them at the Seven Forks Diner."

"Nell, you're not making any sense!" Cally bit her lip. "I'm sorry, I..."

As if she had heard Cally's thoughts, Nell stopped walking

and turned to offer her hand. "Cally, I don't know if I've ever told you how much I appreciate the way you show me so much respect despite my illness. It's no small thing, and I thank you for it. Come on, let's go. You'll be alright. Errin told me she taught you how to see the real roads."

Cally took Nell's hand, and followed.

21 - The Reading of the Cards

The "real roads" Nell had called them, but Cally was increasingly unsure, these days, what the word "real" even meant. It occurred to her she was beginning to sound a lot like Nell, at that.

She tried, as they reached the bridge across the little creek at the bottom of the hill, to see the other roads, the way Errin had taught her. She had been practicing this skill for months, out in the meadow, or along the country road running south from Woodley to old Blackthorn. She'd had some success, but she had never thought to try this inside Woodley itself. She couldn't see anything different, now, when she did. Maybe, she thought, it was because she couldn't see how any of it was going to help George.

Past the bridge, the road sloped up again and, at the top where it ran nearly parallel to the weed-grown railroad tracks on their right, she could glimpse the diner's parking lot. Trees partly obscured the sign but, as they stepped across the tracks, the words "Seven Forks" came into view.

That was when Cally remembered, suddenly very clearly, her previous visits to the diner, and her conversations with the two old women who ran it. Their names...well, she didn't know their real names, but she remembered they called themselves Willow and Raven, an unusual sort of affectation for women their age.

She shook her head as Nell stepped off the pavement and took a shortcut through the underbrush toward the parking lot. "Why are we here, again?" she asked.

Nell held a bent branch to keep it from whipping back into Cally's face as they stepped out of the woods onto the pavement. A glittering row of motorcycles was parked in the sun along the front of the diner and, as Cally and Nell approached, the machines' riders all came out the door. One by one, each engine came to life and each rider turned his bike onto the blacktop, until they all poured out of the parking lot in a gleaming river of color and roar. Nell waved at them until they were out of sight, heading for Interstate 85. Cally reached the door first and held it open for Nell.

The inside of the Seven Forks was cozy and rustic. Forest-themed murals on the walls all around evoked a sense of having entered a sun-dappled woodland glade, albeit one filled with the aroma of french-fries instead of wildflowers. Cally had always felt at peace here, she remembered now. The two old women who ran the place were like surrogate mothers to her – to all their customers, she imagined – nurturing with more than just food. One of the proprietors was tall with long, straight silver hair and the other was short with a round head of white curls. They ran their business and served their patrons in a comfortable choreography of long acquaintance.

The taller, thinner woman appeared in the kitchen doorway, waving to Nell and Cally as they entered. "Just sit wherever you like!" she called. Cally thought she remembered the woman's name was Willow.

The other proprietor, the shorter, rounder of the two, appeared as Nell and Cally slid into one of the booths. She was carrying four sweating glasses of tea, which she placed in the center of the table.

"Hi, Willow," said Nell, pulling one of the glasses toward herself.

The woman pushed her way into the booth and sat down next to Cally. She nodded across the table to Nell. "How are you doing, Doctor May?"

"I'm not a doctor yet," Nell reminded her. "Medical school is a long slog!"

The tall woman who, Cally struggled to remember, must therefore have been Raven, sat down in the seat beside Nell and handed her a straw. "We know you'll make it through just fine!" she said.

"I appreciate you telling me that." Nell nodded solemnly. "Sometimes it's the only thing that keeps me from giving up."

While Raven made sure everyone who wanted one had a straw, Willow reached into her apron pocket and pulled out a square packet wrapped in yellow cloth. This she unrolled carefully, revealing a deck of cards. She used the cloth to wipe away condensation rings before she set the deck in the center of the table.

Nell reached out and drew the cards closer to herself. She fanned the deck out in her hands, looking at the images printed on them. "Oh!" she said, pausing to peer more closely at one of them. "I haven't painted that one yet. Nice job, me."

"Sorry, dear!" Raven took the cards and folded the deck together, handing it back to Willow. "We're getting old. Sometimes it's hard to keep track of which what is when, or where."

"That's hardly surprising." Nell nodded. "There's a lot of when and where to keep track of. Maybe someone should write it all down in a book." She winked across the table at Cally.

Cally grasped her cool glass with both hands. She took several long sips, and the sweet tea calmed her stomach, which had started to feel like it was flipping over and over. There was not enough caffeine in the tea to clear her head, however.

"I..." She struggled to come up with words to describe her dilemma and ask the questions to which she wanted answers, but her mushrooming sense of disorientation was turning her brain into a "404 File Not Found" page.

Raven reached across the table and patted Cally's hands. The old woman's touch felt warm and surprisingly solid to Cally. "You're alright, dear," Raven assured her. "Here, look at me. You know who I am. It's alright."

Cally looked. Raven was tall and sat remarkably upright for a woman her age. Her silver hair was straight and long, and though the skin of her face was crêpey and blotched with age, her green eyes were clear and sparkled with life. The longer Cally looked, the more she could see the young woman Raven had once been. Young and beautiful and full of optimism. Not just optimism, but naiveté, perhaps outright silliness. Even as Cally watched, the silly young girl transformed back into the old woman before her and Cally saw how Raven's girlish silliness had eventually proved to be her greatest strength.

"Now do you see?" Raven asked.

Cally did not, yet, but she held up a hand to ask for silence, because she sensed she was about to. She looked away, as if she could see through the back wall of the diner, back down the blacktop road into Woodley, to where the trees gave way to the business district and the sidewalk began, where the Wyrd Systers Books and

Gifts Shoppe stood beside Main Street with its door propped open to welcome all and any open-minded visitors.

"Willow and Raven..." Cally was muttering more to herself than to the others, but when she re-focused her eyes on the women beside her at the table, she said, "I always thought you two had the wrong names. I always thought that was why I could never remember them."

"Understandable." Willow nudged Cally's shoulder companionably with her own. "You'd think my name should belong to someone tall and thin. More willowy as it were, like my lady here." She reached across and took Raven's free hand in hers. "While someone shorter and darker with dark eyes, like mine, should be named Raven."

Raven elaborated. "We chose our names, not to reflect our appearances, but to name our natures: the one who survives because she can bend, and the one who flies afar to bring stories home to the other and then rests sheltered in her arms. It's no coincidence our names are one another's opposite. It shows how we belong to and depend on one another."

Cally had a sudden, clear vision of a raven alighting in the branches of a willow tree whose roots and branches embraced both earth and sky, and she wished – not for the first time – that she could paint like Nell did.

Slowly and deliberately, she unstuck her tongue from the roof of her mouth and said, "You are Raven and Willow, the proprietors of the Seven Forks Diner, and you are Raven and Willow, the proprietors of Wyrd Systers Books and Gifts, and you are both of these things at once."

"Well, not at *once* at once!" Willow giggled. "That would cause all time and space to implode!"

"Though we have snuck down to the road, a time or two," Raven confessed, "to peep at our younger selves and cheer them on."

Cally thought how nice it would have been, when she was a much younger woman, to have her older self cheering her on.

"They really were very silly, we realize now," Willow said. "But they woke up, because someone had to. Someone had to take on the job of manning the switch, of regulating who goes in and out. And they have you to thank for setting them on their true path before it was too late."

"And when did I do this wonderful thing which caused you two to get so woke?"

Willow tapped her fingers on the tabletop, counting softly to herself. She glanced out the window and squinted.

"Next week, I think."

Raven straightened the edges of the stack of cards, then pushed it across the table. Willow turned the top card over.

Cally had seen this card before. It depicted a blue pond in the center of a green field and, except for the mythical creatures frolicking in the trees around its banks, it closely resembled the pond at Vale House.

Raven tapped the card with one finger and said, "Callaghan McCarthy, you need to acquire allies. You need to seek and accept help from those you trust."

Cally noticed even Nell looked up with a quizzical frown. It was good advice, of course, and it was not the first time she'd heard it, but it was not what the card seemed to depict. Willow picked up the card and scrutinized it. "Oh, I forgot. We didn't have either of you cut the deck." She picked the deck back up and began to bury the card.

"No!" Nell reached across the table. "Don't cut them. Don't shuffle them." She put her hands around the outsides of Willow's. "The board is set. We have to move the pieces as they lie. Just let us know where they lie."

Raven gave her a long, considering look but Willow nodded. "Right!" She set the cards carefully back down in front of her and regarded them quietly without even re-straightening their edges. The picture of the pond she placed face up at the far end of the table.

Willow turned over the next card. It depicted a stream flowing across a green field, out of (or into, depending on which way the card was turned) a tunnel of stone. A set of tracks – animal or human, it was hard to tell – followed along the bank of the stream. Raven set the card on the table so that the stream ran from the pond already on the table, and into the tunnel.

"Well, that seems pretty straightforward," said Nell. "Oh, sorry." She looked up at Raven, then back down at the cards. "Sorry, didn't mean to bogart your reading. Don't let me influence your interpretation!"

Raven laughed. "But you're right. Yes, this is absolutely the path to the darkened portal."

"Do you mean Eladha's portal? The culvert under the railroad tracks?" Cally nodded. "The stream from the pond at Vale House does pass through it." This would make sense, she thought, if the cards were meant to be a map, but she didn't see what the broken portal had to do with George or the other ghosts.

"There are more cards," Willow reminded gently.

Raven reached across the table to turn over the next card. It was a lovely miniature painting of a waterfall, much like the one on which Nell was currently working, flowing from a rocky height in a forest. "You have to be careful not to fall," Raven interpreted.

Cally snorted. "That's rather literal, don't you think?"

Both Raven and Willow shrugged. Raven said, "I don't question what the cards say. I am merely a conduit."

Cally shook her head, waiting for Raven to go on. She had already doubted this would be helpful, and she was not feeling any more hopeful as the process went on.

Willow turned the next card over. It took Cally a moment to make out what the image was meant to depict. At first she thought it was some sort of decorative pattern, like a Celtic knot or a mandala, but on closer inspection she could see the pattern was not symmetrical. It looked more like...no, it actually was, a finely detailed depiction of tree roots. They curled over the ground, passing over and under one another in different directions, much like the twisted real and also-real roads Cally was learning to see.

"It looks like you'll need to go in circles for a bit," Raven said.

Cally laughed and shook her head. "Story of my life."

"No, I mean, this time you have to. Go around and around, or you won't get anywhere."

"That makes just exactly the opposite of sense."

Raven stood and removed the napkin holder and salt and pepper shakers from the table to make room for more cards.

"There you are," said Willow, setting out a card depicting a soft, green hill against a starry sky, and Cally said, "Ah!" She had seen this hill before, she was sure, except the one in the card did not have a tree growing on its crest. Instead, a wooden door was set in the side of this hill, carved with cosmic patterns and standing partly ajar.

"Ohhh..." Raven spoke in a hushed tone. "That is the Fortress of the Dead."

Cally stopped doubting the relevance of this whole reading venture, then. She leaned over the card and peered at it closely. Only blackness was visible beyond the door – she could almost feel the cold of it reaching out to press an icy finger between her eyes. "Is that where I have to go to find George?" If it was, she knew, she would certainly go there, no matter how dark the way might be. She only hoped she could find it in the first place.

Neither Raven nor Willow had any reply to her question. Raven held up one finger in a "wait" gesture while Willow silently turned over the next card. This was not one of the fanciful naturescapes Nell usually painted. Instead this card, crowded with details, depicted the interior of a dim, gray room lit only by a single lantern dangling from a wire. The little room was cluttered with small tables, empty wooden boxes, and baskets lying on their sides. Cracked pitchers and kegs stood on most of the tables, and a thick layer of gray dust covered everything, Even the walls were gray and dusty, as was the closed wooden door in the center of the far wall. Cally assumed this was the other side of the door from the previous card.

Willow nodded. "The Lighted Chamber" was all she said, and Raven turned over the next card. Cally sighed with relief to see another section of stream flowing across this one; all the dust in the previous picture had started to make her feel like she needed to sneeze. The water depicted in this card was a darker shade of blue than in the others, almost black, and instead of a grassy field, it flowed through a starry night sky.

Raven and Willow looked at one another. Willow patted Cally's hand. "Pay for your tea with cash, when we're done here," she said. "Normally, I wouldn't charge you. But you'll need the change."

While Cally wondered why Willow would bring this up at such an odd moment, Raven turned over the final card and placed it at the end of the row. It was solid black.

"Well, fuck," said Cally.

Nell laughed into her tea, spluttering it across the table. Then, giggling, she hurried to dab paper napkins over the cards and Cally's forearms. While Raven ran to fetch more napkins, she said "No, no, it's a good card!" She wiped her chin and the front of her blouse. "Just be glad it wasn't the white one. That would've meant you'd find nothing at the end of your search."

"There's a lot in the black card," Willow explained, pushing it closer for Cally to inspect. "If you look carefully, you can see it only appears to be black because it's full of so many things."

Cally peered closely at the black square, but the most she could make out was, perhaps, the hint of fine brushstrokes from the original painting.

"I made this painting shortly after I was diagnosed," Nell recalled.

Willow picked up the card and held it out to Cally. "Would you like to take it with you, to study?"

"What? Oh! No, no, I'd better not. It wouldn't be good to break up the set."

The three other women all looked at her with solemn regard, then, until Willow said, "You know, she is becoming a lot wiser than she thinks."

Nell pressed Willow's hand down until the card lay once again in its place at the end of the table. "Leave it there. So she doesn't get lost."

Willow nodded, patting the card back into place. "All these cards are staying right here until you get back," she said to Cally.

Nell took her cell phone from her purse. Holding the phone as far back from the table as she could, she snapped a picture of the scene, then typed in a caption with her thumbs. "I'm titling it: Directions," she said.

22 - The Reading of the Will

Cally and Nell arrived back at Vale House to find Dave Reid, of Johnston and Reid, Attorneys at Law, rocking back and forth on his heels at the top of the porch steps.

"Oh, the reading of the will is supposed to start at three!" Cally ran up the steps, extending both hands in apology. "I'm so sorry!"

"Was supposed to start," Reid corrected, and Cally continued to apologize as she opened the door and waved him into the house. "Don't worry, everyone is gathered in the study, and Katarina is serving her famous lime cookies. Everything's alright, Ms. McCarthy."

Digging through her purse, Cally ran through the parlor and the service porch, then down the back hall to Ian's study. Nell and the lawyer followed at a more normal pace.

The five wing chairs in Ian's study, ranged around the small fireplace, had once been frequently occupied by the boys in the band: Ian, Jud, Doc, the Captain and Merv. Now only Jud, Doc and Merv remained, each seated in his accustomed place. They looked up as Cally burst into the study. "Sorry, everyone," she said, crossing the room with her key to open Ian's old desk.

"You're fine, Cally," Katarina assured her. She was sitting between Ignacio and Bethany in kitchen chairs they had brought into the room. Trays of sweating tea glasses and small platters of cookies graced the desk and all the little tables in the room. Nell encouraged Reid to sit down in what had once been the Captain's chair, then crossed the room to sit in Ian's chair beside the swept hearth. The only seat left was the desk chair, and Cally sat down in this as she opened the envelope containing the will.

Reid produced his own copy of the will from a pocket inside his jacket. "Now," he explained to everyone, "a reading such as this is an archaism. It's not normally necessary, in these days when most people are literate. But Ian May specifically asked me to hold one for his household, due to concerns arising from the identity theft incident I'm sure you all remember." Everyone in the room nodded. They remembered the incident all too well. "He left two copies of his will: one with me, and the other you have all just witnessed being removed from his locked desk. Ms. McCarthy will read along silently as I read out my copy. She will call it to our attention if she notices any discrepancies."

Cally fanned out her copy of the document and did her best to focus on it as Reid began to read aloud.

It came as no surprise to anyone that Ian had left, to Ignacio and Katarina, the stone cottage in which they were living, along with the patch of garden Ignacio had been tending for so many years. "This will require me to subdivide the May property," said Reid. "Again."

Cally knew Ian had been one of the wealthier landowners in Woodley, but she was surprised, as Reid read off one disbursement after another, at how extensive his holdings had been.

He had left a cottage on Bell's Road, which Bethany had been renting from him for decades, to her, along with every cent she had ever paid him in rent. "It was Ian, you see," Merv explained to Cally, "who developed the land along Bells Road, and sold it off as a subdivision."

"But being as how it's so hard to get people to move into Woodley," Jud put in, "he still owned quite a few of those cottages."

Everyone approved of this bequest, though it brought tears to many eyes, Bethany's not the least. They were also surprised, but not quite as pleased, to hear how much money Ian had left to Joan Cromwell, the former office manager at Vale House. Many pairs of eyes flicked from Reid to Cally and back again, sure there must be some discrepancy between the two wills. There was not, so eyes turned to Nell to see her reaction. She did not seem to disapprove, and in fact Cally remembered, then, Nell telling her about this on the day Joan had left Vale House. Ian had never been one to hold a grudge.

Ian had left Reid himself a parcel of land, as well, and had left various assets to just about everyone in town. Portions of the meadow were distributed to so many families, creating such a crazy patchwork of property lines, it would be almost impossible, now, to turn it into a mall or to turn Main Street into an I-85 bypass. Jud Thornton scowled his silent disapproval, even though he was the recipient, himself, of a sizable tract right in the middle of the meadow. More than a few winks circulated the room at this.

The only point of contention was the distribution, at last, of Vale House itself. Cally had expected this to be bequeathed to Nell, but as her eyes ran across the words on the paper, she drew in a sharp breath. They said: "Vale House itself, along with the remaining acre of land on which it stands, I leave to Callaghan McCarthy."

Cally looked up at Reid, sure the wording in his copy must say something else. He read off, however, exactly the same words she had just read. She put the paper down in her lap and looked, wide-eyed, around at the other faces in the room. None showed any shock or disapproval, as she would have expected. In fact, she witnessed several nods and smiles, including a happy grin from Nell herself.

"Congratulations!" said Ian May's only living heir.

"No!" Cally put the paper on the desk and stood up. "This isn't right. This is Nell's *home!*"

Nell laughed. "Yes, it is," she said. "And I have no fear you'll be throwing me out of it any time soon."

"But..." She stood, looking around the room for at least one person to take her side, but saw only smiling faces looking up at her. "With all due respect to Ian, I can't accept this. I'm the executor of this will. I can...I don't know. Do whatever I have to, to set this right." She turned an imploring look to Reid.

"I can talk to you about it, later, if you insist," he said. "But it won't be a simple process."

He concluded by reading off the remainder of the will, a list of holdings so considerable Cally had to sit down by the time he had finished. All of these assets Ian had, in fact, bequeathed to Nell.

"See?" Nell leaned over the arm of her chair toward Cally. "He's left me with more than enough for me to finish my education and live out my whole life in comfort, even if I never make a dime from my medical practice. Which I will."

Reid folded his copy of the will, then passed out business cards, reminding them all to call if they had any questions. Bethany offered to see Merv, Doc and Jud to the front door but Merv and Jud reminded her they knew how to exit through the side garden, leaving her to walk Doc to the front door alone. Everyone else gathered up glasses, trays, and chairs to carry back to the kitchen.

"I still don't like it," Cally told Nell, following her to the kitchen with a nearly full tea pitcher in her hands. "It's your family home. It should stay in your family."

"Cally, my family ends with me." Nell took the pitcher from Cally's hands and placed it on the worktable. "I do not intend to have any children. Vale House needs to remain in a family who understands how to take care of it. The responsibilities that go along with it. That's your family." She looked at the south wall of the kitchen as if she could see right through the house to Gardens Road, to the Yellow House and the expanding family within. "Dad was a wise man, and his wisdom didn't fade with age. He knew what he was doing."

Cally had to agree, at least in part, when she saw Katarina and Ignacio come into the kitchen. Katarina put down her burdens and crossed immediately to the door to look out across the garden at the stone cottage. Ignacio followed, placing his arm around her as they gazed together at what was now their own home.

Nell poured herself another glass of tea and saluted the couple with it. "Congratulations on becoming landowners!"

"Hear, hear!" Cally agreed. "You've more than earned it." She considered pouring herself a glass, too, but she wished, at the moment, that the pitcher contained brandy instead.

Katarina turned back to the table, a thoughtful smile on her face. "Thank you both. I mean, I would gladly give it up if it meant we could have Ian back for just one more day. But I can't imagine ever living anywhere else." She looked at the mostly untouched platter of cookies. "Please, everyone, eat these up! I would hate for them to go to waste."

The cookies did look good, but Cally couldn't bring herself to take one. "Well," she said, "I can't imagine living here, anymore, myself."

The room filled with a sudden silence, causing Cally to look up and see horrified expressions on the faces all around her. "Oh!" She hadn't meant to say it out loud, and now she backpedaled quickly. "No, I don't mean that! I mean, yes, I don't feel right inheriting a house that belongs to someone else, but what I can't imagine is... What really isn't right is... Well, this house just feels like a big, empty barn without its ghosts."

23 - Vaya con Dios

The kitchen at Vale House had always felt like a safe haven to Cally. Though it was vast and equipped with shiny, industrial stoves and refrigerators, the row of windows all along its west wall, as well as Cally's many memories of talking with Katarina and Ignacio here, filled it with warmth. Right now, it felt like the only warm spot in the whole world.

Bethany, still blushing from her goodbye with Doc, had entered in time to hear Cally's remark about the ghosts, and she climbed up onto one of the stools at the worktable to join them.

"I agree with Cally," she said. "Something feels very wrong around here." Bethany eyed the cookies, but only poured herself a glass of tea.

Katarina had crossed herself when Cally had said the word "ghosts," but now, even though her face was pale, she nodded and stepped closer to the table. "I feel stupid saying it, but I've been thinking about the line from that movie. You know, the one about feeling a disturbance in the force. That's how I've been feeling since I woke up this morning. Well, since yesterday, more like." She looked up at Ignacio. "I'm sorry your wife is going loco," she told him, but he only smiled and tightened his arm around her.

Cally had had enough of not allowing herself to speak freely with the staff at Vale House. No, she told herself, they were not just the staff. They were her friends – her found family. She made up her mind to start treating them as such. She poured herself a glass of tea, at last, if only to give herself a moment to think. She took a sip, then took a deep breath.

"That woman wasn't just speaking metaphorically," she said at last. "That Geraldine Toller. She really did mean to remove all the ghosts from this house. And she did what she said she would do. She clearly was not a charlatan. But somehow, I still feel like she was a liar. I don't think our ghosts are 'in the light' or any place like it."

She told them about her dream, and then Nell told them

about her similar dream.

There had been a time when this might have happened in the opposite order. In the past, if Nell had described a dream about her childhood ghost-friends being in trouble, it would have taken the corroboration of a neurotypical ally to validate her testimony. Now it was Nell's validation that made everyone take Cally seriously.

Bethany looked around the room sadly. "I think she took Doctor Boojums, too."

"Your cat?" Katarina crossed herself again. "That orange tom you used to have, who died about ten years ago?"

Bethany nodded. "I mean, I was never sure. I never actually *believed* he was here. But sometimes, I still felt him nearby. Keeping me company like he always did. Or I would think little Cindy was rubbing against my ankles and I'd look and see nothing. But now I don't feel him there anymore. I feel his... his absence."

Cally made up her mind. "What I'm thinking," she proposed, "is that we should call the Tollers. We have their home phone number in the register. Tell them we want our ghosts back – demand it, if we have to."

Bethany shifted uncomfortably on her seat. "We take guests' phone numbers down in case we need to contact them about their reservation," she said. "But we're not supposed to use that data for anything else. It wouldn't be legal. It's a privacy thing. That's why it's not legal anymore to ask guests for their home addresses."

"I don't care if it's legal or not," said Cally. "It's not just that I miss our ghosts. I hate the thought of them being kept against their will like that. All of them – there were so many in my dream, and in Nell's. It's not right. They may not have bodies anymore, but they're still people with rights. They don't deserve to live like that. Ha. Live. I don't mean live. It's no kind of life. Well, maybe some of them do."

She regretted her words when Nell looked sadly at her. "It's not for us to decide what Foster deserves and does not deserve," she began, but then she heard the back door slam.

Through the window over the sink, Ignacio could be seen sprinting across the yard toward the stone cottage. Cally thought it odd that he would be more bothered by ghost-talk than the rest of them. Maybe he had just noticed the chickens getting into the tomatoes or something.

"I'm calling them," Bethany said resolutely. She got up and headed out through the swinging doors. Cally, Nell, and Katarina followed.

They crowded around the desk in the Hall while Bethany thumbed through the register until she found the Tollers' reservation. It was one of only two on the page for that day, a day which felt like it had been a long time ago, now. "Cally, you do the talking." she said as she pushed buttons to put the telephone console into conference mode. Then she dialed the number.

The connection was atrocious. A scratching sound on the line, like branches against a window in a high wind, ebbed and flowed. Cally was about to ask Bethany to hang up and try again but the ringing stopped, and a female voice spoke through the noise. It sounded like it might have said something like, "Thank you for calling the Spirit Encounters helpline. Please remain calm – I can help you."

"Hello?" Cally called over the static. "Mrs. Toller? This is Callaghan McCarthy from the Vale House Bed and Breakfast."

"Oh, yes! The one who writes fictional paranormal stories!" The hissing and crackling rose and fell, but Geraldine was speaking loudly, as if aware of this. "How nice to hear from you. I trust things are much better now at your establishment. But I sense you, yourself, are troubled about something. How can I help you?"

Cally rolled her eyes at the deliberate jab about her fictional understanding of the paranormal, but she got right to the point. "You can help me by giving back my ghosts. Our ghosts. We miss them and we want them back."

The cacophony swelled as she spoke. She wasn't sure Geraldine had heard most of what she'd said. She prepared to repeat herself, but the racket subsided in time for her to hear "...and they are beyond your reach, now."

"I'll reimburse you for the objects you bought, and any other expenses you incurred," Cally offered. "I'll even come and collect them myself."

"Don't be silly, dear. It's more than a three-hour drive!"

"Nevertheless..." The line noise grew in intensity until it sounded like an entire auditorium full of people all arguing about something. Cally felt like she was back in the dream she'd had; she could almost distinguish individual words. Bethany's and Katarina's eyes grew wide as they put their hands up to their ears, and Nell looked like she was about to burst into tears.

"...understand your business depends on ghostly manifestations," came clearly through the console speaker as the noise faded to a dull hiss. "But spirits are not to be used for entertainment!"

"I realize that. I feel that way too, but..."

Buzzing sounds drowned out the rest. When these died down, Geraldine was saying, "And that's why I can't help you with this. They must stay here with me, where I can help them. Thank you for your concern. Is there anything else I can help you with?"

Cally set her jaw. "I think I've found out what I needed to know."

She thought she heard the click of Geraldine hanging up her end of the line, but it was overwhelmed by a gust of voices – she was sure they were voices, this time. And this time, at least one of the words they were saying was "Cally." All eyes in the Hall turned to her – they'd all heard it.

Cally felt like she'd been punched in the stomach. She sank down, as she exhaled, until her arms leaned on the reception desk, and she put her head down on them. Bethany hung up the phone.

Cally thought she might just stay right where she was for several weeks, but she heard the screen door open beside her. She straightened to see Ignacio had come back into the house, through the front this time. He held a yellow sticky note in one hand.

"I called the sheriff." He was panting, as if he had run all the way from his cottage.

Bethany's face went red. "Ignacio! I know it wasn't legal for us to make that phone call but..."

He grinned. "I was calling in a favor. Dunn owes me a few."

Cally let out a weak laugh at that. "Do you think he'll be able to pull some legal strings for us, and demand the return of our ghosts?"

Ignacio gently shook his head. "No. But he was able to trace the Tollers' license plate number for us. This is their home address." He handed the sticky note to Cally. *"Vaya con dios,"* he said.

24 - Something Crazy

It took Cally more than a few more minutes to convince everyone present that none of them should come with her. Finally, Nell gave her a side-hug and said, "We're all with you in any case, whether we're physically beside you or not. Think of that, if you find yourself feeling lost."

"And call us!" Katarina called to her back as she ran down the porch steps. "We'll be worrying about you the whole time!"

She stopped, on her way out of town, at the news store to tell Ben she would not be at the gate at dusk to see him off. She left her engine running outside the news store and yanked hard on the door until it reluctantly opened. Ignoring Bree's scowl, she walked straight to the back of the store, where Ben was cutting open bundles of newspapers to set out in preparation for the next day.

"I'm always tempted to read them," he said, straightening and glancing at the stack of papers. "But it just seems a little dangerous, reading tomorrow's news." He looked at her, then. "And speaking of news. You've discovered something."

"I have, and I'm sorry I won't be here to meet you at the fence this evening." She explained where she was going, and why. "We'll just have to say our goodnights now. I probably won't be back tonight, but I promise I'll pull over at a rest area and take a nap if I get too tired."

She could almost see the various worrisome scenarios playing behind his eyes, but he succeeded in not speaking any of them aloud. "If you can wait until tomorrow morning," he suggested, "I'm sure I can talk Bree into letting me go with you." He smiled but did not turn his head toward the snort that came from Bree's end of the store.

Cally recalled that Raven and Willow had advised her to accept help from those she trusted. "But I can't wait," she said. "If I try to stay home tonight, I'll only be awake all night fighting myself not to hop in my car and go. I've been so worried. Not just about

George, but about Melissa and Boo, too. And there are spirits at Vale House I've still never met. Well, there were. I'd always hoped to get to know them someday and... Well. Now that I know where to go, to help them get home, I can't not go." She tried to smile bravely for his benefit. "You know I'm not very good at not doing something crazy."

He sighed, nodded, and walked her back to her car. Shutting the door for her as she fastened her seat belt, he stooped to kiss her through the driver's side window. "I'll see you in the morning."

She made a U-turn in the middle of Main Street and left Woodley, USA.

Because it was a weekday evening, the interstate was choked with eighteen wheelers. It had been a long time since Cally had driven on the interstate; she'd become quite spoiled by the nearly non-existent traffic in and around Woodley. Even though she knew truck drivers possessed orders of magnitude more training than she did, the size and proximity of all the gigantic vehicles, along with the fading daylight, made her grip the steering wheel so hard her knuckles literally turned white. By the time she reached the Virginia border, her arms ached. By the time she reached the outskirts of Warrenton, she felt like she had been bench pressing her own weight for hours.

Her GPS had promised the drive would be less than three and a half hours, but with traffic it turned out to be closer to four. The sky was fully dark by the time she pulled off the interstate. The muscles in her back and shoulders finally began to relax as, in relative quiet, now, her phone's metallic voice directed her along less crowded surface-streets. When it finally instructed her to turn into a tidy suburb, she opened her window and allowed the sound of night insects to flow in on the warm night air.

The GPS directed her past row after row of nearly identical Cape Cod style homes, each clad in vinyl siding in various shades of beige. At the side of a lamp-lit cul-de-sac, the phone's voice finally said: "Your destination is on the right."

She made note of the two-story house with white shutters, nestled amid well-trimmed shrubbery, then drove all the way to the end of the cul-de-sac and turned around so she could park facing the exit. Shutting off her engine, she looked at the Tollers' house and felt suddenly unsure of herself. The decorous home, with lights glowing from its downstairs windows, did not look a thing like a Fortress of the Dead. It did not look like a place where any self-respecting, famous ghost-hunting medium would live. Where, she wondered, was the mystical "spirit workshop" of which Anderson Toller had spoken? No glowing plasma flashed behind the arched windows of the two-car garage; she didn't see an eerie glow in any of the upstairs windows.

She did, however, recognize Danya Barry's car parked in the driveway.

"What the hell is she doing here?" Cally's stiff legs protested as she got out of her car and stood staring at Danya's. "Well, at least that's a solid sign I'm in the right place."

She stretched her aching back. It was a little too late for polite persons to be knocking on someone's front door, but all she could do was try. If she were rebuffed, she would park somewhere else and sneak into the back yard and... She didn't know what she'd do then, but she'd figure that out if she came to it. She shouldered her purse, straightened her clothing, and effected her best imitation of nonchalance as she followed the sidewalk to the small, flat porch.

The doorbell was in the center of the side-lighted door; she pressed it and waited. When she didn't hear any footsteps inside, she ventured a peek through one of the sidelights. Danya Barry's face was staring back at her. The younger woman's eyes were, if possible, wider than Cally had ever seen them before, and that was going some.

When Danya saw Cally looking at her, she ducked out of sight. Growling under her breath, Cally prepared to ring the bell again, longer this time, and repeatedly if she had to. Before she could press the button, however, the door opened a crack.

"You can't be here!" Danya's voice came in a hiss through the narrow opening. Cally tilted her head to peer through the crack and saw one of Danya's eyes staring, intense and frightened.

Cally conquered her urge to push the door open forcefully. While she was trying to decide whether to ask, "Why not?" or just "What are you doing here?" she heard Geraldine's voice calling from further inside the house.

"Who's there, dear?"

Danya didn't close the door, but she didn't open it any wider as she turned away to call back in answer. "Don't worry, it's just that McCarthy woman."

Cally made up her mind, then. *"I'll show you That McCarthy Woman!"* she thought, and gave the door a firm shove.

Danya stepped back as the door swung open, but she didn't say anything. Cally knew her silence was not meant to be an invitation, but she took it as one anyway. She stepped quickly into the small entry foyer.

Danya backed up another step, shaking her head, and Cally heard the door slam shut behind her. She turned, startled, and noticed it was painted black on the inside. Geraldine was calling from a brightly lit room – it appeared to be the kitchen – at the end of the foyer. "Well, ask her in!"

Still staring at Cally, Danya held both hands out, palms up, and mouthed something soundlessly. Cally could have sworn it was "help me."

"This is such a pleasant surprise!" Geraldine appeared in the kitchen doorway. "Danya, dear, don't just leave our guest standing there. Invite her to come in and have a seat!"

Danya still did not move or speak, so Geraldine extended a hand toward a doorway at the side of the foyer. Through it, Cally could see overstuffed leather chairs and a sofa. "Please sit down, Ms. McCarthy. Danya will go and let Anderson know you've arrived. He was just opening a bottle of chardonnay!"

Cally did her best to keep her voice civil. "It's alright, Mrs. Toller. I really can't stay. I've just come to collect my friends."

"Oh, now, dear." Geraldine stepped forward and wrapped a bony hand around Cally's elbow. She tugged with a strength Cally would not have expected, and Cally found herself stumbling into the living room. "It's as I've told you. Your friends are alright. I understand. You miss them. But it's for the best. They are in the light, where the living should not follow."

Cally stopped just short of sitting down in the brown leather armchair toward which the woman was drawing her. "I understand that's not strictly true," she said, and she thought, *"Okay, I guess this is a confrontation, after all."*

Anderson Toller came into the room behind them, then, bearing a tray with a wine bottle, three glasses, and a cellophane-wrapped packet of cookies. "Well, now!" he said, beaming. "I had a feeling we hadn't seen the last of you, Ms. McCarthy!"

"All I want..."

"Danya, bring another glass, please." He put the tray on a side table, then to Cally he said, "Sit down."

Cally sat, and sighed in frustration with herself for doing so. Danya walked backward out of the entry hall. She didn't take her wide eyes off Cally until she had turned the corner into the kitchen.

"Now," Anderson continued as he sat down, himself, on the sofa opposite Cally. Leaning toward her with his fingertips pressed together, he said, "I assure you, the spirits we removed from your establishment are much better off in our care. Some of them possessed deeply negative energy, and it is for the best that we protect the world from them."

"That may be so," Cally said, hating the tremor she heard in her voice. She thought she had learned, a long time ago, not to let herself be intimidated by self-aggrandizing louts. She cleared her throat and sat forward in her seat, as well. "But some of them are my friends. I won't leave here without them."

Geraldine laughed as she poured pale wine into one of the glasses. "Isn't that precious!" she said, handing the first glass to Anderson. "A girl who thinks she can be friends with the dead! Maybe we should apprentice her, too. Andy, what do you think?"

Danya came back into the room. She held the additional wine glass out to Cally, but she didn't quite let go as Cally reached to accept it. Cally tugged, giving Danya a puzzled frown. She could have sworn she saw Danya shake her head, ever so slightly, before releasing the glass. Was Danya trying to warn her the wine might have been tampered with? At this point, she would not have been surprised.

Geraldine filled Cally's glass, and then her own. Danya sat down on the edge of the other chair, gripping the stem of her glass with both hands, while Anderson went into his spiel about how long he and his wife had been working with spirits at very little profit for themselves. Cally didn't know what else to do – she took a cookie from the tray. She kept her purse close at her side, and she did not drink the wine.

While she waited to get a word in edgewise, she thought she saw movement from the corner of her eye. A fat, gray cat emerged from behind the sofa and sat, cleaning its paws, under the side table. Cally tried not to look at it directly, but she was sure it was Doctor Boojums. Even in her side vision, its color began to shift from gray to orange as the air in the room grew colder.

Geraldine also noticed the chill. "Damn, it's that cat!" She spun where she stood, looking into every corner of the room. When she finally spotted him, Doctor Boojums ran, pink tongue still hanging out, between her legs and out through the foyer into the kitchen.

"We just shouldn't even mess with cats!" the old woman declared, following the four-legged ghost. "They're impossible to control!"

Anderson stood to follow her. With Cally and Danya close behind, they all crowded into the kitchen as a streak of orange skidded around the end of the dinette table and then vanished through a closed door beside the stove. The door, Cally noted, was also painted black, like the inside of the front door.

Anderson stopped in front of this door, but he did not open it. "Cats are always the most difficult ones," he admitted in a philosophical tone. Letting out a sigh, he turned around and returned to where Geraldine stood beside the table. "Don't worry." He gave his wife's hand a gentle pat. "He's gone back where he belongs, now. A little adjustment to the wards should do the trick."

"It had better!" said Geraldine. "He's disrupting all of them!"

"All of them?" Cally looked at the black door. "How many have you got in there? Why are they not 'in the light?' Isn't that where you keep saying you've sent them?"

Anderson left Geraldine's side and stepped closer to Cally. "It's just a matter of terminology, my dear." He reached out and wrapped a hand around her upper arm. "Let's all sit down and talk about it. I'm sure you'll soon understand."

Cally stiffened. She measured, with her eyes, the distance between herself and the door, wondering if she could get to it before either of the Tollers could stop her, and whether or not it was locked.

"Ms. McCarthy, don't." Danya had squeezed between Anderson and the table, laying a hand on Cally's other arm and giving her another of those maddening wide-eyed looks.

Cally was done with it. Done with being polite to smarmy weasels, and done with this silly girl's complicity in whatever it was they were up to. In a single movement, she twisted herself out both their grips and flung herself across the room at the door. The knob did not turn when she first grabbed it; she twisted the button in its middle.

She didn't have time to try the knob again. The door pushed back into her hand, sending her spinning backward. A blast of icy air roared out of the dark stairwell beyond the door, pushing her into Danya and Toller, who in turn fell back against the table as chairs scattered and fell.

Cally rolled to her hands and knees, scrambling to put distance between herself and Toller, but he didn't seem to be interested in grabbing her arm again. Instead, as she stood up, he flung himself at the open doorway, reaching a hand into the roaring darkness. Cally could see he was clutching a metallic object, probably some kind of religious artifact, she guessed, and both he and Geraldine were chanting words she didn't understand. She didn't have time to make out much more than that. Danya was at her side, tugging at her arm again.

She looked around for something to use as a weapon – possibly one of the fallen chairs – but Danya leaned her head close and whispered, "We have to get out of here!"

Cally found herself agreeing wholeheartedly with that. The front door was only a few strides away. She could make a break for it while the Tollers were otherwise occupied and come back to find the ghosts another way. Maybe a little stealthy breaking and entering was in order, but for now, she headed for the front door.

Danya whispered again urgently as Cally fled. "Take me with you! Please!"

"Stop her!" Geraldine's voice was as hollow as the wind roaring out of the cellar door. Danya caught up, and then ran past Cally, pulling her along with her through the entry foyer. They got in each other's way as they both grabbed at the knob. Cally could swear she heard more than two sets of footsteps coming behind them. They finally succeeded in pulling the door open together; they both squeezed out through it at the same time.

As they tumbled out onto the porch, the voices and noise and roaring inside the house seemed to cease as if they had been switched off. The suburban night air was peaceful, full of crickets, and now Cally could hear only one voice inside the house, calling her name.

"Just keep going!" Danya thrust Cally's purse into her hands. "Don't look back!"

Cally didn't argue. She fumbled in her purse for the car keys as she ran the few yards to the curb. Yanking open the door, she thought about all those horror movies where the fleeing person is unable to get their perfectly functional car to start. As she put the key into the ignition, the passenger door opened and Danya flung herself into the seat. Cally ignored her and turned the key. The Corolla started as smoothly as ever.

Cally put the car into gear and glanced up to see the Tollers standing arm-in-arm just inside their front door. With one foot on the gas and the other on the brake, Cally turned to Danya. "OK, you can come with me, but what about your car?"

Danya simply said, "Drive!"

Geraldine's voice, much closer to the side of the car than her physical presence inside the house, spoke almost in Cally's ear. "You'll be back," it promised sweetly.

25 - The Road Home

While Cally pulled away from the curb, Danya twisted in the seat, watching behind them. She kept saying, "Don't stop. Keep going," until they had gone around several quiet suburban corners and the Tollers' house was no longer in sight.

"Do you think they're going to send...something...after us?" Cally wondered.

"Just keep going," Danya advised, then "Oh my god, stop!"

Cally stopped for the red light she had nearly driven through. Then, when it changed to green, she turned out of the subdivision onto a four-lane road lined on both sides with fast-food restaurants. Nothing seemed to be following them except the light, nighttime traffic. All she could hear through her open window was the sound of tires on pavement. A sign on the right informed her that the I-17 on-ramp was a quarter mile ahead.

"Okay, Danya, listen. Don't panic. I'm going to turn around and drive back to the subdivision. I'll park at the far end of the Tollers' street. We can sneak back on foot to get your car."

"I'm not going back there!" Danya put her hand on the door handle. "Thanks anyway for getting me out." She sat forward as if she were about to open the door and step out of the moving car right into traffic.

"Alright! Alright we won't go back, but for heaven's sake, Danya, what on earth is going *on* back there?"

Danya slowly released the door handle. Once she seemed confident Cally was continuing toward the interstate, words poured out of her in a torrent.

"They offered me, Toller called it, an apprenticeship. Geraldine is getting on in years, they said, and they want to pass all their knowledge on to someone. I thought that was a great compliment, a real opportunity. But it also seemed like a huge responsibility, so I told them I'd like to stay just a few days, at first. See what the setup was, see if we were a good fit, mentor/apprentice-wise, you know. But after the first night I knew it was not for me. I didn't like the way they... you know, they treat everyone. The ghosts and spirits, too. Like you always tried to tell people. They don't treat them with respect. They don't treat the living with respect, either. Anderson is a control freak! Geraldine, well, she's not intimidated by him at all, but she's a control-freak in her own way. She uses him as leverage, for his salesmanship skills, and he uses her for her spiritual insight. It's all really very cute, in a sick kind of way. And together they use the spirits for their own ends. Cally, I think what they're doing, well, it's what my grandmother used to call *necromancy!*" The last word came out of her throat in a strangled whisper, as if she was afraid just saying it would put her in danger of hellfire.

Cally stopped, this time, for a red light. She was in the correct lane to get back on the interstate, but she was thinking about making a U-turn, despite Danya's objections.

"So I said thanks but no thanks," Danya went on. "I declined their offer as politely as I could. But they said I wasn't thinking straight, that I just needed time to think things through. That was when I noticed my purse, with my car keys and phone, had somehow disappeared. I freaked out! But only on the inside. I had a feeling if I showed it, I would be locked in the basement with the ghosts. So I pretended to go along with it and just waited for my chance to make a break for it. Then you came along... I'm so glad you came along... Oh, my god, Ms. McCarthy, this is all my fault!"

Cally was inclined to agree, but she didn't say so. The light turned green.

Danya continued talking as Cally stepped on the gas. "I wish I had never got it into my head to bring those two to Vale House. I keep trying to do something good, and I only ever end up making bad things happen. And your friend George is so sweet!"

Cally hit the brake. "You've seen him?"

A car horn honked behind them and its driver swerved to go around, waving with one finger as he passed. Cally seized the steering wheel and turned abruptly into the empty parking lot of a big-box store. "You've talked to George? Is he alright?" She set the parking brake and turned to face Danya.

"I haven't seen him, no," the girl explained. "But I heard

him. Whenever I was in the Tollers' kitchen I could hear the spirits whispering, or crying, beyond the door. Geraldine said that was proof of my awesome natural talent that she wanted so badly to mold and nurture. Co-opt and control, is more like. I can see that now. Anyway, George...oh, he's so sweet!"

"For God's sake, Danya, what did he say?"

"He said to tell you not to worry."

"Well I *am* worried!"

Danya pushed her head back against the headrest and squeezed her eyes shut. "I am, too. He said he was determined to find a way to help his friends."

"Well, that's not going to happen as long as the Tollers have anything to do with it."

"No," Danya agreed, letting her head fall forward. She closed her eyes and shook her head. "No, it's not."

Cally's dream replayed over and over in her head, and a sick feeling tied her stomach in knots. Even with her eyes open, she couldn't stop seeing George and all the people trapped with him, George trying to reach her through invisible bars. "Danya, when you said you thought the Tollers were practicing necromancy, what exactly did you mean?"

"I don't know. It's not something I ever wanted to learn anything about. It's too...wrong!" She shuddered. "But those ghosts they've been going around busting all these years, they aren't helping them cross over, like they say. They're keeping them. All of them. They've got them stockpiled in their cellar. There must be hundreds. Toller seems to think he has collected nearly enough for something. I can't even imagine what. He kept talking about 'when Geraldine goes' but at the same time he spoke as if he felt he, himself, would still be around to ...mentor... me for years to come." Danya wrapped her arms around herself and fell silent at last.

Cally squeezed her eyes shut to halt the visions in her head. She took a deep breath and turned off the engine.

"I'm sorry, Danya, but I have to go back. You don't have to come with me. I don't know what to tell you about how to get home from here." She dug in her purse. "I'll give you my Triple-A card and some money. Maybe you can..."

"Ms. McCarthy, you can't go back there! Not now! Now that

you know so much about them. Haven't you been listening to me? You'll get to spend more time with George than you expect!"

Cally felt trapped in the tiny car. She wanted to throw her arms in the air and scream. She settled for pounding the steering wheel with both palms. "I'm not going to just turn my back on him! Not on any of them, not Melissa or Boo or even the Preacher. And all the rest of them – they deserve a better fate...well, most of them do, anyway."

"You're talking about single-handedly rescuing an army of ghosts!"

"I suppose I am. What else am I supposed to do?"

"You can get some help, for one thing."

Cally opened her mouth to explain why she couldn't do that, but then she slowly shut it again, because she realized Danya was right.

"Luke could help you," Danya offered in a calmer voice. "He knows more about these things than you give him credit for. And the, um, the cat. He said someone gave you a paper that shows you the way. I'm guessing he meant a map."

"The cat said? Doctor Boojums spoke to you?"

"All cats talk to me." She shrugged. "They always have."

Cally regarded Danya silently while she tried to think of what to do next, but all the thoughts going through her head seemed to consist mostly of swear words.

Finally, she said "Wait. I do have a map. At least, I know where one is. Danya?"

"Yes, Ms. McCarthy?"

"Please, call me Cally. And put your seatbelt on."

When Danya hesitated, hand still on the door, Cally took her phone out of her purse and started the GPS app. "Take us to Woodley, USA," she told it.

26 - Directions

Just across the Virginia/North Carolina border, Cally pulled off the road to refill her gas tank. She handed Danya some cash to get them each a sandwich and some caffeinated beverages in the station's all-night convenience store. While she waited, she called Katarina's cell phone, as she had promised to do. She told her she was alright and that she was on her way home but didn't want to talk about any details until she'd arrived. When they got back on the road, Cally ate her sandwich with one hand as she drove.

It was going on 3 a.m. when they both spotted the exit for Woodley, even though the GPS signal had been lost for over an hour. There was no sign, nothing to call attention to the two-lane blacktop road turning off between the pine trees, but after all the times Cally had had to struggle to see the roads around Woodley, she had become so adept at it, she suspected she wouldn't be able to miss the exit now if she tried.

Her heart, though still troubled, lightened considerably as the familiar smell of moss and leaves drifted through the open car window.

She saw the lights of the Seven Forks Diner glowing welcomingly ahead. The diner should have been closed at this hour, but there was a motorcycle parked near its door. Cally pulled into the next parking space, and saw Raven and Willow standing in the open door.

"Oh, you poor thing!" They came running, arms wide open, across the parking lot.

Cally got out of the car. "It's okay, I'm..."

But it was to Danya's side of the car they ran. They enfolded her in hugs and concerned exclamations. "We're so glad you're alright. What you must have gone through!" They drew her toward the doorway, in to the warmth and light of the diner. Cally followed.

Raven and Willow waved to the leather-clad motorcyclist and encouraged him to keep enjoying his chili-cheese fries as they led Danya to a table. While the two old women sat down with Danya and made sympathetic noises at her, Cally turned to the table with the tarot cards still spread upon it. It had been pushed to the back of the dining area but was otherwise undisturbed. She sat down at this table and took a pen out of her purse. Carefully, on a napkin, she wrote:

    1: Pond ("you need to collect allies") (pool your
        assets?)
    2: Stream
    3: Tunnel
    4: Falls ("don't fall")
    5: Tangled Roots ("you'll go around and around")
    6: Hill with Door
    7: Room with Light
    8: River
    9: Night

She checked her list carefully against the cards on the table, then checked it again. Satisfied, she folded the napkin and put it in her pocket.

She walked back to the table where Danya and the Wyrd Systers were sitting but did not sit down to join them. "You should call your bank when it opens in the morning," she told Danya, "and have them put a hold on your credit card. Bethany can help – she has a lot of experience now with this sort of thing. You can stay at Vale House until this is all settled."

"And where are you going?" Raven asked.

Of course Raven knew she was going somewhere, even though she hadn't said so. Cally patted the napkin in her pocket. "I've copied down your map. I'm going wherever it leads."

Gesturing for Danya to follow, she nodded to Mr. Chili-Cheese Fries, then left the diner with a much surer step than that with which she had entered.

27 - Sausages and Hash Browns

There were a few hours left before dawn, when Ben would arrive as usual at the edge of the meadow. As Cally drove between the darkened storefronts along Main Street, she considered whether she should wait for him, or just hop the fence and follow Raven and Willow's "directions" straight into the meadow.

She was yawning when she drove between the masonry pillars into the darkened Vale House parking lot. She let herself and Danya in with her manager's key and checked the register to make sure no guests had arrived after she'd left. None were recorded in the register, so she scribbled out a sticky-note for Bethany and wrote Danya's name under "Rose Room."

"You'll remember where it is," she said, handing Danya the key with the pink rose on its fob. Danya nodded, then hugged Cally hard before she turned to trudge, sans luggage or any personal possessions, up the ghost-free grand staircase.

Cally knew she should get some sleep, but the list of "directions" was burning a hole in her pocket. She went back out onto the porch, instead, to the wicker chair the Captain had once loved to sit in on fine summer nights. The growing clouds, along with the impending dawn, meant she couldn't make out many stars above the hills. The part of her mind not suffering from sleep deprivation reminded her that some paths, some roads, only appeared at night, and there wasn't much night left. Sometime before the sun began to illuminate the bottoms of the clouds over the meadow, she did finally fall asleep.

Ben woke her gently, touching her shoulder, brushing her hair back from her face. She hoped she hadn't been snoring.

"How did it go?" he asked.

It was nice of him to ask, but his sorrowful expression showed he already knew she had come back empty-handed.

"They've got George," she said. "I didn't see him, but Danya says she spoke to him. I couldn't get him out. I barely got away, myself. I don't think I would have, if Danya hadn't been there. How did it go with you?"

"I'm so sorry, Cally." He sat down in the chair next to hers and leaned across to take both of her hands in his. "Rianwynn has asked me to please remind you that she has no jurisdiction over anything in the human realm, but that she still wishes to speak with you."

Cally felt only mildly irritated at this. She didn't have time for Rianwynn anyway.

She started to stand up, but Ben leaned closer, looking into her eyes. "Are you okay?"

"Not really," she admitted. "But I'm not giving up. Ben, they have a lot of ghosts there. Dozens of spirits. Maybe hundreds. Just like in my dream."

"Bree told me she dreamed the same thing." He took a deep breath, sitting back to rub his hands against his thighs. "So, what do you mean to do?"

She stood, turned, and reached down for his hand. "For now, let's have some breakfast."

☾

Katarina spun around with a relieved smile when they pushed through the swinging doors into the kitchen. "Eat!" she said. "You can tell me how it went after you've eaten. I'm pretty sure I already know, anyway." Turning back to the wide, industrial stove, she scooped sizzling sausages and hash browns onto plates. "If all I can do to help is feed people, then that is what I am going to do!"

As Katarina set the plates on the worktable and returned to the stove, Cally thought she saw her cross herself. *"Querido Dios,"* she muttered. "I miss Ian and Sofie so much. I don't even remember how to cook small meals!"

Cally tried to offer a little comfort. "There is in fact one guest this morning to cook for," she said. "But I don't think Danya will be coming downstairs in time for breakfast. We had a very long night." She wasn't hungry, herself, but she ate because she knew she was going to need her strength. Copious refills of her coffee cup helped drive back the fog of sleeplessness. Ben, as usual, enthusiastically devoured anything Katarina set in front of him.

Cally was halfway down her fourth cup when Ignacio came in through the garden door. He set two baskets, one containing brown eggs and another heaped with glistening red strawberries, on the drainboard of the sink. Katarina filled a plate for him, too.

He sat down beside Ben, giving Cally a sad glance. He, also, seemed to already know how Cally's quest to Warrenton had gone. Digging into his breakfast, he did not ask her for details of her trip but, between bites of fried potato, went straight to "What's the plan, now? What can I do to help?"

Before Cally could think how to answer, Bethany burst through the swinging doors. Her car keys were still in her hand and she was breathing hard because she had, apparently, run all the way from the front desk.

"You brought Danya here?" She waved the note Cally had left on the desk. "That's unexpected! Sorry, that came out wrong." She reached out to accept the coffee cup Katarina handed her. "I'm fine with unexpected guests, of course. It's just I wouldn't have expected you to be hanging around with Ms. Barry."

"I brought her back with me late last...well, early this morning," Cally explained to everyone while Bethany pulled herself up onto one of the stools. "She's going to need our help, for a while. I've put her in the Rose Room."

Bethany waved away the plate Katarina tried to set in front of her, and the cook gave way without argument. Bethany never ate breakfast. "So, did you have any luck?" She looked around the kitchen, even though nothing had ever haunted that particular wing of Vale House. "Are our ghosts back home, now?"

"I'm afraid not," Cally admitted. "I'm going to have to try something else."

"Well, that stinks. You know, I think we should sue those Tollers!"

Katarina nodded her emphatic agreement. "I say we should all go up there!" Balling up both fists, she shook one of them in the general direction of the Virginia border. "Knock their door down and demand the return of our property!"

Cally had to smile at that. "I feel the same way. But I'm guessing most courts would not consider ghosts to be property. Come to that, I'm pretty sure most ghosts wouldn't, either."

"I don't care! I..." Katarina cocked her head as Cally took the napkin out of her pocket and unfolded it on the table. "What's that?"

"I have a couple of ideas." She felt much calmer, now, safe at home with the soft morning light creeping through the window over the kitchen sink. "It's directions," she said. "Sort of a map, based on a tarot reading the Wyrd Systers did for me yesterday. It shows where the Tollers have imprisoned our friends. And it's not in Warrenton, Virginia, if you know what I mean. I failed, last night, because I failed to follow the directions. I'm going to try to find out what these directions actually mean, today."

Katarina did not nod in understanding, but she joined Ignacio and Bethany in studying the list of notations. "Well, the pond business is pretty clear, anyway," she mused aloud. "But the rest of it doesn't make much sense."

Ben pushed back his plate and stood. "Thank you, Mrs. Munoz," he said with a satisfied grin, just as he did every morning. He gave Katarina a side-hug, then carried his plate to the sink, adding, "You are a goddess among women." Ignacio looked over at his wife and smiled in agreement.

Cally picked up her scribbled-on napkin. "I'm going to show this to a few people, see what they think. Merv, and maybe Bree." She also hoped to consult Rum, if she could raise him at this time of day. If anyone knew anything about the paths beyond the fence, it was the local land-wight.

She folded the napkin and put it back into her pocket, then stood and carried her plate to the sink. "I'll walk with you to the store," she told Ben, even though it wasn't anywhere near time for him to report for work.

28 - Telling Her

Bree looked up sharply when the door made its customary *whunk-rattle* in protest at being forced open.

"Well, this doesn't bode well!" She slapped her newspaper down onto the counter as Cally and Ben entered the store.

"It's nice to see you, too, Bree!" Cally called back. She kissed Ben's cheek, and he ducked down the candy aisle toward the back door. Brandon was standing in the open doorway, signing for a stack of cartons Ennilangr the delivery driver had just wheeled in.

Bree was still glaring at Cally. "I'm starting to think there's little point in assigning any important tasks to you," she muttered as Cally neared the counter.

Cally ignored this. She spared herself the coffee-sipping ritual, as well, and got right to the point. "What do you know about the Fortress of the Dead?"

Bree's already pale face went paler. "The Nocksgall. Is that where Emerald is?"

"What?" Cally frowned. She remembered Aileen having said something about "the Nocksgall" a few nights ago. "No. I was referring to where they have George. But you're giving me the impression you know a whole lot more about Emerald's story than I do. I don't understand why you've been asking *me* to figure it out for you. Anyway, no. That is not where Emerald is. It's where all the rest of the Vale House ghosts are being held, against their will. Emerald is, in fact, pretty much the only one they didn't get."

"Because she's not a ghost." Bree murmured this more to herself than to Cally.

"I know that."

"What else do you know?"

"It's just that, at this point, I'm pretty sure she doesn't know who *you* are, Bree."

Bree shut her mouth, jaw set, eyes glittering like sapphires. Cally took a quick step backward. She had seen what could happen when Bree got upset, and it was one of many things she was not in the mood to deal with today.

But Bree did not go into a rage. When next she spoke, her voice was almost that of a little girl.

"Will you tell her?"

"I might," said Cally. "But only if you want me to."

The old woman was silent another moment. "Okay, listen. The faerie people, they have a place they call the Nocksgall. It's where their own dead go, sometimes. It's more like a prison than your human 'heaven' or whatever. But I don't think humans can go there, dead or otherwise. Why don't you ask my brother? He knows all about..." She tilted her head toward the back of the store and let out a snort. *"That* sort of thing."

"I don't want him to worry about me."

"Huh."

"I'm sure he already has a pretty good idea what I'm planning on doing. I promise, I'll tell him the whole plan, after I figure it out myself."

Bree only nodded, continuing to stare at Cally.

"I have more investigating to do." Cally turned away from the counter, pausing to blow Ben a kiss as she headed for the door.

Behind her, she heard Bree clear her throat. "Cally!"

It was the first time Bree had ever called her by her name. She turned around slowly.

"Yes, Bree?"

"If you're sure it won't hurt her, go ahead and tell her."

Cally nodded, bowed slightly, then kicked the bottom of the door and let herself out of the store.

29 - The Switch

Merv Arkwright was, as usual on fine mornings, sitting in a lawn chair on his loading dock across the street from the news store. He was not, however, reading his morning newspaper, because the dock was surrounded by people. As Cally crossed the street she waved to Jud, who stood at the bottom of the steps, and nodded to Sheriff Mahon leaning against his patrol car at the curb. Standing on the dock beside Merv was a young woman who reminded Cally a lot of herself a decade or so ago, though with darker and more manageable hair.

"Ms. McCarthy!" Merv called out as Cally stepped up onto the sidewalk. "Have you met my daughter?"

The young woman smiled at Cally from behind huge retro-nerd glasses but didn't make eye contact. She had been edging toward her car, parked in front of the sheriff's, but now Merv had obliged her to stop and make more small talk. "I believe I recognize you from Mr. May's funeral," she said to Cally. "But it was such a hectic day. If we were introduced, I'm afraid I've forgotten already."

Merv regarded the younger woman with an affectionate smile. "Callaghan McCarthy, this is my daughter Geddy Leigh."

"I'm so pleased to meet you," said the younger woman. Cally couldn't help but notice the sudden tension in the woman's body. Clearly, Geddy Leigh Arkwright had come to expect, at this point in an introduction, comments about her name. Cally wanted to say she thought it was an awesome name, clearly bestowed by Merv with great love, but having gone through life herself with an unusual first name, she understood how the younger woman must feel. She chose a different topic of conversation.

"I'm afraid I can't stay long," she said. "I just need a quick word with your dad."

Geddy's posture relaxed noticeably, and Cally turned back to Merv. "I'm thinking about taking a long walk through the meadow today," she said. She couldn't show him the note in her pocket, or otherwise talk openly to him in front of the others, but she kept an eyebrow lifted to let him know she wasn't speaking about an ordinary walk. "To find...some inspiration. Do you think I could get there by going under the old railroad trestle?"

Jud jumped in and answered the question before Merv could think of a subtle way to reply. "The inspectors have been over and over that section of tracks!" he said. "There's no reason the trains can't resume using it, and certainly no reason why you can't walk under it. You'd have to wade through the creek, though. Why don't you just use the gate at the end of Main Street?"

"Well I... I just hoped it might look a little different, off the beaten path."

"Careful, you could get lost out there! We did, a few times when we were kids, didn't we Merv?"

The sheriff pointed to the phone hanging from his belt. "Take your cell with you," he advised.

Jud laughed. "Too bad we didn't have those, back then, eh? Kids today have it too easy!"

"Yes, but..." Merv looked over his shoulder, eastward along Main Street toward the residential section, whose oak trees hid the gate and meadow from view. "You might not be able to get a signal out there. Ms. McCarthy, do you have a map?"

"I do." Cally patted her the pocket of her skirt. "Just making sure I understand it properly."

"Well." Merv cleared his throat and gave Cally a level look. "Be careful. The paths can look different, in the daytime, from how they do at night."

"Yes," Geddy murmured, almost as if to herself. She, too, was gazing toward the east end of Main Street. "They really can. Dad, I have to get going. Thanks so much for everything." Merv started to get up from his chair, but his daughter bent down to kiss his cheek. She straightened and descended the steps, and as she passed Cally on the way to her car she said, "Be careful, Ms. McCarthy."

Cally turned the corner around the east side of Merv's store and followed Church Street to where it ended at the empty rear parking lot. From there, she followed the railroad tracks back toward the meadow. This took her behind the Vale House property (*Your property, now*, said a voice in the back of her head. She waved it away.) When she passed the white picket fence around the May family cemetery, she saw a strange pickup truck parked on the grass just outside it. Two men were unloading a shiny, new tombstone from the back of the truck. She didn't pause to read it or watch them install it.

Instead, she ducked into the trees surrounding the pond, pushing aside springy branches to make her way to the water's edge. There, in the shade of river birches and white willows, Ian's boat slumped, permanently now, finally finishing its deterioration on the muddy bank. Cally vividly recalled sitting, on summer days just like this, beside Ian in a lawn chair on the boat's tilted deck. She could almost hear his gentle voice expounding on all the esoteric facts he'd collected over his lifetime.

The water, she noted, was greener than that of the pond depicted in Nell's painting, the first card from the Wyrd Systers' deck of divination cards. As well, no derelict fishing boat had been present in Nell's rendition. Cally suspected the Pirate Ship probably had a separate card all its own. She was certain, in any case, that this was the right pond.

Leaving the boat behind, she circled around the pond on its northern bank until she encountered the little creek flowing out from it. It curved, after a short distance, to follow a level stretch of rocky, mowed ground that had once been part of Bells Road, and this in turn followed the fence between Woodley and the meadow. As it approached the culvert, the creek sank down between steep, bramble-covered banks until it passed under the stone archway which served double duty as both culvert and railroad trestle.

The three: fence, creek, and railroad, all converged here, marking not just the boundary of Woodley, USA, but also a passage from one realm into another. Just a symbol – Cally understood that now – but a very real one whose significance she was only just beginning to grasp. She clambered down the bank, through blackberry canes and jewelweed, until she could rest one hand on the side of the stone arch and look underneath.

A slender crack meandered from the underside of the tunnel,

through the mortar between the stones and all the way up to the tracks, but Cally was inclined to agree with Jud's assessment that the arch itself was still quite sound. She ducked her head into the cool, damp air flowing out from beneath it and looked along the stream to a framed view of sun-dappled trees on the other side. "Pond, stream, tunnel," she murmured, reciting the list in her pocket from memory. Everything, so far, matched the "map" laid out in the cards. She was pretty sure there was no waterfall on the other side, though. At least, she couldn't see one from here.

But she'd been around long enough to know that what she saw, via her constricted view of the other side of the tunnel, might or might not resemble what she would see should she wade through the stream to the other side. Too, as Merv had reminded her, it could all become a completely different story after nightfall. Rough lumps of rock under the water looked like uncertain footing, to her, and none of them jutted above the surface enough to make themselves available as steppingstones.

"You'll have to be careful not to fall!" called a voice above her head on the opposite bank. She looked up, smiling because she knew that voice.

"Rum!" she called back. She had to look in both directions along the weedy slope before she saw a clump of brambles next to the fence wink at her with shiny black eyes. Once she focused on it, the anthropomorphous undergrowth took on the semblance of a very short, very whiskery old dark-skinned man. He was leaning on a gnarled stick, much longer than he was tall.

"Just the person I need to talk to!" Cally called up to him.

A wide grin split the gray whiskers covering Rum's face (and most of the rest of him, as well). "You aren't thinking of going through there, are you?" He gestured toward the culvert with a thin hand that resembled a bundle of twigs.

"I think I may have to." She sighed and glanced into the dim depths. "I'm not sure. And even if I were sure, I don't know when, or what to do once I get there."

Instead of enlightening her as she was sure he could, Rum shaded his eyes and gazed quietly back across the pond to where the men who had installed Ian's headstone now started their pickup truck and drove up the slope of the lawn.

"I am sorry for your loss," Cally heard Rum mutter to her.

"And I am sorry for yours." She began to climb the bank toward him. It had been Ian who had first introduced her to Rum, just about a year ago now. Before that, the two old beings had shared many years working together for the good of Vale House and the surrounding Vale. It was this responsibility, more than anything else, that Cally had inherited from Ian. "Mostly," she said as she arrived at Rum's side, "I'm sorry I have no idea how to step into his shoes."

"Come look here." As the sound of the pickup truck faded away, Rum turned back to the fence and clambered between the two bottom rails. Cally had to duck under the top rail, herself, to join him in the grassy field on the other side, as her Wyrd Systers skirt did not allow for graceful vaulting.

The meadow was a fresh shade of green, at this time of year, and the late spring grass reached to the just below Cally's shins. Intermittent sun shone between breaks in the clouds above, revealing white and yellow wildflowers amid the grasses. Rum led her along the fence to where it ended in a tall, thick post embedded in the railroad embankment. Shuffling across the tracks where they crossed the culvert, he leaned over and looked down. Cally followed him carefully; she had always been afraid of heights, and even though this was not much of a height, she was glad of Rum's shoulder to rest her hand on.

There was no waterfall here, not even a hint of one, not even a shelf of rock for water to gurgle over. The stream merely flowed out of the culvert below them, and then bent gently, finding the path of least resistance between two rising stretches of ground, until it disappeared into the woods to the north. Cally thought of Merv's story of his boyhood journey along that stream, and smiled almost the same way she had once smiled at Ian May's old stories.

"Have you found the switch yet?" Rum asked.

"Switch..." Cally stood back from the edge. She recalled Merv asking her the same question that night, just a few yards from this very spot. She turned her head, now, to gaze along the tracks toward town. "It's just one, straight stretch of tracks," she pointed out. "It doesn't need a switch. But, to answer your question, no. I haven't found one."

Now she did, at least, wonder where one might be, if there were or ever had been one. "The most likely place," she guessed, "would be inside a building close to the tracks. If there was ever a railroad depot in Woodley, it probably would have been what is now Merv's feedstore, or maybe Jud's hardware store."

She looked down to see Rum's dark eyes regarding her solemnly. "You're good." He drew the words out thoughtfully. "Yes, very good. Jud's store was indeed once a railroad warehouse. That's not what I was referring to, but I'm pleased you could see it, anyway. I was referring to a different kind of switch. Look."

He planted his stick in the gravel between two ties and began waggling it back and forth. "The thing," he said "you see, is..." He pushed the stick forward, away from himself. "It's a matter of perspective. And it's your job to decide what that perspective should be. By 'your job' I don't mean just you, but the whole team."

Cally remembered what Merv had said to her, about what Katarina had once referred to as the White Council. "You mean, the elders: Ian and the Captain. Merv and Doc and Jud."

"It used to be them. The torch is passing. That's not an event, but a process. You are part of it, now, along with the rest of your team."

"Oh, Rum, I don't think I have a team." She didn't mean to sound whiny. It was, as far as she knew, a simple fact that all of this sat pretty much squarely on her shoulders alone.

"Don't be such a big baby." He was still pivoting his stick back and forth on the ground, as if it really were a railroad switch. She looked up and down along the tracks, just in case he actually was switching something, somehow; she'd seen him do stranger things. She couldn't see anything moving, though. There was nothing to move, along the single set of tracks.

She did notice, however, that where they had become weed-grown and rusty, lately, they were now better tended and in good repair. The gleaming iron rails ran perfectly straight in either direction until they disappeared into tunnels of trees on either end.

Except, she suddenly realized, the trees were much closer than they should have been. The fence had disappeared, as had most of the cottages along Bells Road. She turned further, and saw Vale House across the pond, just where it should be, but where she should have seen the tops of Main Street's oak trees beyond it, and some of the residential district's shady porches, now she saw only a vast, tilled field. The town west of that consisted only of two large, wooden buildings and a rustic gas pump alongside a dirt road.

She reeled, a little dizzy, back to face Rum, and looked at his hand on the stick while he continued chiding her. "There are plenty of people on your team," he was saying. "You only feel alone because you won't let them in. You push them away because you don't trust them, and then you try to do the work of six because you don't even see them standing right there." Rum concluded his lecture with a sharp nod that slapped his beard against his chest.

"That's not fair!" Cally felt like he might as well have slapped her with that stick of his. She thought she knew which friends of hers he was talking about: Nell and Katarina, Merv Arkwright, Ignacio, and maybe even Luke and Ben. "I do trust them. I just don't like to become too dependent on people. It's not a good idea. I mean, it's one thing to delegate, to let people do what they're better at than you are. To share the burden. But if one day those people are just not available, for whatever reason, then you're unable to..."

She had to stop, because Rum had pulled his stick toward himself, now, and the terrain around them was changing again. The encircling fields were rolling back, to be replaced by downtown Woodley once again. The tracks ran, once more, through a sunny, mowed field between Main Street and Bells Road. The cottages along Bells Road came back into view, too, but as Cally watched they grew more and more crowded. In no time, they were replaced by tall, ugly beige buildings many stories high. The field itself, on both sides of the tracks, dwindled under pavement until even the tracks disappeared to be replaced by four lanes of concrete. Traffic whizzed by on both sides, blowing Cally's hair back. Rum's beard flew in the wind as the four lanes became six, then eight. Cally looked eastward and saw there was no meadow anymore, nor forest, nor anything but endless steel and glass buildings, spreading out in every direction and closing in upon them.

"Okay, I get it!" Cally shouted above the noise of whining tires and roaring engines. "I get it. Stop!" She put her hand on top of Rum's and pushed, tilting the stick forward until the noise subsided. She kept her eyes on her pale hand gripping Rum's knobby, brown one until the noise of tires on pavement faded away. Slowly, birdsong returned to the world around her, and the high-pitched hum of a cicada rang from the woods to the north. A dog began barking somewhere on Bells Road as a warm breeze caressed her skin. She let go of Rum's hand. He was grinning up at her, eyes sparkling like dark pools reflecting a forest canopy.

"Honest to God, Rum," she said. "Every time you give me advice, you scare the hell out of me."

He laughed. "But now you know why it takes a team to maintain this gateway. These decisions are too big for just one person to make. Choose one way, you set one chain of events in action, choose another way, something else happens. It's hard to tell which is better, which is worse, where to stop. That's why you need one another. There should always be someone pushing the other way."

"Merv told me he and the rest of the guys, Ian's team, they were never sure they were doing it right."

"And that's exactly what was right about what they were doing." He held the stick out to her. "Your turn, now."

She shrank back as if he were trying to hand her a hot poker.

He laughed. "It's not the actual switch, you know. It's only a symbol. And anyway, I'm just lending it to you. You'll need it tonight, so you don't fall. I can't go where you're going, but at least you can take this! I expect you to bring it back to me. That way, I'll know you're coming back."

She took a deep breath, let it out, and accepted the stick. It was just a little shorter than she was tall, and the feel of the rough bark covering it was strangely comforting in her grip. She leaned on it and said, "Thanks, Rum."

He had turned away, gesturing with one gnarled hand toward the pond. Cally followed his gaze to where she could see just a glimpse of Ian's boat, a patch of faded blue paint amid the beeches. "One day," he said, nodding. "Someday, not today, but someday you and I will just sit and talk. There. We'll sit and talk the afternoon away."

"I'd like that," she had to admit.

He walked southward along the fence. Cally thought she

heard him say over his shoulder, "The real switch is you."

30 - Separate Ways

She walked along the fence on the meadow side until she was abreast of Vale House, then ducked back through. Walking across the front lawn, she thought she could hear voices on the porch. One of them sounded like Danya. Cally was delighted to hear her laugh but couldn't imagine what she might be laughing about. It was not until she reached the bottom of the steps that she saw Luke, sitting in the wicker chair next to Danya's, that she thought she understood.

He had a pizza-warming box across his knees, and a hand on top of one of Danya's on the armrest of the chair. She was laughing at something he had said – probably a lame pizza joke. Danya looked up and waved, and Cally had to smile when she saw the light in her eyes. Life really could bring happy surprises sometimes, she thought, even when things seemed darkest. She nodded in greeting but left the two young people alone together and went inside.

Bethany was on the phone. Cally walked quietly past her and slipped into her office. She put Rum's stick into the umbrella holder at the base of the coat rack beside the door, then sat down at her desk. There were no new messages from Emerald, but she took a moment to scan her email in-box. With a few much-practiced keystrokes, she deleted all the spam. Then she sent a quick reply to an email from her agent, assuring her she would be able to complete the needed revisions before the deadline. This was, as far as she knew, a barefaced lie, but she could worry about that later. Finally, she closed all the computer's applications except the chat program. Into the ancient text-on-black chat box she typed a message she did not mean to send until after she'd had a good, solid nap.

> **Cally>>** So, I'm going to head out to try to find the
>
> Nocksgall tonight. I've talked to Rum, and I'm pretty
>
> sure now I should go at night. In any case I only got two

hours of sleep last night and I don't want to try to do this under the influence of sleep deprivation! Should you not hear from me by, let's say, tomorrow evening, try contacting Errin, or maybe Mima or Zenbe. You've sent Errin to fetch me more than once! ☺ Well, providing she can go where I'm going, anyway. I'm going to leave my password with Nell, as well, so she can get in touch with you if she gets worried. She hates this old computer, but I know she'll rise to the occasion if she has to. Probably none of this will even be necessary. I fully expect to be back by morning but, you know: just in case!

She checked and re-checked her message, tweaking some of the punctuation and grammar. Leaving the unsent message with the cursor blinking at the end of the line, she tore a page from one of her notebooks. On this she penned a quick note to Nell, telling her what she planned to do. If she told her in person, she knew, Nell would probably try to come with her, and too many of her best-loved friends were already in enough danger. She jotted her computer and internet passwords at the bottom of the note, placed it in an envelope, wrote Nell's name on the front, then laid it across her keyboard.

When at last she stuck her head out her office door again, Bethany was still on the phone, laughing about something. Cally guessed she was informing the entire town that Luke and Danya were, apparently, an item now. She cleared her throat and waited for Bethany to put her hand over the mouthpiece and look up.

"Hey, Bethany. I only got a couple hours of sleep last night, so I'm going to take a quick nap. If you don't mind, please put my phone on Do Not Disturb. Thanks!" She went back inside her office and wrapped herself in the crocheted throw from the back of the sofa. Propping herself up on the sofa's arm so she could see through the window, she allowed herself to fall asleep staring at the clouds passing above the meadow.

The sky had gone gray by the time she woke. She threw off the coverlet and crossed the room to her desk. Rubbing sleep out of her eyes with one hand, she checked to make sure the note to Nell was undisturbed on the keyboard, and pressed the Enter key to send her message to Emerald. Then she glanced at the coat rack beside her office door. It was going to be a warm night, she was sure. She wouldn't need a sweater. Pausing, she patted her pocket to make sure her list of directions, as well as the irksome glamour-busting talisman, were still there. In her other pocket, the change from her visit to the Seven Forks formed a lump against her thigh. She considered stopping to dump it out onto the desk, but now she knew she was just procrastinating. Taking a deep breath, she stepped out of the office, leaving the door unlocked behind her.

"Better hurry!" Bethany was no longer at the desk, and Katarina was walking around the parlor and the Hall, switching off lights. "He's out there waiting for you. Been there for almost half an hour, now, but I hated to wake you!"

Cally saw, as she walked across the lawn to where Ben stood leaning on the fence, a single star (probably a planet) shimmer into life above his head. He turned when he sensed her coming, half-smiling with one eyebrow raised.

"You're going to do something crazy, aren't you?"

She wanted to laugh, to respond with a joke. Something like "What makes you think I'd ever do anything crazy?" It was the kind of thing she normally would have said, but right now it just didn't seem very funny.

The moon, perhaps a hair over three quarters full, rose higher behind Ben's head and began to disappear into a cloud while his gaze remained fixed on her. The square of his shoulders told her he was not going to leave for the night until she told him what she was planning, even if it meant returning late and risking the ire of Rianwynn and all Faerie. Slowly, while she tried to think of the most reassuring way to explain, the hard lines around his mouth melted away. He reached out and pulled her into his arms, tucking her head under his chin. She wrapped her own arms tightly around him, gulping in great breaths of his warmth. As he stroked her hair, every familiar movement of his hands and the muscles moving under his shirt were a comfort to her. She didn't want to let go, but after a moment she did loosen her embrace enough to lean back and look into his face.

She could detect no judgement in his expression, only concern. She reminded herself she had vowed never to deceive him again.

"I guess we both know I do absolutely plan to do something crazy."

He stepped back from her but, before she could panic, he held out his hand. "Come with me, then. We can do something crazy together."

A rush of visions filled her head. She saw herself and Ben walking along all the bent roads in the lands beyond the meadow, untangling the pathways with their very footsteps, discovering new worlds, or just sitting quietly together under some amazing ancient tree. It all seemed so delightful, she nearly reached back. But none of these wonderful adventures would bring George home.

"Let's plan on it," she said. "Another night. For many other nights. We'll do it just for us. We can piss Rianwynn off by running around unchecked through her country and not eating or drinking anything while we're at it." This thought actually made her smile. "Right now, though, I don't see how it could help." She looked past his shoulder, down the hill toward the culvert. "Right now, I need to find George."

She forced herself to tell him her plan, her whole plan, not just selected parts of the truth designed to reassure him. "I am going to try to follow Willow and Raven's instructions, tonight, and find this Fortress of the Dead, whatever it is. I may or may not find it, and I'm not sure what I'll do if I do find it. I guess I'll know when I get there. In any event I promise to be careful. I won't bite off more than I can chew. I'll just sneak in the back way, grab George and the others, and get out. If I can't do that, I'll return with my tail between my legs." She knew this was not strictly true, so she added, "For now."

Ben was still standing with his hand extended to her. He did not lower his hand, but he looked away toward the moon.

"Rianwynn has asked to speak with you," he reminded her. "There might be something she can do to help."

Cally thought of Sofie's parting words to her, about how someday the queen of the Sidhe would owe her a favor. But how could even the most powerful of the Sidhe help with this particular problem? "Unless she can find some sort of loophole that allows her to reach across the miles and slap that Toller woman, I don't see what she can do."

He let out a low chuckle and shook his head. "She can't do that. But she has allies, and friends of friends of allies, who can reach across miles and even dimensions on her behalf. I just wish..." He looked at her again. The moonlight was bright enough, now, to illuminate the china blue of his eyes. He didn't say what he was wishing for, but Cally could guess. He was wishing he could come with her. Maybe, she thought, he was just as tired as she was of wishing for things that could never be.

"I know you're always with me," she said. It seemed like a lame platitude, but it was all she had to offer. "All the time. All day when you're working in Bree's store. Even at night when you're on the other side of the meadow, I always feel you with me. You'll be with me tonight, too. In the morning, I'll let you know how it went. I'll let you know everything."

The moon sailed clear of the cloud around it. Ben sighed, and nodded, and wrapped his arms around her again. He kissed the top of her head; he kissed her mouth. Then, without another word, he crossed the fence and headed off across the hills, just as he did every night.

Except, she realized only after she'd watched him disappear into the shadows, this time he hadn't said "I'll see you in the morning."

31 - A Stray Sod

She ran down the slope of the lawn to the pond, then skirted the bank to where the stream passed between the stone walls of the culvert. She balanced herself with one hand on the arch and ducked her head inside. A cool, moss-scented breeze flowed out from the darkness inside. The tunnel seemed a bit longer than it had during the day, she thought, but moonlight still found its way through from the other side, shining on the water at the other end and casting rippling reflections onto the ceiling above.

This was all as Cally had expected. What she had not expected was that she could hear, or thought she could hear as she stepped under the arch, the crying of the spirits trapped under the iron rails above her head.

The bank was narrow here, so she had to step into the water to continue. She didn't mind getting her shoes wet, but the rocks underfoot were slippery, with some kind of algae or moss growing on them. After her first attempt to step on one almost sent her foot flying from beneath her, Cally laid her right hand on the stone wall for balance. The cracks between the stone blocks were wide enough for her to grasp with her fingertips as she slipped and stumbled forward, but she didn't want to dig her fingers too far into them, for fear something living there might resent the intrusion.

After a few more careful steps, she did see movement behind the cracks in the wall. But it was not spiders or centipedes, or even camel crickets (which she loathed). A faint bluish light, deep inside the cracks, expanded and contracted, over and over, almost as if the wall were breathing.

She let out an involuntary yelp and let go. As soon as she did, her foot slipped and jammed itself between two of the rocks under the water. She landed on her back in the streambed, with her trapped foot painfully twisted in a direction human feet were not meant to turn.

Taking deep, deliberate breaths to stop herself crying out

again, she took a mental inventory of her body while the water gurgled beneath her. She did not seem, she reassured herself, to have landed on any particularly sharp rocks. Thankfully, both her head and her back were alright. She sat up in the streambed and gently extracted her foot from between the stones. This sent sharp shocks of pain all the way up her leg. She didn't think she'd broken anything, but something amidst all the small, complicated bones and tendons inside her foot was not as it should be.

Mindful to avoid submerging the written directions in her pocket, she gingerly lifted herself out of the stream and sat on the narrow bank with her feet still in the water. She shook her head, recalling all the times she had scoffed at female movie heroines for always, inevitably, falling down and twisting their ankles. Worse: she was even, unlike them, wearing practical shoes.

Now she peered through the dripping dimness toward the far end of the culvert, wondering how she could possibly make it that far, with the footing so treacherous and one foot already injured. If she slipped again – and she didn't see how she couldn't – her quest would end quickly and pathetically with her lying in the water, shouting for help until someone came to fetch her and take her to the hospital.

She uttered a particularly ugly word and listened to it echo up and down the tunnel. Then she heard another voice, calling her name. It came from outside the culvert behind her. She froze, listening as it was repeated over and over, growing nearer. It was Nell's voice.

"Damn!" Cally sat back on her haunches. "She must've found my note already!" Nell's calling voice was soon joined by Ignacio's, much closer by. Cally didn't know if they were looking for her to stop her or to join her, but she didn't want them to do either.

Rising painfully to a crouch, she tried to take a step toward the far end of the tunnel and almost slipped again. She swore loudly enough that she was sure, now, her beloved interfering friends had heard her. The fact that Ignacio's voice was quickly replaced by the sound of running footsteps confirmed this.

She realized she might as well give up, if only for now. As she sat back down to await her well-meant capture, she saw the silhouette of a head emerge into the dim arch of night sky at the end of the tunnel.

"Cally!" It was Ignacio. He was whispering. "I think you forgot something!"

He stepped into the water, using a stick to balance himself.

"Dammit! You're right, I did." If she had remembered to bring Rum's stick, she would have been halfway across the meadow by now, instead of sitting here listening to Nell calling her name outside, growing nearer by the moment. "How did you even know..."

"Shush." He sat down on the bank next to her. "Here you are." He pushed the stick into her hands. It was the one Rum had given her – she'd left it in her office.

"Oh, Ignacio, I think it's too late for that, now. I've already hobbled myself." She indicated her gimpy foot as Nell's voice grew nearer and more frantic.

Ignacio leaned forward and laid a hand on the top of her wet shoe. "No, I think you're alright," he said. He began to mumble something in Spanish, his voice soft and prayerful. The warmth of his hand penetrated the cold of her damp foot, and she thought it actually did soothe the pain. "See?" he said. "Just twisted – not even sprained. You got this."

She stared at him, as best she could in the dark. "You're letting me go?"

"I understand what you're trying to do." He spoke quietly as Nell's voice called from much closer. "And you are right. You should not let our Nell come along. Very soon, she'll be needed here." He nudged Rum's stick in her hand. "Don't fall!" She thought his whisper held just the hint of a chuckle.

Cally shook her head. Maybe she really was the wrong person to be trying to do something like this. Nobody was as good at anything as Ignacio was.

He was already standing up, one foot on the bank and one in the water. "I'll distract Nell," he said. *"Mi reina, vaya con dios."*

Before she could thank him, he was gone. Outside, in the direction of the pond, she heard him call, "Nell, do you see her anywhere?"

She wiggled her foot experimentally. It didn't hurt quite as badly, but it still ached enough to make the goal at the end of the culvert seem impossibly far away. Not to mention, even if she did make it that far, a gimpy foot would complicate the almost certainly long walk beyond. She scrambled to a crouching position, laying her hands only lightly against the breathing stone wall. "Well, here goes, quite possibly, nothing." She turned again, carefully, toward her goal.

With three legs, now, instead of just two, she was able to feel her way along the slippery stones in the stream bed without losing her balance, and without having to put too much weight on her hurt foot. She made her way more confidently toward the arch of moonlight at the tunnel's end.

Only after she had passed out into the moonlight at the other end did she look back. The sound of Nell's and Ignacio's voices had ceased altogether, as if a door had shut at the other end of the tunnel.

She climbed up the embankment to the railroad tracks, crouching low so that, if they were still there, Nell and Ignacio would not see her. She had a strong hunch they would not be there, though, and she was right. Looking back across the top of the trestle, through the fence to where she should have been able to glimpse the Vale House front porch light, all she could see was trees. The thick forest running along the north edge of the meadow curved all the way around to the west, blocking her view of Woodley (or, to be more precise, her view of where it should have been). She had expected this but, even so, she felt like the earth had been tugged from under her feet.

Gripping Rum's stick tighter, she dug its tip into the ground until the dizziness passed. Straightening, then, she reached her free hand into her damp pocket. The crescent moon amulet was still there, as was the napkin on which she'd written down the Wyrd Systers' "directions." She drew it out carefully, unfolding and squinting at it in the moonlight. The ink had not run too much. She could still make out the words well enough, and she couldn't help laughing at what she saw. She had written it down, herself, next to the listing for the card depicting a waterfall. "You'll have to be careful not to fall."

She waved the paper in the air to dry it out, then put it back into her pocket and turned to limp along the tracks in the direction leading toward the woods. Her wet shoes squeaked with each step, but the warm breeze soon began to dry her clothes.

Any resemblance the railroad tracks retained, on this side, to steel rails faded after just a short distance. Now they looked – and sounded, when she tapped them with the stick – more like well-hardened wooden beams, and now, after a few more steps, they ceased to run parallel, or even straight at all. Curving around to her right, they traced the edge of the shadow of woods.

The further Cally followed them, the more they twisted and buckled, roughening and rounding, until they looked more like gnarled tree roots crawling along the ground. She nodded. That, she recalled, was what the cards had said would be next: tangled paths.

Feeling much more confident, now, she used Rum's stick like a cane in her right hand, and put her left shoulder to the woods to orient herself as she walked. The border between the woods and the field was quite distinct and appeared to curve gently all the way around the northern edge of the meadow to where, in the distance, the tree line curved southward. Between the dark boles on her left, she could hear night creatures going about their business just as they did in Woodley. Insects and frogs, and the occasional larger and heavier creature, squeaked and snuffled and scampered in the shadows. The familiar night noises were a comfort to her, even though she was not surprised to feel she was being watched from somewhere within.

What did surprise and concern her was that the tree-root tracks she was following, as they led onward, soon began occasionally to burrow into the ground, as roots were wont to do. They would always emerge again a short distance away, but the intervals at which they did became longer as she continued.

After just a few more steps, her concerns were validated as the roots branched and thinned into many fine tendrils which quickly faded, disappearing one by one into the ground. She stopped, wondering what she was supposed to do next. The cards had not said anything about this. She took the napkin out of her pocket again. The next instruction, after the one about the tangled paths, referred to a lone hill, but the terrain around her only rolled gently. No part of the rising and falling ground could truly be called a hill.

She turned in slow circles, looking from the woods to the

fields. Maybe she was supposed to enter the woods, here? But she didn't see a path of any kind, under the shadows of the branches, so that was right out. She'd read enough fairytales to know better than to enter an enchanted wood without keeping to a path. Was she meant to venture out into the field under the moon? Was she supposed to continue along the forest border, in the direction in which the root track had been leading?

Reluctantly, she withdrew the moon amulet from her pocket and put it up to her eye. She hated to use it, anymore, but maybe it would reveal a path, or perhaps the door she was supposed to see at this point. It didn't show her anything different from what she already saw, however. Through the crystal in the center of the silver crescent, the encircling woods, the rising and falling fields, looked much the same. The only difference was that now she could see what was watching her from within the forest. Everything was watching her. Eyes shone out from the shadows under the canopy, some small and narrow, some large and round like lanterns, some low to the ground, and some hovering singly or in pairs near the tops of the trees. Almost all of them stood completely still, regarding her with slow blinks. She quickly shoved the amulet back into her pocket. She put the directions back more carefully.

It occurred to her that if she could regain the track, she could sight along it to form a beeline, perhaps, to a distinctive star on the horizon. She went back the way she had come, zigzagging a little and watching the ground, prodding at it with Rum's stick to find the roots, but they were completely gone now. This didn't surprise her, but it was not encouraging, either.

She turned back around to reorient herself with the woods on her left. She turned and turned, slowly realizing the dark line of the forest now stood at every hand, encircling the moonlit field. She was standing at the edge of a broad rise of grassy ground completely encircled by thick, dark trees.

Looking to the stars for direction was no help. Though the sky was utterly cloudless, now, she didn't see any of the constellations she knew. Nor could she make up any constellations of her own from starry patterns above, as they were scattered uniformly like confetti around the moon. The moon itself stood directly overhead, so there was no way to determine direction from it, either.

"I suppose I could wait for it to start to set," she thought aloud. "At least that way I'll know east from west." As she spoke, she heard an edge of panic creeping into the pitch of her voice. She shut her mouth quickly before she could add that the moon appeared to be in the wrong phase. It had been gibbous, waxing to full when she'd stood with Ben at the fence; now it was completely full. She had to admit she had never seen it hanging so directly overhead, either. She had a feeling it never set, here, or rose, or changed phase, either. There was no such thing as "east" or "west" here. There might very well be no such thing as "then" and "now" here.

She forced herself to stand still lest she start running in panic. A dead certainty crept over her that if she did that, she would find herself running endlessly around the perimeter of a field that never changed, while the moon stared silently overhead. She struggled to control her breathing and tried to think. She cleared her mind and half-closed her eyes, trying to see the paths under her feet the way she had learned to do, but she could not see or sense anything resembling a path, here or anywhere near her.

At least the clearing in which she was standing was slightly mounded. It wasn't much of a hill – just a rising and falling field, really – but it was what she had. She should, she decided, try walking toward the highest point of ground.

She looked at Rum's stick and it crossed her mind that she could plant it in the ground to at least help her find her point of reference again if she ended up having to come back and try something else. She shook her head quickly to rid it of this notion. She had no doubt, if she let go of anything she owned, here, she would never find it again. Anyway, she had promised Rum she would bring it back. Most of all, she was reluctant to let go of the comforting feeling of it in her hand. It was a precious reminder of the world behind.

She gripped it tighter instead, and turned her back to the trees, aiming her feet toward the bright, moonlit circle and the rising ground at its center. She had not stepped away from the shadow of the trees, however, before she spotted a dark shape moving under the moonlight ahead. At first she hoped it wasn't one of the well-meaning friends she'd been determined to leave behind, now caught in this predicament with her. Then, as the shape began to lope toward her, she recognized its hunched posture, and she knew it was no friend.

She considered turning around, then, and running to what suddenly seemed like safety under the dark, encircling trees. Even with her gimpy foot, she thought she might make it, but what good would that do? This beast, she knew, could see perfectly well in the dark, and would enjoy watching her run and stumble before he inevitably caught her. The least she could do was defy him. It was probably all she could do, but she did it anyway, planting the stick in the ground in front of her and gripping it with both hands, more as a declaration than as any kind of shield.

The approaching figure stopped just before reaching her, but this was not because Cally had succeeded in intimidating him. The Fomorian straightened, where he stopped, to his full height and roared out a hot breath of frustration. A line of silvery light stretched behind him, between his ankle and the center of the field, quivering and taut like a chain tethering a watchdog. He strained against it futilely for a moment and then stood, drawing back his shoulders and lifting his head to try to regain some semblance of dignity.

He said: "You appear to have stepped on a stray sod, your majesty."

32 - The General

In the moonlight, Eladha's visage seemed to form and re-form constantly. Like a radio tuned improperly between two stations, his face wavered and shifted between that of a red-faced beast with yellow eyes, wide jaw full of sharp teeth, and that of a fair-haired young hero. Only the eyes remained the same, glowing like molten gold. Cally knew this was not because she was seeing through his glamour but, based on what she had learned from Aileen, because Eladha was not sure anymore, himself, what he wanted to be.

Except free. He clearly wanted to be free, to reach beyond the limits of his silvery bond to Cally. Leaning forward, reaching with both hands quivering, his fingers closed just inches from her. Balling them into fists, he fixed his gaze on her and drew himself up to his full height.

She thanked Rum fervently for the stick, because her grip on it helped her stand steady without flinching.

"Hello, Eddie," she said.

The straining of massive muscles under the skin of his neck reminded her how unwise it was to be flip with immortals. Eladha managed, however, to regain control over himself. He drew back enough to loosen the slack on the silvery line, and his face settled down to that of a human man with, perhaps, a jaw that was just a little too wide.

"I would not have expected a visit from you here, your majesty," he said. Only a few teeth showed when he spoke, and his voice was low and smooth. "You appear to be lost."

"And you appear to be confused about who I am."

His voice shifted back to a growl, long and low, and he took another step backward. "Come into the circle. I'll show you who you are."

"I assure you, again, General: I have still never developed any intention of becoming your queen."

She knew he didn't believe this. He had steadfastly

demonstrated his refusal to do so, numerous times before, but he did appear to be mollified by her having referred to him by his proper title.

His posture relaxed and he sat down, cross-legged, in the grass. Patting the ground between them with what was at once a talon and a long, fair hand, he said, "Come, Lady, let us talk, then. Nobody comes here without a reason, and I hardly think you came to visit my prison out of the kindness of your heart. If you aren't lost, then you must be looking for something."

"I am." She did not sit, but she moved the stick to one side. "I was told there's an entrance into a hill, here. I'm guessing it might be that hill." She nodded toward where the rising ground in the center of the field could be loosely construed as a hill. "The directions I was given were... ambiguous."

He threw back his head and said "Ha!" and for a moment, his laughter made him look like a carefree youth, though one with a sneering smile. "You're looking for the Fortress of the Dead! What on earth would a nice girl like you want in that place? Being queen of two realms isn't enough for you?"

She ignored this. "A friend of mine is in trouble," she explained simply.

He spat on the ground between his feet. "You always were too soft-hearted."

"Maybe so." She nodded. "Maybe so. Apparently, you know of this fortress. I don't suppose you'd care to point me in the right direction, would you?"

"What's in it for me?"

"Not a damn thing. That's why I didn't suppose."

He rocked back on his haunches to let loose a laugh which became a chilling howl running through the trees around the field. "You know," he said at length, "I always did like you. It's a shame things didn't work out between us." He gave her a sideways look, something between a conspiratorial grin and a blatant leer. "It's not too late, you know."

"Thanks just the same." She looked past him to the shoulder of the hill in the moonlight. It definitely looked like a hill now, low and softly rounded at its peak. Even so, was it the right hill? She didn't see a door or an opening of any kind anywhere, but she knew that was irrelevant. She wished Eladha would go away so she could take the amulet out of her pocket to look more closely.

"Alright, listen." He stood, leaning as close to her as he could without straining at his bond, and pointed back toward the rise in the ground. "I can show you the way. All you have to do is step into the circle."

Cally looked down at her toes. She didn't see a circle, but she could describe a circle based on the limit of Eladha's tether.

"I'll find another way."

"Suit yourself." He scrubbed his hands together in a washing motion. "You won't make it there on your own, but that's not my problem. Say goodbye to your friend!"

She looked in both directions along the line of trees surrounding them. This had to be the right place. But even if she could somehow find the door, she couldn't very well get to it with Eladha tied to the hill like a dog to a tree.

"If I give you a gift, though..." Her mind had begun to churn, and now she could feel the talisman in her pocket almost as if it were burning her thigh through the fabric of her skirt. She had brought it with her imagining she might end up giving it to the People of Shannish beyond the meadow, or maybe to some King of the Dead or something, or even just leaving it lying under the stars to let fate decide who should find it next. But, maybe, it occurred to her, she was meant to use it as a gift to bind Eladha to his word.

"If I make a bargain with you," she said. "If I give you a gift in return for a favor, you will be bound to honor your end of the agreement. Am I right?"

The growl rumbling in his chest let her know she was. "It offends me that you would even ask. I honor my agreements, to the letter. Unlike some..." He glowered down at her. "What is this gift you offer, though? I mean, I would only be bound if I actually accepted whatever it is, after all."

She reached into her pocket. Eladha's eyes fastened on the silver chain as soon as she began to draw it out, as if he had realized what was at the end of it. When the silver crescent swung out into the moonlight, a sound escaped his lips which seemed, to Cally, like the sigh of a young lover who had just caught sight of his beloved. His voice was so soft and wistful it nearly melted her heart.

He didn't waste a second in asking her where she'd got it, or what she wanted in return for it. He simply said, "I'll do it. Anything."

"Within reason, I assume."

"Reason be damned."

A chill ran down Cally's spine. Anything Eladha wanted that badly had to be something he really shouldn't have. But the way he gazed at it, like a forlorn child, made him resemble more and more the handsome young warrior he had once been, long before the tales began to speak instead of his fall into greed and lust for dominance. He wasn't even trying to remind Cally that to refuse would be to damn her friend to limbo forever. He merely held his breath and did not speak, awaiting her request.

"All I want is for you to let me cross the circle to that hill without hindering me."

"Done!" He reached out a hand, palm up, toward the pendant. His arm trembled as the silver crescent swung on its chain inches from his fingertips. Cally wondered, if she looked through the crystal now, if his hand would look as slender and soft as it appeared to be.

"If you would show me how to find the door in the hill, as well, that would be amazing."

"Yes, yes. Of course." He didn't move, but turned huge, shining eyes to her. "Agreed."

"The right door. No funny stuff, no tricks."

"I always honor my word," he said. "I am incapable of doing otherwise." Even having to remind her of this did not cause him to revert to his usual arrogant growl; it seemed to be all he could do to get the words out through his bated breath.

Maybe, she thought, the pendant had once belonged to someone he had loved. All the stories she'd ever read about Eladha had spoken more of his breaking hearts than of having his own broken, but perhaps there were much older tales she had never heard. Anyway, what harm could he do with it, here in this isolated place with nobody at whom to look through it? Letting out her breath, she leaned forward and let the chain slide through her fingers.

As soon as it touched his palm, he seized the hand with which she had reached into the circle. "Come!" he roared, drawing her by the arm to stand beside him.

She swore at her own stupidity, holding up the flimsy stick instinctively to defend herself, though she knew it would be useless. But Eladha had already let go of her and turned aside. Lifting the chain over his head, he dropped it around his neck and let the pendant fall against his chest. He stood with both hands pressing it to his skin, eyes closed, and face turned upward to the moonlight. Cally was so struck by his beauty she forgot to take the opportunity to flee.

When he opened his eyes and turned again to look at her, his smile was radiant. "Go ahead and run, if you want to," he said. "You humans don't have to keep *your* promises, after all." The way he said the word "humans" made it seem like it should rhyme with "swine."

"I'm not going to run." Cally lowered the stick to the ground. "We humans are loyal to our friends, and we help them when we can."

He snorted. "Come on, then."

33 - One Chain (Don't Make No Prison)

He led her more or less straight toward the highest point of ground. Even before they drew near it, the slope grew steeper. The silver-blue line that shackled Eladha dragged like a chain behind him across the grass. It made no sound, but it seemed to shorten as they neared the peak, as if some winch within the hill was taking up the slack. When the rising ground looked more to Cally like a true and proper hill, its peak now high above their heads under the overhanging moon, Eladha turned left and began to circle around it.

He had nothing to say to Cally as he led her on around the hill. She had expected a continuing stream of snarky remarks about the nature of humankind and the traitorous fae who consorted with them, or at least prying questions into her personal life and the nature of the friend she was trying to save, but his mind seemed far off beyond the lifeless stars glittering coldly overhead. He merely led her around the hill, and around it again.

She figured this must be some sort of trick of the twisted nature of all fae roads, but after the third time around, she began to wonder if she had unwittingly agreed, somehow, to just follow him around this hill forever. She could see no trampled path repeating in the grass in front of them and, when she paused and looked back, she did not see any tracks behind them, either.

"Getting nervous, my dear?" Eladha had stopped, too, and it was almost a comfort to see him sneering as usual. "If I were going to throw you to the ground and do something unspeakable to you, I would have done it by now."

"I was just wondering how much farther to this door," she said.

"It isn't a door, per se." He resumed walking. "Or, if you must, then call the entire hill a door. You are the key that opens it." He waved toward the hillside as he walked on. It had grown still taller, Cally thought, and also seemed to have changed shape somewhat. The hill had narrowed, partway up, so that it now resembled a mushroom more than a mound.

Eladha ducked his head and peered into the deepening shadow forming around the hill's waist. A darker line circled within it and, as they walked on, Cally watched this resolve into an opening, a cavern splitting the hill in two all the way around. From within this darkness, a cold, damp-smelling breeze now reached to chill her skin.

"Oh! I see!" She turned away from Eladha and began to walk toward the opening. "The way in. I get it, now. General, I will say, you have..."

He grabbed her arm and drew her back. "I wouldn't." His teeth flashed behind his grin. "The trick is to keep going until you can walk under without stooping. I tell you this out of the generosity of my heart and not because our contract obligates me to. You do *not* want those dangling roots to touch you."

He looked at her as if waiting for her to ask why, but she had a feeling she would not enjoy hearing his answer.

"Thank you," she said, and turned back to continue with their trek around the hill.

By the time Eladha deemed the opening beneath the hill to be tall enough, the cold air it exhaled was sharp as winter. It smelled of earth and rock, as a cavern should, but also something else, heavy and cloying, like old perfume that had been drying in the bottom of a bottle for too many years. Cally tried to listen for any sound of running water or the scurrying of any creatures deep inside, but only a massive silence issued from within.

Eladha stopped at last. "Well, you're on your own from here," he said. "I couldn't go with you even if you asked me to." He glanced ruefully and pointedly at his tether.

She had no intention of asking him to come with her. Every minute in his presence felt like borrowed time, as it was.

"I'm good," she said. "I acknowledge that you did indeed keep your word to me, General. The directions didn't tell me what to do after I found the way in, anyway, and that was all I asked of you."

He stepped backward down the slope until he was looking up at her. "It's been a pleasure doing business with you, your majesty."

"Don't call me that."

He had already turned to walk away. Cally looked inside the cavern and saw, aside from a few wide, flat rocks just inside the entrance, only darkness. Supposing her eyes would adjust soon enough, she felt her way with the stick to the nearest rock and sat down. Outside, she could still see Eladha in what seemed, by comparison now, to be bright moonlight. His back was to her as he walked around the slope the way they had come, and she hoped he'd be far away by the time she came back out. Now that she knew of his presence here, maybe she would be able to sprint to the forest's edge before he spotted her again.

Then she saw him stop and take the pendant from around his neck. Crouching low to the ground, he looked through it to the shackle around his ankle. Before Cally had time to realize this should horrify her, the silver line vanished. *Of course,* she thought with sudden clarity. It had been a glamour. And now that he had seen through it, Eladha had no further reason to consider it real. It had no further effect on him.

He ran and disappeared around the curve of the hill before Cally could say, "What have I done?"

34 - Cold as the Grave

Her first thought, as she stood up and began to make her way across the floor of the cavern, was to wish she had brought a sweater. Her second thought, as she rubbed her arms and saw her breath pluming gray in front of her, was that a sweater would not have been enough.

Though she couldn't hear a breeze rushing, or any air stirring at all through the overhanging rocks and roots, she could feel the cold moving all around her. It tugged at her hair like little, frozen hands, brushing across her bare arms with warmth-stealing caresses, jabbing icy fingers through the seams of her clothes.

"I hope it's not far," she said into the darkness. There was no echo.

The moonlit slash behind her, between the ground and the roof of the cavern, was the only directional reference available. She put her back to it, using Rum's stick to feel her way into the dark. The footing was fairly level inside, but boulders and large rocks, which had probably fallen from above, covered the ground and made the path forward a twisted one. Her eyes slowly adjusted to the darkness as she went, but each step also carried her deeper into coldness.

She turned just once to look behind her, and wished she hadn't. She told herself it was just that she had walked too far away from the opening to see the dim night outside anymore, but it looked more as if the hill had simply closed up with her inside it.

"At least that would mean Eladha can't follow me." It was small comfort.

It didn't matter. The only way was forward, in any case.

She was able now to make out some details in the dimness around her. This was clearly not the lighted room depicted in the cards the Wyrd Systers had laid out for her. Instead of tables, large boulders appeared as great, crouching shadows. After a few steps, though, she did begin to perceive a dim light far ahead in the depths. She even fancied she could make out the general shape of the interior of the cavern. It arched far overhead, and seemed to curve around into the distance ahead, sloping gently downward.

The faint light in the depths might have been more reassuring if those same depths did not also seem to be the source of the cold, now battering against her exposed skin in a rising breeze. She breathed on her fingers to warm them and tried to rub some of that warmth into her icy cheeks and nose. She noticed she had begun to hurry, picking her way around the rocks as quickly as she could. It reminded her of the way she sometimes drove too fast when her car was low on gas and her mind's subconscious, but incorrect, logic urged her to drive faster, to make it to a gas station before the gas ran out.

The rocks grew smaller and the slope shallower until both finally ended in a rough but fairly level stone floor. Here the cavern bottomed out into a wide cathedral of stone. Pale stalactites reached down, from inky depths far above, all the way to where some of them met and merged with stalagmites projecting from the ground. There was sound at last, here, too: water dripped, somewhere in the distance, perhaps into a pool of water. She thought she could make out faint ripples of reflected light dancing among the stone pillars.

The light itself emanated from behind a particularly large pillar, almost a wall of rock. Cally made her way around it less cautiously than she should have. She didn't expect it would be a source of warmth, but she was eager to be able to see better.

"George, are you here?" she called as she rounded the pillar. He was not there – nobody was – but she did see the source of the light.

It was a glass lantern, resting in the bottom of a small, wooden boat. The boat itself rocked gently at the edge of a broad, black river, causing the shadows it threw to also rock eerily back and forth amongst the pillars of rock.

"Oh." Cally's voice echoed across the dark water. "Oh. Of course."

She squinted across the water into the distance, but all she could see was pitch blackness.

"Well, I suppose it's a good thing I still have the change from my tea," she mused. She put her hand into her pocket to finger the cold coins clinking there. Some part of her mind was alarmed to realize the inside of her pocket felt no warmer, now, than the air outside it.

"You don't have to pay me," said a voice from further along the shore. "Not yet. Not until we get to the other side."

He came, cloaked in layers of gray cloth that hung from him like cobwebs, into the light of the lantern and lifted a booted foot to rest it on the stern of the little boat. His face appeared to be a perfectly normal human face. In fact, Cally thought, his expression was even pleasant, peering out at her from swaths of gray wrapped around his head like the hood of a cloak. He raised a finger to his brow in salute. "Hail and well met, Lady. I must say, I wasn't expecting to see you here."

"I can't say I expected to be here." Her teeth chattered as she spoke, and then she found she couldn't stop them chattering even when she wasn't speaking. "But I have read about you, and I can pay. I need to find a place called the Fortress of the Dead. I've reason to believe... I've been told..." She gestured across the water. "Is that where it is?"

He followed her gaze. "I can get you across. But I have to be honest with you. I'm not sure you're going to make it." He looked back at her and gave his head a little shake.

She wrapped her arms around herself and stamped her feet to try to get warmth to flow back into them. "How far is it?" She didn't dare ask if it might be warmer there.

"It's not far." His voice was much gentler, kinder than she would have expected it to be. "We don't get many like you here. The cold doesn't bother most of my passengers. Here."

He unwound a length of gray fabric from around himself and draped it over her shoulders. She would have liked to think the gesture warmed her, because the fabric certainly did not. She wrapped it around herself anyway and nodded her thanks as she clutched it to her chest. The ferryman put a hand under her elbow and helped her step into the boat, showing her how to sit, with her back to the prow, on the wooden plank that served as a seat.

He laid Rum's stick along the gunwale beside her and took up his own long, gray pole, which he used to push them off from the shore and out across the water. Cally gazed at the shore until it faded into the general blackness of the distance. By then, she was shivering so hard it made the little boat itself vibrate, causing tiny ripples to radiate out around it, glittering circles expanding away from the lantern light. She was tempted to put her hands above the lantern to warm them, but she stopped herself. She was pretty sure if she moved any nearer to the light, she wouldn't be able to stop herself enfolding it in her arms and either setting herself on fire or, worse, putting out the light.

She chanced a look behind her to see if she could see the other shore yet. What she saw there made her rock the boat in her effort to turn around. An orange blur appeared to be hovering above shore in the distance.

"I'm sure you've also read it's a bad idea to jump into the water," the ferryman said with the slightest hint of a laugh in his soft voice.

"Sorry, it's just..." She picked up her numb feet and lifted them, one at a time, over the seat so she could turn around more carefully to face the prow. The orange blob grew ever brighter, more solid. It was the only touch of color in this entire black and gray world. As she stared, four legs appeared beneath it and it started to walk along the edge of the far shore.

"Boo!" Cally's voice echoed over the rocky hill ahead.

The ferryman did laugh, then. "It's not usually the living who say that!"

"No, it's Doctor Boojums," she explained. "It's what we call him. Called him. He's a cat, well, he was. Boo, wait!"

She grabbed Rum's stick and stood up, fighting to keep her balance as the boat tipped to one side.

"Do not touch the water!" The ferryman's voice no longer held any trace of humor. He thrust his pole against the bottom of the river to steady them until the boat ground with a soft crunch against the gravel of the shore. The orange cat was already walking away, up the gray hill ahead to what appeared to be a dark, squat building at its top.

Cally jumped onto the shore, stumbling and crying out as the sudden impact of her cold feet on the ground stung like an electric shock all the way up her legs. Behind her, she heard the ferryman clear his throat with a rumble that was much deeper, and far less friendly, than the voice with which he had previously addressed her.

She stopped, nearly falling over, and turned back to him.

"My apologies, sir." She had to look down at her pocket, as she could no longer feel it, to shove her stiff fingers in and draw out a handful of coins. Even if she had been able to use her fingers, she didn't have time to count out two pennies. She cupped all the change in both hands and held it out to him. He was barely able to put his own hands underneath before she dumped the coins and turned away, running back up the hill toward the quickly retreating spot of fuzzy orange that seemed to her now like her last receding spark of life or hope.

The building toward which the cat ran didn't look anything like a fortress. It was a long, plain rectangle, not at all tall or imposing, but its silhouette was grim. It squatted at the top of the hill above her like a gigantic, menacing toad that would not ever be moved from where it clung to the earth. She saw Doctor Boojums reach the crest of the hill, and she forced her legs to keep bending and unbending in pursuit. Her lungs burned like dry ice on bare skin, though she wasn't sure she was actually breathing anymore. By the time she reached the top of the hill, her running was so mindlessly automatic she nearly toppled over where the ground suddenly flattened out.

The cat had paused, beside the wall of the building, to turn around and look back at her. He seemed to be slowly fading back to his usual, ghostly shade of gray, or was it just Cally's own vision fading? She had stopped shivering, because she no longer felt the cold. She couldn't feel her legs anymore. She couldn't feel her arms, either, but she did seem to still be able to move them because she saw one of them reach out and lay a hand on the wall of the building. She was vaguely perplexed to realize the wall was clad with pale, horizontal ridges. It was, in fact (she verified this by running her lifeless hand along the ridges and listening to the hollow, plastic rattling sound it made) gray vinyl siding. She was too cold to be amazed or confused.

She heard her voice say "Boo, I have to get inside." She knew she wasn't going to last much longer if she didn't get warm soon. She wasn't sure what was inside, but warmth was now her number one priority, even though she wasn't entirely certain that would help, now, either.

The gray cat, faintly illuminated with some sort of inner glow of his own, turned and walked along the wall to her right. She followed, half stumbling and half falling, until he turned the far corner of the building. He stopped at last a few steps beyond this. Sitting down beside a small, barred window set into the building's foundation, he looked up at her and blinked his wide, moon eyes.

"Boo, I can't fit through there."

If he understood, he made no sign of it.

She looked along the wall. There were no other windows or doors, and she wasn't sure there would be any even if she could round another corner. In fact, she could not take another step.

Despairing, she fell to her knees. She imagined she must have injured her knees on the gray rocks, but she couldn't tell. She did her best to lean over and peer into the window. Somewhere in a distant part of her mind, she realized she was done. She had spent all her warmth, all the strength her body possessed. She wasn't going to make it, and she didn't even have enough energy left to be dismayed about this. Unable to command her body anymore, she fell slowly onto her side, and from where she landed, she could at last see through the small window.

Dozens, maybe hundreds, of nebulous figures milled, crowded together, in the dark chamber inside. Crying words she couldn't understand, dead faces peered up at her. At their forefront was George, the sheer mass of the rest pressing him close to the window. He looked up at her with an expression more of concern for her than of distress for himself, reaching both hands up to the bars. He could not reach through them, though, and she could not reach back. In her mind, she apologized to him for having failed him.

35 - Soft and Heavy

She felt a weight on her legs, soft and heavy, rumbling like some kind of engine. She couldn't actually hear it, but it reminded her of a distant train rumbling along its tracks. This feeling was the sum total of her entire world for a long time.

Gradually, over many aeons, sound seeped back into her perception of her existence. Now, in addition to the pressure on her legs, there were voices, several of them, but she couldn't make out what they were saying. She couldn't remember, it occurred to her, how to understand what words meant anyway. She felt herself being moved, as if she were enveloped by something soft and heavy, something that was, itself, moving, and she was merely going along as part of it.

When memory began to return, she imagined she must be dead, and that this movement must be the beginning of her induction into the same dark chamber of dead spirits that had been the last thing she'd seen. She wasn't sure how she felt about this. Sorry, mostly, she supposed. Sorry for having let so many people down purely through her own stupidity.

Though she couldn't move, herself, or see, some of the voices around her began to make sense. They seemed to be arguing.

"Well, I can't do it. I have to go arrange for the..." The voice trailed off into the distance. It seemed, Cally thought, to have been feminine.

A deeper voice nearby said, "I'll do it, then."

"You? What do you know about mortals?"

That voice was also feminine, and familiar. Cally struggled to match it with a memory of a name or a face, but she couldn't remember any names or faces.

"More than *you* ever will know," said the deep voice again.

"Well, at least you can give her warmth. That's not something I can do."

"Yes. That is what she needs right now."

Something lifted her body – she perceived, now, that she actually had a body – and she felt warmth as if another body lay beneath hers. As if in response, Cally felt herself shivering as she again sensed that she was being borne forward. She gave herself up to this and let her perceptions fade.

At some point – she wasn't sure how long it had been – she felt herself being lowered again to the ground. A cool hand brushed her forehead. She opened her mouth in an attempt to speak, but the air she drew into her lungs stabbed like a knife. She shut her mouth and opened her eyes instead. Aileen's face filled her vision – her fairy form, alien and beautiful, not her human glamour. Stars and moonlight filled a deep blue sky behind her.

"Good morning!" said Aileen. "Isn't that what you say to a human who has been asleep? I don't know much about sleep."

Cally tried to say, "Only when it's actually morning," but it came out an unintelligible mumble, as did "Anyway I wasn't sleeping." She struggled to gain control of her body, to turn and look around her, but her limbs would not obey. She felt like she was caught up, once again, in the dream she'd awakened from, that morning so long ago in a different world. She wondered if she was going to keep waking up in this dream again and again forever.

Aileen helped her sit up, and then Cally knew she wasn't dreaming, or at least this wasn't the same dream. She was sitting on a grassy hill under the moon, under normal stars. She choked back a sob of relief when she realized the moon was in its proper phase, gibbous and waxing. A gray ghost cat lay curled, seemingly asleep, in her lap. A massive black horse stood in the grass behind Aileen, craning its muscular neck around to peer at Cally with huge, indigo eyes.

"Welcome back," it said.

Aileen stood, brushing grass from her knees, and looked away into the distance. A long sword seemed to be swinging from her hip, but Cally couldn't be sure. The fairy woman's human glamour seemed to be coming back in patches or, more likely, Cally realized, her own susceptibility to glamour was slowly returning. Aileen's sword, like Ben's, was not visible behind the glamour. That thought reminded her of Ben, and both remorse and sorrow stabbed through her body like an invisible sword of her own.

Determined to stand, then, she reached down to brush the cat to the ground. Needles of ice shot up her arm as her hand went right through it. Giving her a baleful side-eye, the gray cat sprang from her lap to the ground. Cally felt as if she had been lying under a weighted blanket. She felt lighter, without it, but she also felt the grip of cold dread returning to clutch at her heart.

Aileen nodded toward the top of the slope on which they were gathered. "We are going to Shannish to regroup," she informed Cally. "Doctor Boojums is going back to Woodley to run recon."

Cally turned her head and body enough to follow Aileen's gaze. At first, she thought the hilltop above them was on fire, but the flames arched skyward in shades in which fire did not usually occur. The yellows and reds tended more to the gold and magenta end of the spectrum. Many blue and purple shades also let Cally know she was not, in fact, sitting near a fire, which explained why she still felt so cold. A jewel-like city crowned the hill with buildings resembling tumbled gems of all colors, softer and more rounded than gems made of stone, each glowing with hundreds of windows, as well as from light within the walls themselves.

"The People..."

"Okay," said Aileen. "Let's get you back up."

The faerie woman's long, slender arms lifted her as if she were a child and set her upon the horse's back. Cally tried to sit up properly, but soon found herself slumped forward onto its neck, both hands clutching the thick mane. The horse turned, gently as if it cared whether or not she fell and began to walk up the slope toward the city. She wrapped her arms as far around its neck as she could reach, soaking in the warmth of its body.

She awoke once again and saw that she was now inside one of the buildings. Its walls glowed like amber; she was fairly certain she had been here before. The tables and chairs which had filled the hall, then, laden with a perpetual celebration of food and drink, had been pushed to the margins of the room. Cally lay in the middle of the floor, upon what felt like a thick fleece. It had been tucked around her shoulders and legs, but it offered little warmth, as she had little warmth in her for it to reflect back. The People stood, gawked, scurried and murmured all around her. They were dressed differently, she thought, from last time she had seen them. Instead of long, pale robes they were wearing what looked very much like some of Nell's hand-painted t-shirts.

"She needs heat," one of them was saying. It was a tall, wizened individual Cally thought of as vaguely female, perhaps because of the yellow flowers painted on its front. "We can't give her that."

"Don't worry. He's on his way." Cally looked toward the deep voice and saw the black horse standing just outside the doorway. It was looking over its shoulder into the street, where hoofbeats could be heard growing louder and nearer. "They are all on their way," said the horse.

36 - Shannish

Her next waking awareness was of Ben. She recognized his shape, his scent, and most of all his warmth, before she even managed to get her eyes open again. He was kneeling beside her, his blue eyes puffy and rimmed with red. He had raised her to a sitting position and wrapped the wooly rug around her.

"No," said one of the People. "Put your own body against her."

He sat on the floor then and wrapped the blanket around both of them. Cally found herself able to lift her arms, to clutch at him, drinking in his body heat as if it were water in a desert.

"That's nice," said one of the People. "But there is still a lot of cloth between them. They should remove their garments."

Aileen spoke up for them. "It's good enough." Cally saw the faerie woman, clad in full glamour once again, kneel in front of her. "These humans, they prefer to keep their glamours intact, except in private circumstances." She reached out to pull the woolen mat closer around both Cally and Ben. Ben murmured his thanks and held the blanket shut around them with one hand, tucking Cally's head under his chin.

"Cally." She heard his voice through his chest as he held her tight to him. He spoke her name gently, but his voice was thick. "I thought I'd lost you for sure this time."

No, she thought. *That scene is yet to come.*

He pressed his lips against her forehead, and returning warmth continued to fill her like a slow tap filling a frosty vessel.

While each breath she drew grew gradually less painful, Cally could hear the People scurrying all around her. They would draw close from time to time, holding long, thin sticks against her for a moment, against the length of her legs outstretched along the floor and then, moving, they would press them against her arms, her shoulder, her knees. All the while they spoke in whispers. Cally opened her eyes to see them nodding to one another.

"What are they doing?" she managed to ask in a thick, cracking voice.

"They're measuring you," was all Ben said, pulling her closer.

"For what?" It occurred to her that in an ordinary fairy tale, the protagonist should be concerned that little fae beings were checking to see if she'd fit in the oven. She had met the People before, though. She knew they were a gentle people and, as far as she could tell, vegetarians. Anyway, at the moment, the idea of an oven seemed pretty good, to her.

When nobody replied to her question, she suddenly found the strength to sit upright. "For what?" The only other thing she could recall, at the moment, that a person could be measured for was a coffin.

Aileen laughed. "For your wedding dress." She bent down to straighten the fleece Cally's movement had tugged from her shoulder. "Shush. Be still."

Cally was done being still. At least, her mind was. Her body was still disinclined to obey her commands, but she shook her head and turned her face to Ben.

"I found the place." She managed to scramble onto her knees, and the blanket fell from her. She swayed unsteadily and thought she might lose consciousness again, so she spoke quickly, while she still could. "The Tollers have hundreds of spirits trapped there. At least hundreds. I can't imagine what they plan to do with them, but it can't be good."

"I can," said Aileen. "And it isn't."

"I've been so stupid."

"Yes," Aileen agreed. "But not completely. You did find what you were looking for."

"But for what? I wasn't able to help them!" Cally admitted her failure in a long wail that made the People nearest her step back. "It was all for nothing! Except."

Resolutely, then, she admitted the profundity of her failure, because they needed to know for their own safety. "Except, I also turned Eladha loose."

She braced herself for the outburst of anger and dismay she surely deserved, but the room filled only with soft laughter. Aileen said, "Well, sure you did. Who do you think told us where to find you? It's just a good thing you didn't give him that stick, instead, or that list in your pocket."

She only tried for a moment to make sense of this. It would have to wait.

"George is still there," she said, looking at Ben but appealing to all of them. "And not just George. I have to help them. I can't just leave them there! But I can't..." Her teeth shut, seemingly of their own volition. She slowly forced herself to open them again. It took her several more deep breaths to get the words to come out of her mouth. "I can't do this on my own. I need help."

Aileen applauded.

Ben leaned back from her so he could look into her eyes. "You're asking for my help?" A mischievous smile played on his lips, but then his expression softened. "Of course you have my help. And all the forces at my command, as well."

"Don't go throwing your weight around, your lordship." Aileen glared down at him. Then she patted the invisible sword hanging from her hip. "Of course you have my aid, as well, Callaghan McCarthy."

"I'm in." The black horse had stepped through the doorway, but by the time he reached Cally's side he had only two legs, as well as two arms and a head of long, black curls human women would kill to have. His eyes, however, still sparked like blue fire as he sank to one knee before Cally, looking levelly into her face. "Guacanagarix, whom you call George, has been my friend for a very long time, as you count years, and even as I count human lifetimes."

Cally felt tears stinging her eyes. "Zenbe, you've just said more words to me than I've heard you speak since I met you."

He smiled and lowered his eyes. "I am much better at singing than I am at speaking," he admitted.

Cally struggled to climb from her knees to her feet. Her heart hammered out an irregular rhythm and black clouds closed around the edges of her vision. The People crowded around her, protesting loudly and gesturing that she should sit back down, but Ben stood and offered her his hand. She caught herself deliberately eschewing his help, until she reminded herself of the lesson she had only just claimed to have learned. Accepting his hand, then, she pulled herself to a standing position beside him. Swaying from side to side, she clutched at his arm and willed herself to remember how to balance.

When she did not fall down, the People gradually subsided, continuing to gaze up at her, all arrayed in their new crazy quilt of colors. Some of them, she noticed now, were also wearing scarves of dark gray cloth as insubstantial as cobwebs.

Her legs still trembled beneath her, but her heart began to beat more regularly, pumping strength back into her body. As soon as she felt this strength returning, she also noticed she was hungry. Very hungry, her body's fuel having so recently been completely depleted. As if they sensed this, the People now began to offer her pitchers of drink, handing her morsels from the tables around the room. Ravenous as she was, she knew better than to eat or drink anything here.

When she finally felt able to take her hands from Ben's arm, a Person who seemed, to Cally, to be quite young, ran to her and held a stick out to her. It took her a moment to understand it was not another of the People's measuring sticks. It was much too crooked for that. The last of the haze in Cally's brain finally cleared when she recognized it. "Rum's stick!" He would have forgiven her, she knew, if she had lost it, but she would not have forgiven herself. She grasped it with both hands, not sure whether to hug it or use it to help herself remain upright. She chose the latter.

"I'm so grateful for your help." She turned slowly, looking all around the room as she spoke, not just to the People, but to everyone in the room: Human, Fae, Person, and ...whatever Zenbe was. "And I do need it. Your help. I have no idea how to proceed, but I have to go back. I have to set this right."

"Well..." Aileen spoke up. "The thing is. There are some complications."

"I don't care!" Cally had little patience for complications at the best of times, and she was in no mood to entertain them now. "I can't imagine anything more complicated than this already is."

Aileen turned to the door as a clatter of metallic footsteps arose, grew louder, and then, quite suddenly, stopped just outside. The People in the room, for the most part, fell back from the door, but a few stood their ground. One of them, Cally noted, was wearing a lavender t-shirt painted with letters spelling out "Ghosts are People, Too!" He or she glared defiantly at the figures gathered in the softly glowing street. The ranks of armed Daoine Sidhe outside stood silently, unmoving as statues, but Cally had a feeling only a fragile thread of diplomacy kept them from marching right through the door to seize her bodily.

"Yes, well." Aileen walked past Cally and stood in front of the doorway. The silver-clad faerie soldiers outside saluted her and held their salute until she returned it. Then she turned around and nodded to Cally. "As I was saying."

37 - A Talk with the Queen

"Those are the queen's personal guard." Though Cally managed to prevent herself using foul language, her voice was a bit screechy when she asked, "Why? What has *she* got to do with it?"

"Quite a lot, as it turns out," Aileen answered.

"She sent me here to fetch you," Ben confessed. "She demands to speak with you. Alone, she said, but I'll go with you. She can get over herself."

Cally had to laugh, if weakly, at that. She turned to smile her gratitude. His willingness to defy his mother for her sake was no small thing. Rianwynn was no ordinary mother. "Thank you," she said. "But no. If she knows something about this situation, I need to know what it is. I'm more likely to get results if I play the cooperative lesser life-form."

Outside the door, the Sidhe parted soundlessly to form an aisle leading into the street. Cally handed the blanket to Ben and kissed him, then turned back to the door. Aileen followed closely enough to speak into Cally's ear as they walked between the rows of armed Sidhe.

"Here's the gist of it. The place where Anderson Toller is holding the spirits – the Nocksgall – it's not for mortals. Neither the living nor the dead. The fact that a human is using it, somehow, for purposes of his own, has raised great concern. It's the kind of collision of worlds we're all stationed here to prevent. When Eladha came and told us where to find you, he also told us about Toller. There are some among us who um, hypothesize, that you might be somehow to blame for all this."

"Shit." Cally couldn't control her tongue this time, but she did keep her voice down. The rows of Sidhe fell in behind and marched with them between amethyst and citrine buildings. "Damn Eladha. That means Rianwynn also knows it was me who turned him loose...and how, as well."

Aileen placed a hand under Cally's elbow to help her keep

pace. "He didn't tell her that part. For whatever reasons of his own. I would keep it that way, if I were you."

They passed a building which glowed red and yellow just like the Motherboard Pizza storefront in Woodley, and Cally heard her stomach rumble. She would have given anything, at the moment, for one of Luke's spinach and feta focaccia. She would have given anything to actually be on Railroad Street, to be entering Luke's shop and sitting down with ordinary human friends on an ordinary evening or, at least, as ordinary as an evening in Woodley, USA could ever be.

Instead the Sidhe, with Cally in their midst, turned the corner onto a side street emptying straight out into the hills under the starry night. Aileen touched Cally's arm lightly, then fell back to the rear of the escort.

Atop one of the hills ahead, a pale pavilion had been erected. It seemed to glow softly from within, silvery curtains swaying in the breeze. Cally couldn't tell whether this illumination came from some sort of magical torches, or actually from the Sidhe, themselves, gathered inside. A darker figure stood at a distance outside it, near the bottom of the slope. Something about this figure's stance, the proud silence of its lone vigil, made Cally think of Michael Dawes. The soldiers accompanying Cally did not seem to see him or, if they did, they did not acknowledge his presence in any way.

A shaft of light separated itself from the general glow inside the pavilion and stepped out into the grass. Cally recognized Rianwynn, dressed in green and silver faerie regalia. The slope emphasized her stature as she gazed down at Cally.

Cally was too distracted by her own concerns, and too exhausted from her recent ordeal, to be much intimidated by Ben's mother. As she climbed the hill, Rum's stick in her hand felt, to her, like a much greater symbol of status than the silver sword at Rianwynn's side. She did remember her place, however, and stopped a few steps in front of the queen, bowed, and waited for her to speak first.

"Come with me." Rianwynn turned and, to Cally's astonishment, extended a hand as a mother might to a child. Cally didn't know what else to do but accept it. The Queen of Faerie closed long, cool fingers around hers and led her away from the pavilion, making a wide berth around the quiet sentinel standing in the shadows. In silence, Cally and the queen walked through the soft summer grass, down the slope of the hill, across a dark, shallow valley, and up to the crest of the next hill.

There were no city lights, out here, to dilute the darkness of the sky, and the moon, though nearly full, was sinking in the western sky behind them. The Milky Way flared above in a wide blaze of blues and reds more majestic than the city of Shannish. In spite of herself, Cally stopped with her head thrown back, open-mouthed, staring. This was no faerie magic, no otherworldly manifestation. It was the perfectly natural night sky beyond the influence of civilized persons, mortal or immortal. It was the world she knew.

Rianwynn sat down, her silver skirts billowing in the grass around her. Cally understood she should sit, as well, and when she did, she followed Rianwynn's gaze to the eastern horizon. At first, the only way to discern where the sky met the dark hills was by noting where the stars ended. After a time, however, Cally began to notice other lights on the horizon, growing sharper in focus the longer she looked, just as the city Shannish might slowly appear sometimes at the utmost limit of her vision if she gazed long enough across the meadow. The jewel colors of Shannish, however, were behind them, and this City – if it was a city – shone only in white upon brighter white. Cally perceived a great darkness beyond it, and the sound of the breeze over the hills grew to a hissing sigh. Cally thought it sounded a lot like the sea.

"It is the sea," Rianwynn said, not as if she had read Cally's thoughts, but in a voice full of longing. Cally turned to look at the queen. She had never before seen such a soft expression on the Sidhe woman's face.

The coast of the Atlantic Ocean was over two hundred miles east of Woodley, USA. The sea of which Rianwynn spoke, the one Cally could hear clearly, now, was not the sea of the world she knew.

"Is that a star?" she asked at last, as a particularly bright point of light caught and held her attention. It was hard to tell whether it was in the sky, just above the horizon, or perhaps the beacon of a lighthouse at the edge of the distant city. She knew it could not be a planet, because of the way it twinkled. Whatever it was, it seemed somehow to hover much nearer than all the rest of the celestial host.

"You can see it?" Rianwynn's voice was sharp, and Cally tensed, anticipating a verbal assault. But when Rianwynn turned to look at her, the queen's eyes seemed more sad than angry. "It is the Star back to Inverness," she said.

Cally had heard this expression before. Every time she had heard it, it had brought tears to her eyes, even though she didn't know what it meant. She couldn't speak her reply, past the lump in her throat, so she simply nodded.

"I cannot see it," Rianwynn admitted. "Not yet. But I have felt it growing nearer for a long time, now."

"What is it? What does it mean?"

"When it comes," said Rianwynn. "When it appears, here in this world, I will leave these shores."

"I'm sorry to hear that." To her surprise, she actually was.

She noticed Rianwynn was gazing, not at the light on the horizon, but back down the slope up which they had come. The dark figure still stood, bowed and silent, at the bottom of the hill. The queen gazed quietly at it for a moment, then turned away, seemingly unconcerned.

"Don't be sorry," she said, looking to the horizon once more. "I miss my home so deeply my bones ache with it. My heart breaks continually."

Ben had told her, once, that the Sidhe did not usually feel things like romantic love for one another, but they did feel love for things like beauty, honor, and lands. The tremor she heard in Rianwynn's voice was definitely one borne of a profound love.

"You and I are bound to one another." Rianwynn turned, then, not just her head but her entire body to face Cally. She pressed her palms against the ground between them, softly illuminating the little, pale wildflowers amid the blades of grass standing up between her fingers. "We are bound by blood, you and I, through our mutual grandson. It is you who has brought me to this, just by your being. I should be grateful, but I am torn. It should have been my daughter's daughter who would reign here after me. That was never to be, but because of you, at least now there will be a granddaughter's son, a king, and when he takes his throne, I may return home knowing my duties have been discharged. I should thank you for this. I cannot bring myself to speak the words, but I can promise you a favor, should you ever know what to ask for."

Cally could think of several favors she would have liked to ask of the Queen of Faerie but, at the moment, only one of them occupied her full mind.

"Can you rescue my friends from the Fortress of the Dead?"

Then Rianwynn became once again the imperious, all-business leader of the warrior Sidhe with whom Cally was more familiar. "I can help," she said. "I will help. But the actual breaching of the Nocksgall is your own task, and once you have done it, I will be even more in your debt."

"I've already failed at that," Cally reminded her. "Unless you can tell me how to get inside. Unless you have a key, or something?"

"Getting inside will be pointless unless you have others with you who can hold the line, who can hold open all the doors so that you can get out again. You must take others with you, those you can trust. Also..." The queen pressed a long, pale hand against the base of her throat. "I had a key once, but it has been lost."

The Faerie Queen turned her head to look down the hill, to where the silent figure still watched from the shadows. A sick bolt of fear shot through Cally's heart. *Oh, god,* she thought, *she knows about the amulet. She knows Michael had it, and that he gave it to me – and that means she knows it was me who gave it to Eladha.*

She began to draw back, looking around and trying to decide in which direction to flee, though she knew flight would be useless. She would not get far. But Rianwynn did not strike, either with enchantment or with her pale sword or with her voice. She simply went on speaking.

"I and my guard will be waiting outside the fortress," she was saying. "In the shadows. When you get the door open, however you do it, once you have entered, we will be there. We will have your back in any fray that might ensue, and one will certainly ensue. We will take back what rightfully belongs to Faerie. The Toller man himself, you may do with as you wish."

It took Cally several seconds to reassure herself Rianwynn really did not know about the amulet. She took a deep breath and nodded. Eladha, for some reason, had not betrayed her. This didn't answer the question of how she was going to actually get inside the Nocksgall, but at least she could be reasonably certain she'd survive long enough to try.

Rianwynn was still gazing at the shadow at the foot of the hill. Though Cally did not ask, the queen said, "Yes, he is there. He is always there."

"Michael Dawes," Cally said. "Ben and Bree's father."

The queen nodded. "He, also, will never be free until I leave these lands." There was no emotion in the queen's voice as she said this. She was simply stating a fact.

Cally, lost in mixed feelings, was too slow to bring her common sense to bear, and the words were out of her mouth before she knew she was going to utter them. "Did you ever love him?"

A blast of icy air did not actually sweep over the hill, but Cally felt a chill as if one had. Even if Eladha had not betrayed her by telling Rianwynn how he had come by the moon-shaped amulet, Cally seemed to be doing her level best to betray herself. "I'm sorry," she said in an attempt to backpedal. "That was impertinent of me. You know how obsessed we humans are with romance."

"He taught me a lot about love." Rianwynn's voice did not exactly soften, at this, but it remained sincere. "I will not be the same person, when I return to my home, that I was when I left so many ages ago. Mortal love is very hard. It's one of the few things your people can do better than we can.

"You should take my son with you to the Nocksgall," she added, seemingly out of nowhere.

"He wants to come with me," Cally admitted. "But I don't think it's such a good idea, and not just because of his obligation to spend every night here in your land."

"You could keep one another warm."

"It only means both of us would succumb to hypothermia more slowly. I need to take someone with me who doesn't have to worry about body heat. May I borrow Aileen?"

"The lieutenant will be needed on this end. You will be glad of this, in the end, if you can manage to do your own part." Rianwynn tilted her chin downward, then, so that without lowering her head she could gaze directly into Cally's eyes. "Your species, in general, is under the misapprehension that its females cannot do great things without the help of its males, and you and I are in agreement about the idiocy of this primitive instinct. So, please know this: I am not advising you to depend upon a male to keep you safe, or to rescue you. You are a proud woman, but there are some things at which my son excels, his gender notwithstanding. Things at which you are simply not very good. I am not talking about the ability to lift heavy objects."

As Cally looked at Rianwynn sitting rigidly in front of her, she realized she, herself, was sitting just as rigidly. "Humility, for instance," she suggested.

The unexpected ring of Rianwynn's laughter echoed from hill to hill all around them. "Just keep thinking," the queen said at length. "There's more, you can be sure.

"Go to the Lighted Chamber, tonight when the moon is full. The people in the War Room will show you where the door is. You have a key to that door. This way, your journey will be greatly shortened, and you won't have to march through the long cold. That should help. There will, of course, still be no source of warmth available once you get to the Fortress, so you will have to get in as quickly as possible."

Cally was looking back to the pavilion, wondering whether this was the War Room or the Lighted Chamber of which the queen spoke. "But I don't..." She might have failed to stop herself before saying she didn't have the key anymore, but Rianwynn stood suddenly, both her posture and her expression announcing the audience was over.

"Show her the way back," she said as Aileen appeared, walking up the hill toward them. Rianwynn walked back to the pavilion, once more giving Michael Dawes a wide berth.

"I see you're still alive!" Aileen drew Cally to her feet and led her, also skirting the shadows in which Michael stood, back toward Shannish. The People's city glowed more softly, now, as night edged toward morning.

"Still alive, yes. By the skin of my teeth." Cally sighed. "She doesn't seem to know anything about the amulet. Can she really be that obtuse?"

"I doubt it," said Aileen.

"She said I have a key. Surely that means she..."

"You're overthinking this, Cally. Here. This is the War Room." They had stopped at the edge of the town, within the glow of the red and yellow building that had reminded Cally so much of Luke's pizza parlor. The sight of it wrung her empty stomach with pangs of hunger.

"Honest to God, Aileen, if I hadn't promised to bring it back to Rum, I could eat this stick right now."

"I wouldn't do that, if I were you," said Aileen. "Or you won't have a key anymore."

"I didn't mean it liter... Oh. Oh, you mean..."

Aileen laughed. "Come on. Let's get some food inside you, before you bring on the apocalypse."

38 - Motherboard War Room

The stars above the glowing, jewel-like rooftops grew dimmer as the sky shifted from black to deep blue. Aileen had stopped just in front of the building whose front glowed with the familiar, appetizing colors of Luke's Motherboard Pizza. Looking at the building, Cally could even distinguish convincing facsimiles of the printed paper signs Luke always taped to the insides of his windows to advertise daily pizza specials and low, low rates for software installation. She admired the People's mimicry skills but felt a pinprick of concern that her visits here might be interfering with, even diluting, their wild, fae culture.

Ben and Zenbe and several of the People were standing in front of the building. Ben reached out to Cally, his face grim but relieved to see she had returned apparently unscathed.

"You go ahead." Aileen saluted smartly. "Get on back to your mortal world. It's nearly morning, anyway. I'll report back to Rianwynn and run interference for you if the queen or anyone else has anything to say about it."

Ben's face softened as he bowed to the Sidhe woman. "You have my gratitude, Lieutenant, officially and unofficially."

"Thank you, Aileen," Cally seconded. "For everything."

Aileen bowed, but perfunctorily, cutting the gesture short and waving them toward the door of the Shannish pizza parlor. She turned to head back into the hills but spoke over her shoulder as she departed. "I'll see you all when evening falls." It sounded more like an order than a friendly goodbye.

Cally wanted to ask Aileen to wait, to come back and explain just what, exactly, the plan might be for that evening, but Ben and Zenbe had already opened the door of the building and were waiting for her to enter. A half dozen People nudged her from behind, and she found herself entering the red and yellow shop before she could try to discern what was actually written on the paper signs in its windows.

The inside was well-lit, but not with the soft, organic light of Shannish. Cally glanced up, flinching at the harsh, fluorescent glare overhead. She looked down at the single table beside the window. Danya Barry and Luke were sitting there, in rickety, wooden folding chairs, hands joined across the paper tablecloth. They looked up when Cally entered, their expressions more relieved than surprised, as if they had been waiting there a long time.

"Good morning!" Luke stood, nearly bowling Cally over with an enthusiastic hug. He turned and reached down with one hand to indicate Cally should take his seat. "I don't normally turn on the ovens this early, but Zenbe told me you need warmth. I'm going to go ahead and assume you'll be needing food, as well."

"Thank you, Luke." She was glad to see him, in spite of her confusion. She was doubly glad to hear him speak of food. She noticed, as she sat down and propped her stick against the table, that her hands were shaking. It was not due to cold this time, she knew, but to severely low blood-sugar.

Ben sat beside her in one of the two remaining chairs. Zenbe accompanied Luke to the counter, discussing what to put on the pizza. Danya reached across the table to Cally. "Are you okay?" Her eyes were as wide as ever, but this time with genuine concern.

Cally was still a little confused about what Danya was doing here in Shannish, and more than a little confused about how closely this building resembled its model in Woodley. Everything matched her memories of Luke's shop, right down to the way the slats of the wooden folding chair dug into her bottom. Glancing out the window, she could swear she even saw a black and white plaque on the building across the street which, in the real Woodley, would have read "Johnston and Reid, Attorneys at Law."

"I'm okay, I think," she answered at last. "Though I feel like there are places deep in my bones that will never be warm again. But hey..." She leaned forward to take Danya's proffered hand. "I'm so happy for you and Luke! You two are so cute together."

Danya sat up and pulled her hand back. "What? Oh!" She laughed. "Oh, no, it isn't like that. I'm not exactly Luke's type." She smiled and looked toward the counter, where Luke was pounding a ball of dough into a flat circle. "And, well, he's not my type either. But my God, Cally, it is so nice to have found a friend who, you know, understands. Someone who is as different as I am, in so many ways."

Cally didn't know what to say. She had, so far, been completely wrong about every single thing she'd ever assumed about this young woman. She smiled stupidly and nodded. It seemed to be enough; Danya looked happy and content even though, Cally knew, she still had a hard row ahead of her to hoe.

Luke slipped the newly constructed pizza into the mouth of the oven, then gave Zenbe the stepstool from behind the counter to make an additional seat at the table. "Be right back," he said. "We need one more seat. I'll fetch a produce crate."

Before Cally could point out to him that they already had enough seats for all of them, Luke had dashed down the narrow hall at the back of the shop, past the restroom with a Helen May Original sign on its door depicting a multi-gendered cephalopod unicorn and the words "Whatever. Just Wash Your Hands." When Luke opened the steel rear door of the shop, Cally was sure she could smell leaves and moss on the breeze that blew in.

"If I didn't know better," Cally said to nobody in particular, "I would think I really am back in Woodley right now." Nobody replied, while she looked out the front window at the morning light beginning to fill the street outside. She could see the corner, now, of the building facing what would be Main Street, and she was sure if she stepped out through the front door, she would be able to smell Andi's locally-roasted, organic artisan coffee brewing at the Bean Garden.

When Luke came back inside, Nell was with him. She bent down and gave Cally a quick side-hug. "Thought you could get away from me, did you?" She smiled good-naturedly and sat down in the fourth wooden chair.

Zenbe and Ben scooted aside to make room for Luke to place the blue plastic crate as his own seat. "Pizza should be ready in fifteen minutes," he promised.

"Sorry to turn your shop into a war-room," Ben apologized to Luke.

"I'm happy to be of use," Luke said. "I was starting to think the Old Guard was never going to let me in on any of their secrets."

Nell nodded. "Luke, you've always been able to see so much

more than they ever could!"

He stood and peered across the room at the timer on the counter in front of the oven. The room was filling with the aroma of fresh bread and wild mushrooms, and Cally had to swallow repeatedly to stop herself drooling. "Seeing is my specialty," Luke was saying, "but I still have a lot to learn about how this place works."

"Don't we all." Cally looked out the wide shop window as the growing daylight continued to illuminate what resembled Woodley, now, down to every last detail.

Nell said, "At least now we understand the map better."

It took Cally a moment to grasp that Nell was not referring to conventional maps on which Woodley never appeared, but to the spread of divination cards she'd been using as directions. She took the paper list out of her pocket once more. It was wrinkled and the ink was smeared, but it was still readable.

"All I've come to understand about it," she said, spreading it out on the table, "is that I don't understand it at all. I mean, I seem to have been able to follow it alright. But it didn't lead to any answers, or to a solution. I'm no longer convinced it was ever meant to." She tried to smooth out the flimsy paper with the palms of her hands, as if that might help.

Nell shook her head, laying a hand on top of Cally's. "Don't talk like that. You gave us a good start. And you saved the cat!" She winked as if this were a private joke between them, but Cally was too distracted and hungry to get it.

"Much good it did," she mumbled in reply. "Except for the cat, I guess. But all the rest of them..."

"No, Cally, it's just that you didn't follow the directions properly."

"I did." Cally turned the napkin around so Nell could read it. "I followed them exactly. All the landmarks were there."

Glancing from time to time at the pizza timer, she told them the details of her story of her journey, including her fatal blunder with Eladha, and her subsequent conversation with the queen of the local faerie court.

Nell listened patiently, but when Cally finished, she brushed her curls out of her face and shook her head. "You did follow the directions, for the most part. But not exactly. Look." She took her phone out of her pocket and began thumbing through its camera roll.

Cally bent over the list and squinted at it. "I don't know, maybe I went in the wrong direction. Maybe I should have followed the tracks the other way, toward the western end of Woodley. Maybe it's a figurative tunnel, referring to the tunnel of trees instead. Rianwynn said I need to get in before I freeze, and..."

Nell held the phone up so they could all see the photo Nell had snapped of the table at the Seven Forks Diner. "There's just one thing you missed," she said.

Cally's stomach was growling loudly, and she was losing patience. "No. Not at all. See?" She turned the napkin again and again, pushing it across the table to urge everyone to compare her notes with the cards in the photo.

Luke gasped, and opened his mouth to say something, but the timer went off. He jumped up to fetch his pizza peel.

"Cally. Look!" Nell's voice was uncharacteristically assertive. She held the phone right up to Cally's face.

Cally did her best to humor her. "Right. Yes, see? Pond, stream, tunnel..."

"Look closer."

Cally sighed and took the phone from Nell's hand. It was hard to see any real detail in the cards depicted on the tiny screen. She saw the table, the row of nine square cards, four tea glasses, and herself, Nell, Raven and Willow all seated together around the table. She used her thumb and forefinger to zoom in on each card in turn.

"Everything's the same," she confirmed.

"Look again!"

Cally shook her head and started to hand the phone back to Nell. That was when she finally saw it. Reflected on the screen was the image of the interior of the pizza parlor: herself, Nell, Ben, Danya, and now Luke with a pizza tray in his hands, all gathered around the table. It almost precisely aligned with the image in the photo of herself, Nell, and the Wyrd Systers sitting around the table in the picture.

"Oh." Cally finally said. "Yes, I see it now. It's all the people."

"Yes." Nell smiled and took the phone from Cally's hand.

"That's what you did wrong. If you are going to find the way, in the end, you can't do it alone."

39 - The Lighted Chamber

The close interior of the parlor filled quickly with the sounds of chewing. "When the Faerie Queen said you need to get in fast..." Nell spoke with her mouth full, then swallowed to continue. "Cally, I think she was using the plural form of 'you,' not the singular."

"Okay, I understand that but..." Cally didn't want to talk anymore. She just wanted to keep stuffing pizza into her body for a few more hours, and then lie down and sleep.

"The Lighted Chamber..." Luke murmured thoughtfully, wiping his mouth with a fresh napkin while gazing down at Cally's annotated one. He turned to ask Nell if he could look at the image on her phone. "I think... I mean, I recognize that reference."

"It was the chamber where the ferry was docked," Cally explained. "The ferryman had a lantern in his boat."

"I don't..." Luke was trying to enlarge the photo in the phone enough to see the image on the card, but he gave up, handing the phone back to Nell. "Well, I just think you should come and talk to my sister."

Rising, he balled up his napkin and threw it onto the table. Cally looked up at him but kept on chewing as he went to the door and looked back at her with his hand on the handle. To her dismay, Danya stood and followed Luke, then Nell and Zenbe followed her. Ben did not follow, but Cally could see, when he looked across the table at her, his body language was all about standing up.

She sighed past the food in her mouth and glanced out the window. The top of the wall across the street was now illuminated with sunlight, creeping slowly downward as the sun rose behind the pizza parlor. She had to admit, she did want to know what would happen if she went out that door now. Grabbing another slice of pizza with one hand, she pushed back her chair and took Rum's stick in the other.

Ben retrieved her written directions from the table. "We don't want this to fall into the wrong hands," he said.

Luke pushed the door open. Cally excused her way past the people lined up behind him and poked her head out into the morning light. Thunder rumbled in the distance; the air smelled of damp pavement and rain. A poignant memory passed through her head of Ian May saying there was a word for that smell. She couldn't recall what it was, at the moment. At the intersection of streets to her right, a car passed by, going west. She gave up trying to pretend she didn't know what was going on.

"This really is Woodley, isn't it?"

"Good thing, too." Nell stepped past her onto the sidewalk. "Because if you were still in Faerie, all that pizza you've been devouring would mean you could never go home again."

Luke followed Nell, still wearing his sauce-splattered apron. "Far be it from me to use my culinary genius to trick mortals into becoming faerie slaves," he said, giving Cally a distinctly pixielike wink. "Come on, we need to go talk to Willow." He led the way to the intersection and turned left onto Main Street. Cally could definitely smell coffee – good coffee –as they neared the open door of the Bean Garden. Inside, she saw Andi serving bright orange drinks to Errin and Mima. Zenbe waved to the girls, and Andi waved a white towel at Cally.

Cally had finished her pizza by the time they reached the Wyrd Systers storefront. The shorter and rounder of the two proprietors (Willow, Cally knew now with confidence) was just lighting the first of the day's incense cones in a Buddha-shaped burner on the sales counter. She and Raven both looked up with delighted smiles as everyone crowded into the shop.

Willow ran to give Luke a hug. "To what do we owe this honor, baby bro?"

"You're going to love this," he said. Grinning, he slipped behind the sales counter and indicated, with a flourish, the blue and purple bohemian tapestry hung on the wall there.

"That doesn't look a thing like something I would paint," Nell pointed out.

Cally agreed. She squinted and tilted her head to one side, then the other. "It doesn't look a thing like a Lighted Chamber, either."

"Oh!" Raven and Willow cried out in unison. Luke smirked

with satisfaction and wasted no further time. Grasping the edge of the tapestry, he drew it aside with a rattle of curtain rings. Behind it lay a door, held shut with a steel hasp and padlock.

"I'll get the key," said Willow. She opened the cash register and lifted out the drawer.

"When Jud sold us this place," Raven explained as Willow sorted through dozens of keys on a ring, "we asked him what this room was originally built for, but he clammed up and wouldn't answer. We thought we could turn it into a meditation room or something, but he just advised us to keep the door shut. We soon decided not to use it at all, not even for storage, because everything inside it gets so dusty so fast."

"Still," Willow said, holding up the single key she had detached from the ring. "We always sensed it was important. We always knew the answer would come to us in time!"

"Guess it's time." Luke held the tapestry aside while Willow unlocked the padlock.

As the Wyrd Systers triumphantly opened the door, Cally stepped closer and peered over their shoulders. A bare bulb was already on, inside, illuminating a small room about ten feet square. Raven and Willow stood aside so she could see several small wooden tables standing, some on only three legs, all around the room's perimeter. Stacks of empty baskets tottered on the tabletops, and small, wooden kegs were turned bottom-up in the corners. A stack of packing crates partially blocked a crude, wooden door at the back of the room.

"That light bulb has been burning ever since we first moved here," Raven said. "It hasn't burned out in all these years. There isn't even a switch for it..."

"Nell, look!" Cally turned and called back over her shoulder. "It looks exactly like the card in your deck."

Nell squeezed past Cally, and then everyone else squeezed into the room, pushing Cally into the middle, under the bare light bulb.

"It does look a lot like that card," Nell agreed. "Mostly. I've never got the hang of painting realistic dust."

"Do you mean a tarot deck?" Willow's ears did not literally prick up, but Cally had the distinct impression of a puppy that had heard a can opener. "I know you're an artist, Nellie, but I never knew you'd painted a deck! Would you let us stock it in our store?"

"I'm sorry," said Nell. "There's only one copy."

"Can we at least look at it?" Raven asked. "Where is it?"

Cally grinned. "Try the diner."

Raven made a dismissive gesture toward the west wall of the room. "Pfft, that place! It's never open. Not when we've tried to go, anyway. It's a wonder they haven't gone out of business by now."

Cally thought *"It's a wonder all of Woodley hasn't gone out of business, and yet, somehow..."* She shook her head and looked around the little room. "It's probably just as well," she assured the Systers. "We don't want to accidentally cause all time and space to implode. Not today, anyway. Where does that door lead?"

She walked the rest of the way to the back of the room, soft dust underfoot muffling her footsteps. The door was apparently made for people shorter than any of them, except perhaps Willow. In the dim light of the overhead bulb, Cally could tell it had been painted many times. Green, white, red, and black chips showed through deep cracks in layers of old paint. An iron handle, wrought in the shape of an owl, was bolted to one side, but it didn't have a thumb lever or a latch of any kind.

"I'll show you where it leads!" Willow laughed, reaching past Cally to grasp the owl's head. She dragged the door away from the wall, drawing a dusty semi-circle on the floor because the door had no hinges. Where it had been leaning against the wall, the bricks were still red, having been protected from the accumulation of dust.

"We just keep it there because it looks so cool," Raven explained. "A doorway to nowhere."

Cally ran her hand over the door-shaped silhouette of red bricks.

"Maybe nowhere," she mused. "Maybe somewhere. At the right time and place, for a person who has the right key."

She turned to where Willow stood balancing the door with one hand and held Rum's stick against its unpainted back side. The door was made all of one piece of wood, with a pale grain swirling through dark knots from top to bottom.

"Oh, my goddess!" Raven's voice rose to a high squeak. She and Willow both leaned closer, gazing wide eyed at the stick, though neither made a move to touch it. "It's beautiful! Look at the natural grain – it matches the door perfectly! Where did you get it?"

"From a friend," Cally said. "Willow, would you please close it again for me?"

Willow dragged the door back into place, bumping it with her hip to make sure it stood snug against the wall. Then she stood back and gestured from Cally to the door and back again. "Go for it! See if it works!"

"But there's no keyhole." Raven squinted at the door handle.

"I don't think it works like that." Cally did the only thing she could think of to do with a stick and a door. She knocked.

"Nothing's happening," Raven observed.

"May I?" Cally put out her free hand. This time, Willow stepped back quickly, even as Ben hurried to stand at Cally's side.

This time, when Cally dragged the door open, a wet breeze flowed out from behind it, stirring up tiny dust-devils in the room. The red bricks had gone, replaced now with deep blackness. A sound of rushing water could be heard beyond the doorway. Handing the door itself to Raven, Cally put her hand into the arch of darkness.

"Careful, don't fall!"

Cally turned, startled not so much by the panicked squeak of Raven's voice, but by the memory of her having said something so similar two days ago. The image of Raven's older face, in Cally's mind, superimposed now over the younger version standing before her, made her so dizzy she might actually have fallen over if not for Ben's quick hand reaching out to steady her.

She put her hand into the doorway again, balancing herself this time with Rum's stick, and felt the water rushing by in the blackness. It was a lot of water, cold and falling fast, down into nothing Cally could see.

"Nell, this is like one of your paintings, too," she said. "Only we seem to be on the back side of the canvas. Behind the waterfall."

"Maybe too much like it," Nell pointed out. "It's so dark. You could slip and fall, if you stepped out there. But the queen did tell you to go when the moon is full tonight. Then you'll be able to see, see?"

Cally did, or at least she was fairly certain she did. She took the door from Raven's hands and pushed it back against the wall.

"What time are you closing tonight?"

"Are you kidding?" Raven stared at the closed door, running the fingers of one hand wonderingly over the cracked paint.

"We'll be here waiting for you!" Willow said.

"We want to go with you, wherever that door leads."

Cally shook her head. "I don't suppose I can stop you. But listen." The Wyrd Systers stepped closer together and joined hands, smiling broadly at her. "I would strongly advise against it. This isn't some kind of fun adventure to go visit a talking lion. This is a march straight up to the gates of hell. Only colder."

The young women's smiles remained, though somewhat plastered onto their faces. They nodded their claim of understanding.

"Well, just think about it." Cally heaved a sigh and turned to go back out into the shop.

Daylight, if a little gray, now filled the display windows, and Cally found the fragrance of patchouli a great improvement over the dust of the small storeroom. Errin and Mima were waiting in front of the sales counter, watching as everyone emerged from the door behind it. When they saw Zenbe step out of the little room, they ran to hand him the neon blue smoothie they had bought for him.

"We'll be ready tonight when you are." Errin turned to Cally. "Where are we going?"

Cally looked around at all the people standing amongst the shelves of books and glittery pagan sculptures. It reminded her, only not, of the scenes in movies where the motley questing party all stands gathered, ready to set out. She knew she should have been moved to gratitude by the thought of all these people so eager to support her, but she only felt a nagging guilt, and the weight of responsibility for their well-being.

"Oh, but Cally." Nell emerged last from the little chamber and shut the door quietly behind her. "I'm sorry, I won't be able to come with you. Doc has promised to give me a short crash-course in some, um, conventional medical procedures tonight. Don't worry. You'll be okay without me."

And then Cally was surprised at how disappointed she was to hear this. Despite her misgivings about leading others into danger, and especially after how hard she'd worked to prevent Nell accompanying her on her last misadventure, she had begun to at least accept the idea of having someone with her who seemed to have a clue what they were doing.

"Okay, Nell, it's fine..."

"Until then, you should probably spend your time thinking about what the queen said. About what Ben is better at than you are. Hey, Willow, do you have any Black Cohosh or Vervain?"

Willow led Nell to the glass cabinet displaying various dried herbs in jars, while Raven assumed her station behind the cash register. Ben whispered into Cally's ear. "What did my mother say about me? What am I better at than you?"

"She told me to figure it out."

Errin and Mima winked (with distinct smirks, Cally thought) and then grasped Zenbe's arms between them and walked back outside. A gentle rain had begun to splotch the sidewalk outside the door.

Cally nodded to Raven. "I'll be back tonight," she said, turning toward the door. She paused and amended her promise. "*We* will be back. After moonrise. Dress warmly!"

40 - Ignacio Opens a Door

Luke and Danya accompanied Cally and Ben, through occasional spattering bursts of raindrops, to the intersection of Railroad and Main, and from there they headed back to the pizza parlor. "See you in a while!" Luke called, waving as he went, as if they were merely planning to meet later for vegemite sandwiches.

Cally waved back anyway, and then waved to Brandon, further along Main Street, where he was unlocking the door to Dawes News. He seemed to open the door with no effort at all, holding it with one hand while helping Bree up the single step. Cally nodded to Bree but slipped her arm through Ben's and kept on walking. She had still not figured out what Ben might be better at than she, but she had definitely thought of some things at which he was very good.

When they came downstairs late in the morning, Bethany chided them for having completely missed breakfast, just as she always did. Then she told them, as she always did, they would have to go and see if Katarina could scrape together some leftover sausage for them. Bethany was just a little startled when Cally paused to lean over the desk and kiss her on the cheek. She almost petted Doctor Boojums, as well, where he lay asleep on top of the filing cabinet, but remembered to just smile at his not-really-sleeping form before following Ben down the back hall to the kitchen.

Neither of them was hungry, after Luke's breakfast pizza, but they accepted the fluffy, rosemary-scented scrambled eggs Katarina set on the work table for them. Cally, at least, drank quantities of coffee, while Katarina bustled about the kitchen, humming, glancing out the window at Ignacio in the garden.

"We just want you to know," Katarina said, without looking at them, "we've got your back, tonight, Cally. All of us do."

"What?" Cally didn't know how Katarina already knew what

was planned for that night, but she wasn't exactly surprised, either. What surprised her was hearing Katarina talking so frankly about it. Katarina had always, though she seemed to know a lot about what made Woodley so different, preferred not to speak of such things openly, as if all the Christian saints might be listening and would disapprove.

Ignacio came into the kitchen, then, carrying a flat basket loaded with some kind of greens. Collards, Cally guessed. He continued Katarina's line of thought as if he had been listening all along. "I'll be standing in the door for you," he said. He nodded back the way he had come. "This door, right here. I'll hold it open for you, so you'll be able to get back." He put the basket on the drainboard of the sink, then turned to stand solemnly in front of Cally. "The chain runs through Vale House," he said. "Don't let go of it."

Cally had always known Ignacio was wise, but as she looked into his dark brown eyes, she realized he had always known, just like his wife, far more than he ever spoke of out loud. She felt like she should stand, before addressing him, as one ought to do in the presence of a member of a royal court.

She didn't stand, but she put a hand over her heart when she answered. "I won't let go," she promised. "I see you." Tears stung her eyes. She blinked them back.

"I guess I'd better get going," Ben said, just as he always did in this kitchen as noon was approaching. He stood and carried his plate to the sink, gave Katarina a side-hug, then shook Ignacio's hand perhaps a little more firmly than he normally did.

He turned back, then, as he always did, to kiss Cally before going out through the garden, but she had already stood up with her own plate in her hand. "I'm coming with you," she said. "There's one more conversation I need to have with Bree before tonight."

41 - A Final Chat with Emerald

Emerald<< I'm so sorry - - you were so close!

Emerald<< But at least you know where he is and that he's
OK and how to get back there

Emerald<< Third try's a charm, right?

Emerald<< And you saved the cat

Cally>> Saved the cat. Aha, I get it, now.

Emerald<< I didn't mean it as a joke

Cally>> OK, well, I know where George is, yes, though I
don't know he's OK.

Cally>> But I do understand better, now, what to do.

Cally>> I think I can get back there. Get in fast, like the
queen said. And this time I'll have allies at my back.

Cally>> But I've maxed out my capacity for self-deception,
over the past couple of days.

Cally>> I still don't know how I'm going to get in, once I get
there.

Cally>> Or how to get them all out, even if I do get in.

Emerald<< That's what you're on your way to find out!

Emerald<< I have every confidence you'll figure it out

Cally>> I hope you're right. Because Rianwynn says
Anderson Toller has plans for all those spirits.

Cally>> And I have this awful feeling he's going to go ahead

and enact his plan sooner than later, now that the cat's
out of the bag.

Emerald<< Hah - - cat's out of the bag

Cally>> I didn't mean it as a joke.

Cally>> Listen, Em. I need to tell you something before I go,
in case I don't come back.

Emerald<< I love you, too, my dear friend

Emerald<< And you WILL be coming back

Cally>> It's about your story.

Emerald<< Oh! Cally, no

Emerald<< I'm sorry for whining so much about that - - you
have much more important things on your mind right
now

Emerald<< At least I really am safe - - whatever or
wherever I am

Emerald<< At least I'm not trapped in some ghost hunter's
trophy collection

Cally>> Because you're not a ghost.

Emerald<< Right

Cally>> Because in order to be a ghost, you would have to
have died.

Emerald<< Yes and in order to have died I would have to
have been born

Emerald<< I understand all that

Emerald<< Was that what you needed to tell me? Because
I do know

Cally>> Good. Well. What I need to tell you is, I know who wrote the story that brought you to life.

Emerald<< Was it you?

Cally>> No. Nothing that simple, I'm afraid.

Emerald<< Of course not 😐

Cally>> See, the thing is. This person, this woman, she was going to have a baby.

Cally>> A daughter, who would have become a great queen, just like in your story.

Cally>> But things happened. And that's an entire story, in itself.

Cally>> The upshot of it all was, the baby died before it was born.

Emerald<< And that was me

Cally>> Yes.

Emerald<< I understand

Cally>> Are you OK?

Emerald<< I'm fine

Emerald<< Go on - - you were going to tell me who my - - author was

Cally>> Well, that woman came here to Vale House to recover. From her many wounds, physical and spiritual.

Cally>> She stayed here for several months, right here in this office, and while she was here, she taught herself to use the old computer they had at the time.

Cally>> In her attempts to heal, she made up a story about the daughter she would have named Emerald.

Cally>> It was her way of trying to give you some form of

life after all, of seeing you experience all the things you

should have, and never would.

Emerald<< But she never finished the story

Cally>> She never did. I think she lost heart.

Emerald<< I guess that makes sense

Emerald<< I should probably resent her for leaving me in

limbo like this - - but I don't

Emerald<< I just hope her life was better after that

Cally>> Em, you have a heart of gold. I think maybe you got

it from her.

Emerald<< Maybe

Emerald<< But Cally, who was she? You said you know

A knock came at the office door. Before Cally could call out, the door opened and Bethany put her head in.

"Just letting you know I'm leaving for the night. Doc and I are going to dinner."

"That's wonderful, Bethany!"

"Yes. Well, also, you have a visitor. She says you invited her."

"I did. Would you mind showing her in, please?"

Bethany's head withdrew, and then the door opened wide enough to admit a shuffling, hunched figure. Bree hobbled just far enough inside for Bethany to shut the door. The old woman stood at the end of the desk, clutching her sweater across her chest with both hands.

Cally nodded to her and turned back to the computer screen.

Cally>> Emerald, I would like to introduce you to Brigid

Dawes.

She stood up and swiveled the chair around toward Bree. "I understand you know how to type."

Cally stepped away as Bree sat down in the chair and raised her hands to the keyboard. Light from the screen filled her face with weird, angular shadows as she squinted into the chat window. Slowly, her crooked fingers began to press the keys, growing swifter after a moment.

Cally took her warmest jacket from the coat rack beside the door. "Stay as long as you need to," she whispered as she went out and shut the door behind her.

42 - Take On Me

Ben stood in the Vale House front yard, next to the fence. His back was to Cally as he gazed across the meadow toward the most distant hill in the darkening distance. Cally had stepped out the front door to see this many times, in the past, but everything seemed different this time. Not just because, this time, Aileen was also standing there looking at her from the other side of the fence.

"Come on, you two," she called out as Cally descended the porch steps. "Do your kissy-thing so we can get moving. We have names to kick and asses to take, tonight! Isn't that how you say it?"

Ben turned around as Cally reached the fence. She stood close enough to feel the warmth of him, far enough away to look into his face. Neither of them replied to Aileen.

Cally had still not thought of what Ben could do better than she could. Except wield a sword, and that was why Aileen had come to collect him. He would be returning to the queen's court when the sun set, as usual. Together he and the Sidhe lieutenant would lead whatever charge Rianwynn was planning to send from the Faerie side of the fence against the Fortress of the Dead.

They had talked about this before, more than once. About how they really were working together, toward the same ends, just from different sides of the fence. They hadn't discussed it today in particular, but the words remained, unspoken but true as ever. She looked up into his eyes, now, blue as dawn, while the fitful, rain-scented breeze from the meadow blew his hair into them. She thought his expression looked expectant, or else he was (very likely, she thought) struggling to keep from saying what he was thinking. Sighing resolutely, she tipped her head up to kiss him goodnight. Aileen let out a little grunt and turned to leave.

Ben didn't move. "Lieutenant, hold," he said. "I need you to take word back to the queen. Please report to her that her wayward son has defied her tonight."

Over Ben's shoulder, Cally saw a smirk spread across

Aileen's face. She winked at Cally as she said, "Very well, your lordship." The armor-clad Sidhe warrior executed a poor imitation of a curtsy.

Ben stepped back and held his hand out to Cally. "I'm coming with you."

"But..."

"It doesn't matter. I'm coming."

Cally could still see Aileen grinning at her. Both the human and the faerie woman knew Rianwynn had suggested Cally take Ben with her tonight, but Ben himself hadn't been present to hear this. Cally had intended all along to ignore the queen's advice, because the consequences of breaking the Faerie laws binding him were dire, especially now that the Fomorian General was at large again. Ben's offer to defy (or so he thought) his mother and accompany her moved her much more deeply than any hope of help his presence might bring, and she didn't want to ruin his gift by telling him it was unnecessary.

She swallowed. "Are you sure? Eladha is still out there, and..." She didn't realize she had reached her hand back to him, until his hand closed around it.

"See you at the gates of hell!" Aileen called cheerfully, saluting with her sword as she turned away and headed off into the darkness.

43 - That Damn Rabbit Hole

Mima, Errin, and Zenbe stood at the crossroads, where Main Street ended at the meadow gate. Zenbe was dancing in the middle of the street, whipping his incredible hair back and forth, playing air-guitar as he sang. *"...falling down that damn rabbit-hole, where I know you can't be SAAAAAVED...!"*

Cally and Ben stepped out from between Vale House's masonry pillars, onto the sidewalk under the oaks.

"But if you ask me," Zenbe sang, *"you can't spell slaughter without laughter..."*

"Zenbe!" Cally made slashing motions across her throat. "That's so inappropriate! Don't you know any songs with more positive lyrics?" This, she thought, was a classic example of why she always wanted to do things without other people's "help."

Errin and Mima both gave her "god you're so old!" looks. But Zenbe carefully put away his air-guitar and apologized. "It's just that I have a feeling the bass is about to drop," he said.

Cally had the same feeling. "It *is* a good song," she had to admit. She looked south along Gardens Road, wishing more than ever that she and Ben were really just on their way to old Blackthorn to enjoy a burger and a rock show. "Alright, let's go rescue our bass player," she said at last.

Errin led the way along the sidewalk toward town. The other two teens followed her, and Ben walked beside Cally, bringing up the rear.

Cally had walked this way with Ben many times before, but always in the daylight, never at night. Even so, just as they always did, the people inside the houses they passed opened their doors to – ostensibly – let their cats out onto their porches. She had always assumed all these small-town folks were just keeping themselves up-to-date on the Woodley gossip grapevine. This time, though, the denizens themselves came out onto their porches and stood, accompanied by their cats, silently watching the little procession pass beneath the trees. Cally looked up just once at their silent faces gently regarding her passage and, though none of them spoke, she felt like they were cheering her on. Simple gratitude smoothed some of the tension from her shoulders.

They walked on silently, their footfalls barely audible on the warm concrete, to the end of the residential part of town and on into downtown proper. As they passed the feedstore, Merv Arkwright, sitting on his loading dock, stood up, and watched, and did not wave. The news store was closed, illuminated only by the light in the beverage cooler at the back, but when they passed onward to the intersection with Railroad Street, they could see Motherboard Pizza still brightly lit. Luke and Danya were standing just outside it, and Luke waved for them to stop.

"I'll be staying here," he called out to them, hurrying to meet them at the corner. "I'll be holding the door open. But Danya wants to come with you."

"Please." Danya looked at Cally with big, desperate eyes, unaware that Cally had completely given up, by now, saying no to this kind of request. "I need to do this." She was wearing a flannel shirt and carrying a ski jacket that probably belonged to Luke. "I need to face my fears. And beat them, this time."

Cally nodded, then turned to Luke. "Ignacio also says he's holding the door," she recalled. "The back door at Vale House, to be precise. What door are you holding?"

"The door of my shop, of course." Luke nodded as if he believed she would understand and approve of this plan. "Merv is also holding a door for you. Lots of us are. We'll all make sure you can get back. Did you remember to open the gate?"

Cally was trying to imagine how all these doors could help her get back, and almost missed the part about the gate. "What?" she asked. "The meadow gate? No. Why?"

"Don't worry. Nell can open it – I'll text her."

"Are you sure that's such a good idea?"

"Trust me, it is."

Cally didn't understand what he was talking about, any more than she ever understood what he was talking about whenever he diagnosed and fixed her computer, but she did know he was an odd and wise young man she could trust. She looked back, saw the limb of the moon jutting above the roof of the buildings behind them, and let it go. "Okay. I have to get going. We have to get going," she corrected.

Danya hugged Luke and crossed to the other corner of the intersection. Cally hugged him, too, and followed. Only one more person stood between them and the Wyrd Systers Gifts and Books Shoppe. Andi ran out from the Bean Garden to give Cally yet another hug.

"I don't understand what's going on," she said. "Merv tried to explain it to me, but Jud was standing there, and he couldn't talk. Anyway, I guess the whole town is praying for you tonight."

Cally held onto Andi longer than she meant to. "I promise," she said into her friend's hair. "If I get back...when I get back, I'll tell you about it. All of it. It'll be really nice to have a friend my own age to talk with about these things."

"Thanks a lot!" said Errin. "I'm a lot older than you think!"

Cally stood back and looked into Andi's eyes. "She's telling the truth," she told her with a low laugh. "An understatement, but a true one. See you."

Raven and Willow were waiting in the doorway of their shop when Cally and her companions arrived, but they were not dancing on tiptoe with giddy anticipation, as she'd been dreading. Only Raven was dressed for cold weather as Cally had instructed. When everyone had gathered inside the store, Raven shut the door behind them and locked it. Willow flipped the sign from "Open" to "Closed."

"So, here's the thing," Raven said while Willow pulled back the tapestry and unlocked the door to the dusty, lighted chamber. "I'll be coming with you, but Willow won't. She'll be..."

"Staying here to hold the door open," Cally finished for her. "No, don't panic, I can't read your minds. Just there's a lot of that going around, tonight."

Willow laughed nervously. "I guess so. Well, and it's the raven who flies afar. It's the willow that stands as the steadfast home so the raven can return. It's teamwork." She and Raven stood with their arms around one another in more of a grip than an embrace, as if they were unconsciously afraid to let go.

Cally said, "Alright, then," and ducked into the little

chamber beyond the door. She waited until everyone else had crowded in before she raised her stick to knock on the door at the back.

Raven coughed. "I just remembered something."

Cally breathed out an exasperated noise and lowered the stick. "Can it wait?"

"I don't know. Just that Bree gave me a message. I went over to her store to buy a granola bar, earlier, and found her closing up shop early. She told me to tell you she has swept her hearth."

"That's nice." Cally waited for Raven to elaborate, in case this had any relevance to the task at hand. She doubted it did.

"It's just..." Willow and Raven exchanged glances.

"Well, it's just, that's a witch's way," Willow explained, "of telling people she's decided it's time for her to die."

Cally's heart fell into her toes. She looked at Ben, who was not looking at her, now, but out through the door to the glimpse of Main Street still visible through the shop window. Ben, who was standing beside her now, at night, in Woodley, just as she had always wished he could, would have to return to Faerie forever once Bree had passed away. But that was not, Cally realized now, the only reason she would miss the old woman.

"I hope she plans to wait until we get back." She winced at her own words, because they were absolutely not the right thing to say. She had last seen Bree at Vale House, typing into the chat-screen on her computer. That would probably be a long conversation. Maybe it would last long enough, because Cally knew turning back now from her current task was not an option.

It was Errin who seemed to react with uncharacteristic panic. "Oh my god!" She stiffened and looked back through the door into the store. "That means I can't come with you. There are...things. I need to do." She turned to Mima and Zenbe. "I'm sorry, I have to go."

Mima waved a hand. "You go. We've got this. Go!"

"I'll see myself out," said Errin. And then she was gone. The little bell over the shop door jangled, though the door had not opened or shut.

"Alright." Ben's voice was thick, his eyes shut, as he turned away from them all to face the little closed door at the back of the dusty room. "The moon is getting higher. Let's just do this."

Cally didn't know what else to do. She grasped Rum's stick in both hands and knocked.

Again, the cool, damp breeze rushed out of the opening, blowing Cally's hair back from her face. Zenbe's long, black locks, though, put hers to shame the way they billowed like some kind of shampoo commercial when he leaned forward to peer under the lintel of the doorway.

"It's alright," he said. "There are stars."

Cally felt reassured to hear this, but it was the moonlight she found most comforting. She couldn't see the moon itself, not exactly, but she knew it must be the source of the light shining on the water. The aqueous curtain, falling down over the other side of the doorway, shimmered now like silver. She couldn't help putting her hand out to touch it.

"Don't..." Willow began.

"I won't fall." Cally pushed the tip of her stick through the water to tap the ground she could see, also reflecting moonlight, on the other side. It was solid, and mostly smooth, though she suspected it was also wet. She put her jacket on and turned, stretching out her free hand behind her, and said "Let's go."

Ben grasped her hand and followed as she ducked into the waterfall. The force of the water seemed, at first, strong enough to knock her off her feet, but she steadied herself with the stick and stepped through until the cascade was little more than mist floating all around her. Her hair was wet, but the water had not penetrated all the way through to her clothing. Turning, she saw Ben's hand and arm, and then the rest of him, emerge from the falls. Behind him, Raven followed, clutching Ben's hand determinedly, and behind her Zenbe, and Danya, and Mima.

She watched them emerge, a human (and not-quite-human) chain, hand in hand and link by link. Before Mima finally stepped through, Cally thought she could see beyond her to more hands holding hers, linking all the way back to the shop, to Willow in the doorway and on into Woodley, through Luke in his shop to Merv at the feedstore to Ignacio in the Vale House cellar and on, and on, to Rum at the culvert at the edge of the Vale House grounds, to the People in Shannish and on to where Aileen stood... wherever she was standing. Somewhere on the top of a dark hill, under strange stars...

"They aren't the only people in the chain. Just the ones I recognize."

"Cally. Are you alright?" Ben was grasping her by the shoulders; she opened her eyes.

"I'm sorry. I was just trying to see it all." She wiped moisture, warmer than the mist of the falls, from the corners of her eyes. "I'm ... grateful. And humbled."

"I wish Willow could see this!" Raven had turned around, tipping her head back to stare, up and up, along the silvery ribbon of water. Crowned by the moon itself, the water twisted like a silver dancer, seeming to float in slow motion down the side of the dark stone wall before shattering into mist at their feet. "It's beautiful!"

"And wet," Danya added. "And cold." She wrapped her arms around herself beneath her oversized jacket.

"Right," said Mima. "That's what *we're* here for."

Danya screamed. Raven looked to see what she was screaming about, and also screamed. Without looking, Cally guessed what they were screaming about. Mima's words had come from the mouth of a white horse.

"Don't panic," Raven said in a panicky voice. "I read somewhere that upsets horses!"

"We're not horses," Zenbe said in a voice much deeper than, but just as soft as, his usual voice. His black mane flew, as he pawed at the hard, wet ground, more splendidly than even the magnificent hair of his human head ever had.

"Oh my goddess!" Wonder replaced fear in Raven's voice. She started forward, hand outstretched to pet Mima's face, until Mima stopped her with a cold, blue stare. "You're a..."

"They probably aren't," Cally said. "But they're here to help us hurry through the cold so we don't die. We should get going."

"There are four of us," Danya pointed out, "and only two of them."

"Hah!" Mima snorted. "Come on." She turned her broad,

white side to Cally, and craned her neck around to speak to Ben. "Help them up."

Ben seemed to know exactly what to do. He bent beside Mima's flank and linked the fingers of both hands together. Handing her stick to Danya, Cally demonstrated how to step into his hands. She gripped fistfuls of white mane and pulled herself up, then swung her leg over the white horse's back. She couldn't help feeling pleased with herself over how good she was getting at this. The familiarity of the broad, white back was almost comforting, but she was careful not to go so far as to pat Mima's neck as she had seen riders do in movies. Ben helped Danya onto Mima's back behind her.

"I get it," Danya observed as she settled behind Cally, putting her arms around her for balance. "We three can help one another conserve body heat."

Cally realized she was right. Maybe, she thought, this thing was actually do-able, after all. Maybe this time, by the time she reached the Nocksgall, she might still retain enough presence of mind to figure out how to get in. Taking the stick back from Ben and holding it across Mima's withers, she began to feel a bit more optimistic.

Ben put his left hand on Zenbe's back and, in a single motion, lifted himself onto the black horse's back. Then he reached down to Raven and pulled her up behind him.

"Why can't I drive?" Raven asked.

"Because you ask questions like that," Mima snorted, but Zenbe blew out a great breath of air Cally recognized as a horselaugh.

"Alright. Which way, then?" Cally looked around them. The waterfall filled all their view in the direction she could only think of as "north" (though she knew it probably wasn't actually north at all, anymore.) The cascade struck stony black ground that reminded her of asphalt pavement, flat and fairly smooth. There the water split into two wide streams flowing away down either side of the hill.

Looking away from the falls, she saw the slope falling gently away from them, down through a forest of mature trees. Far below, black outlines of branches were etched against dim, white lights. The lights, four or five of them, ran in a row too straight and regular to be anything found in nature. They reminded her, in a vague, sentimental kind of way, of the times she had seen old Blackthorn ahead through old-growth forest at night. But she didn't dare to hope that was where they were going as Mima and Zenbe headed into the trees.

45 - Dead End

The black, paved ground was wet with mist from the waterfall, but Mima and Zenbe didn't seem to find it slippery at all as they carried the party forward into the shadows. When the sound of the waterfall dissolved into silence behind them, Raven made disappointed noises and turned to look back. Cally didn't bother. She knew she would see only forest, now, stretching behind them as far as the dappled moonlight could show.

Here, at least, the ground was covered with leaves, and Mima's and Zenbe's steps softened to a rhythmic rustling Cally found calming. The mature trees stood fairly wide apart and they passed between them easily, but Mima and Zenbe didn't walk straight toward the lights ahead. They seemed to turn right or left for no apparent reason, at times, and sometimes even went around to double back on a way they had already taken. Cally knew better than to question Mima's choice of route anymore, but Danya's patience ran thin quickly.

"I thought we had to get in and get out fast?" she complained. "This is only taking up extra time, and my nose is already starting to feel numb."

"They'll get us there faster than we could ever get there ourselves," Cally assured her.

Danya let out a sigh only Cally could hear, but Raven gasped.

"Look!" She leaned over to point at the ground, almost unseating herself. "Look at the path. It's a Celtic knot!"

Danya clutched at the back of Cally's jacket and tipped her head to look, but she sat upright again quickly.

"It's more of an alchemical circle," Zenbe corrected.

Cally didn't have to look directly at the paths, anymore, to see them. She could see, in her mind, which ones matched the turns in the card lying on the table in the diner back in Woodley. She always knew which way Mima was going to turn, and she knew when they had come to the end of the maze. Now Mima and Zenbe stepped out of the leaves and onto the stony ground, once again, at the other side.

This time, Cally couldn't help turning around to look, causing Danya to clutch nervously at her. Behind them, now, instead of forest, stood two charming, well-tended Cape-cod style houses clad in beige siding. Similar houses, all with lights in their windows, surrounded the wide circle of pavement at their feet. In front of them, the pavement stretched out to become a lane enclosed on both sides with more houses. The streetlights along this lane were the lights they had seen from the other side of the wood. The pavement at their feet did not just resemble asphalt: it was asphalt, damp with a recent rain, sparkling under the lights. Cally struggled once again to remember the word Ian had taught her for the smell of rain...

"Did you know," Raven said, twisting in her seat behind Ben, looking all around the cold, silent place, "that *cul de sac* literally translates from the French to 'dead end'?"

Cally felt Danya, behind her, press her face into the back of her jacket to muffle a scream.

"I understand if you don't want to go any further," Cally told her quietly. She did understand, or thought she did. Reluctantly, now, she jammed herself into the role of leader, the delegator and giver of orders, and tried to think of who should stay behind to keep Danya from falling into hypothermia.

"No, I'm alright." Danya's teeth were already chattering as she spoke, but probably not, Cally thought, from the chill in the air. Not yet. "I'm the one who insisted on coming along. I need to do this."

Ben was already standing at Mima's side, reaching up to help them dismount. Danya reached down and grasped his arm while he talked her through swinging her leg behind her, then he caught her as she slid down the white horse's side. Cally dismounted as well, and by the time she turned to see how the others were doing, there were zero horses and six humans (or at least people who resembled humans) standing in the black, paved circle.

"Last time we were here." Danya lifted her chin and took a deep breath. "Cally, you said something about sneaking through the back yards, to find a back way in. In to the... You know. Their cellar.

His spirit workshop, he called it. Is that still your plan?"

Cally hadn't really had a plan, because she hadn't known what she would encounter when she went through the door in the back of the Wyrd Systers Books and Gifts Shoppe. She'd mostly been expecting to see the hulking, dark building she'd encountered before, sans doors or windows, at the crest of the cold stone hill. Of course that would have been too simple, her cynical mind reminded her now.

Here, only the vinyl siding remained the same. That, and the all-pervasive, life-sucking cold. Turning slowly, she looked at the lights glowing in all the front windows of all the houses along the quiet street. Glowing, or glowering? Because, as much as this place resembled the subdivision she and Danya had recently fled, Cally knew it was not the same place at all. The light coming from these windows was harsher, and Cally had the distinct feeling someone inside each one was watching them.

"Oh, Cally!" Mima said with a silly, little laugh. "I've a feeling we're not in North Carolina anymore!"

Danya failed to take the bait. "No," she agreed. "No, we're not."

Cally looked around at the faces of those who had come with her: Mima rolling her eyes and looking bored, Raven wide-eyed with wonder and Danya wide-eyed with terror, Zenbe and Ben regarding her silently, awaiting her decision. "Still," she said at last. "I guess my old plan is just as good as any.

"The Tollers' house is the fourth one down on the left. There."

She pointed along the road to a house, halfway along the lane, that looked more or less exactly like all the others, set back on a small patch of grass with its square, flat porch and neat balls of boxwood at either side. Its door was shut and Cally did not, at the moment, see anyone standing in the sidelights. But in her mind, at least, she still heard Geraldine Toller saying, *You'll be back.* She empathized with Danya; she wanted to scream, too.

She stepped off the pavement into the dark wedge of lawn between the two houses at their left. The frost-coated grass crackled under her feet. Leading her little party between the two houses, she stayed low and tried to keep to the edges of the side yard, in the shadows of the shrubbery, though she knew this was ridiculous. Just by virtue of being a warm-blooded creature, she felt as exposed, here, as a bright green caterpillar crawling along a white porch railing. No dark birds dove from the cold sky to seize her and the others, but she could almost hear them snickering in the darkness all around.

"No wonder the Tollers thought everything was a demon," she mused under her breath, turning, once they'd reached the back of the house on their left, into the first of the four backyards between them and the Tollers' house. "They're all around us, here."

"You can see them?" Danya asked. "Oh, of course. I should have known you could."

"I can't," Cally admitted, though she had a feeling she would see something soon enough.

"Luke calls them Watchers." Danya followed her through a gap in a hedge. "He's seen them all his life, he says, though it only started for me when I was a teenager." While Cally stood and held the branches of the hedge aside for the others to pass through, she watched Danya with new eyes. The young woman was definitely seeing something, as she looked around the backyard in which they all now stood. "They're everywhere in the world," she continued. "At least, everywhere I've ever been. Though there are fewer of them in Woodley, and *way* more of them here!" Even as she said this, Danya stuck out an arm to divert Ben, who was about to crouch into the shadow of a toolshed where she, apparently, saw something already standing.

Cally put a hand on Danya's shoulder. "I'm glad you're with us," she said with a sincerity that felt like a balm to her heart. She turned and led on.

46 - The Bass Drops

Cally could definitely see her breath, now, forming white plumes in front of her. She reached the back porch of the next house and crouched down into the shadows next to it. They were just two doors away from the one she supposed was their goal. She stood to move on to the next yard, and her movement triggered a motion-sensing floodlight on the corner of the porch next door. She said a bad word and crouched back down.

"I know this isn't a real subdivision," she muttered to the others crouching there with her. "But whoever created this glamour paid close attention to detail!"

"Not really." Raven stood up and looked around.

Cally wanted to grab her and drag her back down to where the rest of them all crouched, but she heard Ben, behind her, say "She's right." He stood, now, too. "Something's missing."

"It's the dogs." Danya nodded. "That floodlight should have made every dog within a quarter mile start barking. But I don't hear anything."

Cally had to admit she, in fact, didn't hear anything at all. It was this silence which made this entire place feel so eerie and hostile. Slowly, she stood up, and the rest of them joined her. There was no point hiding in the shadows of shrubbery that didn't actually exist.

Mima laughed. "But you all looked so precious, skulking around like that!" Zenbe jabbed her in the ribs with his elbow.

Cally ignored them both. Looking around her, now, was like looking through the amulet she'd once had. The conventional subdivision didn't exactly disappear. It simply wasn't there anymore, because there was no further point in it being there. Even the frozen grass no longer cracked underfoot, and only the damp, black pavement remained, stretching out as far as Cally could see. The only feature still left in the cold, empty landscape was the house which had been their goal, and it was no longer charming, or tidy, or a house.

Instead, a broad, blank wall stretched across the horizon, just as had the Fortress of the Dead the first time she'd seen it. Beyond and above it stretched a black sky that looked like a painting done by someone who had never really looked at a night sky: the stars were all uniform dots, spaced evenly, forming no constellations. Cally knew, if she looked up, she would see a full moon hanging exactly at zenith. She did not look up.

Cold seemed to roll across the dark hilltop in a syrupy wave. Danya, standing beside her with her arms wrapped around herself, looked nervously from side to side. Apparently, the Watchers were still with them. Cally couldn't make up her mind whether that thought unnerved her or comforted her.

"Let's keep moving," Raven advised.

Cally agreed. She stepped forward and began to close the distance between herself and the dark wall in long, brisk steps. She noticed she had begun to shiver, now, but she reminded herself she was ahead of the game this time. By the time she reached the wall, she was still able to move her arms and legs, and to think.

The others, following closely, gathered around her. She didn't bother reaching out to verify whether or not the wall was covered with siding, this time, but led on around the corner of the building. The small, barred window was where it should be, at the base of the wall, illuminated from within by a pale, cold light that seemed to pulsate, waxing and waning like flame.

"I've seen this place..." Danya rubbed her hands together and stamped her feet as she stood looking down at the little window.

"Yes. In a dream." Raven said. "It was cold in the dream, too."

"All we have to do is figure out how to break through."

"And what to do afterward." Cally knelt next to the window, laying Rum's stick on the ground in front of it. She didn't see George – or any other spirits – inside, this time. She did see many small objects, random knickknacks and gadgets crowded along shelves stretching away, on either side, into darkness beyond the reach of the light. Some of them had tumbled to the earthen floor, which lay about four feet below the window. All of them looked particularly dull and lifeless in the sallow light within. Cally hoped she wasn't too late, and that Toller hadn't already put the spirits to whatever dread use Rianwynn had warned her he meant to put them to.

The pulsating light came from an open doorway directly across from the window. This stood at the top of what looked like a perfectly ordinary, open stringer wooden stair she might expect to see in any earthly basement. A wide, wooden crate stood across the bottom of the stairs and a shadow, the silhouette of a man, stood at the top.

Certain she knew who's silhouette it was, she looked away, down to the stick lying on the ground at her knees. It was a key, she knew. She wondered if it could somehow unlock this window. Maybe if she inserted it through the bars, she could pry...

"Someone's here." Mima's voice was less insolent than usual.

"I know," Cally said, assuming Mima was talking about the figure at the top of the stairs. Then she heard everyone's footsteps shifting, backing toward the wall until they surrounded her. She grabbed the stick and stood quickly, turning around to follow their gazes.

Two tall shadows stood opposite the window, about thirty yards away. She immediately recognized one of the shadows by its hunched posture alone, and by the gleam of white teeth in its too-wide mouth. Her grip on Rum's stick tightened. She thought she recognized the other, as well. Its erect but weary posture reminded her of Michael Dawes, and in the center of his chest, something shiny threw crescent-shaped reflections back at the counterfeit moon above.

"Fucking hell," said Ben.

She turned to look at him, not just because she had never heard him use that kind of language, but because of the tremor in his voice when he said it. He was staring at the two figures with a look she had only seen a couple of times before, and in the tainted moonlight, the shadows of his face seemed darker and much more angular. The two figures did not approach. They simply stood, motionless and watching.

"Now I understand," Ben was saying. "They've been working together all along. It explains everything."

"I don't..." Cally didn't know what it explained, or maybe she didn't agree, or maybe she just didn't want him to be right.

"Cozying up to you was just his way of helping Eladha get free. What he's been given in return, I don't want to imagine."

He hadn't turned to look at her, but Cally shook her head. "This can't be what it looks like."

"You know he has betrayed me, in the past," Ben said. "I got over that. More recently, he betrayed us. I can get over that and I know you can, too. You probably already have. But Bree spent her whole life hoping to find out he hadn't utterly abandoned and betrayed her."

He did look at her, then, and the ice in his eyes made the chill of the air seem balmy by comparison. It was all Cally could do not to step backward. "Well," he said with a grin that was not in any way comforting. "I think we've figured out what I'm better at than you are."

She could barely breathe. "What?"

"Anger."

47 - Let the Walls Fall Down

Ben turned back to face the shadows, and Cally heard the soft scrape of a sword being drawn. The sword he always carried, the symbol of his rank which Cally almost never saw but which was always there, now glittered in his hand.

Before she could protest, Zenbe spoke up. "Your lordship." He had not moved, but he was somehow now at Ben's side. Ben gave him a moment to finish, but throughout that moment, he raised the sword slowly, until Cally could see the reflection of Michael Dawes' silhouette in its blade. Eladha spread his feet and crossed his arms. Michael still did not move.

"Your lordship, it's just..." Zenbe struggled to find words, something that was always difficult for him unless he was singing, and it took all the self-control Cally possessed not to interfere. "Well, I'm just wondering. How could he have forced Eladha to give the moon-talisman back to him? He is no warrior."

The sword wavered; Ben's shoulders sank. "Your point is taken." He lowered his hand until the blade was parallel to the ground. "He is no warrior. It would be dastardly of me to bring this blade against him." He took a deep breath and nodded. When he threw the sword to the ground, sparks flew up from the black stone.

He turned and looked once more at Cally. His eyes were no softer than they had been, and his hands were clenched in tight fists at his side. "I'm sorry," he said. "This is for Bree."

Before the ring of metal on stone had died away, Ben had closed the gap between himself and the man in the distance.

Michael Dawes went down like a train-wreck. He didn't seem to make any attempt to fight back at all, and Eladha, only pausing for a moment to leer at the violence taking place at his feet, turned away from both of the men and strode toward Cally.

Cally's eyes went to Ben's sword; she considered exchanging her stick for it, but Zenbe moved first. He stepped between her and the blade, lifting it gently. Cally hoped he had a better idea what to do with it than she did, but he merely gazed at it, turning it over in his hands.

The battle, if it could have been called one, between Ben and Michael Dawes was over before Eladha even reached Cally. She saw Ben kneeling with one knee on his father's chest, reaching to Michael's throat. With a quick jerk of his fist, he snapped the silver chain. Cally watched him rise to his feet, the silver crescent spinning slowly in the moonlight at the end of its broken chain. She held her breath, watching to see if Michael was going to be able to get up again, until Eladha's approach blocked her view of him.

Then she moved to place herself between the Fomorian and the others, instinctively raising her stick as if it could be any defense. Eladha paid her no attention. He had eyes only for the sword in Zenbe's hands.

"I'll take that," he said.

To Cally's utter horror, Zenbe handed him the sword.

"Oh, don't look so betrayed." Eladha sneered into her stricken face.

"No, I'm sorry," Zenbe said. "It's rightfully his, now. That's what he's doing here. In exchange for the amulet, the queen's consort must have promised Eladha he could persuade Ben to throw down his sword."

Cally looked from Zenbe to Eladha, trying to piece this together in her mind. "How can he promise something that doesn't belong to him?"

"The prince released it and walked away," Eladha growled. "It's all correct and in order, according to the laws. For these kinds of swords, anyway. Finders keepers!"

Unable to think of words choice enough to describe Faerie and its laws, Cally could only watch while Eladha tried to put the sword into the empty scabbard at his side. It was too large, and jammed halfway in. Eladha looked over his shoulder at Ben, now walking toward them with the amulet dangling from his hand. "I don't suppose you could hand over that invisible scabbard as well, your majesty." He said the word 'majesty' as if it should rhyme with 'scum.' "It only makes sense to keep the two together."

"Get stuffed," said Ben. He gave the sword the merest glance as he shouldered past Eladha to stand before Cally. He was trembling but probably not, she thought, with the cold, as sweat streamed down his brow. "I couldn't take the sword with me," he explained almost apologetically to her. "I would have killed him."

She looked past his shoulder to where she could see Michael, now struggling to rise. Her relief turned to heartbreak when he stopped, on hands and knees, making no further attempt to stand. "He had faith that you wouldn't kill him. Ben..."

Ben held the amulet out to her. "Taking something in fair battle is also irrevocable according to the law," he said. "As is giving it freely."

She shrank back. "No!" Even had the shining, spinning thing not been dripping with blood from Ben's hand and, probably, Michael's neck, she would not have wanted to touch it. "No," she said again. "I want nothing to do with that thing anymore!"

"I understand." Ben was still fighting to catch his breath. "I hate it as much as you do. But it's the only way we're going to get inside, and we have to get inside. Soon."

She knew he was right. She willed herself, with all her strength, to lift her hand and take the pendant from him. The best she could manage was to take one step forward, but her entire body recoiled with the memories of all the harm it had caused.

"I can't." Her chest was so tight she could barely speak. "I can't bring myself to touch it, let alone look through it again." She felt more frozen, in a different way, than she had the last time she'd been here, and even more of a failure.

Eladha laughed, standing back with his arms crossed, shaking his head at the entire scene. Everyone did their best to ignore him. They made encouraging sounds to Cally instead, though in their voices she thought she could detect the chattering of teeth. Even Mima was starting to shiver, snorting frosty air and stamping her feet.

It was Raven who finally reached out to the pendant in Ben's hand. "Let me try." She opened her hand under it and Ben, after looking to Cally for her nod, let go of the chain.

"Come on." With her free hand, Raven tugged at Cally's arm, gently urged her toward the little barred window. "Show me how to use this."

Behind them all, Cally heard Mima say, "Damn it, I wish

Nell would get that gate open!"

Cally paid her no mind. Putting an arm behind Raven, she said, "You just..." She waved a shaking hand toward the window. "You just look through it."

Despite her loathing of the object, Cally stayed close when Raven stepped nearer to the window. She did hope this would work, even if she couldn't bear to do it herself. As Raven stretched her hand toward the wall, the light from within the window flared brighter, as if someone had thrown fuel on a fire. The shadows of the bars stretched across the ground like a fanged mouth gaping wider.

Cally could hear voices, now, stirring to life inside the building. Like the ones in her dream, they murmured and whispered, at first, then rose to a clamor. By the gasps and alarmed expressions on Raven and Danya's faces, she realized they, too, recognized the sounds of the trapped spirits from dreams of their own.

Danya stood on Raven's other side and laid a hand on the small of her back. "You've got this," she encouraged. "Go ahead. But, um, hurry!"

Raven took one last step toward the wall, holding the amulet low, level with the top of the window. The sepulchral light inside waxed with each pulse, until it shone like a yellow eye through the crystal in the center of the silver moon. Cally began to wonder if this was such a good idea, after all. She opened her mouth to say so, but before she could speak, Raven had ducked her head and looked into the center of the amulet.

The light seemed to strike Raven's left eye like a laser beam. She cried out, a brief "ah," and fell to her knees on the dark ground. Cally knelt beside her. "Are you alright?" She felt even more ashamed of herself, now. "I'm sorry, I shouldn't have let you do that." She could only imagine what such a thing could do to the silly girl.

The amulet had fallen from Raven's fingers to the ground, but she was laughing. "It's just the moon," she said, gasping in deep breaths of the cold air. "It's alright. It worked. We're all on the moon!"

"Oh, God." Without touching the talisman itself, Cally picked the pendant up by its chain. She was never going to be able get rid of the damn thing. Stuffing it into her jacket, she wrapped her arms around Raven and raised her to a sitting position. Raven was still giggling about the moon. "Mima, help me with her! We have to get her back to..."

She didn't finish because, as she stood, she felt a booming in the dark ground that shocked her through her numb feet right up to her collarbones. The barred rectangle of light at the bottom of the wall had begun to spread, wider across the ground, and taller as the opening itself shuddered and expanded. Even Eladha stepped back as the light reached the feet of those gathered around the window. They stepped back again, and then again, but the sulphurous glow soon surrounded them. The window's iron bars snapped in the middle as it yawned wider still, until the opening resembled nothing so much as a ravening mouth full of jagged teeth, a dragon's maw preparing to belch fire.

Instead of fire, though, shadows seemed to be moving inside, moving faster as they increased in number, and above them all, a voice began to chant. Cally didn't recognize the language, but she did recognize the voice. It was Anderson Toller's and, as its volume rose and fell, gray forms, some nebulous and some alarmingly solid, began to issue from the opening. They emerged a few at a time, at first, and then in a great mass, squeezing through the opening like gray floodwater vomited from a storm-drain.

Clutching at Raven's and Danya's clothing, Cally reeled backward, though she didn't expect to be able to do anything but watch helplessly while she and the others were trampled or had their souls ripped from them by howling shadows. The entities issuing from the fortress, however, seemed to pay no mind to her or to her companions. They ran, instead, or flew or crawled, right past the mortals in their midst, outward in all directions, toward the black horizon all around.

As the last of them exited the building, the light inside dimmed until the inside of the fortress was once again lit only by a sullen glow. In spite of herself, Cally couldn't help turning round and round to watch each spirit passing by her, hoping to recognize one of them as George.

She didn't see him, but she saw Michael Dawes, like a fish swimming upstream, limping through the shadows toward her.

When he reached Cally's side he said, loudly enough for them all to hear above the clamoring voices, "It's alright. The queen is here!"

He was right. The host of shadows had paused in its rush to the outer reaches of the dark landscape. Some of them even shrank back, as silver flame erupted from the horizon all around. The shadows were unable to stop long, however. As they hesitated, Toller's voice shrieked insistently from within the fortress, driving them onward once again into the advancing faerie forces.

Mima, at least, was not dismayed. "Looks like our Nell got the gate open, after all!!" Reassuming her equine form, she whinnied a piercing cry and ran to join the advancing Sidhe ranks. Zenbe remained, in his human form, at Cally's side.

"Well, listen." Eladha was turning in circles, clutching the flat of his newly won blade to his chest and looking from the faerie army to the ghostly mob and back again. "I'd like to say this has been fun. But it hasn't. I've got places to go and people to do..."

Zenbe and Ben stepped sideways to block his retreat though it was unclear, in the chaos all around, to where he could have retreated. Ben growled, "I hope you can use that thing better than you could your last blade. Otherwise, you're not the only one who isn't going to make it out of here alive."

"You counsel me to throw in my lot with yours, now?" The Fomorian looked from him to the quickly closing front lines. "If I had my army at my back," he growled, "I would choose the side of the dead." He cast a glance toward the open maw of the Fortress, and then he turned his golden eyes to Cally. "Come with me." It was not a demand, as was his wont. It was an invitation.

He grunted out a low "hah" when Cally responded by shrinking toward Ben. Then, in less than a moment, he had disappeared into the glowing opening in the wall. Toller's voice, inside, boomed out a command, but this was abruptly cut off in its midst to be replaced, once again, with strange chanting.

"He's not wrong." Michael Dawes, blood and sweat flowing from his brow to mingle together in his beard, was looking to the horizon where the encircling silver flames advanced from every direction. The gap between the fae army and the ghost army closed in a hushed clash of blade upon ether. Only the cries of the Sidhe warriors and the undead spirits reminded Cally that this was, in fact, a battle. "You need to go, now. All of you." Michael nodded past her, into the light of the opening behind her. "This is your chance to help your friends. If you can stop the necromancer, you can stop this entire business. But you must go now."

48 - The Devil's Workshop

Cally was unable to take her eyes from the attacking shadows and the Sidhe battling them. Every blow horrified her, regardless of which side had struck it or who was struck. The spirits, it was clear, had no choice but to obey Toller's voice, but the Sidhe could not by any means allow them to pass, to go where the necromancer was sending them. That could be anywhere, or everywhere. If George was among them, Cally was glad she couldn't tell him apart from the rest of the seething mass.

She turned to Michael. "Come with us," she urged him.

He smiled but shook his head. "My place is here." He turned away to gaze across the battlefield, to where the tallest and brightest of the Sidhe stood like a gleaming tower amid crashing waves of shadow.

"But you don't even have..."

There was no time to argue. Behind her, she could hear Raven's voice already inside the fortress. The silly girl was apparently attempting to do something heroic. Cally turned and ran to join the others climbing into the opening.

Zenbe reached up through the broken bars to help her lower herself to the dirt floor below. There, she saw Raven standing on the other side of the room, between the base of the stairs and the long, wooden crate. Her face was lit by yellow light as she looked up, holding one hand, palm facing outward, up to the dark silhouette in the doorway. Wherever Eladha had gone, he had apparently not removed Toller from the picture on his way.

Cally's instinct was to run to the foot of the stairs and tackle Raven, but Ben had already positioned himself behind the crate, where he could grab and drag her back across the top of it if he had to. Cally realized this was the right thing to do. She left him to it and turned to help Zenbe lift Danya down into the room.

"Water by water," Raven was calling, with no trace of tremor in her voice, up to the dark figure standing in the midst of the glare.

"Evil begone through time and space!" Toller held both arms above his head, and Cally thought she recognized the relic gripped in his right hand. "Fire by fire," Raven intoned, "evil begone without a trace!"

"That's cute." Anderson Toller stopped his chanting to laugh gently. "Nice one."

"And it might work," Danya called to Raven, "if he were a demon or something. But he's not. He's just a man!"

This last she spat between her teeth into the light at the top of the stairs, but she shrank back when the dark figure lowered its arms and stepped forward. Ben was quick to reach across the crate, then, but Raven was quicker. She had already ducked into the shadow of the stairs.

As Toller moved away from the light at his back, it became easier to see his face. It was the ordinary face of the ordinary man Cally had met before, his expression as calm and congenial as always. He resumed chanting softly, holding his relic in front of him, and he looked from one to another of them as if he was happy to see them all.

Cally glanced up and down along the littered, hard-packed dirt floor. Though the sides of the room extended away into what seemed like infinite darkness at either end, the place reminded her otherwise of an ordinary basement. They were standing, she realized, in the Tollers' cellar, in Anderson Toller's so-called "spirit workshop," which she had tried to enter once before from their kitchen. She was not surprised, looking behind her, to see an ordinary cinder-block wall, dingy and gray, with a gaping hole in its middle.

Cold air poured in through the opening, stirring the cobwebs draped along arching joists above her head, but this space was not itself preternaturally cold. The chill here was only the ordinary dankness of any basement. Even so, she could still hear the sounds of a ghoulish battle going on outside. She knew they were not, as Mima might say, in Warrenton anymore. They were inside the Fortress of the Dead. They were in the very heart of the Nocksgall.

She recalled how Bree had once referred to the Nocksgall as "more of a prison, really." Looking along the walls at all the objects stacked on moldy shelves, some four or five deep, Cally knew somewhere in this place were the items Geraldine Toller had used to trap George and the other Vale House ghosts. She had no idea which one George's spirit was bound to, let alone where it might be stashed, but that was not the only reason she made up her mind, in that moment, to take all of them with her when she got out of this place. Every single one of them.

And she knew the way out was not behind her, back into the black battle plain. If they were ever going to get out of this place, they would have to get past Anderson Toller.

She was glad she realized this before Toller ceased his chanting all together, because when he did, the opening behind them closed so swiftly the ground shook beneath her feet. Only the little window, obstructed with stubs of broken iron bars, remained. Through it, Cally could still hear the sounds of crying spirits and battling Sidhe outside. As Toller stepped down the first stair, the Sidhe battle-cries rose in a victorious roar all around. With his next step, the tide of the fight turned again, and now the deep moans of unwilling spirit soldiers overwhelmed the faerie voices.

Cally didn't, couldn't, wish for either side to win or lose. "You have to stop!" she shouted to Toller. "You have to let them go!"

He lowered the relic, holding it almost carelessly at his side. She thought it looked like some kind of four-armed cross, made of a dark metal like iron, with long claws at the end of each arm. "In life they served men," Toller said. Though he spoke in English now, he still seemed to be chanting. "In death they serve me. I command them now." Even as he spoke, the sounds of the dark army outside waxed louder. He leaned over the stair railing. Peering down at Cally, he looked for all the world like an ordinary older gentleman, gently smiling with well-tempered reason. "You see? To serve is the only hope for life."

Cally didn't want to dignify such an absurd idea by arguing with it. "Set them free," was all she said.

"Or, my dear, you'll do what?"

Cally looked at her companions, most of them gathered, now, around the wooden box at the bottom of the stair. She knew Ben or Zenbe could probably make it to the stairs and take the object from Toller's hand most quickly, if that was what they were planning. She hoped that was what they were planning.

Toller let out an aggrieved sigh and resumed his descent. Raven crawled the rest of the way under the stairs, while Ben and Zenbe darted to either end of the crate, blocking his way out from behind it. Toller showed no indication of wanting to advance any further, however, once he reached the bottom step. Instead, he set the iron artifact on the lid of the box as if he had no further regard for it. Spreading his empty hands in a demonstration of harmlessness, he turned to face Cally.

Danya stared, open-mouthed, at the relic while Toller resumed speaking. "It's kind of you to come," he said. "Geraldine always said you'd be back, but, you know, it might have been kinder if you had come while she was still alive."

"What happened to her?" Danya didn't sound shocked. She sounded like she was certain she already knew the answer to her question.

Toller answered without taking his eyes from Cally. "It was her time," he said gently. "She made the great sacrifice. She gave the last of her life energy so that we might finish our work."

"I bet you..."

She didn't finish her accusation as, outside, the battle cries of the Sidhe grew much louder. It sounded like the entire battle had moved to within a few steps of the building. Cally couldn't help turning to look through the opening at the base of the wall. She couldn't see anything, and the sounds of the battle moved away again, into the distance.

A loud clang rang through the room, then, but it had not come from outside. Cally spun back around to see Danya standing beside the crate. She was clutching one hand in the other, looking with horror at the metal relic lying, now, at her feet on the hard earthen floor.

Without turning to her, Toller closed his eyes. He vanished, then, but for only a fraction of a second. When he reappeared, he was standing directly on top of the iron cross, looking down at Danya.

"You probably shouldn't touch that," he said, smiling gently.

Ben managed to catch Danya as she reeled backward. Toller made no attempt to pursue her, but quietly bent to pick the artifact up. "It's called a Hand of God," he explained, tucking it into his belt. "It takes years of training, and many wards and protections, to be able to handle one properly. And Ms. Barry, as I recall, you have declined my offer of appropriate training."

Ben and Zenbe dragged Danya back from the crate, and Raven dashed at last from under the stairs to crouch at her side, uttering exclamations of concern. Cally let out a breath of provisional relief when Danya covered her face with her hands and curled into a ball on her side.

"Alright," Cally said. "Please, nobody else try to do anything heroic!"

She saw Ben throw a small, ironic grin over his shoulder at her. He did not need to speak for her to hear his sarcastic reply to that, and he quickly returned his attention to Danya.

"Heroics are not required, here," Anderson Toller assured them all as he laid both hands on the lid of the wooden box. "Come, pay your respects." He lifted the wooden lid with one hand, and with the other he gestured welcomingly toward its interior. A dim, white glow seemed to emanate from within.

Ben stood quickly, his arm held out at one side as if he still held his lost, mythic sword. Instead of looking into the open box, he turned to look at Cally. He was waiting to see what she intended to do, she realized, but if she didn't do something quickly, he would certainly do something himself.

She glanced past Toller to the top of the stairs, where sallow light still waxed and waned in the doorway. Eladha had probably gone that way, she knew, but she had no idea where the door led.

Raven saved her having to make up her mind, for the moment. "It's a coffin!" she said, standing up and walking toward the open box. She reached a hand out to Cally as she paused beside the box. "He's right. We should pay our respects."

Cally didn't want to go anywhere near the box, and not just because she didn't have much respect to pay to Geraldine Toller, dead or alive. But she stepped closer to Raven while Anderson held the lid of his wife's ersatz coffin open with one hand. His other hand rested lightly on the iron cross in his belt, and Cally thought maybe she could use Rum's stick to fling the object far enough across the room that everyone would have time to get up the stairs before

Toller got back from rejoining it.

Even as she rolled her eyes at herself for even thinking she could pull off a complicated kung-fu move like that, she looked down into the box. Her free hand she kept on Raven's arm, in case the body lying there wasn't, strictly speaking, dead.

"Poor, old, sweet thing." Raven smiled kindly down into the open crate. The body, dressed in white silk, was resting atop what appeared to be a deep accumulation of bleached bones. "She was so kind to Willow and me," Raven went on, not seeming to notice this. "When she visited our store, she told us she admired our work." While Raven leaned over the coffin, Cally tightened her grip, prepared to act, but the poor, old sweet thing remained where she lay, the same stiff smile on her face as she'd had in life. Her thin, blue-veined hands were folded across her chest; a white rose had been tucked between them. It was from this rose that the gentle glow came.

As the sounds of the battling fae and ghosts continued to wax and wane outside, Raven straightened and nodded to Toller. "You should have bought her a nicer coffin," she said. "But you've done a nice job of honoring the body." Cally wanted to shake her.

She shook herself, instead. Raven's blathering had reminded her of Geraldine's account of visiting the Wyrd Systers shop, and now Cally thought she had figured out which object, somewhere in this dismal pit, George might be bound to. He had never shown any interest in toy trains, or in vases. He had come here to try to rescue his friend. He would have been attracted to an object that would allow him to be close to another soul.

She stopped eyeing Toller's iron cross, stopped glancing up to the door above. She wasn't going anywhere without what she'd come here for.

Turning away from the ghastly display in the crate, she spoke loudly enough for the others to hear. "Raven, we need to look for those stones, the two halves of the geode you sold to this woman." Then she faced Toller as squarely as she could. Her voice shook as she spoke, because she had every idea how foolhardy she was being, but she said, "If you'll excuse us, sir, we're here for our own Dearly Departed."

Toller nodded, a patient, resigned expression on his face.

"I'll do you one better." His voice was no longer gentle and decorous. "You can join them." The lid of the box shook as his grip on it shifted. He glanced up, listening through the joists to the sounds of the battle. "You can all join them. They could use the extra help."

He heaved the lid open the rest of the way, letting it fall with a boom onto the floor on the other side. The soft glow emanating from the rose in Geraldine's hands waxed quickly to pure, white brightness.

49 - Give Us Iron, Give Us Rope

Cally pulled Raven away from the coffin. Toller didn't seem enthusiastic, himself, about sticking around. He scurried sideways around the end of the crate, heading for the stairs, but Ben reached the stairs first, blocking his retreat. With a grunt, Toller turned his back to Ben and glared through the white light at Cally instead.

Even empty-handed, Cally knew Ben could take Toller down in less than a moment. The only wild card was the iron relic Toller had pulled from his belt. This he gripped at its center, with its iron spikes extending from his fist in an X. He held it at arm's length across the crate toward Cally.

"Don't make me do this," he said in a somewhat rushed attempt at a reasonable voice. His eyes had grown wide and round, and as he spoke his glance flicked downward into the glow above Geraldine's body. "I am not warded against mere physical attacks, you see." He turned his head, nodding, to Danya, Raven and Zenbe each in turn. When his gaze settled back on Cally he said, "If any of you were to attempt to touch me, I would have to call back some of my spirit thralls to defend me. They seem so close to victory, now, out there." Without taking his eyes from her, he tilted his head toward the opening in the wall. "But if they have to rush back here to protect me, their strength will be weakened. The fae would destroy many of them. Maybe all of them. I know you don't want them to be destroyed, do you, sweetheart?"

"I'm not your sweetheart." Cally had to squint so see him through the white glow that continued to brighten above the open box. She thought she could perceive movement near the center of Geraldine's reposing body, but when she glanced down, it was not Geraldine who was moving. A slender darkness, like a black tendril, seemed to be emerging from the heart of the rose itself. Wrenching her attention back to Toller, she said, "And I don't think your ghost army is all that devoted to you, either. Are you sure you really want them to come back here now?"

"Ah." Toller seemed to have noticed her glance at the rose. "Yes. It is beautiful, isn't it?" Though his voice had regained its deceitful calm, Cally noticed the hand holding the iron artifact had begun to tremble. "Geraldine always loved roses. There is only one like this one in the entire world, you know. A fitting tribute. My wife devoted her entire life to our dream of a new world order, one where the dead may walk freely in the light, even holding positions of authority, in all realms, not just that of the dead. A beautiful garden where roses are kings and queens. Ms. McCarthy, please don't let her death be in vain."

Cally realized he would, if they let him, keep on talking like this until his spirit army outside either defeated, or was destroyed by, the faerie army.

The glow suffusing Geraldine's body, meanwhile, continued to intensify until Cally couldn't help risking another look at it. The black tendril in its midst had grown, taking on the shape of a wisp with inky arms and legs. As she watched, it developed the equivalent of a head, flame-shaped, with tendrils of its own. Its blackness was so deep it began to seem like the only solid object in the room. Cally didn't understand how nobody else was staring at it, and the only thing that kept her from becoming completely mesmerized was her annoyance as Raven chose that moment to wax eloquent about roses.

"A rose is a symbol of purity," Raven said. "Of perfection. They say the scent of roses means angels are near."

"The rose is also a symbol for the brevity of life," Toller added, nodding, still watching Cally, still holding the iron cross before him in his trembling fist.

"I don't smell any angels," Zenbe pointed out.

"Exactly," said Raven. Then she went on talking about rose aromatherapy. Cally considered strangling her while Toller, wide-eyed and nodding at Raven's words, began visibly to sweat.

And then, suddenly, Cally understood what Raven and Zenbe had been hinting at. She looked past Toller's shoulder to Ben. He stood on his toes three steps up, locked and loaded and ready to go off. With Toller facing her, she couldn't afford to wink or nod. She could only hope Ben understood from her expression that she had a plan and needed another moment to enact it.

He met her eyes and nodded. Slowly, he moved one foot down to the step below him, but otherwise held his ground.

While the rose-light continued to spread into the far reaches of the room, Zenbe took half a step forward, himself, raising one fist and drawing Toller's attention to him. Cally refrained from looking at the box again, and used her stick instead to feel her way, edging slowly closer to the coffin. The stick made just enough of a soft, scraping noise to earn her a sharp glance from Toller. She froze.

Ben, also, flicked a glance in her direction. He reclaimed Toller's attention by sharply drawing in his breath and taking one more step down, audibly this time.

Toller spun to face him. "Now, that is a shame." His eyes flitted from Ben to Zenbe. "I guess this means our little standoff is over. Very well. Have it your way." He turned toward the window and began chanting once again, but in a shrill voice this time.

Ben held his position, neither advancing nor retreating, while the sounds of the battle outside grew nearer and louder, almost overwhelming Toller's voice. Cally resumed edging toward the coffin.

When she felt the stick touch the side of the wooden box, she risked another glance into the midst of the white light. The anthropomorphic shadow was sitting lotus-style just above Geraldine's still body, many tendrils draping and oozing, now, down over either side of the casket. The black bulb serving as its head turned from side to side. It might have been looking at Cally, or at Toller. She couldn't tell, because it had no eyes.

She looked away because the temptation was strong to fixate on it and never look away again. The rose – her goal – lay beneath it. Making sure Toller was still not looking at her, she reached into the casket and laid a hand on the bony knee beneath the silk dress. She had no fear of touching the corpse, but as she felt her way up the body toward its folded hands, she knew she would have to reach very close to, and possibly even through, the black shadow itself to grasp the rose. When her questing hand encountered Geraldine's cold elbow, she shut her eyes. She felt one of the shadowy tendrils brush across her hand like a feather made of ice. Drawing in a breath and holding it, she stepped forward one more time, until her hand found the corpse's cold fingers and the thorny stem of the rose clutched within them. Now she could feel shadow tendrils, several of them, waving softly through her arm like cold wire slicing through skin and bone. She clenched her teeth to stop herself crying out, but she must have made some kind of noise, just the slightest whimper, because Toller's chanting suddenly ceased.

"No!"

Her eyes flew open. Toller had come no closer, but white rose-light reflected menacingly in his eyes as he glowered at her over the top of his iron artifact. "Don't!" he commanded.

Moving no part of her body but her hand, Cally pried the dead woman's fingers apart and reached between them, seizing the rose's stem. The stiff hands seemed reluctant to let go of it, but she twisted it free and slowly raised it, through the shadows and tendrils surrounding her now, and held it between herself and Toller as if in answer to his iron cross.

The noise of the battle outside had ceased. All Cally could hear, now, aside from her own gasping, was a dull groan from the stones of the building itself, as if a weight pressed heavily against its walls. From the corners of her eyes, she could still see inky tendrils curling on either side of her. Some of them wrapped around her, others reached past her.

"What do you think you're doing?" Toller's free hand reached toward her like a talon, but he still did not step forward. "You must stop!" His jowls shook as he seemed to struggle between his need to attack her and his fear of getting any closer to the shadow around her. All pretense of reason was gone now from his voice. "Put the rose down, you idiot! You have no idea what it is!"

"You're right." Instead of releasing it, Cally raised it above her head. "I don't. But I bet you don't want anything to happen to it. Let the spirits go. Let them all go, or I'll destroy it."

She expected Toller to laugh and say something like, "You have no idea how to do that," and he would have been right, but the way he looked at the object in her hand made her think he was wishing she actually could make good on her threat.

"Stay back!" His voice had been reduced to a strangled plea. *"Immundus spiritus, parere!"* He raised the iron relic above his head like a hammer, as if he was unable to think what to do with it anymore besides throw it at her.

That was the limit of what Ben could take without acting. He broke like a river through a dam and landed upon Toller from behind. As he rolled Toller onto his back and pinned his arms to the ground, the relic flew from his hand and landed with a dull clang on the packed earth floor.

Cally took a step toward it. She didn't expect Ben would be able to hold Toller long before he vanished and rematerialized where the cross lay. Holding the rose before her like a shield, she reached out with Rum's stick, intending to fling the artifact further away, down into one of the dark ends of the room where none of her friends were standing.

But Toller did not vanish, and he did not make any other attempt to reunite himself with his Hand of God. Even as Ben straddled his chest and raised his fists to pummel him, Toller twisted around to turn his wide-eyed stare to Cally.

Her lungs burned, she thought her heart stopped, as a black tendril shot from her chest. More tendrils reached around and through her, all of them curling toward Toller. They pulled her forward with them while Toller screamed and struggled to escape the inky wraith.

Ben let him go. He leapt to his feet and ran to Cally, now, his eyes wide with horror, reaching out through the shadowy tendrils toward her. She tried to tell him she was alright, that he should keep away from the shadows, but the voice that came from her mouth was not her own, and she didn't understand the words it said. She didn't know what might have happened if Zenbe had not appeared at Ben's side and pulled him away as if he weighed no more than a child.

Toller, having scrambled to the bottom of the stairs, was trying to climb them but in his terror he seemed to have forgotten how to use his legs. As he pulled himself up the treads with his hands one, and then two, of the tendrils whipped out to wrap around his legs.

Cally felt strange words in a strange voice coming from her mouth once more: *"Sequor quo pergitis!"* It was a female voice, but only the hollow echo of one. *"There is nowhere you can go that I will not follow."* Masses of shadowy tentacles flailed out all around her to draw Toller back down to the bottom of the stairs.

She didn't watch as he landed screaming on the ground,

enveloped in a writhing cloud of blackness. Whirling around to face her companions, Cally was not surprised to see them all staring at her. More precisely, they were staring at the rose still clutched in her hand. Its light was blinding, now, and the wisps of shadow emanating from it were blacker than the pit of Hell. She wondered where the human-shaped figure at their center had gone. It only took her a moment of looking around, not at the tendrils but at the horrified faces of her friends, to understand where it was, now. It was standing where she was standing. Its shape and hers had become one.

Released from Zenbe's grip, Ben ran to her side. He was unable to bring swords or fists to bear upon what was happening to her, so he simply wrapped his arms around her. She wanted to tell him she was alright, but she was afraid of what might come out of her mouth. This was not what she had meant to happen when she'd seized the rose. She had only wanted to use it as leverage to coerce Toller.

Toller's cries grew softer and less frequent, muffled by tightening ropes of shadow. As the whimpering mass slowly began to sink into the ground, taking what was left of Toller with it, she felt a voice pushing at the back of her throat. She pressed her face into Ben's chest and refused to let her mouth open.

Deprived of her throat, the voice spoke from the air all around instead. "Finish it!"

It was Geraldine Toller's voice. "Finish it now!"

Cally twisted around to look at the coffin. The body still lay there, waxy white, cold and unmoving. Even the white glow that had suffused it with what had passed for postmortem serenity was gone. All the light was concentrated in the rose.

She threw the rose down at her feet. It lay there completely undamaged, perfect, radiating black shadows amid pure, white light that was just a little too bright, just a little too pure.

Cally had told Toller she would destroy it. She didn't even know if it could be destroyed, but instinct and horror drove her to attempt to keep her promise. Her other hand still gripped Rum's stick. She raised this above her head and then jabbed it down, through the rose, into the dirt floor beneath it.

50 - The Moon Bridge

Though she jerked her hand back, then, the gnarled stick continued downward into the ground beneath the rose, pinning it to the packed earth. She gladly let Ben pull her backward into his arms. Everyone in the room watched, riveted, as the rose seemed to writhe where it was impaled, twisting itself around the stick. Both stick and rose seemed for a moment to be locked in some sort of wrestling match, or perhaps a passionate embrace. Tendrils and vines wound their way up the crooked stave, while roots springing from the stick's tip wrapped around the rose, spreading through the packed earth floor. Cally stepped back as the roots reached her feet, pushing Ben back in turn, into the midst of their comrades.

What remained of the stick above the ground began to grow, taller as the roots sank deeper. It sprouted tendrils of its own, green and white, twisting upward and outward. Cally could feel rumbling beneath her feet where the roots delved deeper, pushing aside the packed earth, growing thicker and twisting outward. The stick itself thickened, bark splitting along its length, until it resembled the trunk of a twisted tree.

Step by step, everyone backed away as the ground rose in a mound under them. The crown of the tree quickly reached the joists, and it did not stop there. The floor above them broke away from its foundations like a lid being lifted from a box. Fresh, cold air poured into the space beneath, and Cally saw flashes of blue light slipping in, like branching lightning, through widening cracks all around. Dust and cobwebs rained down into her hair while blocks of masonry tumbled around the edges of the room. The gap between the floor and the wall widened until the night sky was clearly visible through it. The stairs, at the base of the tree, tipped over and fell as the tree's growth devoured the bottom steps.

When at last the upheaval stopped, a breathless whispering noise filled the underground chamber, intermittently interrupted by dull thuds of crumbling masonry and lumber still falling around the perimeters of the room.

Cally, her back held tight against Ben's chest, looked around at her companions. They were all looking up into the branches of the tree, watching as tiny leaves, and then small, white blossoms, began to glow softly at the tips of the twigs. Cool, fresh air swirling all around made the little blossoms sway like bells, making everyone in the room inhale deeply, over and over again.

Gently and with a smile of reassurance, Cally peeled Ben's arms from around her. She stumbled, lacking Rum's stick to steady her, through the rubble to the side of the room where the window had once been. The night outside was quiet and still. The ground all around the building rolled in small rises and falls, softer than it had been, and tinged with green. It reminded her, just for a moment, of standing inside the hill where Eladha had once led her.

She saw no sign of Eladha, or of Michael Dawes, or of the battle that had been going on. The entire horizon, as far as she could see, shone silver, not with the sunrise that would never come here, but with ranks of Sidhe standing silently all around. The fae army was all she could see under the black, star-sprinkled sky.

"Where are the ghosts?" she asked no one in particular.

Ben was at her side, but he had no answer to this, and he didn't bother looking out at the Sidhe. He only put a shaking hand out to her and said, "I thought I'd lost you for sure, that time."

She stood back from the wall and looked down at herself. She didn't see any dark tendrils protruding from her torso. She looked across the ruined room to her companions. Their faces no longer bore horrified expressions. In fact, most of them were not even looking at her. Danya and Zenbe were picking through the rubble.

"I think our ghosts are back," Danya called across the room to her. She had gathered an armload of knickknacks and was looking around for someplace safe to put them. "See?" She held up a brass candlestick. Cally didn't see anything about it to indicate it was inhabited by a spirit, but she was not about to question Danya's instincts on these matters anymore.

The tree in the center of the room seemed to have stopped growing, at the point where its trunk was so thick all of them together might not have been able to join hands around it. The stairs had been completely obliterated. The stairs were a moot point, anyway, as there was no longer any door at the top of where they had once been.

"The queen did tell me getting home again would be the real trick." Cally looked back at the landscape outside. That was a way out but, she knew, it was not the way home.

"Speaking of the queen..." Ben began, but he didn't finish. Zenbe and Raven were noisily dragging the wooden crate, empty now because it had been tumbled several times in the course of the upheaval, across the room to position it against the wall. Here, Zenbe held it steady while Raven climbed onto its upturned bottom.

"It's nice out here," she reported, stepping out onto the ground. "Not as cold as it was."

Ben held out an arm, apparently to help Cally do the same, but she shook her head.

"We can't leave them here," she said. "The ghosts. The objects they're bound to." She looked across to see Danya nodding in agreement.

"No," Ben agreed. "We won't. I promise. But..." He nodded over the top of the wall, to where they could see Rianwynn and a retinue of her ladies approaching across the empty hills. "It would be more politic to be standing on her level when she arrives."

She let him help her clamber up to the ground, then, and turned back to help him do the same. Raven was right: the air, while not exactly warm, was pleasant, the breeze mild. The ground at her feet was flocked with short grass and a sprinkling of pale, tiny flowers.

She dared a glance upward. The only thing that kept her from succumbing to the illusion of being back in her own world was the stars. Those were the same uniform dots of light, forming no constellations, just as she'd seen on the night she'd first tried to cross the meadow to the Nocksgall.

But the moon itself was in its proper place, between the horizon and zenith, not at zenith itself. It was full but that, now, was as it should be.

Danya crawled last out of the hole in the ground. "I guess we could collect everything into that old crate," she called to Cally, gently piling her armload of knickknacks in the grass, "since the bones have been dumped out of it. But I still don't know how we would get it home. She gave Zenbe a long, considering look. "Maybe we could make it into a makeshift..."

"Don't!" Mima, running ahead of the Sidhe contingent, arrived first. By the time she reached Cally's side, she had resumed her human form. "Don't you dare say it out loud. It's bad enough having to carry you pathetic humans so often. But we will not pull wagons. We are not beasts of burden!"

"I would..." Zenbe began, but Mima cleared her throat loudly as the queen and her ladies drew near.

"Well," Cally mused quietly to Ben. "The queen does owe me a gift, now. I was hoping to ask for something a bit less prosaic, but..."

Ben smiled and drew her to his side, turning to face his mother. "Try to save it," he advised from the side of his mouth. "There may yet be another way." He bowed as Rianwynn stopped before them.

Cally bowed, as well, as the queen's ladies arranged themselves to her right and left. Aileen was among them, and she smirked at Cally while the rest of them stood silently, eyes forward.

The queen left them there, walking left and then right along the rift in the ground, inspecting the darkness below with a critical eye. She finished by looking up at the tree reaching well above the ground, now. Her expression softened as she tilted her head back to gaze up into the branches and the blossoms at their tips. There was no longer any trace, in the tree's crown, of a floor or ruined building. As Cally followed Rianwynn's gaze, a soft wind shook the branches and a rain – she couldn't tell whether it was raindrops or pale, insubstantial petals – showered down on them all for the briefest of moments.

A gentle smile was playing at the corners of the queen's mouth by the time she looked back at Cally and Ben. "Well," she said. "That is quite something."

Her words reminded Cally of what Ian May had used to say, whenever he couldn't think of what to say, and she found herself fighting importune tears as she tried to remember the word he'd once taught her to describe the smell of rain.

The queen returned to the head of her personal guard and,

adjusting the sword at her belt, reassumed her imperious posture and expression. "There have been losses on both sides," she informed.

"We were all on the same side!"

Cally looked around to see who had blurted this defiant remark, but the queen's ladies had turned their eyes to her, and she realized she was the one who had spoken.

Aileen winked at her. "It's been nice knowing you, Cally."

Rianwynn did not blast her for insolence, however. She merely nodded, saying, "It seems you would make a good queen, at that, Callaghan McCarthy. Perhaps I shall allow my son to marry you after all, regardless of what the Fomorians may think."

Cally opened her mouth, then shut it and thought for a moment before speaking again. "If it please your majesty," she said, "there's actually something else..."

Rianwynn did not seem interested in hearing what it was. She turned to address all present. "This tree which the McCarthy woman has caused to be here," she said, "is our path home, now. But for the humans in our midst, there is little time left. The moon will soon pass its full and begin to wane. We must hurry."

With a single, graceful flick of her wrist, she waved the assembled Sidhe toward the opening around the foot of the tree. Immediately, they all began leaping into the pit, dashing into the darkness and gathering items from the rubble within. With a little cry of gratitude, Cally joined them.

She followed the shelves, tumbled now, along the far wall of the pit. She knew it was wrong of her to ignore most of the figures and baubles spilled there in her search for two specific objects, but she assuaged her guilt with the knowledge that the Sidhe were very thorough, gathering everything into their arms and carrying it all back outside.

Though they ignored the bones scattered across the ground where the stairs had once been, the faerie warriors took a moment to arrange Geraldine's tumbled corpse more decorously in a hollow between the tree's roots. To the iron Hand of God, still lying nearby, they gave a wide berth. Cally saw Zenbe stoop to look closely at it. When he reached down and picked it up, it did not seem to hurt him in any way. She still wanted to suggest to him this might not be such a good idea, but as he straightened, it seemed to vanish in his hand.

Then her foot kicked something, which rolled away from her across the packed dirt.

She fell to her knees, scooping it up in both hands from where it rolled against a broken shelf. It was half of a geode, but of course she could not be sure which half, or whether it housed George or the Preacher. Stuffing it into her jacket pocket, she continued searching on hands and knees all around the place where it had lain.

"Here." A slender, white hand lowered into her view, holding the other half of the stone sphere. As soon as Cally had tucked it, also, into her jacket, Aileen grabbed her arm and pulled her to her feet. "We have to get going. You go in front." As Sidhe scoured the ground all around her, picking up the items she had not, Aileen gave Cally a shove toward the line of already laden warriors climbing out onto the grass.

The host had assembled in ranks facing the tree. As the last of the Sidhe emerged from the hollow, Cally saw Ben waving her toward him. He and the other humans in their company stood just behind the queen and her personal guard. Cally hurried to her place beside him, while the rank and file of the Sidhe continued to form ranks behind her, each bearing random objects in their hands.

As if on a command Cally could not hear, the entire assembly stepped forward. Cally and her friends hurried to keep up. They followed the queen in a steady march, clockwise around the tree. As they circled, once around and then twice, the tree seemed to grow both taller and farther away. By the time they had made three full circuits around, Cally felt she was looking at it from across a wide meadow. It stood now at the crest of a low mound, holding the moon and strange stars in its arms.

Heading away from the tree, the company passed down a broad slope to where Cally could see the reflection of the moon glittering on water below. A broad river flowed between the hill on which they stood and the next. The slope rising beyond appeared to be cloaked with trees.

Rianwynn and her ladies stood aside, leaving Cally and her companions standing alone, facing down the slope with the fae army at their backs. The queen waved a hand toward the bright water and said, "You must hurry. The moon bridge will not last much longer. In order to cross, you will have to tell the truth."

With that, she and her guard turned away and marched back up the hill. The rest of the Sidhe army, continuing downhill to the water, parted to walk around Cally and her friends. They walked silently to the edge of the water, each still carrying inhabited objects in their arms. There they paused only a moment before walking on, across the reflection of the moon as if it were made of mithril rather than water and light.

"The goddess is alive," Raven breathed, staring down at the river and the reflection rippling across it. "And magic is afoot!" She began walking down to the riverbank. "It's so beautiful!" she called back over her shoulder.

"It is," Cally agreed. She glanced back at the others to make sure they were following, then hurried to catch up with Raven. "Let's go tell Willow about it."

She meant to go first, to make sure it really was safe for mortals, but Raven was already walking across the rippling circle of moonlight. The Sidhe who had gone ahead of her vanished about halfway across, but Raven continued smiling after them, as if she could see them walking up the hill, through the trees on the far side. She glanced back at Cally once, nodded and smiled, and then stepped forward, vanishing into the night above the water.

51 - Dead Honest

Cally wasn't sure, but she thought she could see silver shadows slipping through the trees on the far side, making their way up the hill. Maybe she just hoped she was seeing them. As the remainder of her party gathered around her, she swore and said, "Alright, let's not let Raven get too far ahead of us. We don't know what's in those woods over there, after all."

She turned and stepped out over the water, where the ripples glittered most brightly. There, her foot seemed to encounter a barrier, solid as a stone wall but soundless. She reached forward. She didn't feel anything, but she was still unable to extend her hand beyond the edge of the water. Behind her, she heard Ben laugh.

"I don't see what's so funny," she said as he came to stand beside her.

"You heard the queen," he said. "You have to tell the truth. Raven is honest to a fault, so it was no problem for her." He was still grinning as he put an arm around her and looked across the water.

"My kind are incapable of lying in any case," Mima said, walking around them to the edge of the water. "But I'm sure that still counts." She stepped out onto the bright water and walked away across it.

Zenbe paused to look at Cally. "She's lying," he said. "No barrier can stop her. Or me. I'll make sure Raven is okay." Then he, too, was treading softly across the water. As he caught up with Mima, they vanished together from Cally's view.

Danya stood on the bank, now, looking across with a worried expression. "Well I certainly can't say I've never lied, so I hope..." She hesitantly put out her hand. "Oh," she said. "Oh, I see." Extending her hand fully, she looked up as if she were looking into someone's face. "Yes," she said, and then, "Well, no. It was actually me." She smiled, looking sheepishly back at Cally and Ben as if she thought they'd heard her confess to a grave sin. "Sorry. But I guess that's all you have to do. Just answer truthfully." She shrugged and turned away, stepping out onto the water to disappear halfway across, just as the others had.

"What are you grinning at?" Cally found her irritation growing as she saw Ben still looking at her with amusement in his eyes.

He shook his head. "It's nothing," he said. "It's just that we've finally figured out what I'm better at than you are."

"Well I knew it wasn't anger." She was starting to feel like she might soon demonstrate how good she could be at that.

His grin turned to a gentle smile and he took both her hands in his. "It's truth," he said. "I lost the heart to lie a long time ago."

She opened her mouth but couldn't think of a good defense.

"I'm not saying you're a dishonest person," he went on. "But you still don't fully trust yourself or others, so you still hide yourself sometimes. Well, a lot. But I see you, and I love everything about you.

"I'll tell you what," he said, pulling her into his arms. "I'll tell the truth for both of us."

"Oh, you're *that* honest, are you?" she snarked, but he stepped sideways, taking her with him, and then she had to admit he was right. They encountered no barrier and she saw their feet, when she looked down, standing toe to toe upon the bright ripples.

Without letting go of her, Ben turned his head toward the water. When she followed his gaze, she saw a tall, hooded figure standing a few steps away on the moonlight bridge. "Oh," she said. "That's what Raven was talking about."

The hooded figure didn't frighten her. She'd seen it many times before. In the bright moonlight, its robe seemed lighter in color than Cally remembered, more blue than gray. But it still carried a lantern above its head; a loop of chain, each link bearing keys of different sizes and shapes, still hung from the belt binding the figure's robe around it. The only real difference, this time, was a noticeable gap along the chain where one of the keys seemed to be missing.

"The Crossroads Ghost."

"Cally. You know that's not a ghost."

"No," she agreed. "It's not. That's just what the people of Woodley call it." Raven had been right – it probably was actually a goddess of some sort.

In the past, whenever Cally had encountered this specter, it had held out a hand toward her, and she had learned (after figuring out yelling at it did no good whatsoever) to reciprocate by reaching back. It was their only real form of communication: a gesture of acknowledgement of their mutual tasks in the world.

It wasn't holding its hand out to her this time. Cally tried to extricate her arm from between herself and Ben so she could try extending her own hand first, but he only held her tighter. He was looking up attentively into the darkness of the hooded face, as if he could hear the specter speaking. Cally had never heard this being speak, before, and she didn't hear anything now, but Ben answered.

"Well, yes," he said. "Yes, of course."

He looked at Cally and smiled. "So, there's that," he said. He stepped back and took her hand, then turned to walk across the bridge of moonlight. He vanished from her sight before she felt his hand slip from hers.

She couldn't help the words she uttered, then, not even in the presence of a goddess. If Ben had answered for both of them, this creature must not have accepted both halves of his answer. Cally still stood on the surface of the water, but alone, now, shivering and remembering what Rianwynn had said about the bridge not lasting much longer. Falling into the water was the least of her worries. If the bridge vanished before she got across it, she knew there was no other way to get back to her own world.

The hooded figure still stood upon the reflection, upon the bridge, towering silently between Cally and the far bank, her lantern above her head and her incomplete set of keys at her waist. This time, when the goddess spoke, Cally heard her voice. It reminded her of thunder, and lightning. The breath emanating from beneath the hood smelled like rain.

"Is it your will to wed him?" the goddess asked.

Cally glanced down at the moon beneath her feet, staggering, fighting vertigo. "Of course, I'd be happy to marry him," she said, "but..."

The lantern's light blinded her as the hooded figure lowered it to just inches from her face. "What is your will? Will you wed?" The smell of thunder and rain wafted all around Cally, blowing back her hair.

"I would like to, but..."

The light went out. The goddess turned away, its shuttered lantern still extended as it walked swiftly toward the far shore.

"Wait!"

Cally heard her cry echo through the trees on the other side of the river. She and this goddess may have had a history, Cally knew, but it was not in any way obligated to listen to her. She was a mere mortal, and it owed her nothing. It had not owed her a second chance; it certainly did not owe her a third one, but it did stop. It stood unmoving in the middle of the bridge, its back to her.

"Wait, I do have a Truth for you!" Cally fumbled between the stones in her pocket until her fingers found the edge of the silver crescent. "I think this is the key you're missing."

She dared another step across the moonlight, and she did not fall through. "I'm sorry," she said to the goddess' back. "I do know what truth you wanted to hear from me. But this," she held the pendant out toward the cloaked back, "is the best I can do. And that's the truth."

Not the kind of goddess inclined to laughter, this one paused before turning around, and Cally had the distinct impression something inside that dark hood was at least amused with her. The breath flowing out from it was still rainy, but much warmer. Cally, as she held her offering out at arm's length, suddenly and inexplicably remembered Ian's word for the smell of rain. *Petrichor*.

The amulet was gone from her hand – gone forever, this time, she knew – and now hung glittering brightly from its link in the chain at the goddess' waist. The hooded figure held out its hand, palm up, and Cally reached back, returning the salute, before the figure vanished altogether.

52 - The Keeper

She ran to the end of the bridge and, leaping off before it vanished from beneath her, nearly tripped among the thick, tangled roots sticking up from the mud there. Ben's arm reached out to catch her. He pulled her to him as silver shadows moved away up the hill ahead of them. She could feel his chest expand in her arms as he drew in a deep breath and held it. Tangling the fingers of one hand through the hair behind her head, he said, "I was going to say, I thought I'd lost you for sure that time. Again." She could see his smile flash in the intermittent moonlight through the leaves above them. "I need to stop saying that, don't I?"

She didn't answer. She was looking past his shoulder to a landscape she was certain she recognized. The tangled roots, the trees, the moon, the muddy smell of the bank beneath her feet all reminded her of one of her fondest memories, a memory of when she had first met him. She tipped her head back to look further up the slope, where the Sidhe and their other companions had already reached the top of the hill. Most of all, she remembered the sound of music and the soft, golden light emanating from the doorway far ahead. "Have we been here before?" she asked. "Have we found our way back to old Blackthorn?"

She felt a quiet laugh rumble through his chest. "Close," he said. "Guess again."

He turned, extending a hand for her to follow, and they began to ascend through the forest. The trees ended where the top of the hill leveled out. Here, a cobbled terrace paved the ground between the trees and a tall, fieldstone building with lighted windows all along its front. The door of this building stood open to the night, just as the door of the Fountain in old Blackthorn always did. This building was much taller, though, than any in Blackthorn, and the aromas emerging from the doorway were not those of hamburgers and fries. They smelled more like barbeque sauce and moonshine.

"Oh!" Cally squeezed Ben's hand, probably a little too hard.

"This is Seen's Mill!" It was all she could do not to bounce on her toes like an excited child. "I've always hoped to visit Seen's Mill one day!"

A slender man with a neat, gray beard stood in the light of the door. As Cally and Ben caught up to the line of people filing in past the man, he tipped his woolen cap. "Well met, My Lady," he said. "Well met, My Lord."

"Hail, Keeper." Ben bowed low. "Thank you for holding the door open for us."

"Keeper," Cally murmured. Of course he had a name. Why had she never asked? She found herself wanting to hug him. She refrained, and bowed instead.

"I'm sorry you won't be able to stay long tonight, Lady," said the Keeper, ushering them inside with one arm. "Perhaps you can return another time."

The inside of the inn also reminded Cally of the Fountain, but only slightly. The common room was much larger, with forked columns holding up the ceiling beams. Lanterns swinging from these illuminated the space instead of electric stage lights. There was a stage, of sorts, but the players sat upon it in a circle of wooden chairs, facing one another and playing fiddles and pipes. The inn's patrons paid Cally and Ben and their entourage little mind as they all hurried through to the back of the room.

Cally couldn't help looking around for Jerry Garcia as she followed the others. She didn't see him, but she did recognize the biker she'd often seen eating chili-cheese fries at the Seven Forks diner. She couldn't tell what he was eating, this time, but she didn't stop to look. Everyone else (save the Keeper, who picked up a white towel and began wiping the bar) had already ducked through the narrow doorway at the back of the room.

53 - Holding the Doors Open

Lowering her head to duck under the crude lintel, Cally found herself in a small, dusty room illuminated only by a bare bulb hanging overhead. Dozens, it seemed, of fae were crowded cheek-to-shoulder with her human companions in the room. Raven and Danya were picking up baskets and packing crates from the floor and tipping dust out of them. These they set upright on equally dusty tables while Sidhe circulated around the room, dropping the objects they bore into containers. Danya and Raven were sneezing as they retrieved packing crates from the corners; Ben started to sneeze, and Cally felt herself needing badly to sneeze. The Sidhe did not sneeze but moved swiftly to discharge their burdens and leave the room again through the low door at the back.

Sneezing at last, Cally looked across to the far wall, where she knew another door should be. It was there, standing open to the Wyrd Systers Books and Gifts Shoppe just beyond. She could see Willow near the counter, talking to Zenbe and Mima. Beyond them, through gray rain sheeting down over the shop's display window, she could glimpse the softly glowing street lights of downtown Woodley, USA.

As the last of the Sidhe left the lighted chamber, Cally saw a short, gnarled old black man grasp the door in either hand and replace it over the opening in the wall. Turning, he joined the others gathering empty vessels. He was not sneezing.

"Rum!" Cally would have hugged him, but it wasn't apparent to her whether or not anyone else bustling about the room could see him. "Oh," she said, sighing softly. "I'm so sorry. I almost got your stick back to you like I promised, but..." She tried to think of a concise way to describe what had happened to it.

"It's alright," he said. "You brought me something even better."

He stuck a hand behind his beard. From behind the bib of his barbeque-sauce stained overalls, he drew a small, dark object. Cally had to squint to recognize the iron cross Toller had called a "Hand of God." It was much smaller, now, than she remembered, and Rum shoved it quickly back inside his overalls. "I'll make sure it doesn't fall into the wrong hands," he said. Raven reached over his head to set a wooden box on the table in front of him. He ducked, as others began filling the box, out of their way, into the shadows of the corners until Cally was unsure whether or not he was still there.

"Well, I think that's the lot," Raven said, rubbing dust from her hands onto her clothes and smiling happily around the room. She bent to pick a full basket up from the floor, which she carried out into the shop. Willow kissed her quickly and accepted it into her own arms.

Zenbe followed Raven back into the room and lifted two wooden kegs brimming with tchotchkes. Each container seemed far heavier, Cally thought, than someone Zenbe's size should have been able to carry. He turned and handed these to Mima before bending down to pick up two more. Mima settled the kegs, as if they were bags of groceries, onto each hip. "We'll have to hurry," she said. "It's raining out there, and some of these things aren't waterproof."

Not uttering a single word about beasts of burden, Cally picked up the largest basket she could manage and followed the others out of the little room. Willow locked the padlock behind Ben as he came out bearing the last of the packing crates. Raven dropped the tapestry over the door while Willow put the key back into the cash register. Cally followed everyone out into the rain.

Keeping her head bowed to avoid rain getting into her eyes, she almost didn't see Luke as they all crossed Railroad Street. He was standing in his shop door, waving to them as they passed. Merv Arkwright also stood just inside the door of his feedstore, with Andi (Cally assumed, squinting through the downpour) next to him.

It was easier, once they reached the relative shelter of the oaks along the residential district, to look ahead. The wet sidewalk was illuminated by the lights of dozens of porches, where Woodley's citizens and cats stood watching as they passed. All the dogs of the residential district were in evidence, as well, barking as the procession hurried toward Vale House.

"Go in through the back gate!" Cally called ahead to Mima, who had advanced to the front of the line. That, she knew, would save them having to go all the way around Vale House to get out of the rain. As she neared the gate, herself, she could see the warm glow of the kitchen shining out across the back garden. A silhouette stood framed in the light of the doorway, and it brought to Cally's mind all the figures in all the doorways she had faced recently. She wondered, briefly, if she was ever going to finally wake up from this dream, but this time she was far less disheartened as the silhouette waved, and Ignacio's voice called *"Hola!"*

The rest of the company filed in to the yard ahead of her. As Ben turned back to hold the gate for her, she glanced along the street toward the meadow. The gate stood open, as Luke and Mima had thought it should, and in the midst of it, amid flashes of lightning, Cally could see a dark, hooded figure standing with one hand extended toward her.

"Cally!" Ignacio called from the back door. *"Bienvenida a casa!"*

He stepped aside to let her and Ben enter the kitchen. Cally saw Katarina at the other end, holding open the swinging doors as the others passed on through the kitchen to the back hall. "If you don't have enough boxes," Katarina said to them, "I have plenty of baskets!"

"I think we've got everything." Cally wanted to hug both of them, but she hurried through to where the cellar door, also, stood wide to the back hall. Zenbe had already reached the bottom of the stairs. He set down his load and reached up to help everyone else descend the rickety stairs despite their having no free hands with which to hold onto the pipe railing.

Katarina followed them, carrying an armload of dishtowels, and Ignacio followed last, shutting all doors behind him as he went. He had apparently already cleared the workbenches below, as well as some of the shelves nearest the stairs. Katarina distributed dishtowels to everyone as they began unpacking their wet and definitely no longer dusty baskets and boxes.

Cally set her basket down on a workbench and looked around the very ordinary, very safe and familiar Vale House basement, inhaling its perfectly ordinary musty basement smell. She wasn't even disgusted, anymore, by the camel-crickets hopping around her feet. Even so, as she watched the others wiping candy dishes and candlesticks, she had a feeling Vale House was about to become quite haunted again, in ways she could not predict.

"I think most of these are going to have to wait here in the cellar," Ignacio said, holding a red ceramic vase up to the light above him. "Until we can figure out how to safely set them free."

"Yes. Especially some of them." Cally was pretty sure she knew what spirit resided in that vase, and she was equally unsure she wanted to set it free.

Ben left his basket of objects where he had set it and went around to Katarina's side of the table. "Have you seen Bree?" he asked. "Is she...?"

"Still alive!" Katarina laughed. "And cantankerous as ever. She's in your office," she added, looking past him to Cally. "When I went in to offer her a bed for the night, or at least a cup of tea, she just demanded to see you!"

Cally would ordinarily have responded to this by stiffening with dread, but now she couldn't help smiling. "She may have decided to die, but I guess she hasn't specified when."

Ben looked a little dismayed that Bree hadn't asked to see him, instead. "I guess I should go up to her," Cally said to him. "I'll send you up after she's done reading me the riot act."

Feeling in her pocket for the two stone hemispheres still bulging there, she paused at the bottom of the stairs. Turning back, she said to the room in general, "I'll be back to help with all of this." Then, to Ben in particular, she added, "I'll just be a little while. Don't worry about me."

54 - Down to the Crossroads

A soft, blue line of light glowed from under her office door. She opened it quietly and stepped inside. There she saw, in the light of the screensaver dancing on her monitor, Bree lying on the sofa. She was, in fact, still alive, snoring fitfully, but she didn't seem at all cantankerous to Cally at the moment. She'd pulled down the crocheted throw from the back of the sofa and lay tangled in it with one leg sticking out. Her face, paler than it usually was, looked peaceful nonetheless, her brow smooth and her lips pouting. It was all Cally could do to stop herself reaching out to tuck the covers closer under the old woman's chin.

Turning to leave the room, she also had to stop herself reaching out to clear the screensaver as she passed the desk. She wondered if the chat application was still running. If it was, it would be easy for her to scroll backward and read Bree's and Emerald's conversation. The temptation was strong to invade their privacy, but Doctor Boojums was curled up, pretending to be asleep, beside the mouse pad and this helped Cally succeed in resisting.

Besides, she still had an errand to take care of. Removing the geodes from her pocket, she hung her wet jacket on the coat rack. Then, holding the stones against her heart with one hand, she backed slowly out the door and closed it as quietly as possible.

The rain had stopped, and the sky was clearing. As she descended the porch steps, she watched the remaining patches of cloud above the meadow separate into shreds, revealing the stars between them. The light from the moon sinking behind the house lit their undersides with the first truly beautiful light Cally had seen in what felt like a very long time. She had to stop in the middle of the lawn for a moment just to look at it. Then she looked at the geodes in the moonlight. She could not see George's face in them, not at all, not in either of them. She missed him, now, more than she had this entire time.

Passing through the pineapple gate onto the sidewalk, she

saw the porch lights along Main Street had all been switched off, though some of the houses along Gardens Road still had their lights on. The meadow gate still stood open. She didn't see the hooded figure, at first, and thought she had come too late, but when the breeze blew, she was able to make out gray robes swaying gently just beyond the gate, a shadow against the shadows of the meadow.

She stood between the gateposts and bowed. "I need your help," she said. And then words poured out of her in a rush, her heart pouring out to an entity she wasn't even sure had a heart of its own. "I don't know how to free him...them. I know, given enough years, I can learn how to do this myself. And I promise, I will. But I was hoping... I was dreaming when I got him out of there, I would be able to see him grinning down at me from the gallery during breakfast the next morning."

"It's almost morning now." The goddess did not speak out loud, as she had at the moon bridge, but Cally could hear its rainy voice inside her head like the echo of a dream.

It said nothing further, but continued standing, waiting. The rain-washed breeze blew its robes about it like the gray shreds of the ferryman's shroud.

Cally held the geodes against her breast as the goddess waited, and then she cleared her throat. Shifting the stones to one hand so she could hold out the other, palm up, she said, "I've been thinking." She looked down at her feet, then left along the fence, past Vale House and down to the pond, and then back to the figure in front of her. "I'm thinking, some things are going to change around here. Maybe it's time to leave this gate open, for instance. I'll have to consult with the others about this, of course. It's not my decision alone."

The goddess gave no sign she approved or disapproved, or even that she had heard.

"I'm also going to advocate for the removal of the railroad tracks," Cally went on. "Some people aren't going to like it, but the entities trapped beneath the iron need to be set free."

She understood, or hoped she did, these changes in the status quo would make Woodley an even stranger place than it already was. On the one hand, it would become more open to other worlds and peoples and, at the same time, it would become even harder for ordinary people to find.

The breeze grew stronger, and a bit warmer at the same time. The goddess' garments fluttered to one side and Cally thought she saw golden hair flying, if only briefly, out from within the dark hood.

"Very well, then, Callaghan McCarthy," said the goddess at last. There was no hint of thunder in its voice, now, but Cally thought maybe she detected a hint of crashing waves, low and soft. "Put down your burdens and step back."

At first Cally thought the goddess was telling her to step back from the responsibilities she had resisted for so long and had only just made up her mind to shoulder after all. She thought she was being fired. She opened her mouth to protest, but then it dawned on her that the goddess was actually referring to the lumps of stone she was clutching.

She laid them down, side by side, gently in the grass at the goddess' feet. She forgot the part about stepping back. The goddess bowed and vanished, though the sound of the sea on the breeze remained. Cally bent over the stones, trying to determine if they were still inhabited. "George?"

"Cally! What are you doing here?"

She could never have mistaken George's voice, or his unique accent, in a thousand years. She spun around to see him grinning at her just the way he always did, and it was all she could do not to run forward and try to wrap her arms around him.

"George." All she could do was breathe out his name, and even so it took her a minute to speak past the tightness in her throat. "Georgie. Oh, my god, it's so good to hear your voice. Did I ever tell you how lovely your voice is?"

He laughed but, looking around him, said, "You shouldn't be here. What are you doing here?"

"It's fine, Georgie. I went to the Nocksgall to get you, and I've brought you back to Woodley. You're home now. Don't worry, I brought your friend, too. He's here...somewhere, I'm sure. Let's go home."

She knew he couldn't take it, but she put her hand out to him anyway, and turned back toward Vale House. She didn't see the porch light. At first, she thought that must be because it was so close to morning. Bethany must have arrived early for work and switched it off. But she didn't see the pineapple gate, either, or the oaks and crape myrtles. Instead, a long, raised walkway, like a wooden pier, stretched across the ground where they should be. Beyond it lay only sky and stars. She looked back at George, understanding, now, what he had been asking her, but she was still unable to answer.

Moon-limned shreds of cloud still sailed overhead, but where the meadow should have been, all Cally could see was darkness that heaved like a wave. The smell of the sea confirmed for her that that was exactly what it was. She was standing on loose sand, well-trampled and strewn with bottles, broken shells, and seaweed tangled with bits of net and rope. When she turned around, instead of the oaks and front porches of Gardens Road she saw dark silhouettes of low, crooked buildings, some lit, though dimly, from within. Raucous sounds of human voices rose and fell from within the lighted doorways. Cally closed her eyes and clenched her teeth, wondering if she was ever going to wake up from this dream. This time, however, the dream invoked more of her senses. Whenever the stiff sea breeze behind her subsided, the stench of rotting garbage and human effluent swirled around her.

"Woodley is very far away," George said. "This is the settlement of Port Royal in the colony known as Hispaniola."

"Port Royal doesn't exist anymore," Cally reminded him. He had told her this himself, long ago. "Please. What are we doing here?"

"As for myself, I came here for my friend. This is the night Joseph kills me." He went on to explain how he intended to meet his friend's spirit, here at the moment of their discorporation, to help him cross over properly into the afterlife this time, but all Cally could do was mutter "Joseph" to herself. Just like that, the Preacher's ghost had a name, and was a person.

"...and you're right," George was saying. "Port Royal is not going to exist for very much longer. That's why you can't stay here. Anyway, it's not a good place for a nice lady like you."

Cally didn't bother telling him she would have liked nothing more than to not stay here one second longer. She only hoped he knew some way to get them out of there. She certainly couldn't imagine one and, as she tried, a horrifying thought occurred to her. "George! Did you mean not to come back to Vale House at all?"

"Shh." He turned to look at one of the noisome buildings, where the laughter had changed timbre. Now it sounded more like angry shouting. A wave of vomit-scented air emerged from the door as a dozen or more staggering men emerged into the street. They were moving, a dark mass of stomping legs and flailing arms, in the general direction of the dock from which the pier stretched. A handful of women followed, also shouting and waving. At first Cally thought they were exhorting the men to stop, but then she realized they were actually cheering them on.

George, too, began to walk toward the pier, paralleling their progress, along the edge of the water. Some part of Cally's mind noticed he wasn't leaving any footprints, but she followed in their absence, because she couldn't bear the thought of being left behind on this awful beach. As he walked, George said, "Cally, you might not want to watch this. Don't worry; it's okay. I need to be here when it happens. I need to tell Joseph it's alright, so he can cross over."

"No, George, it is *not* alright!" The crowd to her left

stumbled out of the street and began to seethe onto the dock. The men's shouts grew louder, punctuated by the women's high-pitched jeers. Cally couldn't make out what most of them were shouting. At least four languages were represented, and only two of them seemed even slightly familiar to her. The drunken brawl moved from one side of the dock to the other; knives and broken bottles flashed above heads in the moonlight.

When George reached the pier, Cally tried one last time. "Come on, George. Let's get out of here. Let's just go home. Please!"

He merely smiled his gentle smile, then turned away and began to climb the piling where the pier met and then extended out over the surf. Trash-laden waves swirled beneath, depositing broken barrels, boots, and more bottles on the sand around the pilings.

"Stay out of sight," George whispered down to her. "These are not very nice men."

She agreed with him on both counts and did her best to duck under the shadow of the pier. Just as quickly, she stepped out again, because the sounds of squeaking and the scurrying of feet filled the darkness beneath.

At least one of the voices in the crowd changed, then, from a shout to a scream. Cally couldn't say it was George's voice – not really – but it was young and male. It called out three words in a language she didn't understand, before it was cut off mid-word. After that, what had been a noisy altercation became a full-blown free-for-all.

Cally took George's advice and looked away. The shouts, screams, and the sickly thumps of fists on flesh made the faerie battle she'd recently witnessed seem civilized by comparison. She kept her eyes on George, instead, where he stood on the pier against the background of stars, watching quietly.

When one of the women in the crowd shouted a sharp warning, the sound of fighting ceased abruptly. Cally turned to see most of the fighting men now facing back toward the town. There, a tall man had emerged, swaggering, not staggering, from the building they had all so recently left. As he took several long steps toward the dock, the few men still brawling became still, gaping at him. The man put a hand on the curved sword at his hip. He did not draw it, and he did not speak, but one by one, men on the dock began to slink away, scurrying through the shadows, back toward the buildings to resume their debauchery. When only a handful remained, the silent figure barked an order.

The women parted as he turned, letting him pass, and then followed him back into the hovel from which he'd come. When he was gone, the men remaining on the dock began to work together. Some of them grabbed barrels and drew water from the surf, while others bent to lift dark shapes at their feet.

George watched dispassionately as two of them carried a thin, dark body to the end of the pier. The men did not seem to see him. Muttering in low tones, they dangled the lifeless form over the water by one leg before dropping it in headfirst into the sea. The waves accepted it completely as it slipped beneath them with the softest of splashes. The men turned back to fetch more bodies, while other men poured dirty sea water onto the boards to wash gore from them.

The next body they dragged to the end of the pier seemed heavier. The men who brought it had to lay it down parallel to the edge of the pier so they could tumble it in. Moonlit waves swallowed it as willingly as they had the first.

The splash had not yet died away when Cally saw another figure appear beside George. She recognized the clenched posture, the sharp shoulder blades of the Preacher's ghost, before he turned so she could see his long, serious face in the moonlight. He turned and turned, looking first at George then at the sea, briefly at Cally and then at the men dragging more bodies to feed to the waves, pouring water upon the boards beneath their feet.

George ignored them, instead speaking his companion's name gently, several times before Joseph finally looked at him. His answer was a question, a croak in a pinched voice. Laying a gentle hand on the man's shoulder, George began to explain, Cally assumed, what had happened. She didn't understand what either of them said, but she guessed they were conversing in French. From what she retained of high-school French she caught the words "*pardonne*" and "*bien*," repeated several times.

The Preacher – Joseph – straightened, then, and looked across the waves to the sky above the horizon. His mouth fell open, hanging soundlessly as he gaped at the stars.

George laid a hand along the side of his face. "*Bien,*" he said. "*Aller.*" Joseph shook his head sharply and stepped back.

"Oh, God," Cally realized. "He's not listening. He's just going to repeat history all over again. George has gone through all this for nothing."

The preacher's ghost must have heard her, because now he looked right at her, for the first time since she'd become aware of his existence. He asked – apparently – who she was, and George seemed to be trying to explain. When Joseph shook his head, refusing to understand, George gently took the man's face between his hands. "I'm blowing it, Cally," George said in English. "I'm not going to be able to change a thing!"

Cally looked up at George's long, brown thumb gently stroking Joseph's cheek, and she put a hand up to her own face. "I envy you," she said to the preacher's ghost. She didn't expect him to understand, but she needed to say it anyway. "All the times I've wished I could hug this young angel. You've been blessed – you've been able to touch him, in your lifetime."

Apparently, Joseph could understand English. In fact, his accent was distinctly British as he cocked his head to look critically at her with one eye. "Are you an angel?" he asked.

She shook her head, and George tugged at Joseph's arm to draw his attention back to the sea and sky. He gestured with a wide sweep of his hand, out past the moonlit swells, past the horizon to the stars beyond it. "*Beaucoup d'anges...*" he said. "Many angels!"

Slowly, the man raised his eyes to where George was gazing and, just as slowly, he nodded. Then he looked at George, keeping him in sight as he began to fade. For a moment Cally was able to see the stars through him, more and more clearly, until only his outline remained.

She panicked, then, thinking when the other man vanished, George would go with him and leave her here, stranded alone in this wretched, doomed place. But when Joseph was gone, George was still there, grinning down from the pier.

"Now let's get *you* out of here!" He jumped down to stand in the sand beside her.

56 - A Star Back To Inverness

"George, you didn't stay just for me?" Cally followed him along the edge of the surf. "I don't mean here in Port Royal. I mean here in this world. You could have crossed over, too, just then..."

He stopped at last, once the noise and stench of the town were well behind them, and looked down at the wet sand beneath his feet. Cally thought he actually looked dismayed to realize he had left no footprints, but when a wave swept along the shore and erased Cally's footprints as well, and he breathed out a soft, thoughtful "Hm."

"If you hadn't been here," he finally said, "I don't think it would have worked. Joseph might not have moved on from this night. But..." He seemed to be looking right through her, as if she were the one who was the ghost. "I also think you had to come here, so you could see it happen. So you could learn how to help spirits cross over to the next world." He shrugged. "Maybe. I don't know. Cally, my time and your time are not the same. You know that. But the main thing is, this time..." He stretched out both arms, indicating the sea and dunes around them. "This is not your time. Even if you could get to someplace safe that isn't about be swallowed by the sea, you can't stay in 1690. You have a whole life back in Woodley. You have people who love you, and a grandson about to be born."

He might as well have stabbed her in the heart. She kept her eyes on him to stop herself panicking. Would she see Woodley, or Vale House, or anyone she loved, ever again? Her children wouldn't even know what had happened to her. Ben would never get another chance to say, "I thought I'd lost you that time." She would never get to hold her grandson. Adam, she suddenly realized, might already have been born now, back in the real world (or as close to the real world as Woodley ever could be, anyway.)

"Is it Midsummer's Day, yet?" she asked. "Georgie, I don't even know what day of the week it is, right now..."

He laughed softly. "I never did pay much attention to days

of the week. Not even when I was alive. But look. You're close: it's Midsummer's Eve." He nodded at the sky as if it were a calendar. She supposed it might actually be a calendar, for someone like him who had spent so many years at sea. He raised an arm and pointed. "See that star?"

She didn't have to wonder which star he meant. It was the brightest above them. Even as she watched, it waxed brighter. She was too far south of the latitudes she'd grown up in to be able to recognize any constellations, here, or to know what the stars should look like. "Is that, I don't know, part of the Southern Cross?" she asked.

"No, that's over there." He pointed in another direction too briefly for her to be able to follow, and then turned back again, turning his palm up as if to cup the star about which he had been talking. It had grown still brighter, giving the illusion of having grown nearer. "*That* is the star back to Inverness."

This again. Cally sighed. "I keep hearing that term, but I don't know what it means."

"It's easy." When he looked at her, she could see stars reflected in his dark eyes. "Inverness is just a word. And words are only symbols." He shook his head. "I thought writers knew that!"

Of course she knew that. "It's the name of a city," she informed him. "Named for the river Ness. Back in the real world..."

"No, it's something completely different. Inverness is a symbol for Home. Here, take my hand."

"You know I can't..."

"Just do it!" He laughed. "Come on. Just try." He held one hand out to her and reached the other up to the sky, spreading his long, bass-player fingers until the bizarre star shone between them.

She did as he said, or tried to. As she expected, her fingers passed right through his. Then, as the star above them grew brighter, she thought she did feel something in the midst of the mist where his hand had once been.

This, too, felt like a hand, but impossibly small and soft. Its fingers closed around one of hers as the sky and sea and sand fell away. Cally felt she was falling with them. Even George disappeared, until her only anchor in space was the tiny, warm hand clutching hers. In George's place, she saw a much paler face, green-eyed, surrounded by a mad halo of golden curls. This face's grin was every bit as puckish as George's, but it spoke to her in an altogether different voice.

"Grandma! Did you forget my birthday?"

She gasped in air that was not air. "Adam." She tried to look around her, but she couldn't figure out how to move without a body, and she couldn't see anything but the child before her. "I'm sorry, Adam. I've been so..."

The sensation of falling ceased so abruptly she fell over into the long, cool grass. Tumbling once, she put out her hands to raise herself to her knees. Across the tops of the grasses and flowers, she could see through the fence to the lights of the porches along Gardens Road. She didn't see the child anymore, but she did see George, standing beside the fence and smiling broadly into the light of the third porch along the road: the Yellow House. The distinct sound of a popping champagne cork punctuated the night, followed by the cheering of voices, kind and happy voices she definitely recognized.

"Better get over there," George said. "They're saying it's a boy."

57 - More Light

Cally sat on the wooden porch steps of the Yellow House with the baby in her lap. The sunshine, starting to feel a little too warm, now, filtered through the leaves onto the sleeping infant's face and Cally cupped a hand over his soft forehead to shield his eyes. Little Adam slept on. The light didn't seem to bother him.

Nothing seemed to bother him. He had barely cried at all during his first three days of life (although, everyone assured her, he had wailed like a warrior when Nell had held him up to experience his first breaths of earthly air.) Cally felt a little jealous of Rosheen for having such an easy baby to handle, but not too jealous. She had a strong hunch Adam was going to make his parents' life very complicated indeed when he got older.

During his naming ceremony he had not even fussed about being passed around the Yellow House living room, through the hands of thirteen different women as they gave him the requisite number of blessings. He had only squirmed once, when a well-meaning newcomer to Woodley had proclaimed that "All women will love him!" Willow, the next in line, ameliorated that curse with alacrity by saying "He shall love whomever he will." Little Adam had gone back to sleep, then, and had not stirred again until Cally, placed strategically as the thirteenth godmother, had taken him into her arms. She'd known what she was meant to say, then, but was unable to say it out loud until he opened his green eyes and smiled at her.

"He is the Star back to Inverness," she breathed again, now, as the sleeping Prince of Faerie wrapped his tiny fingers around one of hers.

"It's true, of course." Nell sighed. After the baby-blessing ceremony, Nell had placed her easel in the middle of the sidewalk outside the Yellow House, facing the open gate into the meadow. She sat there, now, with her elbows on her knees, her chin in her hands, and guests leaving the Yellow House were obliged to step into the lawn and go around her. "I wonder if that's what this painting needs...a big, bright star? No." She stared through the fence into the meadow as if that could, somehow, inspire her to finish the waterfall painting.

Two of Rosheen's relatives helped Bree out of the house and down the porch steps. They stopped at the bottom, and one of them (Cally noticed she had fox feet peeking from beneath her long skirt) turned to tickle the baby under his chin. "Coochie-coo, your Majesty!" she said, then turned to continue on her way. Bree, face pinched with pain, at first refused to take the arm offered to her. Instead she gave Cally a glittering china-blue scowl and said, "You'd better be there. Don't you dare back out of this now."

And that, Cally figured as Bree let the two faerie-hybrid women lead her through the gate into the meadow, was the last of the guests.

She stood and lifted the baby onto her shoulder. "Oh, god..." Turning to go back into the house, she had to stop and steady herself with a hand on the stair railing. Adam cuddled softly on her shoulder, breathing out sweet milk-breath. "He even smells like a real baby!" Tears squeezed from the corners of her eyes as she pressed her cheek against him.

"Of course he smells like a real baby." Rosheen had come out onto the porch, and she laughed as she shrugged herself into a front-carrying baby sling. "He is a real baby!" Behind her, Brandon, and Brandon's older sister Kelleigh who had come to Woodley for the festivities, also emerged from the house. Brandon pulled the door shut while Kelleigh helped Rosheen buckle the straps at her back.

Cally helped Rosheen settle the infant into the carrier, but she was looking at Brandon and Kelleigh when she said, "I know. For now, he is. But they grow so fast."

Rosheen adjusted a couple more straps and patted the baby's bottom. It was impossible, Cally mused, not to pat a baby's bottom in one of those carriers – no race of beings was immune to this.

"Okay, now." Rosheen took Brandon's hand and gave Cally a serious look. "Are you ready for this?" She nodded toward the meadow gate.

"I absolutely am not." Cally didn't even bother to try to

sugarcoat it. She followed Rosheen's gaze. People – people she knew from town, and other neighbors she barely recognized – were walking up Main Street, now, some of them pausing to wave to her as they walked through the gate into the meadow. As she watched, she saw Katarina and Ignacio in colorful, traditional Mexican outfits, strolling arm in arm through the wildflowers toward the first hill east of the fence.

"I don't know, you guys." Cally looked from Rosheen to Nell to Kelleigh. "I'm not sure this is a good idea. I'm really not."

Rosheen swayed from foot to foot, patting the baby's bottom. "Maybe it is," she said. "Maybe it's not. But it's the right idea."

"It's the queen's gift to you," Nell reminded. "Refusing to accept it could cause... well, there would be repercussions."

Cally turned around to see Nell still glowering into her unfinished painting as she went on. "I don't know Cally. I don't know what you should do. I don't even think the Wyrd Systers could tell you, at this point." She lifted her eyes from the vexing canvas and fixed them, if absently, on Cally. "All I know is, well, you know. I probably won't ever get another chance at my happily-ever-after, in my lifetime. But you. You've been given a second chance."

"Helen, don't say that!" Cally knew Nell was not one to lay guilt-trips on people, and that she was merely speaking her heart. She put a hand on Nell's paint-smeared shoulder. "That's... I mean, you never know. You may yet meet a..." She gave up. It was a trite and useless thing to say, and anyway something about the canvas was distracting her. She bent closer, peering at the patch of indigo sky, between two cliffs, above the waterfall in the painting. Her hand reached out for one of the paint brushes. "May I?"

"Of course." Nell scooted her stool back to make room for Cally to stand in front of the easel.

Cally picked up the brush with white paint on it. (*Titanium White*, she guessed. She'd seen enough Bob Ross videos to know one couldn't go wrong with Titanium White.) With only the image in her mind's eye for a guide, she swirled the white paint in a semi-circle upon the patch of sky above the falls. Pleased with how smoothly the paint flowed onto the canvas, she dipped it again and filled in enough white to make the moon gibbous, waxing to full.

"It should have a reflection..." she murmured, standing back a little.

But Nell, leaning forward, had already taken the brush from her hand. "Yes!" She dipped the brush into a slightly brighter shade of white and then dotted a sprinkling of tiny stars around Cally's moon. Moving faster now, she used the same mixture of whites to duplicate the stars in the falling water, until it became a luminous curtain of diamonds.

Nell stood up, then, signed her name triumphantly at the bottom of the canvas, and slam-dunked the brush into the jar of paint thinner. "Thank you, Cally!" When she turned around to look at them all, her face was radiant.

Brandon stepped closer to regard the canvas. "It's a completely different picture now," he observed in a thoughtful tone.

"It is," Kelleigh agreed. "So many more dimensions, all of a sudden. So much more light."

"And now," Nell said, reaching out a paint-smeared hand. "Now that you've helped me find my answer, let's go find yours."

She seemed so happy, skipping like a little girl to the meadow gate, Cally couldn't help but follow.

58 - There May Come a Day

A delegation of the People was standing in the grass, just on the other side of the gate. They surrounded Cally, stopping her progress while Rosheen and the others waved, muttered some encouraging words, and left her there. As a few stragglers walked through the gate to join the crowd gathering at the top of the first hill to the east, the People tugged at Cally's clothing to draw her attention to a long, white garment some of them were unrolling in the grass.

"I can't put that on," she said. She tried to step backward when they advanced on her as if they were going to put it on for her if she didn't do it herself. "Guys, stop! Everyone is watching!"

The People, as one, turned their heads to look up the hill. Nobody was watching. Human people, some having brought lawn chairs, had assembled on the side of the hill nearest Woodley. They formed a sort of semi-circle, facing across the top of the hill to where another crowd of mostly-not-human people had assembled in another semi-circle to balance them. The People then turned and looked behind Cally, through the fence to Vale House. George stood on the porch, gazing across the meadow, not at the crowd but at the horizon a little to the south of it. She looked past Vale House to the houses along Main Street, but all of them were empty now, their residents already gathered behind her. Everyone's attention was fastened on a handful of official-looking Sidhe forming a line along the crest of the hill. Nobody was watching.

Cally looked at the dress the People had prepared for her. It resembled one of Nell's hand-painted t-shirts, but much longer. On the front, in a style not exactly like Nell's, was painted a beautiful rendering of a tree in full leaf, its branches embracing blue sky all the way up to the neckline, its roots entwined in brown earth at the hem.

"It's lovely," she had to admit. She scrutinized it carefully to make sure there was no cleverly camouflaged lettering about naked unicorns. "Okay, but listen. There's something I want you to promise me."

As they waited silently to hear what she had to say, she glanced up to the line of figures forming along the crest of the hill. Sidhe and other fae were lining up behind Ben, facing the top of the south side of the hill – Cally saw Ben's eldest daughter Ana among them. Facing up from the north side of the hill were Cally's own family and dearest friends from Woodley. Rosheen, she noted, stood on this side. At the very peak of the hill, just in front of Ben, a conspicuous gap remained.

She turned back to address the People. "Do you see that gate over there?" She pointed to the iron gate standing open to Main Street. The People all nodded. "I want you to promise me you will not go through it. Ever. Not even out of curiosity. The gate will remain open. For as long as I live, anyway. But I'm afraid our culture is...infecting yours. I don't want you to lose yourselves. You're precious to me. Do I have your word?"

They gazed through the gateway, down the part of Main Street they could see from where they stood. Though she still didn't understand their expressions well, Cally thought some of them did look curious. But one of them, near the back of the crowd, said, "See? She really will make a great queen!" Then, in different voices and languages, they all blurted their promise to her.

"Alright, then." She skinned quickly out of her jeans and kicked them aside. She barely had time to stand upright before they had surrounded her, pulling the soft dress down over her head. She had to admit it fit her well.

Cheering, then, they half pulled and half pushed her up the hill. Near the top, a few steps away from the line of standing figures and the Cally-sized gap in it, they stopped and backed away. As she watched them blend backward into the crowd, her knees threatened to give way. She swayed where she stood, not sure she could complete the remaining steps herself.

Gasping for air, she looked to where Ben stood facing the gap with his eyes closed, face tilted up to the sun. He was wearing a garment he, also, had probably not chosen for himself. She liked the way it draped over his shoulders and hips, but she suspected he might think it would look better on a glam rock star. Grinning at this thought, she let out her breath and stepped into the space in front of him.

He opened one eye and looked down. "I was afraid you wouldn't come," he said.

"Of course I would have," she almost lied, but stopped herself in time and instead told the truth. "I'm with you."

"And I'm with you."

From the half of the line stretching behind Ben's back, she saw figures step out, turn, and begin to approach. Aileen supported Bree with one hand while holding a silver dagger aloft, like a small scepter, in the other. Rianwynn carried a golden goblet balanced in both hands. The three of them stopped next to Cally and Ben, on the side east of the line.

Cally glanced down to where Bree stood, tottering, dressed in drab, ordinary workaday clothes so unlike the glittering gold and silver of the Sidhe glamour. The old woman didn't look like she should be standing up at all, let alone walking around in a meadow. She looked like she should be lying quietly in a comfortable bed, with loved ones at her side, waiting...

"You're supposed to join hands," she croaked.

Cally and Ben obeyed quickly.

"Your left hands!" Bree corrected. "The ones closest to your hearts."

From either side of the line, then, from behind Cally and then from behind Ben, important citizens of Woodley and ranking fae approached the top of the hill, each bearing long, silken ribbons of different colors. Aileen tucked her dagger into her belt and accepted the ribbons one by one, wrapping each around Cally's and Ben's joined hands while Bree explained, not always in English, what each color meant in the grand scheme of universal love and honor. By the time the last ribbon had been delivered, the multicolored ball wrapped around Ben and Cally's wrists was the size of one of Ignacio's best summer cantaloupes.

Rianwynn stepped forward, then, with the gem-encrusted goblet. Aileen retrieved her dagger from her belt and held it, point downward, above the bowl of the goblet.

Cally choked at the sight of the red wine brimming there. The chalice might as well have been full of her own heart's blood. It was faerie wine, she knew, and she couldn't drink it. Which was to say, she could, but she mustn't. If she did, she would never be able to return from this side of the fence, from Faerie, ever again. She would join the Sidhe court at Ben's side. In Faerie, she would be immortal, but she would have to leave behind all the people standing and seated in the grass at her right hand, her family, her new grandson, and all the people who loved her enough to take the time and trouble to come here today to wish her well. If she drank, she would have to leave Vale House to its fate.

Ben would have to leave the mortal world soon enough in any case, whether he drank or not. She had always known this, as had he. She had always known she would have to face the choice, someday, between going with him and leaving behind everything else she had come to love, or losing him. But now, as she stared at Rianwynn's reflection in the red wine, she understood she faced a slightly different choice, between leaving all she loved, or staying in Woodley and finding herself married to a man she could never see again.

"Let me." Bree's voice intruded into her thoughts. The old woman was reaching up to take the goblet from Rianwynn's hands.

Rianwynn looked down at her daughter, the crone, and did not release the cup. "Your part of the ceremony is over, now. You may go and sit down in the shade." She looked for someone to escort Bree down the hill.

"He's my brother," Bree insisted. "Let me."

Aileen didn't wait for the queen to answer. She reached out to steady the old woman's palsied arms while Bree took the chalice in both hands. Rianwynn did not protest, but she did not step back. She watched with a critical eye as Bree raised the cup between Cally and Ben. With Aileen's help, she didn't spill a drop as she wedged the stem of the vessel between their awkwardly wrapped hands. Through all the ribbons, Cally felt Ben's fingers trying to grip the cup more securely.

Aileen raised the dagger above the wine once more, but Bree ducked her head under the glittering, silvery point to lean into the shadow between Cally and Ben. Muttering so softly only they could hear, she said, "I told you, once, I would dance at your wedding. I wasn't being sarcastic. I will." She tilted her head, left and then right, looking up into Ben's face, and then into Cally's. "But there may come a day I will dance on your grave."

She stepped back again and, as she did, for just one unbelievable second, Cally could have sworn she saw the old woman do something she could never have imagined her doing: she winked.

One of the people from Woodley ran up the hill to offer his lawn chair to Bree, and others helped her settle into it. She slumped there, all her strength spent, not paying any more attention to the ceremony at hand.

Cally looked at Ben and wondered if he had understood what Bree was trying to tell them. She wondered if she had understood it correctly herself. She found herself trembling, but Ben looked quite calm, now. He nodded to her, and she felt his fingers under the ribbons shifting the goblet in his grip and reaching to wrap further around hers.

"Are you ready for this?" he asked.

She didn't know. She nodded.

Slowly, balancing carefully against one another's hands, they lowered themselves to the ground until they were kneeling, facing one another. And then, together, they poured the wine out into the grass.

Aileen threw her dagger down so it stuck, quivering, in the ground. "I was supposed to say, 'Hail to the queen!' here. What am I supposed to do now?"

"You can still say it." Cally was struggling to stand up but, one hand weighted down by Ben, she nearly fell over. Ben, trying not to laugh, did his best to help. Rianwynn loomed over the entire scenario. Cally ignored her. "You can still say 'Hail to the queen.' But say it to Brigid Dawes."

Rianwynn turned her glare to the woman in the chair. "Her?"

"She is your rightful heir, after all."

"She rejected her birthright many years ago. You know that. We all know that." Rianwynn looked from Bree to Cally, to all the people around the hill, and then back again.

"Well I want it back, now." Bree leaned forward in the chair and coughed.

"You can't just waltz in here and take it back now!" Rianwynn said. "Now that you're staring mortality in the face, you can't just come beg for your heritage back because you're afraid of dying."

"I am not afraid!" Bree stood up, pushing her face as close as her short stature would allow to the Faerie Queen's. Her outburst made her coughing begin again, but Aileen stood behind her and kept her from falling over backward. "I am not afraid. It's just that, I have discovered, I have something to live for, now. Anyway, this is my wedding gift to my brother and his...whatever. I'll take his place here."

"As you should have done in the first place." If Rianwynn had been human, Cally thought, veins would be standing out from the sides of her neck. "Do you think you can just apologize to me now, after all these years, and that I will accept it?"

As far as Cally knew, Bree had never apologized to anyone in her life, and she certainly didn't seem to be apologizing now.

"I am asking you to accept it." Cally had finally managed, with Ben's help, to stand up. She stepped toward the queen, awkwardly tugging him along with her. "I'm asking you to accept her apology. I am asking you for this gift."

"I've already given you a gift! I've permitted my son to marry you!"

"I never asked you for that." Cally gave Ben a quick, sheepish glance, but he was smiling at her, nodding, silently cheering her on. "When you said one day I could ask you for a gift, even you acknowledged you would owe me a great one. Well, this is the gift I'm asking for. Let him go, and let Bree take his place."

Seconds ticked by, though to Cally it felt like she saw the sun set, the moon rise and set, and the sun rise again while Rianwynn tried to make up her mind whether to glare at Cally or at Bree with the most ferocity. The wispy crone stood looking into the queen's face without flinching, though her old body wavered sideways from time to time.

"It all checks out," Aileen concluded pragmatically. "It's a fair deal."

The queen's glare turned, then, on Aileen. "I see," she said. "Yes. I see how it is, now." Without surrendering a shred of her pride, Rianwynn lifted her chin in acknowledgement that she had lost this battle. She stepped back.

Bree said "Hmph!" and twisted out of Aileen's grip. Cally didn't know whether it was adrenaline or sheer cussedness, but when the old woman stumped back to where Ben and Cally stood, she seemed to close the distance without a limp. Picking the fallen goblet up from the ground, she squinted into it. Then she raised it over her head and swallowed the few drops of wine left in the bottom. Aileen plucked her dagger out of the ground and held it over Bree's head.

"Hail to the queen!" she said.

59 - The World I Know

When Cally and Ben finally unwound the ribbons from their wrists, they hung them on the fence for the birds to take for their nests.

"So, does this mean you're married, now, or not?" Katarina, still wearing her bright, flowered huipil, was standing on the other side of the fence. Behind her, the Vale House front yard was filling up with cars and people walking across the lawn and up the porch steps. Ignacio held the front door open for all of them, even though many of them were clearly not human. "It's just," Katarina was saying, "people keep bringing food and drinks, expecting wedding toasts to be happening in the parlor."

"Honestly, Kat, I don't know." Cally unwrapped the final ribbon – a red one – from around her wrist and Ben's. "But we are going on a honeymoon anyway."

"Where will you go?"

"Good question. Where should we go?" This she addressed to Ben, who stood beside her smiling the smile she had always loved, the one that crinkled the lines at the corners of his eyes. She didn't know if this was a glamour, still, or if some kind of faerie magic had actually turned him into a Real Boy, at last, and left him at the age he'd always meant to be. She didn't care either way, anymore.

"There's a great burger place in Blackthorn," he suggested.

Cally looked for a moment at the red ribbon in her hand. Instead of hanging it on the fence, she used it to bind back her hair. "I like that idea," she agreed. "For starters. And maybe after that we can go to Seen's Mill."

Ben turned back to Katarina. "Would you and Bethany please pack us one of those amazing picnic lunches you're so good at making?"

Katarina's wide grin spread even wider. "I'll make sure it's a really big one!" She spun around, calling out for Bethany as she ran back to the house. There Cally saw George, still standing on the porch, turn his gaze away from the meadow and nod, smiling, at her.

She and Ben turned back to the meadow, where people and People still milled all around the crown of the first hill to the east. Many of them played pipes or fiddles, and many of them were dancing. Not all of them were fae and, on her way up the hill, Cally stopped to warn any humans she passed not to eat or drink anything here. "Head on over to Vale House if you get hungry or thirsty," she advised in her most serious voice. Many of them seemed to already understand this, though, even as they danced with people they could not have failed to notice weren't human. She thought she saw Ana dancing with Jud Thornton, but she couldn't be sure, as there were many fae present with Ana's preternaturally beautiful features.

Bree was dancing, also, just as she had once promised. She seemed to grow taller with every turn around the hilltop; her back straightened and her hair grew longer and darker, swinging behind her like a cloak of night. At the moment, she was dancing with Ennilangr, the delivery truck driver, at least until Luke cut in.

"Is that flowers in her hair?" Ben wondered aloud as the circle of dancers swung by. "I could swear she's actually wearing flowers in her hair!" With her dark curls, alabaster skin, and sparkling eyes, Cally thought this new Bree looked a lot like her own mental image of Emerald.

Rosheen and Brandon danced just outside the circle, more slowly than the rest, because the royal infant was still asleep between them. When Cally and Ben drew near, Rosheen turned aside and said, "Mom, I'm going to go find a quiet corner to feed Adam. Here, dance with your son before you go."

Cally danced with Brandon, then with Zenbe, Merv, the sheriff, and several Sidhe including Aileen, who whirled her all the way around the hill to the tune of a high-tempo reel. Finally, as the music changed to a waltz, she found herself at last dancing with Ben. They stealthily maneuvered their way through the waltzing couples until they faced the open gate into Woodley. Just outside the masonry pillars of the Vale House grounds, Cally could see Katarina's covered picnic basket sitting on the hood of the Dawes family Daimler which somebody (probably Ignacio) had parked next to the curb there. Nobody, so far, had violated the car's vintage gray finish with shoes or paper flowers.

"As soon as this song ends," Ben whispered into her ear, "let's make a break for it."

Just as the music ended, however, Michael Dawes stepped out from the shadows of the oaks beside the gate and bowed. "I was hoping I would have a chance to dance with you as well, Callaghan McCarthy."

Ben didn't seem to be able to find any words to say to his father, not yet, but he did step back and bow ever so slightly as he placed Cally's hand in Michael's. "I'll wait right here," he promised.

Cally looked back into the meadow, to where the sun sinking behind Vale House sent out golden rays to gild the dancers at the top of the hill. The flowers in Bree's hair blazed like a crown as she laughed and called the next tune.

"There will be many more chances for us to dance," Cally said to Michael. "But right now, I think there's someone else you need to talk to." She put a hand on his shoulder, turning him to face the meadow, and gave him a little nudge in Bree's direction. "And possibly even a granddaughter you need to meet. Somehow, somewhere. Go ahead. You can tell us all about it another day."

Michael followed where his shadow stretched out across the grass in front of him. Cally and Ben grabbed the basket, got into the Daimler, and drove away southward along Gardens Road.

Fin

Playlist and Outro

My friends, as always, I have copied here for you some titles from Cally's MP3 player, which I feel would make an appropriately atmospheric soundtrack for you to listen to on shuffle while you read this part of her story.

This is the last playlist I will make, and I hope you enjoy it. I have been blessed to hear so many kinds of music, in my lifetime, and thanks to my beloved friend Cally I have even been able to play some music myself. I have had a full and beautiful life.

I have waited until after Cally left, so as not to ruin the fun of her special trip with Mr. Dawes, before slipping away quietly to my own next adventure. She might have tried to talk me out of it, but I know she'll understand, in time.

I stayed on this earth as long as I did because I didn't believe I would find a place to belong, were I to join my family in the next world. No more than I belonged among them when I was alive. But when I glimpsed that world at last, I saw that the things which drive people apart, here, no longer matter there. I will be going home, quite possibly for the first time in all my very long life.

Dear friends, until the end of this world, when all things
will be understood,
I remain
Your faithful servant,
Guacanagarix

Green Grass and High Tides - The Outlaws
Seven Bridges Road - Eagles
Seven Turns - The Allman Brothers Band
Close Action - Big Country
Come on Eileen - Dexy's Midnight Runners

Come Sail Away - Styx
Country Roads - John Denver
Don't Let Him Go - REO Speedwagon
Drift Away - Dobie Gray
Ghost of a Chance - Rush
Home - Edward Sharpe and the Magnetic Zeros
Home - The Smashing Pumpkins
I'll Stand By You - Pretenders
I'm Gonna Be - The Proclaimers
I'm Your Moon - Jonathan Coulton
In Your Eyes - Peter Gabriel
Long Train Running - The Doobie Brothers
My Only Friend - Gregg Allman
Never Die Young - James Taylor
Not Dead Yet - Styx
One Chain (Don't Make No Prison) - The Four Tops
One of these Nights - Eagles
Ordinary World - Duran Duran
Porrohman - Big Country
Ripple - Grateful Dead
Rivers and Roads - The Head and the Heart
Soulshine – The Allman Brothers
Stone Cold Believer - 38 Special
Take On Me - A-ha
Talk to Me - Stevie Nicks
The Chain - Fleetwood Mac
The Parting Glass - The High Kings
Thunderstruck - AC/DC
Time Stand Still - Rush
Traintracks - Adar Nasiykh
Truckin' - The Grateful Dead
Whenever I Call You Friend - Kenny Loggins

ABOUT THE AUTHOR

Kim Beall started sneaking into the basement to read her parents' massive collection of Science Fiction, Fantasy, and Gothic Romance when she was nine years old, which resulted in her spending her teenage years writing dozens of novels. This might have worked out better for her if she had not written them during math class.

She sincerely believes every adult still yearns, not so deep inside, to find real magic in everyday life.

Other Books by Kim Beall

Seven Turns: A ~~Ghost~~ Love Story – May 2018
Moonlight and Moss – May 2019
The Pizza Delivery Boy's Tale – September 2018
A Midnight Clear – *the Woodley, USA Christmas Episode,*
Coming soon!

www.kimbeall.com
www.kimbeall.com/blog
amazon.com/author/kimbeall
goodreads.com/author/show/18012965.Kim_Beall
facebook.com/kimbeallauthor
@KimBeallsGhost